MURDER IN THE SENATE

WILLIAM S. COHEN
AND
THOMAS B. ALLEN

NAN A. TALESE

DOUBLEDAY

New York London Toronto Sydney Auckland

Murder

in the

Senate

PUBLISHED BY NAN A. TALESE
an imprint of Doubleday, a division of
Bantam Doubleday Dell Publishing Group, Inc.
666 Fifth Avenue, New York, New York 10103

DOUBLEDAY and the portrayal of an anchor
with a dolphin are trademarks of Doubleday,
a division of Bantam Doubleday Dell
Publishing Group, Inc.

Library of Congress Cataloging-in-Publication Data

Cohen, William S.
Murder in the Senate/William S. Cohen and Thomas B. Allen.
p. cm.
I. Title.
PS3553.O434M87 1993
813'.54—dc20 92-16769
CIP

ISBN 0-385-26678-2

To the men and women in blue

O, that a man might know
The end of this day's business ere it come!

—*Julius Caesar*

Acknowledgments

WE ARE INDEBTED to many people for their assistance and encouragement in the completion of this novel.

First, our gratitude to Bill Adler, who lent his support to this joint effort. A special word of thanks to our editor, Nan A. Talese, who embraced the project from its inception and contributed greatly to its refinement. She was assisted ably by associate editor Jesse Cohen and copy editor Liz Duvall, who can strike a dangling participle from a hundred paces.

To Frank Kerrigan, the former chief of the Capitol Police; Deputy Chief of Police Robert Howe; and Robert K. Langley, who served as Acting Chief of the Capitol Police—our thanks for familiarizing us with the workings of the department. We are also grateful to George "Irish" McLain, U.S. Senate Liaison, and to Officer Raymond L. Dextradeur for relating some of their experiences in maintaining security in the United States Senate. A special note of thanks to George Mueller, former Chief Engineer of the Senate, for providing us with information and materials that explain the structural plans and operations of the Capitol.

To Angela Dellafiora Ford, we owe a special debt of gratitude for lifting the veil that conceals the world of the paranormal.

Finally, we thank Kevin Cohen, writer-at-large in Los Angeles, for many thoughtful insights and creative contributions.

CAST OF CHARACTERS

IN THE CAPITOL POLICE DEPARTMENT

JEFFREY P. FITZGERALD, chief of police
ALEXANDRA PHELAN, lieutenant
FRED MATHEWSON, sergeant in charge of CERT teams
TED RINGLE, public affairs officer
CATHY OWENS, communications officer
ROY KOCH, lawyer

IN THE OFFICE OF THE ARCHITECT OF THE CAPITOL

WILLIAM R. MASON, architect
JERRY SUMTER, chief engineer
ADAM MORRISON, Senate sergeant-at-arms
IRISH LUNIGAN, deputy Senate sergeant-at-arms
PAUL CONSTANTINO, House sergeant-at-arms
HENRY SCHULTZ, computer consultant

IN THE SENATE

DANIEL LAWSON (California), majority leader
CHARLES C. BRISTOW, senior senator from Louisiana (deceased)
JULIA K. BRISTOW, junior senator from Louisiana,
widow of Charles Bristow
CRAIG HAVERLIN, administrative assistant to Senator Bristow
CARL ROPERS, senior senator from Louisiana
JAMES BARCLAY, senior senator from Wyoming

IN THE HOUSE OF REPRESENTATIVES

MICHAEL ROYAL, representative from Louisiana
GWENDA HARRIS-TOPPING, nonvoting delegate from the
District of Columbia
JOSEPH MARENO, representative from Pennsylvania

IN THE GOVERNMENT OF THE DISTRICT OF COLUMBIA

LYDELL MITCHELL, mayor
BYRON BROWN, Mayor Mitchell's security chief
Dr. LAWRENCE PERKINS, medical examiner

OTHERS

JAMES NADEAU, governor of Louisiana
KYLE TOLLAND, administrator of the FBI laboratory
ELLEN DARWIN, Chief Fitzgerald's landlady
PHILIP DAKE, journalist
JAMES DAVIS, anchorman of Channel 3 News

Monday, April 6

1

IT WAS 11 A.M. and Jeffrey Fitzgerald, chief of the Capitol Police, was smoldering in the gallery of the United States Senate. This was the last place he wanted or needed to be at that moment. But just a little over an hour earlier, he had received a call from Byron Brown, Mayor Lydell Mitchell's security chief. His Honor would be making a surprise visit to the Hill. "Thanks for the notice, Byron," Fitzgerald had snapped, making no effort to tone down the sudden flare of rage in his voice. He knew that no display of emotion or insult would make a bit of difference to Byron Brown or any of the other sycophants who surrounded the mayor.

"Damn," he had blurted as he slammed down the receiver. He had already beefed up security, adding more officers, uniformed and plainclothes, to move around the Capitol grounds. He would have to roust more of his people into double shifts to secure the safety of a man who should be doing time in the slammer rather than pulling strings and calling tunes on Capitol Hill. A visit by the mayor meant a two- or three-car entourage carrying a dozen of Mitchell's boneheads with big guns and quick fingers. Fitzgerald always refused to let any of them onto the Hill while armed.

He wondered about that short notice. Mitchell usually liked to announce his trips several days in advance. That way, he could crank up the press notices, allow speculation on his visit to build in the hope that a one-day news blip would turn into a two- or three-

3

day media bonanza. Something had to be up. It had to be about the statehood for the District of Columbia bill, which was tying up the Senate. And it had to mean trouble.

Fitzgerald sat in the last row of seats behind the mayor, only vaguely aware of the false flatteries being exchanged below on the Senate floor—usually an indication that something nasty was about to be said in a thoroughly civil way. His thoughts drifted to his job. Second thoughts. At first the job had seemed to be a lifesaver: six-figure salary; no heavy lifting; a 1,300-member force to provide security for 535 members of Congress and patrol a land area of about 200 acres. The job was the envy of any big-city cop. But Fitzgerald had soon found out that it was not as cushy as it first seemed.

The violence of Washington, the nation's murder capital, was starting to wash over the walls of this barricaded place of privilege. Robberies on Capitol grounds had increased; a senator's wife had been robbed at gunpoint outside her Capitol Hill home the previous month. Racial tension was tightening, especially now, with the statehood bill filibuster in its third week. Members of Congress wanted more security, as long as it did not interfere with the rights of their constituents, no matter how wacky, no matter how. . . .

The velvet voice of Senator Daniel Lawson of California, the majority leader, interrupted Fitzgerald's thoughts. The police chief looked down at Lawson, who seemed self-assured, almost regal. His chiseled features and silver hair were admired by many of his colleagues. "I see the distinguished gentlelady from Louisiana on the floor, seeking recognition," he began. "I understand that she has an important statement to make, and I now yield the floor." Lawson's voice, ordinarily deep and sonorous, seemed oddly out of pitch. There was an edge to it, which told Fitzgerald that the senator was not at all happy with his distinguished colleague.

Senator Julia K. Bristow, a stunning woman in a light green dress, rose from behind her desk. "Mr. President," she said, addressing the presiding officer sitting behind the ornate dais. "I thank the majority leader for his customary courtesy. As my colleagues know, I have struggled with this issue of statehood for the District for some time, making every effort to be open and fair-minded to all. But I . . ."

Something moved at the edge of Fitzgerald's vision. He turned his head to the left and saw, three rows down and across the aisle, a tall man in a plaid shirt standing up. The man shouted something incoherent and raised his right hand. *Gun.*

As Fitzgerald lunged, his friend Irish Lunigan, the Senate's deputy sergeant-at-arms, charged down from the top of the aisle. Another man, Sergeant Fred Mathewson of the Capitol Police, one of the officers scattered around the gallery, leaped across two rows, bumping aside spectators between him and the standing man.

Just as Mathewson leaped, the man fired three shots. A woman screamed. Fitzgerald felt something graze his forehead, and blood clouded his left eye. Bodies roiled in Mitchell's row. Mathewson had wrapped his hands around the man's right wrist and was trying to keep the gun pointing upward while he pulled the man into the aisle. As Fitzgerald and Lunigan reached them, Mathewson had the man on the marble steps. For an instant Fitzgerald got a look at his face. He was Preacherman, one of the crazies who wandered the Hill.

As Fitzgerald flung himself forward to get the gun, Mathewson crouched over Preacherman, moved one of his hands slightly, and pressed Preacherman's arm against the sharp edge of a step. The arm audibly cracked, and the gun fell from Preacherman's hand. He thrust his other hand toward Mathewson's face, something gleaming in his fist.

Mathewson dodged his head sideways, pinned Preacherman's arms, and spun backward, landing on his back and sliding headfirst down the steps. Preacherman's long, thin body rose from the stairway and flew from his grasp. His head struck the ledge at the end of the aisle, and he somersaulted over the edge, seeming to hang in the air, arms and legs splayed, staring at the domed skylight of the Senate chamber.

"Oh, my God!" Lunigan muttered.

Preacherman landed on his back, shattering the desk of the senior senator from Alaska. The flattened desk slid out from under him and he lay on the blue-and-gold carpet, the sudden hub of a circle of senators, pages, and staffers. He moved his left hand, which still clutched the blade of a linoleum knife between two fingers. The blade was poised over his throat when he lost consciousness. In less than a minute he was dead, his neck and back broken.

Fitzgerald looked first at the Senate floor and then at where the mayor had been sitting. Mitchell's glasses were broken and his nose was bleeding. *Shot? No.* Byron Brown was out of his seat, looking confused and rumpled. Brown, Fitzgerald guessed, had hurled his considerable bulk onto the mayor to protect him. For the first time he could remember, Fitzgerald smiled at Brown, and Brown smiled back.

Fitzgerald wiped the blood away from his face with his handkerchief. "It's a visit to the doc for you," Lunigan said, grasping his left elbow. He began propelling him through the crowd heading up the stairs toward the exits.

On the Senate floor, Lawson declared the Senate adjourned. Senator Bristow still stood at her desk. Without looking toward the knot of people gathered around the shattered desk and body, she lifted the lid of her desk, took out a slim burgundy-dyed leather briefcase, put it under her right arm, pushed open the door leading to the senators' private lobby, and headed for the Senate subway for the short ride to her office.

In the infirmary under the Rotunda, Fitzgerald sat on the edge of an examination table while a physician put the final stitch into a two-inch gash on his forehead. He started to say something to Irish Lunigan.

"I won't be responsible for your looks, Chief, if you don't hold still," the physician said. He snipped the suture, took a quick look at his work, and taped a compress over the stitches. "For the record," he added, "this makes your skull officially harder than marble." He dropped the marble chip he had removed from the wound into his shirt pocket.

"Thanks," Fitzgerald said. "Expect a malpractice suit if there's a scar." He turned back to Lunigan. "What the hell do we know about this guy?"

"Preacherman? He's been here for years, Jeff. Sits in the gallery, hands folded like he is praying. We had no reason to expect that he'd—"

"Nobody expects crazies to act normal," Fitzgerald interrupted. He stood and put on his tweed jacket. "Irish, could you do me a favor and ask Sergeant Mathewson to get our tech boys here on the double. I want all the goddamn metal detectors checked, and if any of them looks bad, shut down that entrance."

As Lunigan opened the door and started to leave, Fitzgerald said, "One other thing, Irish. Tell Mathewson to get hold of that FBI liaison guy, Wheeler. Tell him we'd like a checkout of our crazies against FBI files. He can work with Thomas in Threat Assessment. And—"

Senator Lawson walked into the examining room and slipped past Lunigan, whom he clapped on the shoulder. "Nice work, boys." He looked at Fitzgerald. "You okay?" Fitzgerald nodded. "Good." Lawson paused, his eyes on Fitzgerald, his hand still on Lunigan's shoulder. "Jeff, I couldn't help overhearing what you just said to Irish. Could you hold up on that for a while? There's something I've got to talk to you about right now."

Lunigan shot a glance at Fitzgerald and left. So did the physician, after an exchange of pleasantries with Lawson.

Lawson stood by the closed door. "Jeff," he said. "You know I don't like to interfere with your work. But about the FBI—can we keep them out of this? We can run our own checks, do our own work. The FBI's still mad at the House trying to cut it out of the post office scandal. I don't want to give them an excuse for nosing around the Senate. They like nothing better than finding dirt on the Hill."

"Okay, Senator," Fitzgerald replied. "Threat Assessment will be the lead on it. I just want a stiffer approach to the crazies around here. I want an updated list on them."

"Just make sure you don't put any members of Congress on the list, Jeff," Lawson said with a tight smile.

2

JULIA BRISTOW passed through her reception room and walked past the cubicles of her staff without acknowledging anyone. She went into her private office, closed the door behind her, and sat at her desk. She was trembling, and she did not want anyone to see that she was. She had been shaken by what had happened. The shots. The screams. *Had he hit anybody?* The body, like some acrobat, then smashing down. She was shocked, but frustrated, too, and just shy of being bitter.

That madman in the gallery had robbed her of a moment that she had planned out carefully for days, waiting for just the right time, calibrating the press exposure and public reaction. A shadow had been cast over her day in the sun. But maybe it was just as well. Her speech, if given earlier, would have been diluted by the scene of that man lying broken and bleeding on the Senate floor. And that would have been a pity.

For what she had to say would shock the nation and secure for her a place in the history books. Her speech would be compared to Margaret Chase Smith's "declaration of conscience" during the McCarthy era. But it could wait until tomorrow. Besides, she could use the extra time to be sure she could deliver it without typed or written notes. She wanted her speech to sound as if it had sprung pure and strong from the very depths of her soul. And the apparent spontaneity of her words would have the added virtue of preventing anyone on her staff—including Craig Haverlin, her administrative assistant—from knowing what she was going to say. This was one speech that was never going to be leaked. Tomorrow she would own the airwaves.

She dabbed at the fruit plate that she had ordered from the Senate dining room and sipped delicately on the strong English tea, which was a tad too hot. Her eyes moved around her large office, with its sixteen-foot-high ceilings and wall-to-wall bookcases. She still felt vaguely like a stranger. The office still seemed to belong to her late husband, Charles Bristow. She had inherited it only temporarily, and it was far too masculine to suit her tastes. Too many books, dark mahogany tables, and red leather couches and chairs. And those dreadful abstract paintings and obligatory photographs with Carter, Reagan, Bush, Gorbachev and Yeltsin . . . as if the presence of these former leaders had infused Charles with some intrinsic importance beyond his title.

She had thought it would appear unseemly to redecorate the office, particularly since she was supposed to be a mere caretaker until the next general election in Louisiana. And she also knew that inviting Senate colleagues to her office in its current state might serve her own interests. By playing upon their sentimentality and affection for Charles, she might gain a respect she had yet to earn.

She had always been "focused"—a word infinitely more suitable to her than "calculating." Sixteen years before, right out of graduate school, she had landed a position as a junior legislative assistant on the Senate's Public Works Subcommittee. Almost immediately she had caught the eye of Charles Bristow, who was next in line to become chairman of the subcommittee. Tall, erect as a dancer, with light brown hair, she had eyes that seemed to shift from light green to aqua to gray, depending on the color of her expensive clothes. Charles Bristow certainly was not the only man who had been awed by her beauty.

But she wanted more. She quickly learned that beauty bred envy, along with interest and lust. Other female staffers, who adopted the dress and demeanor of worker bees, resented the presence of a butterfly and plotted in skillfully nefarious ways to undermine her. The men in the office, and other senators who saw her in the corridors, gave little thought to her intelligence or capabilities. They seemed only to notice her long, shapely legs. And so Julia had maintained a delicate balance, moderately toning down her appearance when with her peers, then amplifying it again in the presence of Charles Bristow.

Senator Bristow had lost his wife of twenty-eight years to cancer. Following a year of grieving, he was open to romance. Julia was eager to oblige. At first they were discreet. But Charles, proud of his quickened virility, grew bolder. There were whispers, then persistent rumors. Finally, an item appeared in the gossipy "Personalities" column of the Washington *Post:* "Senator Hears Wedding Bells: December Man to Marry May Bride in June." Initially, the thirty-year age difference raised more than a few eyebrows, but Bristow looked younger than his fifty-eight years and was a man of considerable vigor. He was eager to reenter Washington's social circuit with beautiful Julia on his arm.

For the next fifteen years they lived grandly, occupying a double condominium suite on Pennsylvania Avenue and entertaining friends and important constituents at their large country home in nearby Virginia on weekends. Then, in one shattering moment, it

9

was over. Charles died in a freak accident in Louisiana. The governor, confounding all of his political critics, appointed Julia to serve out the remainder of Charles's term. Again underestimating or ignoring Julia's intelligence and cunning, everyone expected her to be little more than a mannequin in the Senate, following blindly the legislative path that had been carved by her revered husband.

Well, now she would show them—and shake the nation in the process.

She shuffled through correspondence for a couple of hours, then buzzed for Haverlin. She had inherited him along with the office. She did not particularly dislike him, but there was no warmth between them, either. He always seemed to be looking past her, anticipating words before she said them. He was waiting, she suspected, for the *real* senator who would succeed her through an election. Well, she would show them about that, too.

Haverlin opened the door and stuck his head in. It was his way of hoping that all she had for him could be accomplished by a shouting match across the length of the office. He had a pale, thin face made paler by faint eyebrows and light blue eyes. His hair was dark with a streak of blond running across the top of his head. "Yes, Senator?" he asked.

Without looking up from writing on a yellow pad, she motioned with her left hand, pointing to the chair in front of her desk. He sat on the edge of the seat. Slim and about five-foot-eight, he wore a double-breasted suit, cut too sharp for the senator's taste. Everything about him seemed too sharp, too cool.

"Quite a drama on the floor today," he said.

"Yes, and in the air, too."

He looked puzzled. She made a diving motion with her right hand. "Flying. The body, flying through the air."

"Right." He made a noise in his throat. It meant, she knew, *What do you want?*

"I'll be heading over to the hideaway shortly. I'm not to be disturbed." She pointed to two stacks of paper on her desk. "I've scribbled down some notes on this correspondence. Constituent aid business. We're falling behind again, Craig."

He nodded.

"Now, what I want you and Nancy to do—and anyone else you can round up, when they're through gossiping about Preacherman

10

—what I want is for you to supervise cracking through this material. I'll give you a ring around six or so, and I'll want you to get over there with me to sign *all* of this. *All*. Got it?"

He nodded again.

"When I come in here tomorrow morning, I want to see *none* of this correspondence and this—"junk." She gestured toward a stack. "Things are going to get busy around here tomorrow, and I want the backlog cleared up. Got it?"

He nodded yet again, and she resumed writing on the yellow pad.

A few minutes later she went into her office bathroom, and emerged wearing a flat-topped red hat. In a city where women rarely wore them, hats were her signature, as much a part of her image as a bow tie or a full beard on a male senator: a sign of being different, a way of standing out just a little.

She slipped out a side door that led directly to a maze of offices off one of the walkways around the soaring atrium of the Hart Senate Office Building. She took an elevator marked SENATORS ONLY to the basement, where she boarded a subway for the short trip to the Senate wing of the Capitol. When she arrived, she entered a low-ceilinged basement corridor and, her heels clicking on the concrete, headed for her hideaway.

Julia Bristow, a senator for only six months, did not rate one of the seventy-seven offices in the tunnels and vaults beneath the Senate wing and in niches on the upper level. Some were large and grand; others were little more than broom closets. The hideaways were awarded by the Senate Rules Committee to the seventy-seven senators with the most seniority. Soon there would be more, one for every senator. For now, Julia Bristow unlocked an unmarked white door and entered the hideaway that Senator Charles Bristow had been given two years before, when he moved up in seniority—and up from a hideaway with a fiberboard ceiling and a chair and desk that looked like leftovers from a yard sale. Lowest ranking in Senate seniority when she was appointed, she continued to occupy her late husband's main office and hideaway through senatorial courtesy. No one wanted to take them away from Charles Bristow's widow. She knew what they were thinking: *Such a beautiful woman . . . and she won't be around very long.*

The hideaway, about the size of a motel room, was brightly lit by overhead lights. Along one wall was a couch covered by a floral print against a yellow background. Before it was a low table. At the wall on the left was a long, low bookcase with about a dozen books in it. On the yellow walls were dozens of framed mementos too humble for display in the main Senate office suite but qualifying for the assurance of senatorial thank-you notes—"It now hangs in my office": cartoons from Louisiana newspapers and photographs of Senator Charles Bristow with constituents at high school commencements, ribbon-cuttings, barbecues, Cajun weddings, and alligator hunts.

Because the Capitol was built into the side of the Hill, the basement room's two windows looked out onto the stone-railed terrace that bordered the west side of the building. Numerous tourists walked along the terrace every day, unaware that they were passing the hideaways, which were kept so secret that they were entered only by janitors, senators, staffers, and invited visitors, who always needed help in finding them.

Julia Bristow stood at a window and parted the curtain to look down the Mall at the Washington Monument, a view that never ceased to inspire her—to stay in Washington, to stay powerful. Then she picked up the phone, hit five numbers, waited a moment, and said, "I'm in the hideaway. Shall we say about eight?"

Tuesday, April 7

3

JIMMY CULLUM slammed his car door and ran across Parking Lot 16. As he dashed past the wire-fence gate, he nodded to the attendant and pivoted onto First Street Northeast, nearly running into a man racing just as fast toward Union Station. Grass, greenery, and flower beds blurred past as he gathered speed up the long block enclosing the Russell Office Building. At Constitution Avenue he ignored the traffic light and, zigzagging through two lanes of cars, crossed to the barrier of huge potted plants and concrete barricades that guarded the plaza of the Capitol. A Capitol Police officer in a small white guardhouse smiled at him as he whizzed by, veered across the vast tarmac to a ramp, and ran up a set of stairs to a portico along the north wall of the Senate side of the building.

Cullum paused at the massive, bronze-framed glass door and, holding up the metal chain around his neck, dangled his laminated identification tag under the eyes of a Capitol Police officer at the inner door. He stepped through the frame of the metal detector, turned left, and discreetly slowed to a fast walk, striding along the blue, cream, and red glazed tiles of a lavishly decorated corridor. He thought for an instant of how he should bring Denise into this softly lighted cave, whose walls and ceiling were covered with intertwined paintings of birds and flowers.

Just after passing a marble staircase with the brass banister that

15

he occasionally would mount and slide down, he turned left again and ran down another corridor, this one dim and deserted, to a stairway that plunged into the labyrinth of tunnels and hallways beneath the Capitol. For the first time in his run he looked at his watch: 7:33. Damn!

Now he sprinted down the last corridor, a long, shadowy tunnel that always reminded him of the nuclear submarine he had served on for two years. He punched the button of an elevator, stood slapping his hands against the marble wall, and lunged into the elevator before the doors fully opened. When it stopped he burst out into a hallway, through a glass door, and down the stairs that led to the Senate subway: 7:35. Damn! As he ran toward the subway cars, he saw that his first passenger of the day was already aboard. Officially, the subway wasn't scheduled to begin operations until 8:00. But some senators started their day early. And they didn't like to walk.

Like most workers in the Senate, Cullum was required to know every senator by sight, even from the side or back. He would not get a perfect score just yet, but he had no trouble this morning. His only passenger was the senator easiest to identify: she was one of a handful of women in the Senate and she had light brown hair, crowned this morning, as usual, by a jaunty hat. She always liked to get an early start.

Cullum quickly rushed to the driver's cab, without announcing his arrival. *When in trouble, when in doubt, drop your eyes and do not shout.* He had learned that in the Navy. And it was pretty much the same here, if you thought of the senators as the admirals, their uptight staff people as the captains and commanders and lieutenants, and everybody else as enlisted personnel. He surreptitiously looked at his watch: 7:37. Not bad, he told himself. It was the first time he had been late in his three weeks on the job.

He opened the narrow door of the operator's compartment in the middle of the roofless train, which looked like an ornate relative of a carnival bumper car. Painted on the cars' blue sides were large Senate seals. Chrome-framed windows topped the waist-high sides of the linked cars, whose nine rows of seats were just wide enough for three senators (or tourists) of moderate size. Senator Bristow's flat-topped red hat jutted from the corner of the first row of seats; her back was to Cullum.

16

Cullum wore a dark blue blazer and tan slacks, the uniform of subway operators. He knew the uniform gave him anonymity, and he welcomed it this morning. You never knew when one of them would turn you in. He wondered how long Senator Bristow had been waiting. He sat in the operator's swiveling chair and reached for the controls. At the edge of his vision on one side was a gleaming metal shaft reaching up to the power wires that ran along the roof of the brightly lighted subway tunnel. When he turned the ignition key, electricity flowed from the cable to the train's motor, which hummed quietly. A green light glowed on the console in front of him. Cullum flicked a lever, and the cars glided serenely down the narrow set of rails.

About one hundred yards from the starting point, the train reached a V-shaped junction. Tracks to the left ended at the Russell Office Building; the two sets of tracks to the right went to the Dirksen and Hart buildings. The fact that Senator Bristow was sitting in the car that went nonstop to the Hart Office Building made it unnecessary for Cullum to ask her destination. One minute and thirty-five seconds later, he braked at the Hart subway stop. He decided that perhaps he should say good morning. He turned his eyes toward the car where Senator Bristow was seated, but he could not see anyone in the car. For a moment he wondered whether in his panic to get to work he had seen her at all.

Cullum jumped out of his chair and reached the front car in two fast strides. Senator Bristow lay diagonally across it, her head near the seat, her feet against the side of the car. Her dress was drawn up, her legs were together, her arms were at her side. The backrest and seat above her were smeared with blood, and her throat was a streak of shiny red. Her white blouse and green suit coat were stained with blood.

Cullum instinctively stepped toward her, as if to help her to her feet. Then he drew back. "Jesus! Sweet Jesus!" he gasped. His voice at once climbed and cracked. He ran to an elevator marked by a sign that said SENATORS ONLY. He hesitated, looking around for the two Capitol Police officers who should have been on duty at the subway stop. Where the hell were they? He punched the button and went up two flights.

He ran from the elevator, skidding on the marble floor of the vast atrium. Halfway across the sun-splashed space he stopped, by the black metal mass of Alexander Calder's "Mountain and Cloud," which loomed three stories above him. His shouts—"Police! Police! Help!"—echoed across the marble. Three faces peered over the tiers of galleries that ringed the atrium. At the east entrance, two Capitol Police officers turned toward him, and he gestured for them to follow him. He ran back to the elevator with one of the officers in pursuit, a gun in his hand. The other stayed at her post and reached for the radio on her belt to call for a backup.

Cullum hit the elevator button and said to the officer, "Dead. She looks like she's dead." As the door opened, he felt the officer's gun in the small of his back. "Jesus!" he said. "I didn't do nothin'."

They stepped into the elevator, Cullum facing the closing door, the officer at his right side, the gun brushing his blazer. Then the door opened and they stepped out. "There she is," he said.

When the two men reached the side of the subway car, the officer saw Bristow's body and gasped. Pointing his gun at Cullum's chest, he said, "Hold very still, brother. Don't move a friggin' finger." With his other hand, he yanked his radio from his belt, touched the button, and said, "Two twenty-seven from Hart post twelve. We've got a dead senator on the subway."

"Repeat, post twelve."

"Homicide, man. We've got a homicide here. Senator Bristow. She's all covered with blood."

"Ten forty-seven, post twelve. Stand by." The Capitol Police dispatcher paused. Her voice changed from crisply responsive to baffled shock. "Who am I talking to?"

"This is Boomer, Cathy."

"Boomer. What the hell is going on? What's the code for this?"

"Beats me. We don't have no code for murder."

"Ten-four, Boomer. I'm going for the CERT team to the subway, then bucking this to the watch commander. Ten-five."

With one hand, Boomer Hawkins switched off the radio and put it back into its belt holster. His other hand still held his gun, which he lowered so that it was aimed at the middle button of Cullum's blazer. "And now, brother," he said, "we're going to stand right here and you're going to tell me who you are and what the hell happened."

18

4

IN THE COMMUNICATIONS ROOM of the Capitol Police, under the Russell Building, the dispatcher sent a signal to the Contingency Emergency Response Team ready room in headquarters, a block from the Hart Building. Out of the room came Mathewson, the CERT leader, a broad-shouldered man in white sneakers, a blue T-shirt, camouflage pants, and a blue baseball cap. He had gone on duty as usual this morning. The Threat Assessment unit had him scheduled for a hearing this afternoon on the death of Preacherman. He had been looking forward to a typically quiet shift. Now what the hell was this?

Yelling "Go!" Mathewson donned a bulletproof jacket and a camouflage shirt as did the other man in the room. Two others ran in from the gym next door when they heard the signal. While they suited up, the first two ran down the corridor and up a flight of stairs to the roll-call room, where an officer was unlocking the steel door over the counter of the armory room. He leaped over the counter, unlocked a rack, and pulled four M-249s from it. Each of the automatic weapons could fire 1,100 rounds per minute.

The watch commander entered the roll-call room, his face pale. He held a radio in one hand, a cellular phone in the other. "We've got a member down. Dead. Apparently murdered," he told Mathewson, who was handing three of the M-249s to his partner. "In the Senate subway. Bristow. Not in the succession."

The last remark was important information for a contingency operation. If the slain member of Congress had been the Speaker of the House or president pro tempore of the Senate, and thus in the line of succession to the presidency, the Secret Service's CAT, or Counter Assault Team, would have been on the way to Capitol Hill, and Mathewson's CERT would have had to merge forces with the Secret Service. They had done so in many drills, and neither group enjoyed the forced show of cooperation.

The Capitol Police Department is to Congress what the Secret

19

Service is to the presidency. About the size of the police force in Columbus, Ohio, the department applies the most concentrated police protection in the nation to the two hundred acres that encompass the nation's capitol and its outlying Capitol Hill buildings. The Capitol Police also guard the 435 representatives and 100 senators, all of whom are referred to as members. Now one of the members under the protection of the Capitol Police had been killed, and the automatic assumption was that all others might be in peril.

"I pressed the button for the Big Seal, and I'm trying to reach the architect and the sergeants-at-arms," the watch commander continued. "There's a car picking up the chief. The channel is five and the operation is Hilltop. The command post is in Hart."

Mathewson nodded and slung over his shoulder a pack containing extra ammunition, CS riot-control grenades, and stun grenades, which emit a blinding light and deafening explosion on detonation. The other two CERT men were already outside headquarters when Mathewson and his partner appeared with the weapons. They handed them out, and Mathewson said, "Take the vehicle to the Second Street entrance and report to the command post. Radio the plaza and tell them we're going to the subway stop at Hart and don't want anyone else to respond until we say so."

At the plaza, the expanse of tarmac and greensward that forms the east front of the Capitol, heavy metal plates rose from the narrow roadways at the two vehicle checkpoints. On the west front, which looks out on the Mall, officers ran to the top of the broad stairs and set up wooden barricades. At every entrance, doors slammed shut behind officers in bulletproof vests. The white patrol cars of the Capitol Police sped to the six intersections that mark off the boundaries of Capitol Hill. Each car swung to the center of the street and blocked traffic. Within eight minutes, Capitol Hill had been sealed off from the rest of the District of Columbia. A monumental traffic jam began to congeal on Pennsylvania Avenue and the streets leading to the Hill.

Weaving through the traffic, siren yowling, red and blue lights flashing, another patrol car headed south on Pennsylvania Avenue. It made a screeching U-turn in front of the District Building, which housed the mayor and other District municipal officials. On the sidewalk in front of the building was Fitzgerald.

20

He wore the standard dark blue, gold-buttoned uniform, with the insignia of his rank: six narrow gold stripes on the left sleeve of his jacket, arcs of gold on the visor of his cap. Some men are enhanced by a uniform. Fitzgerald was not. The cap seemed perched above his ruddy face, and the uniform seemed to encase his angular body rather than clothe it. He paced the sidewalk, impatience showing in his shifting shoulders.

Fitzgerald had been winding up a breakfast meeting with Mayor Mitchell when the call had come in. The meeting had been scheduled weeks before, ostensibly to wrap up plans for a big statehood rally planned for the following Thursday. The titular organizers of the rally were the mayor and his political archrival, Gwenda Harris-Topping, the District of Columbia's nonvoting delegate to Congress. She had introduced the legislation that had triggered the statehood debate and the filibuster on the Senate floor.

Rally planning was not a typical activity for Mitchell, who spent more time out of the District Building than in it. But he wanted as much political credit as he could get. The breakfast meeting had originally been choreographed as a sleeves-rolled-up photo opportunity with Fitzgerald and other officials surrounding the mayor.

As soon as the cameras left, Mitchell ordered everyone but Fitzgerald out of the room and began the morning tirade. The first reason for it was a harangue about "my brush with death" in the Senate gallery. Fitzgerald tried to explain how he could provide only as much protection as Congress allowed him, how Preacherman's plastic-encased gun had eluded the metal detectors, how he had not aimed at anyone . . . but what was the use? Mitchell was not listening.

Fitzgerald knew what was coming next. "One of your officers is in Metropolitan Police custody," Mitchell told him. "From what *my* police tell me, your Keystone Kop, playing some kind of undercover game, went into an office here in the District Building—the Office of the Assistant to the Mayor for Urban Redevelopment, to be precise—and attempted to buy drugs. Our officers were summoned, and he finally identified himself. Another sorry example of how the white power structure rides roughshod over black politicians. Entrapment! That's what it was. Entrapment! And let me tell you—"

Fitzgerald tried to explain that his Intelligence Section had been

21

sending undercover teams into open-air drug markets of the District to find the sources of drugs flowing to the Hill. Drug sales had been going up. The Capitol Police had been arresting users, who included congressional staffers and maintenance workers. One of the users had been on the staff of the Senate Intelligence Committee. His arrest had brought in investigators from the FBI and CIA.

"I know all that stuff," Mitchell said impatiently. "What the hell does this have to do with what happened in the District Building?"

"We're going after the suppliers," Fitzgerald said. "A lieutenant from Intelligence has been running it. It was called Operation Iceberg. He told me he wanted to have some men go undercover. Bicycle messengers were one of the covers. And one of them—"

"One of them thought he could find drugs in *my* District Building. In *my* town!" Mitchell shouted. He stood and shook a long, bony finger at Fitzgerald. "There's only one town in this town, Fitzgerald, and that's my town. It's mostly black and mostly doesn't give a damn what happens up there on your Hill."

"Look, Mr. Mayor," Fitzgerald said. "I don't want to get into a jurisdictional hassle with you. Let me find out what happened and—" And then had come the call from headquarters.

The car pulled up with the front passenger door open and was heading back up Pennsylvania Avenue before Fitzgerald slammed the door. "What do we know?" he asked.

The driver, who had been quickly briefed by the watch commander, told all he knew: Bristow's body had been found in a subway car when it got to Hart.

"The body was in it when the subway left the Capitol?"

"That's the way I understand it, Chief."

Fitzgerald unhooked the microphone from the radio under the dashboard, switched the channel selector from 1 to 5, and said, "Car one."

"Come in, car one."

"This is Fitzgerald. I want Phelan's crime scene team at Hart. Tell them to stand by for my orders."

"Affirmative, Chief."

"Now patch me through to Metro Police communications on channel one and copy."

"Ten-seven, car one." There was a click, a crackle, the sound of two faint voices.

"Metro. Go ahead, Capitol."

"Metro dispatcher, this is Chief Fitzgerald of the Capitol Police. Please advise your District One patrols that Capitol Hill is sealed off."

"Repeat, Capitol."

Fitzgerald, his voice edgy, repeated the message, then added, "Metro dispatcher, copy to the mayor's command center and advise the watch there that further communications on this matter will be on channel five."

"Request authority for the message, Capitol."

"The authority, Metro, is Capitol Police Chief Jeffrey Patrick Fitzgerald. Ten-four."

Fitzgerald replaced the microphone on the hook and a moment later said, "Pull in here and pop the trunk." The car was nearly abreast of the checkpoint barrier on the Senate side of the east front, where Jimmy Cullum had sprinted less than half an hour earlier.

"But our command post is in the Hart Building," the driver said as the car stopped.

Fitzgerald did not respond. He opened the door and beckoned to an officer at the guardhouse. When the officer ran up to the car, Fitzgerald, without looking at the nameplate on his blue uniform coat, said, "Good morning, Hunt. Get the crime scene tape out of the trunk and come with me."

By the time Hunt had gone around to the open trunk and taken out a roll of yellow tape—CRIME SCENE DO NOT CROSS, endlessly repeated in black letters—Fitzgerald was trotting across the east front. He disappeared into an arched passageway under the broad stairs at the Senate side of the Capitol. As Hunt approached, puffing, Fitzgerald had his belt radio in his hand and was saying, ". . . immediately. Repeat, immediately."

An officer had opened the passageway door she had been guarding and was standing next to it, squinting up at Fitzgerald. Squatting on the narrow pavement near the door was a wizened, barefoot man in a white shirt and stained khaki slacks. Propped next to him was a large sign covered with hundreds of tiny hand-lettered words. The biggest words, painted in red, were NO JUSTICE.

23

Fitzgerald grabbed the man by the back of the neck and pulled him to his feet. "Handcuffs," the chief ordered, reaching out his left hand. The officer removed the cuffs from her belt and handed them to him. He spun the man around, twisted his hands behind his back, and snapped the cuffs onto a pair of skinny wrists. "Book this son of a bitch, Eggleston."

She nodded and began mumbling the *Miranda* incantation.

"Knock off the rights message until I leave. Just listen to this: when the plaza is ordered secured, it means Mr. Bones here gets kicked out. Got it?"

"Yes, sir, Chief," Eggleston replied. "We thought he was harmless. He—"

"Harmless? You tell Mathewson that. Or the people that other harmless bastard could have shot yesterday."

"What . . . what will I book him for?"

Fitzgerald, who had begun walking away, turned to her and shouted, "Buggery, for all I care! Just get the son of a bitch out of here." He took a step toward her. "And remember this, Eggleston: nobody's harmless. Nobody. Got that?"

"Yes, sir," Eggleston said to the broad blue back of Fitzgerald, who had already stepped into the elevator that would take him down to the Senate subway. Hunt squeezed in behind him just as the elevator door closed.

Moving swiftly out at the basement level of the Capitol, Fitzgerald turned right and walked down a short corridor. He passed through two sets of swinging glass doors that were latched open. Just beyond the second set were the doors to a men's room and a women's room. Four wide steps with bright brass handrails led to the subway tunnel and the walkways paralleling the sunken tracks.

An empty train was at the end of one set of tracks to the right, its operator lounging against it and talking to a Capitol policeman. The operator apparently said something to his companion, who turned, saw Fitzgerald, raised his right hand to his visored cap in a kind of salute, and strode over to the platform.

Fitzgerald glanced at the saluting officer and looked back at the puffing Hunt. One end of the crime scene tape trailed behind him. "I want these doors locked and guarded," Fitzgerald said, pointing to the glass doors. "Check in with your regular post and tell them I ordered you here."

Hunt mumbled a "yessir" and fumbled with the doors' locks. He closed each door, twisted its knob, saw that it was not locked, fumbled with the locks again, and tried the doors once more. "They're locked, Chief," he said.

"Well done, Hunt," Fitzgerald said. "Now string that tape all around the platform and down these steps. I don't want anyone going through any of these doors or using the johns until the crime scene team gets through here."

The other officer touched Fitzgerald's right arm and said, "Chief, those doors. I mean, you *can't* just close them. All them people coming in, the tourists, the members."

Fitzgerald looked at the officer's beseeching hand, which he snapped away from Fitzgerald's sleeve.

"You're new here, Maldonado," Fitzgerald said softly, "so I'll just forget that I heard you. Now I want you to tell your friend over there that nobody gets on his train and it goes nowhere without my authority. Tell him I'll be taking a ride later on. Otherwise, he's to do whatever he's supposed to do to shut the thing down. On my authority. Then I want you and Hunt here to stand at those doors. And you aren't going to let a single solitary human being through any of them. You got that, Maldonado?" He turned toward Hunt. "And you, Hunt? You got that?"

The two officers nodded and began draping tape across the handrails and through the door handles. A young woman in a blue blouse and a short black skirt tapped at one of the glass doors. Maldonado opened the door slightly and said something to her. She scowled and began complaining. He closed the door, and to her protests raised a large flat hand and pressed it against the glass.

Fitzgerald walked across the platform to the women's room, took a handkerchief out of a back pocket, and wrapped it around his right hand before he touched the doorknob. He opened the door and, still using the handkerchief, flipped a switch. He took a step into the anteroom, then pushed through a second door and turned toward the toilet stalls. From the corner of his right eye he caught a flash of motion. Startled, he swung his head and saw himself in the mirror that ran above a row of sinks. He smiled at himself, at his jittery nerves.

The map of Ireland is on your face, his mother had said one day when he was about five, and he had gone into the bathroom and looked in the mirror and tried to understand what she meant. He had asked his sister, who was eight, and she had patiently explained that it was just a way of saying that a lot of people who are Irish have blue eyes and red hair like his and hers. *Wrinkles around the blue eyes,* he thought now. *The red hair's more gray than red. Moustache, too. Chin sagging a bit, maybe, but not quite jowls yet.* The map was still there, though showing some folds and creases.

He opened the door of the first stall, peered in, then did the same with the second. There he stopped and, crouching down, saw what he assumed to be flecks of dried blood around the rim of the toilet bowl. Two pink stains ran down the outside of the bowl and ended on the tile floor. Behind the bowl, in the shadow of the toilet tank, he saw a bobby pin. He perched a pair of half-lens glasses on his nose, knelt, and looked closely at the bobby pin. Pinched in it were two long strands of light brown hair.

Fitzgerald rose, pocketed the glasses, and returned to the glass doors, where Hunt and Maldonado stood talking. At his approach, they turned their backs to the door and tried to assume the posture of guards. "Listen up," he said to them as he unholstered his radio and called communications. "I'm about to head for Hart. Tell Mathewson to take his CERT boys back to headquarters but to stand by. Make sure no one touches the body or the subway car. Tell the crime scene team to start here, with emphasis on the women's room."

He walked to the subway car, waved his right hand over his head to alert the operator, and took a seat directly behind him. The car started as soon as he sat down.

Fitzgerald leaned forward and asked the operator, "What's your name?"

"Willis, sir. Loren Willis."

"Know an operator named Jimmy Cullum?" Fitzgerald asked.

"A little, sir. But he's new, real new."

"How new?"

"Oh, like two, three weeks."

"How long have you worked here?"

"A year . . . No, wait. Fourteen months. That's it. Fourteen months. You want the Hart?" Ordinarily the car would have stopped at the Dirksen Building.

"That's right, Willis. How did you guess?"

26

"Well, that officer. Maldonado? He told me about the senator and all, and I figured that's where you'd be going."

"Right," Fitzgerald said. He felt the train slowing down and saw that it was nearing the Dirksen stop. "The trip from the Senate to Hart takes one minute and thirty-five seconds, right, Willis?"

"That's right, sir. Maybe a minute or so to pick up passengers when it's busy. How'd you—"

"So with no one to load on, it's less than two minutes?"

"Yessir. It's not much of a trip. We don't do much more than just sort of sit here. And the motor don't do much more than stop and start."

"The subway shuts down at six, right?"

"Well, when the Senate's in session, like now, and when they aren't staying up all night doing stuff, when it's ordinary days, like now, well, it closes down at six o'clock. On the dot."

"So last night it all shut down at six?"

"Sure."

"That's a long day."

"Well, there's relief operators that come in and give us a spell. And there's a lot of juggling. People going to school and things like that."

"You going to school, Willis?"

"Well now, I was, but I sorta took a break."

"Don't let that break last too long, or you won't go back at all."

Willis did not respond. The Hart stop was in sight. "You get the job through your congressman?" Fitzgerald asked.

"Sure. Like everybody. But I had to be okayed by the architect, you know."

"Yeah, I know. Me too."

Willis smiled at that. He stopped his train, which ran parallel to the one containing Senator Bristow's body, more than five yards short of the passenger platform.

The watch commander ran up to the car. "Lots of trouble, Chief."

"I figured that, Henry. Start with the worst."

"The media. They—"

"I'll pass on that for a minute. Next?"

"Notification of kin. Who and how?"

"Let's start with her administrative assistant." Fitzgerald looked at his watch. Ten after nine. "He should be in now. Go tell him. And give him a chance to start doing what has to be done. Okay? Next?"

"What?"

"Next trouble."

"Right. That, Chief, would be the architect and the sergeants-at-arms. They're in the architect's office."

"I'll handle them. Now, about the media. No one gets in here. No TV cameras, no print reporters, nobody. Tell communications to refer media queries to the public information office. Ringle's on duty today, right?"

"Right. I've already talked to him. He's filled in on her being dead and is supposed to be saying nothing more than that."

"Good. Get the word to him to stay with that. And tell him to set up a press conference for eleven o'clock."

"Right," the watch commander said. "But Chief, you've *got* to talk to the architect and the sergeants-at-arms before you talk to the media."

"I said I'd take care of them," said Fitzgerald, hoping that he sounded more confident than he felt. He had already had a talk with Lawson on the Preacherman incident. That one wasn't over yet. And now this one.

5

BY THE TIME Fitzgerald reached the architect's office, he had heard Jimmy Cullum's story, seen the body, and ordered that nothing was to be touched or moved until his return. At this point, he decided, he knew as much as anyone could know about the crime and could give a decent briefing on it. But when he opened the architect's office door, Fitzgerald began reminding himself of the reality of the coming moments. It would not be enough for him to know about the crime or to be a coolly professional police officer. This was Capitol Hill, and whatever happened here—even murder—had political twists that he would not be able to foresee.

"Don't think you'll be a chief of police," his predecessor had told him. "You're going to be a functionary in Vatican City, where five hundred and thirty-five cardinals all think they're the Pope."

Fitzgerald distrusted analogies, but this one grazed reality. He fought hard not to be a functionary of the Vatican and looked upon the cardinals of Congress as his citizens and his charges, not his bosses. In nine months as chief he had concentrated on building up and running a police force. Yet day after day the reality of Capitol Hill intruded. Now, stepping through the doorway, he again reminded himself that there was no comparison between the Federal Bureau of Investigation, where he had known the rules, and the Capitol Police, where the rules had a way of changing before his eyes or, worse, behind his back.

He closed the door and hesitated for a moment to survey the room. Seated behind a gleaming mahogany desk in a high-backed leather chair was the acting architect of the Capitol, William R. Mason.

Architect of the Capitol. When Fitzgerald first heard the title, he naturally assumed that Mason was an architect. But as he so often discovered on the Hill, titles did not always mean what they seemed. About two years before, Mason had replaced the retiring architect, who *was* an architect. Going back to the earliest times, the architect of the Capitol had been a qualified architect. That tradition was not consistently held to, however, as the post evolved from one concerned with overseeing the appearance of the Capitol to one that dealt with the complex facilities that had been built to serve the members of Congress. The Senate and House leaders who had selected Mason believed that he could bring a knowledge of computer-age communications to a place that still clung to its inkwell desks and pageboy and girl message service.

Mason was not a tall man, but he carried himself with such a sense of command and physical rectitude that he could pass for being over six feet. Much of his presence was due to his military background. A brilliant mathematician and engineer, he had achieved the rank of captain in the Navy and become the commanding officer of the U.S.S. *Puget Sound*, a guided-missile test ship loaded with electronics. Then he had become director of DARPA, the Defense Advanced Research Projects Agency, at the Pentagon. When he had retired from DARPA, he had started his own think tank. By then he was a nationally renowned expert on computerized communications and security.

But he was much more than the product of education and training and career. There was something in the blood. An English father and a German mother had given him a certain air of austerity; indeed, he seemed to have a genetic compulsion for order and detail. The compulsion served him well as architect. He was charged with overseeing Capitol Hill, its vast land, all its buildings, and most of what went into them, from paper clips to computer chips. He liked to say he ran a tight ship.

Mason would forever remain a captain, a thoroughly nautical man. It showed in his office: the ornately carved stand-up writing table against the wall, next to his long, gleaming desk; the brass clock and the sextant that had adorned his quarters aboard the *Puget Sound;* the organizational charts and computer printouts draped across a wooden rack; the maximum utilization of space, the absence of clutter . . . Little wonder that everyone still called him captain. Occasionally, even Fitzgerald did.

Mason nodded wordlessly toward Fitzgerald and motioned him to one of the chairs drawn up before his desk. In the other chairs were Adam Morrison, the Senate sergeant-at-arms; Paul Constantino, the House sergeant-at-arms; and Roy Koch, the young lawyer who was the Capitol Police's counsel.

Fitzgerald was accountable to what in any other city would be called a board of police commissioners. The Capitol Police Board consisted of three people barely known beyond Capitol Hill: the architect of the Capitol, and two powerful congressional appointees whose titles could be traced back to medieval knights charged with protecting the king—the sergeants-at-arms of the Senate and the House. Each had a deputy, several assistants, and a staff. They included men like Deputy Irish Lunigan, who had trained himself to be a keen security officer, and others who performed largely ceremonial duties.

Constantino was a black-haired, black-bearded man who rarely spoke at meetings. Eleven years before, when he had not had a beard, he had been an officer of the Capitol Police. The job had been desperately sought not by Constantino but by his wife, who had prevailed upon her cousin, a member of the House from New Jersey. Constantino, then thirty-three, had been drifting from job to job—assistant manager of a Trenton supermarket, drive-in bank teller, roofing salesman—and Shirley Constantino had demanded that he find what she called a career. He had found it on Capitol Hill.

Two years after his cousin-in-law transformed him into a policeman, Constantino knew he could be more. He had spent those two years not only guarding the House of Representatives but also finding ways to be helpful. This, he soon learned, was most visibly done on the staff of the House sergeant-at-arms. So he got himself transferred, and because of his police experience, he was assigned to manage security in the office of the Speaker. When the House sergeant-at-arms retired, the Speaker made a few phone calls, and Constantino got the job.

Morrison stood six-foot-two and was slim and gray-haired. His face was smooth and his cheeks were touched with the pink of a horseman. As a member of a first family of Virginia, he had inherited a life that included Virginia horses and Virginia politics. After twelve languid years in the state legislature, he had run for Congress. When he was defeated after his third term by a black woman who had graduated from Virginia Tech, he had fallen into a deep depression. Through the efforts of his state's most influential politicians, he had recently been restored to Capitol Hill as sergeant-at-arms of the Senate, a patrician counterbalance to the plebeian Constantino.

Mason, who ran the board, with the acquiescence of Morrison and Constantino, looked away from Fitzgerald. "For the time being," he said, "we will put aside any further inquiries into the incident in the Senate gallery." He turned back, paused for a moment, and said, "There may be some link between the incident and the death of Senator Bristow. I assume you are working on that. But what I am concerned with right now is simply this: how did this happen?"

"The body was discovered hardly more than an hour ago," Fitzgerald said. "I believe that—"

"We know when the body was found," Mason interrupted. "And I don't like hearing *believe*. What I want to hear is *know*. What do you *know?*"

Fitzgerald took a deep breath. It was no secret that Fitzgerald thought that Mason was a pompous martinet surrounded by two political courtiers who, like him, knew little about police work. And Fitzgerald was not alone in that judgment. As part of a plan to expand the territorial jurisdiction of the Capitol Police, the House wanted to remove the architect from the police board and relegate the two sergeants-at-arms to ex-officio members of the board without voting rights.

But Mason had persuaded the Senate leadership to resist the House plan. Yes, the Capitol Police should have greater arrest authority in the District, he conceded, but congressional committees simply did not possess the expertise of the architect and sergeants-at-arms. After a long stalemate, the House finally blinked. Fitzgerald, who had hoped that Mason's role as a police overseer would be history, had no choice but to defer to him. At least for now. Maybe next year, the House would win the stare-down.

Fitzgerald exhaled his anger with a sigh and answered Mason. "Senator Bristow's throat was slashed so deeply that muscles in the sides of her neck appear to have been severed. She was also stabbed repeatedly in the chest. Her left breast was nearly cut off." Fitzgerald paused. Morrison gasped. Constantino was fiddling with a pencil, which slipped from his fingers.

"I'll have to wait for a medical examiner's report before I can say much more," Fitzgerald continued. "But I believe"—as he spoke this word, he looked directly at Mason—"that the cause of death was strangulation. Probably manual."

"But what about the stabbing?" Mason asked.

"Her wounds, if inflicted while she was alive, would have caused a great deal of bleeding. When a person is stabbed, particularly through an artery, the heart keeps pumping and the blood gushes out of the wound in—"

"I take your point," Mason said. "You can cut the anatomy lesson."

Fitzgerald went on as if he had not heard Mason. "—in spurts. It spurts out of the heart. There was relatively little blood in the subway car."

"But what if she were—"

"Murdered elsewhere? The most likely spot would be the women's room at the subway's Senate entrance. I checked there. It looked to me as if the killer took her into a stall, strangled her, then stabbed her and mutilated her after she was dead. Then he carried the body out to the car and cleaned up the stall as best as he could."

"You say 'it looked to me'?" Mason repeated.

"I'm giving you a crime scene assessment. The scene needs to be gone over by evidence technicians. The body must be examined by a medical examiner. There has to be an autopsy." He stopped for an instant, then added, "You can't solve a murder at a meeting. Every minute I spend here is impeding the investigation."

Before an obviously agitated Mason could respond, Koch turned in his chair and spoke directly to Fitzgerald. "There's a question about the medical examiner, Jeff. And about a lot of other things."

Mason, resuming control, said, "I asked Roy to give me an overview of the legal questions involved."

Koch reached down to the open briefcase beside him and took out sets of stapled papers, which he passed to the others. "I've photocopied the pertinent statutes in case anyone wants to refer to them," he said. "First of all, there's Section 351 of Title 18 in the U.S. Code. This is entitled, quote, Congressional, Cabinet, and Supreme Court Assassination, Kidnaping, and Assault, unquote. What is pertinent to us right now is that any crimes covered by the statute must be investigated by the FBI. As I see it, the Capitol Police force is charged with investigating crime on Capitol Hill. And a felony—which this clearly is—*must* be dealt with when it is detected, regardless of subsequent jurisdictional issues. Beyond that—beyond acting under speedy information on a felony—the FBI has jurisdiction. I think we should turn this over to the FBI right away."

"I agree with that, Roy," Fitzgerald said. "As far as I'm concerned, the sooner the better."

"Fine, fine," Koch said. "So far, so good. But we've got a body on Capitol Hill"—he caught Mason's frown—"a senator's body, and the question of a medical examiner comes up." He flipped to another page. "U.S. Code again. When the Congress gave home rule to the District of Columbia, one of the specific issues that was raised was the jurisdiction of the D.C. medical examiner. Congress decided, with this statute, that the medical examiner would be under the control of the mayor. Furthermore, the medical examiner's investigations of unexplained or violent deaths are to be conducted with the aid of the Metropolitan Police of the District

33

of Columbia. But as you know, Congress also decided that felonies in the District would be handled essentially as *federal* crimes, to be prosecuted by U.S. attorneys and tried in U.S. District Court."

"And the point of all this?" Mason asked irritably.

"The point," Koch replied, "is that we must call in the FBI for investigation of the murder. We must call in the District of Columbia to have the body legally examined. And we must call in the D.C. police force"—he looked toward Fitzgerald and shrugged—"the Metropolitan Police, that is, to aid the D.C. medical examiner."

"Jesus!" Fitzgerald exclaimed. "The FBI and the Metro Police don't tell each other the time of day." He leaned forward to confront Mason.

"And," Mason asked, "just what do you propose?"

"I propose that I go back to the crime scene," Fitzgerald replied, standing. "I can handle the preliminary work, until we can get the FBI into this. And if I'm on the case right now, it avoids bringing in the D.C. police. The problem is, I just don't have enough of the right people to deal with a murder case. I—"

Mason broke in. "It's a bit complicated. Senator Bristow's murder may have been the random act of a psychopath. On the other hand, she held a key vote on this whole statehood issue, and . . ." He paused again. "I just got off the phone with Senator Lawson. He suggests, Jeff, that you begin the preliminary work and we hold off the FBI for a while."

"Okay," Fitzgerald said with a sigh of resignation. "I'll give it a shot." He started toward the door and then turned and looked at Koch. "Roy, we've got a senator murdered, Capitol Hill sealed off, a traffic jam, the media in an uproar, and five hundred and thirty-four members wondering if they're next. I'll try to solve those problems while you work out the legal issues."

"One moment, Jeff," Mason said. "Those five hundred and thirty-four members need more from you than an offhand remark. What are you planning to do to step up security?"

"I'll let the sergeants-at-arms draw up recommendations and act on them," Fitzgerald said. He well knew that the sergeants-at-arms rarely agreed on anything. In a recent case involving theft from the House post office, Constantino, with the backing of the Speaker of the House, had argued that Congress was a separate branch of government and had forbidden Fitzgerald to cooperate with the FBI. Most members of the House and Senate, as Lawson had reminded Fitzgerald yesterday, did not want to give the FBI a franchise to wander around the Hill looking for crimes.

As Fitzgerald started for the door, Koch spoke. "There's no way you can legally move the senator's body, Jeff. You *must* call the D.C. medical examiner."

Fitzgerald smiled at him. "That's a binding legal opinion?"

"Yes, it is," Koch said solemnly. "If you need—"

"I'll call you if I do, Roy," Fitzgerald said, closing the door behind him.

Fitzgerald walked up a short set of stairs to the Rotunda and then through the small Senate rotunda to the four-room suite of the majority leader. One of Lawson's staff members, in the required three-piece suit, was at a desk just inside the door. He recognized Fitzgerald. "What can I do for you, Chief?" he asked.

"I need to see Senator Lawson immediately," Fitzgerald said. The aide spoke into a phone, hung up, and ushered him into Lawson's spacious private office.

The senator rose from a gleaming mahogany desk whose top was clear except for a white phone console and a yellow lined pad, which was to a distressed Washington official what a favorite blanket was to a troubled child. He motioned Fitzgerald to a red-and-gray-striped armchair to the right of the desk. Like every piece of furniture in the room, like the drapes on the windows and the thick carpeting, the chair had an aura of flawlessness.

"Jeff! Good to see you. You must be wondering right about now if I really did steer you to a good thing." Fitzgerald did not respond. Lawson never missed an opportunity to remind him who had lined him up for the chief's job.

Fitzgerald waited for the aide to leave before he spoke. "I've just come from Mason," he said. "He said you wanted me to handle the Bristow murder and keep the FBI out. I'm not sure, Senator, if you realize that—"

"I realize that I'm asking a lot, Jeff. You don't have to tell me that you don't have the . . . facilities for handling a murder case. But please, bear with me on this." Lawson walked over to a tall window with a carved arched frame that soared toward the vaulted ceiling. He pulled aside a plush drape and looked out.

35

Then he turned away from the window. "The FBI has tried
Abscam, the House post office. They'd like nothing better than to
get into our knickers. And the murder gives them that chance."
He returned to his desk, sat down, and leaned forward. "I'm trying
to protect an institution. And I'm trying to save your ass, Jeff. You
let a would-be assassin into the Senate gallery. Now you've got a
senator murdered. The press is going to be all over you for being
incompetent—being part of the mess in Congress. You can bet
your last dime that they'll be digging up what happened back in
Yosemite. By the time they get through with you, you'll look like a
reject from *Police Academy III*."

He acted as if he were waiting for Fitzgerald to say something.
When Fitzgerald failed to respond, he raised his voice a notch.
"You're looking at the end of your career. You cash in on this now,
turn it over to the FBI, and you're through. Once the FBI comes
in, if they can't solve it, they'll say you screwed it up. If they do
solve it, they won't share the credit. You of all people know how
they operate."

Fitzgerald felt deep within himself an anger that he knew he
had to throttle, even while someone was driving nails into his
coffin. "I get the picture," he said. "How long have I got?"

Lawson looked up at the ceiling for a moment, then looked at
him and said, "My guess is a couple of days. Maybe a week. No
longer."

6

FITZGERALD took the Senate subway to the Hart subway stop.
On the platform were three phones. One, a direct line to the Democratic and Republican cloakrooms, was used to report that senators were on their way to the Senate floor. The second was used
exclusively for police communications. The third was a regular
phone. Fitzgerald, with Koch's sheaf of photocopies tucked under
his left arm, punched 9 for an outside line and called information

to get the number of the District of Columbia's medical examiner's office. He was soon speaking rapidly to a disbelieving voice.

"That's right. I am the chief of the Capitol Police. Fitzgerald's the name. And I'll say this one more time. Get me your boss and tell him that this is about the murder of a United States senator."

"Hold on, mister," the voice said. "I'll get you somebody."

In two minutes and fourteen seconds, by Fitzgerald's watch, another voice came from the void. "What is this about?" the new voice said. It was the voice of a woman, and Fitzgerald knew that the medical examiner of the District of Columbia was a man named either Higgins or Perkins. Fitzgerald had seen Higgins or Perkins on a local news show two weeks before, lamenting the burden on his office caused by the District's ever-rising murder rate. He was a husky black man whom Fitzgerald had judged to be about his age, and when he lunged forward to make a point, something about the broad face that filled the screen prodded a memory.

"What this is about," Fitzgerald replied, with angry spaces between words, "is an urgent police matter. I am Chief Fitzgerald of the Capitol Police and I am requesting the services of the District of Columbia medical examiner. That's what this is about."

"You are speaking to an assistant medical examiner, and a damn busy one. What can I do for you?"

"You can't do anything, Ms. Assistant Medical Examiner. According to the law, the only one I can talk to about this matter is your boss."

There was a long, theatrically loud sigh, then, "I don't think even my boss deserves *another* cop in his life. But I will try to switch you over. Hold on."

One minute, twelve seconds, then, "Perkins here."

"This is Capitol Police Chief Jeffrey P. Fitzgerald."

"Okay. Well, speak quick, Fitzgerald."

"I've got a murdered senator on my hands. I'd like you to claim the body and conduct an autopsy."

"Are you kidding? What I've got on *my* hands is better than a murder a day. Every damn slab in my morgue is occupied. I've hired part-time pathologists, retirees. Some of them haven't touched a body in years. A couple of them never saw a gunshot wound till they came here. That's what I've got on *my* hands,

37

Fitzgerald. And besides, I got my own chief of police. And I take my orders from the mayor. So maybe you should call him."

"From what I saw on television, you aren't much of a fan of the mayor."

"That's between him and me. And if you saw me on that TV show, then you know what it's like down here. So you get one of them Army or Navy doctors that take care of congressmen's belly-aches. Goodbye, Fitzgerald."

"Hold on just a second, Doctor. There's a personal matter I want to clear up. When I saw you on TV, I thought I recognized you from somewhere."

"From where?" Perkins asked, and Fitzgerald, hearing a long sigh, wondered if Perkins's assistant had picked up the habit from her boss.

"From the emergency room in St. Luke's Hospital in Philadelphia. Am I right? Were you there on June 17, 1982?"

"Well I was there in '82. But I can't tell you exact dates," Perkins said. "Why?"

"Because I think you're the doctor who took a .32 slug out of my shoulder."

"FBI? Some kind of bank shootup?"

"That's right. You leaned down and you said, 'Not bad, Red. Not bad at all.' And then you put me out. When I woke up, the Bureau had some other doctor treating me, and I never found out who you were until now. I owe you a drink."

Perkins laughed. "Yeah, I remember. My first gunshot wound. I was thinking then about going into pediatrics or pathology."

"What made up your mind?"

"A woman, Fitzgerald. As always." Perkins began speaking more quickly. "I've got no time for reminiscing. But you got yourself another minute. What the hell is this all about?"

"Senator Bristow has been strangled and then cut up. In the Senate subway. The law says—"

"Don't give me law, Fitzgerald. Who told you to call me?"

"Nobody. I need a medical examiner who knows about homicide, not a goddamn Army doctor who's waiting for his pension at Walter Reed."

"You know Mareno?"

Fitzgerald had to think for a moment. Joseph Mareno. Pennsylvania congressman. From Philadelphia, Fitzgerald thought. Chairman of the House District of Columbia Committee. Even though the District had home rule, much of its money came from the federal government through appropriations controlled by the D.C. Committee. Mareno ran it so tightly that he was called Washington's other mayor.

"Well," Fitzgerald replied, "I know who he is."

"Your cops get so much money, surprises me you and he aren't buddies."

"Never met him," Fitzgerald said.

"I'll be damned. Okay. Listen up. Get a pencil and write this down."

"That's all right. You just go ahead," Fitzgerald said.

"Call this number: 225-3121. That's his private number. He says okay, I say okay. Either way, you call me back. Now here's *my* private number: 724-5112. Got that?"

"Got it. Thanks."

Fitzgerald hung up and, because he was inside the Capitol phone system, dialed only the last five digits of Mareno's number. A gruff voice answered. "Mareno here."

Fitzgerald told him about the murder and the call to Perkins.

"So he told you to call me?" Mareno asked. Before Fitzgerald could answer, the congressman continued. "Good man, Perkins. But I wish to hell he wouldn't get me involved in this." He paused, and Fitzgerald heard the sound of a cigarette being drawn on.

"I hear good things about you, Fitzgerald. And not from that asshole Mason. We got to meet one of these days." Another puff. "You call Larry Perkins and you tell him that he's to go over there and do his thing. Tell him he should give this one the highest priority. Okay?"

"Okay," Fitzgerald said. "Thanks very much, Congressman."

"No thanks to me, Fitzgerald. You didn't call me. Got it? And you tell Larry to forget he got me into this. Got it?"

"Got it. Goodbye."

"Just a minute. You're having a press conference at eleven o'clock?"

"Right. But how did you know?"

Mareno made a noise that sounded like a snicker. "Christ, you

39

really are a new guy. From media alerts on the AP wire. Anything happens on the Hill or in the District, I know about it. The wire's my secret. Anyway, you're having a conference, you put our boy Perkins in front of the mike. Okay?"

"If it's all right with him, it's—"

"Don't worry. Larry'll love it. It's a wonderful chance to piss off the mayor."

Mareno hung up without saying goodbye.

Fitzgerald called Perkins back and recounted the conversation with Mareno. Perkins said he was on his way.

As Fitzgerald turned from the phone, a young man in a gray suit approached him and said, "Chief? I'm Craig Haverlin, the administrative assistant to Senator Bristow. They told me I'd find you here."

Fitzgerald acknowledged Haverlin with a nod and walked toward the train that Willis had drawn up next to the one containing Senator Bristow's body, which was now covered with a rich blue blanket fetched from the Senate infirmary. Willis discreetly left the operator's seat when Fitzgerald sat down and motioned to Haverlin to sit next to him. Haverlin hesitated, started to say something, then sat down, his eyes cast downward. He took a pack of Pall Malls from his shirt and said, "Mind if I smoke?"

"No ashtray," Fitzgerald replied, sitting back. Haverlin sat on the edge of the seat, looking as if he might tip over. "You've notified the next of kin?" Fitzgerald asked.

"There's a sister and a brother-in-law. No children," Haverlin said. "I'm trying to reach the sister. I think she's in Europe somewhere. I made the . . . arrangements for the late senator—Charles Bristow—and I'll probably be handling it again. I . . . I'd like to know what happened."

Fitzgerald quickly described the finding of the body and watched Haverlin's pale face grow even paler. "Any questions?" he asked. Haverlin, his gaze again toward the floor, shook his head.

"Well," Fitzgerald said, "I've got a couple." He changed his seat to sit directly across from Haverlin. "When was the last time you saw Senator Bristow?"

"Last night," Haverlin replied. "The Senate adjourned about five o'clock. As usual, she worked a bit after that. She called me from her hideaway and—"

40

"Hold it," Fitzgerald said. He picked up his radio and pressed a button. "Communications. Fitzgerald. I want two Patrol Division officers—repeat, *Patrol Division*—to Senator Bristow's hideaway, that's room 279A near our Senate basement station. And I want two more in her Hart office. Seal the rooms and post officers there until further notice." He turned back to Haverlin and asked, "What time did she call?" He had taken a notebook and a pen out of his inside pocket and began jotting notes.

"About . . . about six. Well, a little after six."

"And you went from here—the Hart Building—to the Capitol by subway?"

"No. The subway closes at six. I walked."

"Along there?" Fitzgerald asked, gesturing toward the narrow walkway beside the subway tracks.

"No. It was such a nice warm evening I walked to the plaza and entered the Capitol from there."

"So you arrived at this hideaway of hers at maybe six-twenty or so?"

"About that."

"How did she seem?"

"Oh, normal. Quite normal."

"How's that?"

"*Normal.* I mean, she was the way she always is—*was.* Brisk. Businesslike."

"How long did you work for her?"

"Ever since she got here six months ago. I worked for her late husband, the first Senator Bristow."

"Did you get along with her all right?"

Haverlin smiled. "Getting along with your senator is an AA's basic job. She told me what to do and I did it."

"What did she want you to do last night when she called you to the hideaway?"

"Nothing significant. To bring over the afternoon mail and the folder with the day's correspondence for her to sign."

"Wouldn't it be more appropriate for her secretary to do that?"

"If she had a secretary. We are temporarily without one."

"This has happened before? Not having a secretary?"

"Twice before."

41

"About the mail and the correspondence. Was there anything in it that seemed to upset her?"

"Basically, it was all routine. But . . . well, there was a certain crisis . . . not *crisis*"—he raised his right hand and made a twisting gesture—"but perhaps a turning point. Yes. Turning point."

Fitzgerald leaned back and waited for more.

Haverlin shifted and stretched out his legs. "Some of the correspondence lately has been about fund-raising and about her decision on whether to run on her own. She talked a little about that last night. About what she would do. Not asking for advice, certainly. I mean, she wouldn't ask my advice. Sort of thinking out loud."

"Was she going to run?"

"I have no idea."

"So she was in a good mood? Not acting as if something was preying on her mind?"

"She seemed fine. When I stood to leave, at about seven, she said she was going to be there just a little while more. I offered to wait and walk her to her car. She parked it in the basement here. She said no thanks. I said something about what a beautiful night it was. And she said she'd be driving in it but not walking in it."

"Meaning that she would use the walkway?" Fitzgerald asked sharply.

"She always did. She was afraid of walking on the Hill at night."

7

FITZGERALD'S RADIO beeped. It was Maldonado at the Capitol. The crime scene technicians had finished up there and were wondering if they could take the subway to Hart. Fitzgerald got out of the car with Haverlin and told Willis to pick up the technicians. As the train silently slid away, he directed Haverlin to the command center and told him to give a statement.

Fitzgerald walked over to the other train and looked down at the rumpled blue blanket, trying to focus on the murder. This was what he was supposed to be concentrating on. But he could not take this murder from the shadow of Capitol Hill. He was dealing with the politicians, not with anyone who could help him find out who killed Senator Bristow. And who would those helpers be? Maldonado? Hawkins? Mason?

On the wall of his office, in a black frame, was what looked at first like a genealogical chart strung with interconnected boxes. It was the table of organization of the U.S. Capitol Police. He thought about it now. He had almost memorized it, not dutifully but desperately in those first few weeks on the job, when, assailed by doubt, he had tried to make sense out of his decision to take over what was really only a guard force. He had stood before the string of boxes long enough and often enough to see a hidden message: he was the chief of two police departments, one consisting of genial building guards and one that had at least some of the attributes of a modern municipal force.

He was the top box. The next box down, assistant chief, was empty and would stay that way until he had time to observe and evaluate the candidates. Below the empty box was a line of boxes. The one labeled *Uniform Services Bureau* contained nearly all of his cops. They had their little boxes too—Capitol Division, House Division, Senate Division—and those boxes represented guard and security responsibilities. Hawkins and Maldonado, assigned to the Senate, were typical. They rotated frequently with the other units that were assigned to the House and to the Capitol itself. These were the armed and trained law enforcement personnel. Although often seen standing in front of bronze doors, directing wayward tourists to their destinations, they were fully alert and able to respond to any potential threat or disturbance.

The rest of the cops in Uniform Services were in the Patrol Division: the patrol car cops, the motorbike cops, the CERT cops. They wrote the parking tickets and kept an eye on members' residences or rental properties on the Hill, and lately they had been responding to more crime calls: purse snatches, muggings, sexual assaults. These were the street cops of a company town, the ones you waved to and knew by sight as you went to and from your company job. They made you feel safe, protected by the company, especially when crime filled the nights of the town next door and was beginning to cross the border into the company town.

Less obvious kinds of security were promised by the little boxes under the *Protective Services Bureau* box: Threat Assessment Unit, Electronic Countermeasures Section, Dignitary Protection Unit, Special Investigations Division. From those boxes, which Fitzgerald had helped to create, he hoped to find the people who would form a complete police force.

The subway train from the Capitol pulled up, and two men and a woman in civilian clothes, each carrying a large aluminum suitcase, got off, followed by Maldonado.

"Anything worthwhile over there?" Fitzgerald asked.

An evidence technician shrugged. "Lot of prints," he said. "Bloodstains. Lot of material to sort out." He put down his suitcase and hunkered by it to open it. He was a rangy black man in tan slacks and a dark green jacket.

"And the hairpin. Don't forget the hairpin, Lowell," Sergeant Alexandra Phelan said to the technician. She looked at Fitzgerald, smiling. "Was that a test, Chief?"

"Test? What do you mean, test?" Fitzgerald said, looking at first surprised, then irritated.

"Maldonado told us about your little visit to the ladies' room," Phelan said. She was still holding her suitcase. Maldonado turned and rapidly walked back to the train.

Fitzgerald reached down and lifted the blanket. "See what you can do with this, Phelan. This isn't any test."

Phelan opened her suitcase and from one of the compartments pulled a pair of transparent plastic gloves and several plastic bags. On each bag was a numbered label. As she put on the gloves, Fitzgerald noticed that she did not have on any rings. She was wearing a loosely cut beige suit that had the austere look of a uniform. She reached into an inside pocket of her jacket and took out a little black looseleaf notebook to which was clipped a black ballpoint pen stamped *U.S. Government.*

Without turning to look at Fitzgerald, she asked, "Are you running the investigation? Do we report directly to you?"

"Until you hear otherwise. This is the first homicide this department's ever had, and—"

"It's not *my* first," she said. Lowell, who was taking something out of his suitcase, smiled and slowly shook his head.

Phelan gathered up the bags and walked past Fitzgerald. Leaning into the car where the body lay, she carefully removed the blanket, turned it over, and spread it full-length on the tile floor. "Better give it a vacuum, Stan," she said to the second technician. "Maybe it picked up something from the body."

She stepped back and, eyes on the body, began talking with Lowell about the still and video photography that would be needed. Then she told Stan what spots to dust for prints after the body had been removed.

Lowell swiftly made a video record of the crime scene, carefully replaced the videocamera in its case, and just as swiftly shot the stills. As soon as he was finished, Phelan crouched by the body and began writing and sketching in her notebook. She was gently tugging at a hat under the body when the door of the SENATORS ONLY elevator opened and Dr. Larry Perkins appeared, followed by three white-uniformed attendants with a folded-up gurney. Perkins walked regally from the elevator to the platform, stopped, and said loudly, "Hands off that body!"

Fitzgerald took a step toward him while the two evidence technicians pulled back. Phelan, her back toward Perkins, kept examining the hat.

Perkins pulled a crime scene tape from a pillar and, holding it aloft like a banner, strode rapidly up to Fitzgerald. Not saying a word, he leaned down, slung the tape around Phelan's right arm, and yanked.

Without looking up, Phelan swung her stiffened left hand around and brought it down sharply on Perkins's forearm. As he reared back, she whirled and sprang toward him, her right hand poised high for another blow. Fitzgerald grabbed her elbows from behind, spinning her away from Perkins and pinning her arms behind her back. Her jacket flared open, and Perkins saw her shoulder holster.

"Take it easy, Phelan," Fitzgerald said. "It's the medical examiner."

"I don't give a goddamn who he is!" she shouted. "Attacking a police off—"

"No attack intended," Perkins said softly, rubbing his arm. "I took you for a civilian. *Big* mistake."

Fitzgerald slowly released Phelan and stepped between her and Perkins.

"I am now going to examine the body," Perkins said, his voice

45

once again imperious. He spread a white handkerchief on the floor of the car, knelt on it, took a microcassette recorder from a coat pocket of his European-cut suit, and began speaking: 'April 7, ten sixteen A.M. Hart Office Building, First Street Northeast. The body of a Caucasian female . . ."

Fitzgerald summoned Maldonado. "Here's what I want you to do. This is Lawrence Perkins, the medical examiner. Get one of his people here to go back and drive their ambulance or hearse or whatever they call it to the plaza. Get Hawkins to ride along so the vehicle can get through the checkpoint. Then, when Perkins is finished, lead him and the gurney through that maintenance tunnel that runs from here to the Capitol. Bring them up to the plaza level and through that door under the arch. You got all that?"

Maldonado nodded slowly, then said, "But Chief, the body—those stairs."

"There's an elevator for the handicapped at the bottom of the escalator. If the gurney won't fit, then she'll have to be carried up. Don't worry, Maldonado." Fitzgerald jutted his chin toward the men in white. "Those guys have taken a lot of bodies from places a lot worse than the U.S. Capitol. I'm doing this to keep the press uninformed. Understand?"

Maldonado nodded again, as slowly as before.

Fitzgerald turned to Lowell and said, "When you're through, report to my office." Then, with a nod to Phelan to accompany him, he headed toward the SENATORS ONLY elevator. He knew it always came faster than the ones reserved for John Q. Public. No one was going to charge him with trespassing today.

8

FITZGERALD'S OFFICE was on the top floor of the seven-story Capitol Police headquarters. From behind his desk he could look through a window with vertical blinds to the Russell Senate Office Building and, behind it, the Capitol's magnificent dome. Because the headquarters of the Capitol Police happened to be on the

Senate side of Capitol Hill, the uniformed officers who guarded the Senate were stationed there. The officers who guarded the House and the Capitol were stationed in the Longworth Office Building. In the basement, on the Senate side of the Capitol, there was also a small precinct for the Senate police detachment. It was an odd arrangement, dictated by the leadership of the two Houses, carried out by the sergeants-at-arms, and overseen by the architect.

So be it, Fitzgerald thought now, shifting his gaze from the Hart Building to Alexandra Phelan, who sat before his desk, legs crossed, fingers drumming on the chrome armrests formed by the frame of the chair. Her aluminum suitcase was next to the chair.

"Coffee?" he asked.

"Yes, Chief. Thanks. Black."

Fitzgerald smiled. "That's the way I drink it, too." He rose and went to the cabinet by the door, hoping that Margaret, his secretary, had managed to brew coffee between phone calls. The dark gray coffeemaker sat on a shelf under the sleek metal cabinet, which, like the walls, trim, and carpeting, was light gray.

From the cabinet Fitzgerald took two white mugs bearing the gold, white, and blue seal of the Capitol Police. He poured a cup of coffee and turned to see that Phelan had followed him. He realized that she had not expected to be served. He handed her the cup, and she returned to her chair. He poured himself a cup and pulled up another chair next to hers, shifting it so that he could speak directly to her.

"Lawson wants us to take the lead on this, at least temporarily. We're going to need help. Like the medical examiner." He smiled and reached for his coffee mug.

"And the FBI lab?" Phelan asked.

"We'll need the lab. But let me handle that one. Let's get started with this." He took out his notebook and went over his conversation with Craig Haverlin. "Check out his statement. I've got a feeling that there's more to him than meets the eye. What have you got lined up?"

"Her car," Phelan said. "It's in the Hart basement garage. I think it should be impounded and towed to our garage."

Fitzgerald nodded, made a note, and asked, "Anything else?"

47

"That hideaway of hers—I want to have the team go over it. Then it ought to be sealed right away."

"Done already," Fitzgerald said, smiling slightly. "What else do you see?"

"Whatever paper I can pick up. Any threatening letters that came in and went over to Threat Assessment. Critical letters to the editor in Louisiana newspapers, and all documents on file with the Senate. Her financial disclosure statement."

"And?"

"End of list for now," she said. She hesitated for a moment, then added, "Look, Chief . . . who do I—"

"I want you to run this, Alix, reporting directly to me. Got it?"

"Yes, sir. But I will need help."

"You'll get it. All I can give you. Also, as of right now you're a lieutenant, at least in name. You came out number one on the exam. The budget is what didn't pass. But Lieutenant Dominguez of the Capitol Division retires in June. I'll juggle things around and you can start getting paid as a lieutenant then. So till then you're a lieutenant with a sergeant's pay. Okay?"

"Very much okay. And the team? Lowell, Stan Borstelmann? I hope I get them."

"You get them plus what you need." He looked at his watch and touched a button on the phone console on his desk. "Margaret? Is Lowell there yet? Send him in."

As Lowell shut the door behind him, Fitzgerald motioned him to the chair next to Phelan.

"Coffee?"

"No thanks, Chief."

"You're on the Bristow case and nothing else," Fitzgerald said. "Lieutenant Phelan will brief you. What I want right now is two things: one, the crime scene video absolutely sealed—*no leaks*—and two, still photos of the deceased suitable for publication."

Lowell shot a fast, puzzled glance at Phelan. "Don't worry about the video, Chief. The cassette goes right to the evidence vault. But the stills, well, they're all pretty . . . well, *forensic,* but maybe I can crop—"

"Her dress," Phelan interrupted. "Her legs were exposed."

"Crop it so all you have is the upper body," Fitzgerald said. "I want to release prints. I want people to see it. I want the guy who did this to see it. And I want to establish control over what goes to the media. They'll be screaming for photos." He looked at his watch again. "There's a press conference at eleven. You've both got ten minutes to tell me what we know."

Lowell looked at Phelan, shrugged, and gestured toward her, palm up.

"Right now, Chief," Phelan said, "I think I can give you two things. This isn't someone off the street or one of our friends from your favorite shelter for the homeless. The killer was a man, and he was very familiar with the layout at the Capitol and at Hart. He even put the body in the car going to Hart."

"Familiar with the Hill," Fitzgerald said. "Yes, I sensed that, too. And sure, a man. But you sound awfully positive of that. Why?"

"The hairpins. You saw one in the ladies' room, where you figured she was killed. There was another on the floor of the car, and two in her hair. They were put in wrong."

Fitzgerald looked puzzled. Phelan tore a piece of paper from the memo pad on the desk, took a hairpin out of her hair, and handed it to Lowell. "Lowell," she said, "will you please attach this piece of paper to my hair?"

Lowell fumbled with the paper and hairpin and quickly gave up.

"It's easy for a woman. See?" She deftly fastened the paper to her hair, shook her head to show that it held, then removed it. "The way I see it, Senator Bristow was grabbed near the ladies' room and in the initial struggle lost her hat. The killer took her inside, killed her, and then tried to get the hat back on when he put her in the subway. Why? Maybe he was obsessive. Maybe he saw it as some kind of crazy joke. Anyway, he managed to get it on her head. Cullum remembers seeing it, right? But when the body fell onto the floor, the hat came off, because it had not been properly attached."

"Not bad," Fitzgerald said. "Anything else?"

"Check out the closed-circuit cameras."

Installation of remote-controlled, closed-circuit television cameras had begun several years before, under the direction of Mason's predecessor. The eighty-five cameras were programmed to transmit images to monitors on a relatively random pattern. Opera-

49

tors in the Capitol Police communications room watch the monitors and zoom in with a camera when they see something suspicious. On their own, the cameras respond to motion by immediately transmitting an image to the monitors and breaking into the display. The cameras' images are kept on time-showing tapes.

"There's a camera at the end of that long corridor in the Senate basement, the one that leads to the subway," Fitzgerald said. "Start with that one."

He turned to Lowell. "Get those photos—say fifty of them—to the conference room by eleven." He stood, shook hands with Lowell, and asked Phelan to stay. When they were alone again, he poured another coffee and sat back down. "I can see this is not your first homicide," he said.

"Before I came here I was a detective—they called it special investigator—for the Connecticut State Police."

"That's why I picked you when I set up the crime scene team. I didn't know about your homicide experience. Tell me about it." He sipped the coffee, reached out to put the mug on his desk, and folded his hands in his lap.

Phelan held her mug in both hands and spoke across it. "In two years I had four cases, five homicides. The first one was a farmer who killed his wife and teenage daughter and said they had gone off somewhere. His girlfriend suspected something and went to the sheriff. He called in the state police. I found the bodies."

"How?"

She sipped, put the mug on the desk, and leaned back. "A hunch. He was a pretty dull guy. I figured he would think that he could solve a problem by killing them but he wouldn't do anything remarkable. The farm was up for sale and kind of rundown. He hadn't done much work, except in one spot in the middle of a field. It was all nicely planted and weeded. I went there one day with a shovel and—"

"And a search warrant?"

"Oh, sure. The Connecticut State Police are as straight as the FBI." She laughed, throwing back her head. She had a slight overbite but straight white teeth, and she ended her laugh with a quick motion that rippled her long black hair.

"What about the other homicides?"

"Car in a lake. Driver full of coke. Shift still in neutral. Motor

vehicle murder made up to look like an accident. His partner in a
lawn-care business did it. Then a wife who shot her husband. Used
a .30-.30 deer rifle. No problem who did it, but the state's attorney
wanted a motive so she wouldn't walk with a self-defense claim.
And . . ." Her voice dropped. "And a three-year-old boy. His
father put him under a drill press and drilled him repeatedly. His
little chest, his head . . . A neighbor heard screams and called us.
We could see what had happened through a cellar window." She
took another sip of coffee.

"They sent me in to talk the father into surrendering. He was
holed up in the cellar, ranting and raving about how God had told
him to do it. We didn't know he had a gun. An AK-47." She moved
the coffee to her lips, then put down the mug. Her other hand was
gripping the chair arm.

"He came at you?"

She nodded. "He got off half a dozen wild rounds before I shot
him."

"Dead?"

She nodded.

He stared at her. "Dead?" he repeated, almost inaudibly.

She nodded again, looking puzzled. He suddenly seemed far
away. She stood and asked, "Is that all, Chief?"

He nodded and she left, closing the door softly behind her. He
went back to the chair behind his desk, sat down, and turned to
look out the window. "Dead," he whispered. "Dead." And as he
had done so many times before, he thought of Alice Tyle.

9

DURING Fitzgerald's three years at the FBI field office in San
Francisco, he had never visited Yosemite National Park. He and
Helen had talked about it, but as in so many things, they had
never been able to find the time, mesh their schedules, work it
out. Those phrases, so often spoken past each other . . .

Then the day had come when he did drive to Yosemite, but not with Helen. Seated next to him in the front seat of the black Bureau Oldsmobile was Special Agent Alice Tyle.

"Aren't you going to stop for the view?" she asked as the car rounded a bend on the road to the national park road. Fitzgerald gripped the wheel tighter and turned his right hand slightly to glance at his watch while keeping an eye on the curve ahead.

"No way, Alice. We've got other things to do," he said.

"Come on, Fitz. Stretch your legs. Five minutes won't hurt. We're early."

Fitzgerald turned into the overlook. He pulled the car into one of the parking spaces, nosing forward until it almost touched a low stone wall. He did not turn off the engine. They both gazed for a moment through the bug-splattered windshield at the granite vista spread before them. Tyle reached across Fitzgerald and switched off the ignition. The purr of the air conditioning died. She opened her door and got out. Then, holding the door open, she looked in and said, "Unfreeze, FBI." When he did not respond, she turned and walked toward the point of the lookout. She did not close the door.

Fitzgerald got out of the car, went around to close the other door, and followed her. In her left hand she carried a brown knapsack by its straps. She was wearing jeans, a loose-fitting short-sleeved white cotton shirt, and a rolled-up green-and-white bandanna tied across her brow. As he walked faster to catch up with her, he watched her shoulder-length blond hair moving in time with her stride.

She wore what he knew to be brand-new hiking boots, gray and ankle-high, bought just a few days before. On the drive up he had mentioned them. Didn't they feel uncomfortable? Didn't they have to be broken in? "Not these days, Fitz." She had laughed. "It's a Gore-Tex world out there now." Now, watching her lithe body, he remembered the pang from that remark. Her world, so different from his world of worn leather boots and worn ideas.

A fat tourist, bulging in yellow shorts and a green T-shirt, was following Alice Tyle with his sunglassed eyes, and Fitzgerald felt another pang. *Jealousy—my God.*

She stopped at the edge of the overlook, which arched out from the parking area. Her hand swept the panorama—El Capitan, Half Dome, Sentinel Rock, Bridal Veil Falls, a scrim of shimmering rainbows—and she said, "Beautiful. So wonderfully, wonderfully beautiful." She turned, removed her sunglasses, and squinted up at him. Her eyes were green, and her face was radiant. Her hair shimmered like the distant falls. "Thanks for this, Fitz," she said.

He knew she did not mean the view. And he knew there had been talk at the office about assigning her to the murders. Most of the men resented a woman's getting a crack at a high-profile crime. Careers were made by working on the big ones. "Don't thank me, Alice. Not yet. Today's going to be tough, really tough."

Hardly anyone called him Fitz, he thought. He was going to say something about that. But he didn't. They talked about the case on the half-hour drive to park headquarters.

They met with the park superintendent and the chief ranger in the superintendent's office on the second floor of a building that looked out over the heart of the park, Yosemite Valley. From where he sat, Fitzgerald could see sidewalks crowded with people eating ice cream, dodging bicycles, entering and leaving shops. This, he thought, could be the Saturday morning jam in a small-town mall. The only vehicles were tour buses that slowly made their way through the crowds that spilled out onto the road.

The superintendent was droning on about budget restraints and the problems of crowd control and the lack of manpower. No matter what the subject, Fitzgerald sensed, the litany would have been the same. Maybe yesterday the subject was overflowing garbage cans. Today the subject was murder.

"Superintendent Bennett, if I may interrupt," he said, turning away from the window. "There have been two murders here in a week. Everybody has budget troubles, I can assure you—the National Park Service and the FBI. So, if you will pardon my bluntness, let's get down to the murders."

Chief Ranger Norman Dusko, a slim, white-haired man six months away from retirement, unfurled a topographical map, held it open on the conference table with his outstretched arms, and looked around helplessly. Fitzgerald put a bird guide and an empty coffee mug on the corners nearest him. Tyle commandeered the superintendent's pen-and-pencil set and wood-mounted nameplate.

Dusko pointed to two red X's, each neatly circled in the contour lines of a high-altitude wilderness area. "The women," he said, "were killed along here, on back-country trails off Tuolumne Meadows. As I told you when you were here Wednesday, Miz . . . Agent Tyle, the first one, well, a wolf or maybe even a bunch of marmots got to the body before we found it, and we didn't know it was a murder."

Fitzgerald nodded without comment. The embalmer at the funeral home in Mercer, where they took the body, had found the two hollow-nose .22 slugs in her chest and the abrasions caused by the muzzle of what was probably a .22 target pistol. Fitzgerald, the agent in charge of the San Francisco field office, had sent Alice Tyle to Mercer to check it out. The Bureau had jurisdiction over crimes in national parks. In Yosemite that meant drugs, now and then a knifing, and an occasional murky report about Satanic cult meetings. He assumed that the young woman had been murdered over drugs or had been killed by a boyfriend, a romance gone wrong.

"The second one was here," Dusko said. He pointed to an *X* near the symbol for a campsite. "About two miles from a high sierra camp. It's run by a concessionaire. They have cabins and a central unit with bunks, showers, and dining rooms. The camps are spaced about eight miles apart. People can travel light between them. One of my rangers found the woman early this morning when he headed up the trail to the camp to collect permits. He radioed in. We sent a party in to get her body out, and then we called you."

At Fitzgerald's request, the body had been taken to the funeral home in Mercer, where he and Tyle had seen it on the way to the park. She had been shot just like the first woman: two hollow-nose .22s, up close.

"She still had on her camera bag," Tyle interrupted Dusko to say. "Nikon, extra lens, expensive binoculars. Nothing taken. No sign of—"

"No sexual attack," the superintendent said. He sounded to Fitzgerald as if he were trying to defend Yosemite's honor.

"No sign of a struggle," Tyle continued. She turned toward the superintendent. "We must assume that these murders *were* sexual attacks. A man—size eleven bootmarks were found on the trail—is out there in your park killing women. Not robbing them. Just killing them. That's sexual to me."

Dusko looked up from the map and said, "We think we know where he is. A helicopter pilot saw someone in the meadow, off the trail, heading north. Bushwhacking. The pilot called in. I put rangers on the trail there, and we got the campers out."

"And all this," the superintendent said, "with a personnel force thirty-four percent below authorized level."

Fitzgerald ignored him and asked Dusko, "Armed? Are the rangers armed?"

"All my rangers are sworn lawmen," the superintendent answered. "Weapon-certified."

"We'll need help," said Fitzgerald. "I've made arrangements for a tactical team." He nodded toward Dusko. "Go on."

Dusko looked down at the map again. "The girl—"

"Woman," Tyle said. "She was thirty-one years old."

Dusko and Fitzgerald furtively looked at each other. Dusko shrugged and said, "Yes'm. Woman. Well, she was right on the trail. It looks like he was coming up the trail toward her. She had no reason to be afraid of another hiker on the trail. He was able to get close up, and he shot her, almost exactly the way that other gir— woman was shot. But this time someone else was on the trail and heard the shots. The ranger found her in the camp, all hysterical. That must have spooked the murderer, and he bolted off the trail. Funny he didn't try to get the other one."

"That's not the way he works," Tyle said.

"How do you know that?" Dusko asked.

"I just have this feeling, that's all," Tyle said.

"We'd better get up there," Fitzgerald said.

A helicopter deposited Dusko, Fitzgerald, and Tyle in a clearing near a lodge surrounded by small cabins. They were met in the lodge by Ranger Thelma Evans. Pointing to a spot on a wall map, she said, "I saw an illegal off-trail campsite right there the day before yesterday." Under her broad-brimmed hat, her red hair was gathered in a braid that hung down her olive-gray shirt. On her belt was a holster for what Fitzgerald recognized as a .38. "The pilot who saw the man bushwhacking had him going in that direction." She pointed again.

"How far is that from here?" Tyle asked.

"About a mile and a half up the trail, then maybe a quarter of a mile in," Evans said.

"Can you take us there?"

"Sure."

"Hold on, Alice," Fitzgerald said. "We've got the tactical team on the way."

"How long will they take?"

Fitzgerald glanced at his watch. "Less than an hour. They're coming up in a Marine helicopter."

"Landing *here?*" Tyle asked.

"They'll land near park headquarters, pick up a ranger to guide them here, and then land here," Fitzgerald said.

"That'll spook him. We know he spooks easily," Tyle said. "We can take him right now." She took off her pack, pulled out her shoulder holster and pistol, and strapped it on.

"Too risky," Fitzgerald said, shaking his head.

"*Risky?*" Tyle replied. "With four of us, all armed? Against a nut with a target pistol? Besides, we don't know if there's a woman coming up that trail right now, being stalked by that guy. That's the real risk—that he'll kill another woman while we're standing here."

Fitzgerald looked up at the wall map for a long moment, then asked Evans, "How close can we get to that campsite without being spotted?"

"It's in a kind of hollow," she said. "I can take us to a little ridge where we'd be looking down on it from about fifty yards."

"We'd be able to call for his surrender from there," Fitzgerald said, half to himself. "Little chance of gunplay."

That night, Fitzgerald stood in the small auditorium on the first floor of park headquarters. Around him were glassed-in exhibits of Yosemite animals, and behind him was a black screen. "I have an announcement about Special Agent Alice Tyle. She is—" Someone pressed a wrong button, the lights went out, and in the darkness for a few seconds he was bathed in the flickering image of mountain and sky while a voice boomed, "Welcome to Yosemite National Park." Then someone found the right switch, the film stopped, the lights of the auditorium came on again, and he resumed speaking.

"She is dead."

Members of the press began asking questions. He held up his hands for silence.

"We—I—believed that we would be able to call for the suspect's surrender from the ridge," he said. "I did not think there was much chance of gunplay."

"But there was," a reporter from a San Francisco television station said, and her cameraman swung his camera toward her. "Who was shot first?"

"Ranger Thelma Evans," Fitzgerald said, hearing his voice falter. He tried to strengthen it. "The suspect . . . the suspect apparently heard us coming and circled around behind us. When I called out for him to surrender, our eyes were on his campsite. Ranger Evans was approximately fifty feet to my left. Chief Ranger Dusko was approximately the same distance to my right."

"And Agent Tyle?" another reporter asked.

"She had crawled forward, toward the campsite. At the sound of the shot, she stood and turned toward the sound. Her weapon was in her hand." He paused. "Chief Ranger Dusko and I also turned toward the sound. We could not see the suspect. There was another shot, and I saw Agent Tyle fall. She apparently had seen the suspect, because when she fell she fired. Twice. I turned in the direction she had aimed and I saw the subject coming out from behind a tree. He fired again and hit Chief Ranger Dusko, who had unholstered his weapon but did not have a chance to fire it. I fired at the suspect and he fell backward into the brush."

"Did you know he was dead?" the San Francisco reporter asked.

"I fired six shots," Fitzgerald replied softly. "Three shots hit him in the head and three in his chest. I was quite sure he was dead."

"And so were the others," the reporter said, seeming to mimic the softness in his voice with a dramatic softness in her own.

"Not quite dead," Fitzgerald said, his voice hardly audible. "Dying. All dying. Agent Tyle survived, without regaining consciousness, until . . . until a few minutes ago. She died in the park hospital in the valley here." He paused, and his voice resumed its narrative tone. "The suspect, we believe from initial inquiry, was a finalist in competition for the U.S. Olympic pistol team but had not been chosen for the team. He apparently had some psychiatric background. This is being checked out."

57

Fitzgerald looked as if he were expecting a question. When none came, he said, "The suspect was wounded by Agent Tyle's shot. That was probably why he was only able to get off one shot— the one that killed Chief Ranger Dusko—and not two."

"Or he would have got you, too?" someone asked.

"Yes. Agent Tyle saved my life."

He did not tell them that he had ignored the others and had run toward Alice. He did not tell them that she had said, "Fitz . . . Fitz . . . I got him?" And that he had said, "Yes, Alice . . . Alice." And that he would keep saying it.

The autopsy would show that Fitzgerald had misspoken—that was the word used in the internal notice of censure. He had *misspoken* about the number of wounds in the suspect's body. There were six, and they all had been made by bullets from his gun. Alice Tyle's weapon had not been fired.

One week after the shootings, he was removed as agent-in-charge and transferred to FBI headquarters in Washington, where he was assigned to building security, but his daily tasks consisted of answering questions put to him by tight-lipped inquisitors from Personnel, Agent Training, Weapons, and the Office of the Inspector General. Helen decided to stay in San Francisco, where she managed a dress store. There was little left to the marriage. She, like so many FBI wives he knew, said he was really married to the FBI. When he was transferred to Washington, she began friendly divorce proceedings.

The inspector general's report of what was called the Yosemite incident was kept confidential. It recommended Fitzgerald's "separation without prejudice at an appropriate time." On the basis of Fitzgerald's account of her heroism, Tyle had been awarded a medal, so the inspector general also recommended that the "discrepancies regarding Agent Tyle's actions at the scene be kept a matter of internal knowledge."

Agent-in-Charge Fitzgerald, in addition to having shown exceedingly bad judgment in not awaiting the tactical team, used similarly bad judgment and excessive lethal force in emptying his weapon at the suspect. Had another suspect been present, Agent-in-Charge Fitzgerald would have confronted the suspect with an empty weapon. But this transgression pales beside the tragic offenses in judgment and procedure that led to these unwarranted, unnecessary deaths.

He had turned in his resignation, in response to an unwritten request, eight months after the shooting. On that last day he went to the room he had rented at the FBI-approved apartment house on Connecticut Avenue and was on his third drink when someone from the FBI Office of Congressional Liaison called him, said that Senator Daniel Lawson of California, the Senate majority leader, had been trying to reach him, and gave him a number. Fitzgerald made a cup of instant coffee from the hot-water tap in the kitchen, gulped it down, and called Lawson.

When Lawson had been governor of California, he and his wife had been taken hostage by a disgruntled state employee who killed the governor's bodyguard and driver before kidnapping him and his wife. Fitzgerald had led the FBI hostage rescue team that found the Lawsons, who were being held in a convenience store. He had talked the kidnapper into releasing the store manager and two customers. Then, while the kidnapper stood by the glass door with his shotgun lowered, Fitzgerald had shot him twice in the head.

Fitzgerald walked to the phone next to the bed, took a deep breath, and dialed the numbers he had been given.

"Jeffrey!" Lawson exclaimed over the phone, and his boyish face drifted back into Fitzgerald's memory. "I should be mad at you for not calling me while you've been in town. But I forgive you. I just learned that, as they say in Hollywood, you're at liberty. Well, I also just heard about a job you might be interested in."

And now I'm back in the murder business, he thought, trying to clear his mind of the past and concentrate on the present. He swiveled to the computer next to his desk and, pecking away at the keyboard, opened a file he named BRISTOW and began typing in what he knew.

His phone rang. "This is Mason," said the crisp voice. Margaret always put the architect right through. "I've just heard from the mayor's office."

"And what did His Honor want?" Fitzgerald asked.

"I didn't speak to the mayor directly," Mason replied. "His

assistant told me that you have been talking to the District's medical examiner."

"I did more than talk," Fitzgerald said. "He took the body away to the D.C. morgue. There'll be an autopsy tonight."

"Is there really a need for an autopsy?" Mason asked.

"An autopsy is mandatory in a murder case, Captain," Fitzgerald said, wincing to hear himself use the title.

"I was also told that Mareno's office is somehow involved. Is that correct?"

"Perkins would not do it unless Mareno gave his approval," Fitzgerald said. He quickly recounted his dealings with the two men.

"I hope you know what you're doing, Jeff," Mason said.

"What I am doing," Fitzgerald said, "is getting the best expertise I can find. We need Perkins."

"And why is that?" Mason asked. "I was hoping that we could contain this."

"Perkins is the medical examiner for the District of Columbia, and whether we like it or not, Capitol Hill is part of the District of Columbia."

"These are tense times for the District. And for the Hill's relations with the District," Mason said. "This is a Hill matter. A tragedy that has to be *contained*. I want daily reports on this. I also want a report on that incident involving one of your officers in the District Building."

Mason hung up before Fitzgerald could answer.

10

FITZGERALD walked down the concrete stairwell instead of taking the elevator to the first floor. He told himself he needed the exercise, but in fact he did not want to meet anyone. He needed time to think what he would say about the murder.

An officer stood at the entrance to the conference room. He

saluted Fitzgerald and opened the door. Like every other room in headquarters, the long, narrow room had light gray walls and a gray ceiling fitted with rows of recessed fluorescent lights. Battleship gray was the architect's favorite color.

Fitzgerald walked the length of the room toward a wall that was almost covered by an immense aerial view of the Capitol and its grounds. In the center was the dome of the Capitol, whose exquisite symmetry began with its white wings for House and Senate and radiated out in more and more symmetry—sharp-edged shadows, twinned fountains, broad avenues as evenly arrayed as compass points, perfectly balanced expanses of rolling lawns mirroring curves of sidewalks shaded by matching sets of trees. The image made the Capitol look like a mystic point of equilibrium, a place of unearthly harmony. The viewer, entranced by this portrait of Olympian order, sometimes did not realize that there was no sign of life, no one strolling along the sidewalks, no traffic on the streets. The image was a three-dimensional hologram produced by Mason's computer. He had presented it to Fitzgerald and recommended that he use it as a planning tool instead of the conventional Capitol Hill map that it replaced.

Ted Ringle, the public affairs sergeant, glided over in his three-wheeled electric scooter. He had been paralyzed from the waist down when a car driven by a drunk driver pinned him and his motorbike to the low stone wall surrounding the Hill's greensward. "Setup okay, Chief?" he asked, sweeping a hand around the room. "I got some of Mason's boys to give us what we needed."

Rows of folding chairs faced a platform erected before the Capitol Hill image. In front of it was a lectern bearing the seal of the Capitol Police.

"Looks fine, Ted."

"You sound a little nervous, Chief. Just take deep breaths and think about being somewhere else," Ringle said. "The phone's been jumping off the hook. It'll be a full house. All the locals plus NBC and ABC are sending their big shots. And 'Nightline' wants to set up something with you and Mitchell later in the week. You know, 'city under siege' stuff."

Fitzgerald continued toward the platform. He always seemed to deal with Ringle this way: off-the-top decisions, no planning. He stopped and looked down at Ringle's upturned face. "What does Mitchell say?" he asked.

"The 'Nightline' guy said Mitchell has signed on. The show was set up a couple of weeks ago. It was focused on what the Metro cops are doing or not doing about the murders in D.C. They weren't thinking about you—about the Cap cops—until—"

"A polite no thanks, Ted. I've got enough on my plate." Fitzgerald glanced toward the platform. "Get a good-looking chair up there. I've got a guest lecturer."

"Who?"

"The D.C. medical examiner." He explained about the photos that Lowell would be delivering.

"A suggestion, Chief?"

"Sure." Fitzgerald had taken a step. He stopped and waited for Ringle to come alongside.

"You handle the finding of the body, all the police angles," Ringle said. "Don't let Perkins do more than a walk-on."

Fitzgerald nodded and turned away once again.

"And don't mention the photos on-camera," Ringle continued, again pulling up alongside. "Let me pass them out after the TV boys pack up. You passing them out would look funny on the screen."

"Okay, Ted," Fitzgerald said, not slowing down. He stepped up to the platform. "Thanks for your as-usual good advice." A good man, Ringle, he thought. Ringle had given him two pieces of advice when he had taken over the job: wear your uniform, as much as you hate wearing it, at least in the building, and keep track of what is going on in Congress. "You've got to know a little about politics, just like a police chief in a mining town has to learn a little about mining," Ringle had said. Fitzgerald told himself he could use some education right now.

11

A SHORT TIME LATER the conference room erupted with a babble of cries and an explosion of lights. He could make out "Chief!" and "Here!" and "Bristow!" but all the rest was like one long, undulating shout.

He signaled for silence with hands held aloft. He was sweating under the lights, but he resisted an urge to wipe his forehead with his handkerchief. "All right. Please calm down," he said. "We all know why we're here. Let's get down to it."

After describing the discovery of Senator Bristow's body, he paused for an instant, and the deluge of questions began. He pointed to a pretty face he recognized, a local TV reporter. Her cameraman turned his lens toward her as the cameras of other TV reporters turned away.

"Chief, any suspects? Any drug involvement?" she asked in a breathlessly dramatic voice.

"This is a murder," Fitzgerald said. "The murder of a senator. It's not a street crime."

A deep, penetrating voice cut in: "Do you mean the murder of a senator is more *important* than the murder of a black citizen?"

The TV reporter frowned, her moment on-camera ended. Alongside her, a rival camera turned to the tall, imperious figure of James Davis, the city's leading anchorman.

"I mean exactly what I said," Fitzgerald replied. "Senator Bristow's murder was in the confines of the Senate, not on a street."

"You do not put this murder on the city's murder list?" Davis asked.

"Statistically, of course, this is a D.C. murder," Fitzgerald said. He turned away and pointed to a Washington *Post* reporter who was waving a hand and clutching a notebook. As the *Post* reporter began to ask a question, Davis cut in again: "And you believe your department is capable of solving this *D.C.* murder?"

Fitzgerald spun his gaze back to Davis. "We will solve it," he said, paused, and added, "even though it is a D.C. murder."

"That sounds like a reflection on your brothers on the Metropolitan Police force," Davis said.

"They have a lot of murders to solve. Hundreds. I've got one."

Other reporters started shouting, complaining about Davis's domination of the news conference. He acted as if he were alone in the room with Fitzgerald. He had a gift for that, for the creation of a memorable TV moment for Washington viewers: the black man standing up to the white man.

Ignoring the shouts, Davis continued. "Are you aware, Chief Fitzgerald, that Mayor Mitchell has offered the full resources of the Metropolitan Police homicide squad to the solving of this murder?"

"What I'm aware of at this moment," Fitzgerald said, "is that Mayor Mitchell has told you something that he has not yet told me." He turned to Perkins, who stood and walked toward the lectern. "I would like to introduce the medical examiner of the District of Columbia, Dr. Lawrence Perkins."

Neither Perkins nor Fitzgerald knew what was going to happen next, but at least, Fitzgerald decided, the cameras would all turn away from Davis.

Perkins nodded to Fitzgerald and said, "The Capitol Police *have* some D.C. help on this murder. Me."

12

OFFICER CATHY OWENS was at the central communications console, a semicircular bank of equipment: transceivers for communications with the patrol cars and the hand-held VHF radios carried by officers; a transceiver plugged into the Metropolitan Police communications network; direct telephone lines to the White House Secret Service detail, the mayor's command center, FBI headquarters, the director of the Federal Emergency Management Administration (which keeps constant track of everyone in the succession); lines to the offices of the majority leader of the House and the president pro tem of the Senate and to the architect's office. All the lines fed into an internal switchboard, controlled by a pad of buttons at Owens's left hand, and into an internal tape recorder whose spinning reels were visible through a locked glass panel.

Owens wore an earphone-microphone headset that disappeared in her dazzling crown of red hair. Every word that passed through the headset was recorded on the tapes. She nodded to Phelan. She looked more harried than usual, Phelan thought. She was speaking into the microphone and pressing buttons with her left hand. Three officers at their posts were turned toward the console, watching her intently.

Phelan went into a glass-walled booth outfitted with a sink, a coffeemaker and coffee paraphernalia on a narrow table, and three chairs. Sitting in one of them, drinking a cup of coffee, his eyes riveted on Owens, was a slim, balding officer; Owens's relief, Phelan assumed. She shut the door, closing out the hustle of the communications room.

Owens had said she would wait for Phelan here when the shift ended. Phelan glanced at the digital clock on the wall. The shift had ended ten minutes ago. She pressed a button marked *Loudspeaker*, and Cathy Owens's calm voice flowed into the booth.

". . . extreme caution. Enter through Room 323. Do not attempt to enter through reception area. Member has secured himself in private office. Subject may be armed, but—"

The whispering voice of Sergeant Fred Mathewson broke in. "Ten-four, Control. Entering Room 323. Request backup at east three stairwell. Out."

Owens pressed a button and said, "CERT Alpha. Did you read your unit?"

Another voice: "Ten-four, Control. Proceeding to east three stairwell."

Four minutes clicked past on the digital clock. Then, "Incident ended, Control." It was Mathewson's voice again. "Subject apprehended. We're taking him to a holding cell. Please notify Saint E's for admission of visitor showing signs of abnormal personality."

Owens, grinning, said, "Ten-four, CERT. You did good." She glanced at a list of numbers on a laminated card and called in a request for an emergency admission team from St. Elizabeth's Hospital, a federal mental hospital in southeast Washington.

Phelan was out of the booth and heading toward the console. "Cathy, wait!" she called. "I'll want to talk to him."

Owens turned her head, smiled, and nodded. She punched a few numbers, took a log from a shelf above the curved counter of the console, made a notation, and stood up. The booth door opened and the other officer emerged. Owens ducked out of the headset and handed it to him. "Okay, Sam. It's all yours."

She motioned Phelan toward the booth. "Don't worry," Owens said. "I told the holding cell not to release him until you get to him. But I doubt that he's the guy you're after."

"Why do you say that?"

"Well, he's an old familiar nut. Mr. Bones. You know, the guy from under the stairs on the Capitol plaza."

"What happened?"

"It must be full-moon time. First Preacherman and now Mr. Bones. He went into Representative Mareno's office and started raving and making threats. There was an intern on duty as receptionist. She didn't recognize him and hit the duress button. That means an automatic CERT response and assumption of bodily harm. It's all in the book."

Phelan knew the book. The *Security Awareness* manual. It had been issued to every member, and it covered everything from office security to bomb threats. When a member or someone on the staff encountered what the manual called an "abnormal personality," he or she could make an innocuous-sounding phone call that was actually a coded emergency aid request to the Capitol Police. Or aid could be summoned by pressing a duress button under a desktop.

"What was Mr. Bones's gripe this time?" Phelan asked.

"A complaint about the Chief," Owens said. "It seems Fitzgerald personally arrested him when we sealed off the plaza. Downtown didn't hold him, so he decided to make his complaint." She shrugged and motioned to the booth again. "Now, let's go in there and you can tell me what I can do for you."

Like most women on the force, Owens felt immediately comfortable when she found herself dealing with another female officer, regardless of rank. She knew that they would get down to business without the little jokes and macho remarks that male officers frequently interjected into conversations when they worked with women.

At the door of the booth, Owens stood back to admit Phelan first. "Congratulations, lieutenant," she said, motioning the other woman to a chair. "Glad to see one of us moving up." Owens, a few years younger than Phelan, had passed the sergeant's examination but was still awaiting appointment.

"Thanks, Cathy. And it's still Alix."

"Okay, Alix. I figure this is about the Bristow murder, right?" Owens poured them both coffee.

"Black for me," Phelan said, watching in fascination as Owens added more creamer and sugar than coffee to her own cup. "Thanks. Right, the Bristow murder. I'd like you to go over tapes of all communications starting, say, at four o'clock yesterday and continuing to the call you got from Boomer when Cullum found Bristow's body."

"Okay. But I can tell you right now it was all pretty much routine." Phelan did not respond. Owens quickly added, "But maybe I missed something. I'll go over the tapes right away."

"Thanks," Phelan said. "And there's something else. Senator Bristow walked from her hideaway—it's just off the basement corridor near the Senate police detail's roll-call room—to the subway entrance. She was intending to walk along the walkway to her car in the Senate underground parking garage. But as we see it now, her killer grabbed her and forced her into the ladies' room at the subway entrance and killed her there. Then he put her body—I say *he* because I'm sure it's a man—into a subway car."

Cathy Owens shuddered and put down her cup with a trembling hand. "It's so ugly. So awfully ugly," she said. "You make it so I can almost see it."

Phelan reached over and touched her arm. "It is ugly, Cathy. But it will be worse if we don't get this bastard." She paused and softened her voice. "What I want to know is whether there is any record of a malfunction of the camera at the end of the corridor leading to the subway entrance. Or of any other camera, for that matter."

"Malfunctions?" Owens, grimacing, tilted her head toward the communications center. "We get them all the time. Blackouts.

Lines down. This place is a breakdown heaven lately. Electrical fires. Some guys lost their civilian clothes in that locker room in the Capitol a couple of weeks ago, you know. They're lucky that was all."

Phelan nodded absently. Officers assigned to headquarters knew little about what went on among their colleagues assigned to the Capitol and the House and Senate wings. Many headquarters officers, Phelan included, thought of the others as mere guards who stood around waiting for their pensions.

"Getting back to the cameras," she said, "we'll do a complete check of them. But right now I'm interested in the one at the end of the corridor that leads to the subway."

"Let's take a look," Owens said. "No food or drink around the equipment." She emptied their cups and wiped them with a paper towel, put them back on the shelf next to the coffeepot and led Phelan out of the booth. Across the room from the radio communications console was an array of nine television monitors arranged in three tiers. To the left of the array were two slightly larger monitors.

"We've got our eighty-five cameras scattered around the Capitol buildings. We can also install temporary ones, like in a hearing room, if the members want it. It's done through the architect's office. Unless the operator sets up a pattern on the controls here" —she pointed to a panel of buttons and dials—"the monitors show a random selection of cameras. Each camera has its own videotape. The tapes are removed, replaced, and examined every week. If there's nothing important on them—and that's the way it usually is —we hold them for a month, erase them, and put them in the replacement box to use over again."

She pointed to the two larger monitors. "These are piped in from the television systems of the House and Senate. The basic feed is from the chamber, but the operator can switch over to closeups or other views. Each chamber has about ten cameras in use during a session. We tend not to pay much attention to those monitors because they are not part of the camera security system. And they are being closely watched by the people who run the television setup in the chambers. If they see anything funny, like a guy who keeps moving his seat in the gallery, they call us. They got film of Mathewson flipping Preacherman, by the way."

Seated before the flickering images, elbows propped on a crescent-shaped gray desk, was an officer whose round, florid face was glazed with boredom. Before him was an ever-changing black-and-white mosaic of the Capitol: an empty, dusky subterranean corridor . . . a young woman hurrying down a marble stairway . . . two adults in shorts talking to a guard . . . a well-polished door . . . a blank screen suddenly full of motion as half a dozen high school students lunged around the corner of a hall in the Russell Senate Office Building . . . another subterranean corridor, this one containing a man pushing a cart full of boxes . . . two members, deep in talk, disappearing around a corner of the Rayburn House Office Building . . . a guide lining up a group of tourists at the Rotunda . . . a panel delivery truck pulling up to a checkpoint on the plaza . . .

One of the two color monitors next to the mosaic showed an almost empty Senate chamber, where Senator Lawson, leaning on his desk, was talking to two other senators. The other monitor showed a tall representative standing at a microphone in the well of the House, waving his right hand and clutching a wad of papers in his left.

"How about a smoke break, Dan?" Owens asked.

"All *right!*" he exclaimed, grinning up at her. He spun his swivel chair away from the monitors, sprang to his feet, pulled a package of cigarettes out of his shirt pocket, and, shaking a cigarette loose, headed for a small outer room that Phelan assumed was full of smoke twenty-four hours a day.

Owens slipped into the chair and touched a few buttons on the control panel tilted before her. "Here we go," she said without turning her head. "Your corridor camera is coming up. I'm backing it up to last night." One of the monitor screens went blank, showed streaks of black and white for a few moments, and then slowed down to reveal the gloom of a long corridor whose rounded ceiling was corrugated with conduits and ducts. In the lower right of the screen appeared *4/06 5:30 P.M.* "Okay. What would you like?" Owens asked.

"Go forward slowly until you see an image. Then freeze it."

"Okay."

The tape rolled forward until a dark figure appeared at the end of the corridor. The figure suddenly enlarged. It was a stout, white-haired man in a T-shirt and shorts. "Lost tourist," Owens said. "What probably happened here was that the camera, which is motion-sensitive, detected a movement and the image automatically came on the monitor. Then the operator zoomed it to get a better look."

"It doesn't zoom by itself?"

"No. It just comes on and automatically appears on a monitor, interrupting the pattern and, we hope, waking up the operator." Owens lowered her voice and turned to Phelan, who was leaning over her shoulder. "We don't put our first team on this duty."

She touched a button and the film rolled on to another image. Someone was pushing a cart down the corridor. The process continued through three similar stop-and-zooms as they examined other insignificant images. Then, when the time on the tape was *11:04*, a figure appeared in the corridor, walking toward the glass doors leading to the subway entrance.

"Stop!" Phelan said. "The hat. See the hat? That's Julia Bristow!"

"Good Lord!" Owens exclaimed.

"Okay," Phelan said. "Start it moving slowly, as slowly as you can."

Julia Bristow resumed her walk. She walked decisively, Phelan thought. Even in slow motion there was a determined cadence to her pace. She reached the twin glass doors, opened one of them, and stepped to the top of the stairs that went down to the subway platform. She stood there for a moment. Phelan held her breath.

Julia Bristow turned her head slightly and walked to the left, out of the camera's line of sight. Sensing no more motion, the camera turned off and the tape went blank.

"My God!" Phelan said softly. "Did you see that?"

Owens, her eyes still on the tape, shook her head. She could not speak.

"Roll back," Phelan said, "'and let me see it again."

Once more Julia Bristow walked down the corridor, opened the door, stopped, turned, and vanished.

"Don't you see what happened?" Phelan asked. "She *heard* somebody, *saw* somebody. Her head turned. I thought I saw her lips move. My God! She was seeing her killer. Talking to him."

70

"The ladies' room is there, Alix. On the left at the top of the stairs."

"I know. But there's a little bathroom—a toilet, a sink—right outside her hideaway. She wasn't going to the ladies' room here. She was going to the left to talk to somebody. The man who killed her. That's where he did it." Her heart was racing. "Get this tape to the evidence room, Cathy. Don't tell *anybody* about it. Got that?"

"Got it," Cathy Owens said softly. She was staring at the freeze-frame of a blurry, black-and-gray Julia Bristow a few moments before her death.

13

SHORTLY AFTER six o'clock, Julia Bristow's body lay on a gleaming stainless steel autopsy table. Circular fluorescent lights, concentric in a reflective overhead fixture, bathed the body in a blue-tinted glow. The feet, hands, and head were encased in clear plastic bags that made the nakedness look obscenely clothed. Larry Perkins wore a green surgical gown, a green mask, a tightly fitting green cap, and transparent gloves. "We begin Bristow, case 285," he said to the little cylindrical microphone clipped to his gown and to Alexandra Phelan, who, similarly dressed, stood at his left, a notebook and ballpoint pen in her gloved hands.

As Perkins bent over the table, he flipped the visor of a magnifying light over his eyes. A narrow beam shot out from a slit in the visor, cutting like a knife into the shadows cast across the body by his head and hands. He deftly removed the plastic bag from the head, sealed it, and placed it on a small table that an orderly had silently wheeled into the room.

Perkins leaned close to the light brown hair, the visor's beam seeming to flicker as it passed across the long strands, which moved under his probing fingers. "Some hair on right anterior of scalp forcibly uprooted." He leaned closer, the hair touching his face. "Follicle injury is postmortem. Slight scratches in the subaponeurotic tissue."

"That would be the hairpins," Phelan said.

Without turning, Perkins said, "Other voice is that of Lieutenant P-H-E-L-A-N of the Capitol Police. I am asking her to refrain from comment until conclusion of autopsy." He touched a button on the microphone and, still looking at Julia Bristow's scalp, said, "I meant what I said to the tape recorder. But I am curious, Lieutenant. Tell me about the hairpins."

She repeated what she had told Fitzgerald. Perkins flipped up the visor, turned, and looked at her. "Interesting. I'll add it to the scalp section in my next book."

He turned on the microphone and resumed his examination, moving to Julia Bristow's pale, broad forehead and then to her right eye. Opening it with his left hand and holding the eyelid up, he swept the index finger of his right hand around the edge of the eye. "Indication of contact lens use in right eye. Lens, however, is missing."

He heard Phelan's sharp intake of breath, sensed that she had something to say, and pressed the microphone button. "I think," he said in an exasperated tone, "that you were once again about to speak."

"Sometimes," she said, "in a trauma death, especially strangulation like this, the contacts are expelled by shock-induced ophthalmic reflex. Have I got it right?"

"Close enough," Perkins said. "Where'd you get that?"

"From 'Pathological Evidence Often Overlooked at the Scene of a Crime,' by Dr. Lawrence Perkins."

"Actually, 'at a Crime Scene.' You read the *Journal of Forensic Pathology?*"

"I took a course in it at the University of Maryland last year. And about that contact—"

"Gruneveldt," Perkins said, shaking his head. "I wouldn't let him touch one of my bodies. Too bad you didn't take it a couple of years ago. I was a guest lecturer. Maybe you would have learned something."

"Well, I did learn enough to pick up a contact lens in a stall of the ladies' room at the Senate subway stop."

Perkins turned back to the body, hit the microphone button, felt around the left eye, and extracted a contact lens. "Contact lens removed from left eye and retained in head evidence bag for possible comparison with lens believed found at"—he paused and turned, the beam of the visor rippling across Phelan's face—"the purported scene of the crime."

He bent closer to Julia Bristow's left temple. The beam ran along the hairline and behind her ear. He turned her head slightly and similarly examined her right temple.

Perkins switched off the microphone, flipped up the visor, and looked again at Phelan. "The old procedure was that there was always a detective in attendance at an autopsy in a murder investigation," he said. "One good reason is that I can tell him—sorry, her; you're a first for me—so I can describe things I see that would not get into my autopsy report but might mean something to an investigator. Here's a good example: the senator had a facelift, and a very good one, less than six months ago, I'd judge. From the delicate work, I'd bet the doctor was Wharton, Elliot Wharton."

"She just turned forty-three," Phelan said. "Kind of young for a facelift, no?"

"I've seen them on even younger women," Perkins said. He flipped down the visor and looked again at Julia Bristow's face. "In suicides."

"Women who are trying to hold off age because of something that's happening in their lives," Phelan said softly, as if she were speaking mostly to herself. "A man . . . a younger man." Raising her voice slightly, she added, "Thanks. It's a good lead."

"You're welcome," Perkins replied. He continued his examination, removing the plastic bags from each hand and each foot, placing the bags on the small table, and summarizing his findings. "No evidence of blood or skin tissue under fingertips. Fingernails and fingertips normal. No abnormal bruises on ankles or feet. No indication of struggle with assailant." He spoke a few more words into the microphone. "And quite extensive livor mortis." He turned to Phelan and pressed the button on his mike. "Remember what that means?"

"Settling of the blood into the capillaries of the skin as they become dilated after circulation stops," she said. "The skin is usually purple where this happens. You'll see mention of livor mortis in my crime scene notes."

73

"Not bad, Phelan," Perkins said. He pressed the button and went on. "Live larvae, apparently of blowfly species, noted under eyelids and between lips. An unusually quick appearance."

"That's your specialty, isn't it?" Phelan asked. Without waiting for an answer, or for Perkins to switch off the microphone, she went on. "I read that paper you did in the *Forensic Science Gazette* on using insects to help establish time of death. And how what the cops called scratches on a woman's face were really ant bites."

Perkins nodded, pressed the button, and said, "She was face down in moldy leaves. What the hell did they expect?" Smiling, he pressed the button again.

From the nearby table he took a roll of transparent adhesive tape, picked up the plastic bags one by one, and carefully sealed them. Flicking off the microphone, he flipped up the visor and turned to Phelan. "The next part, Lieutenant, as you probably know, is . . ."

"Surgical?"

"That's one word for it. Also, to be unscientific, gruesome for somebody who isn't used to it."

"I'm staying," Phelan said. "To make up for missing your guest lectures."

"Okay," Perkins said. He gently lifted Julia Bristow's head, exposing a wound that extended from one side of her throat to the other. On the right side of the wound, the white glint of bone shone in his beam.

He described the wound, then leaned in closer. "The knife, applied after strangulation of the victim, was driven with great force," he said, and Phelan thought she detected a deepening of his voice, a hint of emotion that had not been there before. "The blade point chipped the right clavicle, possibly breaking off. I am probing for the blade tip in the wound."

He opened the wound slightly with his left hand and thrust the fingers of his right hand into the red darkness. Something gleamed. He withdrew his hand, motioned to Phelan to hold out her hand, and deposited on her gloved palm the tip of a knife blade. Then he turned off his microphone.

"That's for you," he said. "Evidence. I can keep it here among thousands of things that get misfiled and messed up, or I can give it to you and get a receipt."

"Thanks. I appreciate—"

"Forget it, Detective." He touched the microphone button again and said, "Foreign matter—apparently the tip of a knife blade—turned over to Detective Alexandra Phelan of the—" He turned at the sound of loud voices as the door to the autopsy room opened. "What the hell is that?"

A high-pitched female voice repeated, "I said you could not enter that room."

She was answered by an angry male voice with a soft southern accent: "And I said I have a court order to stop this illegal autopsy."

Perkins whirled around, his body grazing the metal table holding the specimen bags.

"Hold it right there, mister," he said, his deep voice soft with menace. The orderly grabbed the table as it began rolling across the tiled floor. The intruder was sandwiched between the swinging doors. His round face was red; in one hand he clutched a briefcase, in the other a sheaf of papers. The silhouette of another man appeared in the smoky glass panel of one door. Standing just inside, with her back to the doors, was a tall black woman in a long white lab coat.

"Dr. Douglas," Perkins said to her, "will you please explain what this is about?" Phelan noticed that he had not switched off his microphone.

Both Douglas and the man began to speak. "I will listen," Perkins said, "only to Assistant Medical Examiner Douglas." The man stopped speaking.

"This gentleman," Douglas said, "is a lawyer." She managed to make these nouns sound loathsome. "He says he has a court order to stop the Bristow autopsy. I told him the autopsy had already started, and he said—"

"I believe I can speak for myself, Dr. Douglas," the man said, pushing his way past her. "My name is Wendell Gardiner. I represent the . . . interests of the Bristow family. For religious reasons, the family does not want an autopsy on the body of Senator Bristow."

Perkins started to speak. Gardiner raised the hand that held the papers. "The federal court for the District of Columbia," he continued, "has issued a restraining order compelling the District

75

medical examiner to release the body and . . . all remains . . . to the family. It is their wish that the body be removed to the Kirkland Funeral Home for cremation. The funeral service will be tomorrow."

As Gardiner was speaking, the other man slipped through the doors. Phelan recognized him from his videotaped statement. He was Craig Haverlin.

"First," Perkins said in his lecture voice, "this is a murder, and the law requires an autopsy. Second—"

"Excuse me, Dr. Perkins, but the court order waives that requirement. And—"

"On what grounds?"

"On the grounds that the medical examiner made a determination of homicide at the crime scene and examined the body sufficiently to determine a probable cause of death."

"And how, may I ask, was the good judge able to decide that?"

"By affidavit," Haverlin said. "From me." He cocked his head toward Gardiner, as if to gain lawyerly endorsement. "I was at—summoned to—the crime scene. And there were your statements at the press conference."

"Bristow's AA," Phelan whispered to Perkins. She identified herself to Gardiner and said, "As the police officer in attendance here, I must point out that an expert autopsy is vital to this case. Our counsel will want to appeal the decision."

"So will I," Perkins interrupted. "I intend to ask Kirkland to hold the body pending further legal actions. There's a precedent here that I—"

"As the court order clearly states," Gardiner cut in, "the family's wishes are to be carried out."

"And the wishes are?" Phelan asked.

"Immediate cremation at Kirkland, this evening," Haverlin answered. "There will be a funeral tomorrow in a chapel at the National Cathedral. The ashes will be taken, by me, to Baton Rouge, Louisiana, for burial in the family plot."

"I see," Perkins said. "All fixed up." He touched the microphone button and turned to the orderly, who had been gripping the table during the conversation. "Eunice, prepare and pouch the body and remains of Case 283 for removal and notify Kirkland."

"You sure you mean 283, Doctor?" the orderly whispered. Turning her back to the door, she held up a plastic bag marked with the number 285.

"I am positive that's what I mean, Eunice." He raised his voice and looked toward the door. "Dr. Douglas, will you please take these gentlemen to my office? I will join them in a few minutes to sign the paperwork."

As the door closed behind Douglas, Perkins pointed to the body. "Into the cold vault with this one, Eunice."

"And just what's the number on it now, Doctor?" she asked. "Seven-eleven?"

Perkins smiled but did not answer.

"Hold it," Phelan said. "There's still—"

"Stomach contents. Vital organs. Vaginal examination," Perkins said rapidly. "Right. But I don't have much time."

"Fitzgerald is ex-FBI," Phelan said. "He has a pal at the FBI lab. Is there any way we can get the bodily evidence to the lab?"

"I don't know. I need to think," Perkins said. "There's some goddamn fix going on. I've seen it before. I can stall them with the little mistake in the case number." He gave Eunice a glare and a smile. "But they'll get the body as soon as Kirkland unzips the bag and finds—what'll they find, Eunice?"

Eunice took a notebook from her smock pocket and turned to a paper-clipped page. "Black male, eighteen to twenty-two," she read. "Gunshots, face and chest." She closed the book and looked up. "Could've at least sent a female. Like one of them whores."

"Sorry. Wrong number," Perkins said. He removed his light and cap, stripped off his mask and gloves, and tossed them into a container next to the autopsy table. Then suddenly he spun around and leaned down to look at the body. "Damn! Strangulation and chest wounds—the prostitutes."

He slipped a glove on his right hand and pointed to one of four wounds clustered between the nearly severed left breast and the right breast, which bore no wounds. "The wounds," he said, "are in a downward direction—right to the hilt of the knife. The mark of the hilt is very clear right above the wounds. You get the picture of the killer standing over the prone victim. The hilt mark—a bruise, a kind of abrasion—is caused by the hilt scraping the skin. The knife was completely inserted. That's why we got the tip. All the way in, and bang! Snapped against a bone." He turned to Eunice. "The prostitutes. Who did the autopsies?"

Eunice flipped through her notebook. "Dr. Douglas did one. And that temp from Virginia. The old guy? Gates? He did the other two."

"Damn! That guy is an imbecile. But Douglas—she'd have some good stuff."

Perkins switched on the microphone. "As Medical Assistant Eunice Talbot pointed out to me," he said, "the combination of strangulation and postmortem knife wounds on the body of Senator Bristow resemble the strangulation–postmortem knife wound pattern in the deaths of three other women autopsied by this office in the past several months. Details to come and to be incorporated into the 'remarks' section of this report as soon as I can obtain and analyze the records of the other homicides. End." He switched off the microphone. "Get me plenty of photos, Eunice."

"You think whoever killed Bristow killed those prostitutes?" Phelan asked.

"I'm thinking I need to look up the records, the photos, talk to Douglas," Perkins said. "That's all I'm thinking."

Phelan wanted to ask more questions, but Perkins was heading for the wash-up room and motioning for her to follow him. Eunice began arranging a camera rack on the autopsy table.

Perkins and Phelan entered adjacent cubicles and spoke across the partition while they removed their green medical uniforms and donned street clothes. "We've got to talk fast," Perkins said. "If we keep 'em waiting, they'll start thinking we're up to something."

"Well, we *are* up to something," Phelan said. She removed her gown and the shoulder holster she had worn under it. The holster straps left welts along her left shoulder and across her chest, below her bra. She hung the holster on a hook, put on a beige blouse, stepped into a blue skirt, and strapped the holster on again.

Perkins, who had not yet put on his shirt, went to a double sink and rapidly washed his hands and face, scrubbing off the white smear of deodorant salve under his nostrils. "Tough stuff to get off," he said, keeping his back to the cubicles.

78

Phelan stepped up to the sink, soaped her hands, and began daubing at the salve on her face.

Perkins picked up a washcloth and reached across to wipe it off. He held her chin with one hand. "I had planned to use a mirror," she said but did not move her face.

"Just being helpful," Perkins said. "Do you always pack a gun?"

"Regulations. And I couldn't leave it here." She took the washcloth from his hand and stepped to an oblong mirror. Perkins returned to his cubicle.

"We've had three recent homicides that seemed similar," he said. "Prostitutes. Two were picked up in the District, one in Virginia—in Arlington, I think. They were killed somewhere else, then the bodies were dumped in alleys. Strangled, then stabbed, breasts mutilated. The wounds were all similar." Knotting a maroon tie, he emerged.

"That's all? Three murders and that's all you know?" Phelan asked. She turned away from the mirror and looked at him for a moment, not quite meaning to. She reentered her cubicle to get her jacket. Perkins took a step toward her, to help her on with the jacket, she thought. She spun around, facing him while she put it on.

"It's not my job to solve murders, Lieutenant. It's the Met cops' job. And they've got so many murders they just try to solve the easy ones—where the guy is standing there, dumb dope grin on his face, gun in his hand . . . Look. Let's go in there and sign the papers, then go have a sandwich and we'll talk about this. Okay?"

Phelan did not answer immediately.

"Look," Perkins continued, "if you were a male detective I would say, 'Let's go have a sandwich.' This is business, Detective. Okay?"

"Okay, Doctor. A sandwich and business."

Gardiner stood when they entered Perkins's office. Haverlin did not. Before anyone else could speak, Perkins established his turf. He went behind his desk, with its standard pen stand, clock, in and out trays, two phones, and said to Gardiner, "Okay. You're the lawyer. So let's hear what this is all about."

Gardiner sat down and repeated, in quieter, more lawyerly words, what he had sputtered in the autopsy room. "So as you can see, Dr. Perkins, the autopsy you began has been forbidden by court order," he concluded. "But of course you were unaware of the order." He smiled, bestowing exoneration on Perkins.

"My job, Mr. Gardiner, is to look at dead bodies and try to figure out what made them dead. If a judge, and the people who put the judge on the case—if they don't want to know what made somebody dead, well, that's no business of mine." He picked a sheet of paper from a file folder, signed it, and handed it to Gardiner. He glanced at Douglas and said, "I told Eunice to release the body."

"I want a copy of that order and of Dr. Perkins's release," Phelan said. "And I have a couple of questions."

Without looking at her, Gardiner said, "You have no standing here, miss. This is a matter of—"

"I believe you know who I am," Phelan said, stepping toward Gardiner's chair. "But just in case Mr. Haverlin did not tell you, here is my identification." She reached into her jacket pocket, showed him her badge and ID card, then handed him her card. "Please have a messenger deliver a copy of that court order to me at headquarters before nine P.M. tonight."

Gardiner looked up at her. "I repeat, you have no standing here."

"I am surprised, Counselor, that you are not aware of the federal law that authorizes the Capitol Police to protect all members of Congress, officers of the Congress, and any member of the immediate family of any member or officer—anywhere in the United States. I am investigating the murder of a member. *That* is my standing, and if you wish me to demonstrate it by arresting you for interfering with a police investigation, I am prepared to make that arrest. Immediately."

"That bit of melodrama will not be necessary, Officer. I—"

"Lieutenant."

"Very well. Lieutenant. The order will be delivered, as I had intended to do before you made your threat." Gardiner and Haverlin stood to leave.

"One moment, gentlemen," Phelan said. "As I said, I have a couple of questions." She stood in front of Perkins's desk, took her notebook and pen from her pocket, and pointed the pen toward Haverlin. "In your statement you said that Senator Bristow's only kin was a sister who was abroad and unreachable."

"I reached her."

"You spoke to her? Where and when?"

"I sent her a telegram."

"And she responded?"

"Not yet."

"So the court order, the funeral arrangements, the so-called wishes of the family—these are all on your authority?"

Haverlin turned toward Gardiner, who spoke. "Mr. Haverlin, as a matter of course, was given a great deal of authority by the late senator."

"Wasn't Senator Bristow a Catholic, Mr. Haverlin?" Phelan asked.

"No. She was an Episcopalian," Haverlin said. "A convert. She was born Jewish. Her middle initial, K, was for Kaplan."

"Nevertheless," Phelan said, "cremation would be contrary to her tradition."

"Is that a question, Lieutenant? The fact is that she preferred cremation and a funeral service at the National Cathedral. Within twenty-four hours of her death, in respect for her Jewish forebears. She told me all that after her husband was buried." Haverlin stood. "There was no witness, Lieutenant. You just have to take my word." He smiled and tipped his head slightly. "The word of a southern gentleman."

"A slick southern gentleman," Phelan said. "Very slick."

Perkins had meant it when he said a sandwich: paper-thin ham and cardboard-thin orange cheese on thin white bread, in the green-walled cafeteria of the District of Columbia General Hospital, which also housed the office of the District of Columbia medical examiner. Over Styrofoam cups of coffee the color of swamp water, they were finishing what Perkins called their postmortem of the postmortem.

"So," he said, "assuming that you're right and that Haverlin is trying to cover up something about the murder, what am I supposed to go back in there and look for?" His tone was mildly condescending.

"Haverlin's clever—cunning, maybe—but not very smart," Phelan said. "He is the perennial aide, the guy who starts off going for coffee and ends up an administrative assistant. Untalented, somewhat sleazy, harsh on the lowliest, toadying to the highest. I'm willing to bet he didn't set this up himself—calling in Gardiner, figuring what judge to put pressure on, stopping the autopsy—"

"Interrupting the autopsy," Perkins cut in. "We did get something out of it, and it's on the record. And I can still do a little more before Kirkland discovers what they've got."

"Right. Well, here are my two conclusions. One, somebody told Haverlin to do this. Two, that same somebody wanted you not to find out something that her dead body would tell you."

"Okay, picking up your theory, I'll tell you two things her body could tell me. One, what and when she ate last. It doesn't look as if that's important in this case. Two, whether she had sex just before death. If she did, the DNA data could help us identify her lover."

"By now Kirkland Funeral Home is on the phone yelling at Dr. Douglas or Eunice. There's not much time," Phelan said. "Let's forget the stomach contents. Get a vaginal smear and whatever secretions you can and hold on to them until I tell you how to get them to the FBI lab."

"There's something else," Perkins said. "The prostitutes. Is it that guy? Is Bristow number four?"

"It's a big change from whores to a U.S. senator," Phelan said.

"Yeah. And from black women to a white one. Maybe the Hill is going to get a dose of what we're getting in our part of town."

At the end of that long day Fitzgerald was slumped in a leather chair in the small living room of his flat. He lived on the ground floor of a turn-of-the-century Capitol Hill townhouse that had been divided into four apartments. He had a glass in one hand, half full of vodka and melting ice cubes; in his lap and spilling to the floor was a printout of everything he knew so far about Senator Julia K. Bristow and her murder. *Lots of paper*, he thought. *But not much else.*

At 8:45 Phelan called and told him about the interrupted autopsy and the sudden decision for a funeral at the National Cathedral. Fitzgerald called the watch officer, told him to begin arranging security plans for the service, and authorized overtime for the CERT officers the next day and for the statehood rally coming up on Thursday.

Just before ten, Lawson called. "I saw your performance on the seven o'clock news. Very impressive." He let a moment go by.

"I'd like to see you, Jeff. How about breakfast in my office? Seven-thirty. Okay?"

"Seven-thirty's fine. Good night, Senator."

Fitzgerald picked up the remote control and flicked on the television set across the room. A car commercial ended and the ten o'clock news began. The first item was presented in the grim baritone of James Davis: "Murder in the Senate: a victim, a mystery, no suspects." A pause. "More after this." And the screen filled with a baseball manager selling a liquid diet.

The Davis-Fitzgerald press conference dialogue was on-screen when the phone rang again. Fitzgerald hit the mute button on the remote control and watched himself mouthing words while he picked up the phone and said, "Fitzgerald here."

"Chief, it's Alix again. Perkins managed to get something. We'll need the lab. For that . . . and for something Stan got in the hideaway."

"No details on the phone, Alix. I'll set something up with the lab. Anything more on the camera tape?"

"I got a copy over to a lip-reader on the faculty at Gallaudet. She's deaf. She had a hearing colleague call me. The tape is too blurry to get any idea of what Senator Bristow was saying. But the lip-reader felt that from the angle of her head, she was not showing fear. And her lips were moving. We'll get all this in a formal report, and—"

"Right. Right. What it means is that she must have known the person standing there to the left. The son of a bitch must have been aware of the line of sight of the camera. Anything else?"

"For the guy to get in there without being seen by the camera," Phelan said, "I figure he had to reach the subway platform by entering the Hart or Dirksen or Russell Building from the outside, then going down to the basement, staying out of camera range. It can be done, but you have to know what you're doing. I had all the posts checked. No one suspicious entered the buildings."

"Well, that bastard wasn't suspicious. That was the point, wasn't it? Nice work, Alix. Just keep it up. And when you talk to anybody, make sure it's me."

Fitzgerald switched off the television set and picked up the phone. He kept dozens of phone numbers in his head, effortlessly memorizing them and rarely forgetting them. There was one he would always know, the one that reached a person who had been very important to his life: Kyle Tolland.

At the headquarters of the FBI, Kyle Tolland was known as the Godfather. Officially, he was the assistant administrative director of the FBI Forensic Laboratory. Unofficially, he was the fixer, the scheduler, the arranger in and beyond the lab. His job description said he managed the LSPS, the Laboratory Scheduling Priority System. What the description did not say was that he decided when to use the system and when to slip around it without leaving any bureaucratic tracks. It was also Tolland's unofficial job to keep out of the lab anything that would politically embarrass it or scientifically thwart it. When anything in either of those categories did manage to slip past him, he was the manager of damage control.

A lifelong bachelor, Tolland knew generations of influential Washingtonians and was the extra man for the extra woman at innumerable dinner parties. He knew of past blunders and near-misses in all of Washington's many games. He knew the goats and the heroes of countless bureaucratic flaps. He knew secrets—and, more important, phone numbers—that he was not authorized to know. It was Tolland, with a bold phone call to the director's red phone, who had urged that the Navy retain the John F. Kennedy assassination materials and not forward them to the lab. When the worth of that instinctive decision seeped into the political brain of the director, the word went out: Kyle Tolland can do no wrong, can never be denied.

It had been Tolland who had arranged for Agent Alice Tyle to remain publicly the hero who had saved Fitzgerald's life, "because, goddamn it, that was what she died thinking." And when Senator Lawson tapped Fitzgerald for the chief's job, it had been Tolland who had yanked all the derogatory remarks made in the inspector general's report from Fitzgerald's file because, he had decreed, there was no need for Congress to see internal FBI matters.

Now, poking the numbers to reach Tolland, Fitzgerald wondered how long it would be before that report would reach the Washington *Post*. Lawson said a week. Fitzgerald would not bet on it.

Wednesday, April 8

14

THE ALARM went off at 6:15. Ten minutes later Fitzgerald was leaving his flat. As he passed a gleaming mahogany staircase, a door opened, as usual, and Mrs. Darwin, as usual, said, "Good morning, Jeffrey. Have a good run." She held a blue teacup in her right hand, a blue saucer in her left.

Fitzgerald nodded and opened the inner glass door. Near it stood an elephant-foot umbrella stand that held three umbrellas and a black cane that belonged to Mrs. Darwin, the owner of the house. He unlocked the outer door and stood for a moment on the broad stone steps. The air was soft and still damp from the previous night's light rain.

Mrs. Darwin's Red Emperor tulips had bloomed in the last day or so, clusters of red and orange bursting like flames along the narrow walk between the front steps and the wrought iron gate. Her roses would arrive soon. He could see the dots of pink and white and red in the mass of green that arched along the black frame of the fence.

He ran down A Street Southeast to Third Street, then turned left onto East Capitol Street, passed the Folger Shakespeare Library, and jogged in place for a moment, waiting for a car to pass on Second Street Northeast, the northern boundary of the Capitol. An officer at the checkpoint saluted him and he threw back a salute and a "good morning." He continued along the perimeter of a long, low wall that surrounded the Hill and turned left again down Constitution Avenue. The Russell Office Building loomed across the broad avenue. Near the corner, at an opening in the wall that had once been a road, he wove his way past large white concrete structures crowned with shrubs that did their best to make roadblocks look like decorations. Another checkpoint, another salute.

Fitzgerald's pace quickened as the path carried him down the Hill to the huge, green-tinged mass of myth and history that rose from two fountains at the lower edge of the Capitol's land. On his runs Fitzgerald never stopped long enough to decipher who was who in the fountain sculptures. But he always slowed to look up at the Capitol, the great winged bulk of stone and light that seemed to fill the morning sky.

Before he had moved to Washington, Fitzgerald had not taken to running. The hills in San Francisco had intimidated him. His exercise routine then had consisted only of lifting weights with a fellow agent twice a week at a rundown health club. Now, fighting the softening of his forty-four-year-old body, he ran. What had begun as a regimen of physical exercise—and his only recreation—had soon turned into something more. Each morning, he awoke just before the sun broke over the horizon, trumpeting its victory over the night. By the time he reached the Mall, the sky usually turned an intoxicating rose hue. And there, as his feet dropped softly against the crushed gravel that carpeted the paths of the Mall, he knew an exhilaration and serenity that made it unnecessary to seek God through the ritual and liturgy of his church.

Coming up the Hill from the Mall, he saw another jogger approaching him. "Mornin', Chief," the man said, his face half hidden under a black baseball cap that bore the word *Saints* in bright gold script across its peak. Running behind was a puffing, thick-necked young man, his blond hair crew-cut, the bulge of a shoulder holster under his gray sweatshirt. *Bodyguard*, Fitzgerald thought. *But what's the name of the guy he's guarding?*

He began to go through a mental checklist. He knew every member of the Senate on sight. But there were 435 members of the House of Representatives, some of whom looked only slightly older than the pages and interns who served them. Many of them lived in Washington only part-time, for their sessions usually ran from Tuesday through Thursday. So he did not see them as often as he saw senators.

And, of course, the runner was not wearing the gaudy congressional identification button that so many of them wore on their pin-striped suits. *Saints*, his mind said, turning to a word association game he sometimes played. Exaggerate images, mix them. *New Orleans Saints . . . Kansas City . . .*

"Good morning, Congressman Royal," Fitzgerald shouted as he spun around, jogging backward momentarily and receiving a wave from the man heading toward the Rayburn Building. There, Fitzgerald was sure, Royal would make his way to the huge gymnasium facilities in the basement.

Michael Royal, Fitzgerald muttered to himself, surprised that he had been so slow to recognize somebody whom Washington was finding it hard to ignore. Fitzgerald did not know much about Royal, having seen him on television only once or twice. But what he had seen, he did not much like. With his smooth good looks and charm, Royal preached a message that sounded as fair, decent, and noble as Thomas Jefferson's proclamations. But behind the words, the beguiling manner, and the attractive drawl, Royal was exploiting fear and hatred, laying the blame for society's rot at the feet of America's blacks.

Fitzgerald cared little about politics in general and nothing about politics in Louisiana. How could the same state elect a Charles Bristow and a Michael Royal? He shook his head in confusion as he turned left again at Independence Avenue and began puffing up Capitol Hill.

He crossed First Street and continued up East Capitol Street, through the dappled light of thin trees and massive buildings and past the clean white lines of the Supreme Court, its windows ablaze in the low morning light. Slowing, he turned left onto Third Street and returned to A Street, then came again to the tulips and the black iron gate.

His mood abruptly changed as he thought of Royal's bodyguard. Fitzgerald made a mental note to have someone check on that goon. He'd damn well better have a gun permit, and he'd better not carry the weapon into any building on Capitol Hill.

□ □ □ □

Showered, shaved, and in his uniform, Fitzgerald walked down the corridor and knocked at Mrs. Darwin's door. "It's unlocked," she called out. He opened the door and entered what she called her parlor. Greeting him was the bay window with its window seat and red plush cushion. Before the window was a low mahogany table on which sat a silver tray bearing more silver—long-spouted coffeepot, creamer, sugar bowl, spoons. Next to the tray were two blue cups and saucers, two linen napkins, a silver toast rack holding two perfect pieces of lightly buttered toast, and a shallow crystal dish containing, Fitzgerald knew, strawberry-apple preserves made by Mrs. Darwin.

The Persian rug was properly old and of intricate design, faintly golden. There was a fireplace with black lion's head fire irons, a pale green sofa of stern lines and gleaming black feet, two lustrous mahogany chairs on either side of the table, and a side window, lace-curtained. Flanking the window were tall bookcases where gaps and books lying sideways showed that the books were read, not merely displayed.

Ellen Darwin rose from the window seat as Fitzgerald entered. A tall, white-haired woman with a softly angular face and startlingly blue eyes, she wore a vertically striped, red-and-white long-sleeved blouse, its V neck half hidden by the ends of a red scarf knotted loosely around her throat. Her red skirt ended just below her knees.

"I've told you before, Mrs. Darwin, you shouldn't keep your door unlocked," Fitzgerald said.

"Bull tickey, Jeffrey, if you will pardon my French. I *don't* keep it unlocked. I unlocked it when I spotted you coming around the corner." She nodded her head toward the bay window's busybody, a mirrorlike device as old as the house that enabled someone standing at the edge of the window to look up or down the street without being seen from outside. "Besides, I am quite aware that this house is on the 71 List for every shift of your nice little police force, and hardly an hour goes by without one of your white cars cruising past. There are plenty of dummies out there, but I don't believe many of them are dummy enough to try this house."

Ellen Darwin had lived here for nearly all of her seventy-seven years. She moved in when her father, with several others who became known as the Ohio Gang, left their native state to grow rich and powerful in the administration of Warren G. Harding. Arthur Darwin escaped indictment in the Teapot Dome scandal, ran successfully for Congress, and after four terms became a lobbyist. Ellen, the Darwins' only child, grew up in the little Washington of the 1920s and 1930s, when the War Department and the State Department fit in one building, when young girls went to finishing schools in Virginia and had their own horses, when dinners at the White House were intimate and never included movie stars, and when a hostess (which Ellen became after her mother's death) was expected to understand politics well enough to get the right people together at the right time but was not expected to have an opinion on any subject, not even the fortunes of the Washington Senators.

Around the time her father was dying of cirrhosis of the liver, Ellen began to break the mold. She started talking at her parties, started spouting off what she had learned at Wellesley, and started seeing her name in the gossip columns. Surprisingly, her fame as "a sharp-tongued, quick-witted bombshell" (one of her favorite captions under a photo in the old *Evening Star)* did not hurt her father, who met rising New Deal stars through Ellen. She married one of them, an assistant undersecretary of state who joined the OSS when World War II began and was killed as he parachuted to a rendezvous with the French Resistance.

"Kyle called," Mrs. Darwin said as Fitzgerald sat down. She poured coffee and handed him the cup and a napkin before she continued. "He couldn't get you and figured I'd see you before you went off to catch the mad killer of Capitol Hill."

"Did he say what he wanted?" Fitzgerald asked.

"He said to tell you he has set up an informal liaison—now that's a word that used to have a *romantic* meaning—with the lab."

"Now that I know that," Fitzgerald said, "I don't need to call him." He lowered his eyes and concentrated on his coffee.

"You will not leave this room without calling Kyle Tolland," Mrs. Darwin said, rising from her chair. She walked to one of the bookshelves, picked up a yellow portable phone, dialed the number, and tossed the phone to Fitzgerald, who caught it with his free hand and held it to his ear. Tolland always answered on the first ring.

"Tolland here."

"And Fitzgerald here. What's the situation?" he asked, reaching for a piece of toast. Mrs. Darwin slipped a plate under it and sternly motioned to him. He placed the toast on the plate, broke off a piece, and took a bite.

"I've cashed in a lot of my diminishing pile of chips for you and set up a liaison with the lab," Tolland said. "All unofficial. And you can tell your new pal Perkins that if he wants to use a real forensic lab, he should call my private number. If he sends us Senator Bristow's vital organs, we'll give it the priority we call 'congressional courtesy.' "

"Thanks much, Kyle," Fitzgerald said. "And keep your eyes open. I think my pals there may be planning a surprise party for me. Watch your back." He hit the hang-up switch, handed the phone back to Mrs. Darwin, and stood up.

"Not so fast," she said. "I have a question."

"And what's that, Mrs. Darwin?"

"Julia Bristow was not raped, was she?"

"No—well, not from what the preliminary examination showed. No obvious signs. Why did you assume that she wasn't raped?"

"Because, Jeffrey, that is what I . . . what I have reason to believe."

"Well, your intuition was right, Mrs. Darwin."

"Intuition? Someday we'll have to talk about what you call my intuition." She looked at him sternly. "Sex is involved here, but I don't believe this is a sex crime. And there's something else."

"What's that?" Fitzgerald asked.

"I'm terribly afraid this murder is only the first."

15

AT 7:15 FITZGERALD entered the Dirksen Building, exchanged salutes with the officer at the staff entrance, and walked down a long, marble-floored corridor past an open door with a sign saying SENATOR LAWSON toward a closed oak door farther on. Lawson had two sets of offices. As majority leader, he conducted Senate business in an office in the Senate wing of the Capitol. As the senior senator from California, he had an office here.

Fitzgerald knocked and entered, and Lawson motioned him to a table in front of a leather couch. Fitzgerald put his chief's hat on the edge of Lawson's desk, unbuttoned his uniform coat, and sat in a leather chair in front of the table, directly across from the senator.

"You'll never get used to that uniform, will you?" Lawson asked, laughing. Fitzgerald did not answer. Lawson leaned over to pour coffee from a carafe into two cups bearing the Senate seal. He moved with the grace of a tall man who had learned early in life that height was a gift.

Lawson's national record for the pole vault had won him an athletic scholarship to UCLA. His academic record had won him a scholarship to law school, where he began his political career by running successfully for editor of the law review. He learned then a lesson that carried him to the California state legislature, the governor's mansion, and the leadership of the U.S. Senate: people look up to a tall man whether they want to or not.

Fitzgerald had read a number of profiles written about the man whose life he had saved. Most were favorable. They spoke of Lawson's energy, intellect, and powers of persuasion. There were the inevitable psycho-babble pieces that claimed to reveal the interior man. Still, Fitzgerald had the sense that Lawson, like all politicians, never opened up, never disclosed the thoughts behind his striking blue eyes, never dropped the veil that shielded his vulnerabilities.

In previous breakfast meetings with him, Lawson had had a specific request: a constituent wanted to use police cars to run a test on a computer system for tracking vehicles; the Senate's Democratic Policy Committee wanted Fitzgerald to work a little harder on recruiting black officers; could the Capitol Hill townhouse that Lawson had recently purchased be put on the 71 List, the list of residences given special attention by patrol cars. (The standing order said, "Show frequent, irregular presence in street in front of each Code 71 residence, checking door, window, and gate locks.") Today, however, Lawson decided to wait for Fitzgerald to speak first.

Fitzgerald obliged. "What's on your mind, Senator?"

"The same topic that I'm sure is on your mind, Jeff. How is it going?"

"It's too early to tell. And I've got to work with what I've got."

"Have a danish," Lawson said calmly, pointing to a plate with several pastries on it. He leaned forward, broke one in half, and put it on a plate near Fitzgerald. "Come on. Let's split one." He sat back. "I think we should reconsider about the Bureau."

Fitzgerald took a bite of the danish, put it back on the plate, wiped his fingers, picked up his cup, and looked across it at Lawson. Before he had become majority leader, Lawson had chaired the Judiciary Committee, so he was more than familiar with the FBI's capabilities.

Lawson put down his cup, pulled his arm from the back of the couch, reached over, and touched Fitzgerald on the shoulder. "I'm sure you have figured out that I got a call from the director's office," he said. "Someone speaking for him."

"Let me guess . . . ," Fitzgerald interrupted.

"I'm not saying who, Jeff. I'm only telling you something for your own good. They're putting the word out that you're trying to shoulder the Bureau out on this one. Your little pound of revenge."

"That's pure bullshit, Senator," Fitzgerald said angrily. "And you know it. You're the one who wanted the Bureau out of this. I'm the one who wanted it in."

"Easy, easy," Lawson said. "I'm only telling you what the FBI is putting out. And a friend at the *Post* tells me that the Bureau is about to leak the internal report on you at Yosemite. You look like the target of all this, but *I'm* the target. I'm the one who got you the job. The Feds cast a pretty wide net. You've got to stop them. If you solve this, you save your ass—and mine."

Fitzgerald nodded but did not look convinced.

"Look, Jeff. The White House sees me as a potential opponent. They're not going to miss a chance to dirty me up. They play rough down there. The FBI's supposed to be independent, but the White House has a way of using it."

"You're telling me they're closing in already?"

"In terms of time, I'd say it plays out in no more than four days. You know how the *Post* likes to start the big series with a Sunday splash." He used a sip of coffee to create a pause. "So what have you got?"

94

"It looks like she was killed by someone who really knew his way around. Possibly someone who could approach her and not immediately frighten her. She's from Louisiana and she lived in D.C." He paused to make his point. "My money's on a white killer." Then he suddenly leaned forward. "Can you think of any political reason why anyone would want to kill her?"

"*Political?*" Lawson asked, sounding surprised. "I thought this was a . . . a crime of passion, a sex crime, senseless murder. That sort of thing."

"If I've learned anything here, Senator, it's that just about everything around here winds up being political."

"Politics is the art of making things happen, Jeff. Murder doesn't fit in. It's too messy, too . . . final. Murder isn't part of politics." He paused, but before he could continue, Fitzgerald interrupted with "Tell that to Jack and Bobby Kennedy."

Lawson leaned forward, throwing a lean shadow across the rug at Fitzgerald's feet. "But Jeff, you know that assassinations are another matter."

"Not to me they aren't. Murder is killing with a motive. So is assassination."

"Mad motives," Lawson said.

"Every defense lawyer tries that one. 'Temporary insanity' doesn't work with me either. Any cop who has worked on murder cases can separate the crazies from the crazy-as-a-defense types. That's what I'm doing with this one. I don't feel that Senator Bristow was killed by a madman. There's a motive here. There has to be. And I have a feeling that it was mixed up in politics. What was she involved in?"

"Statehood. She was a key vote."

"How was she going to vote?"

"She was playing it coy. I was counting on her to vote with me to cut off the filibuster. I need sixty votes for the cutoff. She was number sixty, by my count. But I couldn't get a solid answer from her. My bet is she was going to switch on me."

"If she was changing, then statehood could be the motive. It could be someone for statehood."

"I think you're really reaching, Jeff."

"Maybe. But right now statehood looks like something I need to know more about it. Is there someone—"

95

"Done," Lawson said. He went to the door leading to the outer suite of offices and called to one of his aides. "Betty, get me that CRS brief on statehood."

In a moment a young woman entered and handed Lawson a Congressional Research Service report. He stepped over to Fitzgerald and gave it to him. "Here's what you need to know," he said. "It'll educate you. But I don't think it's going to help you solve anything. And we're running out of time."

"I know. I know."

16

BACK IN HIS OFFICE, Fitzgerald told Margaret to hold off everyone except Mason and Phelan. Then he put on his half-glasses and began reading *D.C. Statehood: A Brief Background Report.*

The Twenty-third Amendment to the Constitution, ratified in 1961, gave District residents the right to vote for President. Subsequent legislation gave them limited self-rule and stimulated local efforts for statehood. The first attempt failed with the demise in 1985 of a constitutional amendment that would have granted voting representation in Congress to residents of the District of Columbia. The amendment died after the seven-year deadline passed without ratification by the necessary three quarters of the states.

Statehood advocates then turned to a simpler strategy. The District called a constitutional convention, wrote a constitution, and petitioned for the admission of "New Columbia" to the Union. Ever since the days of the western frontier, territories had used this method to become states. Gwenda Harris-Topping, the District of Columbia's delegate to Congress, had led the petition-signing campaign.

A statehood bill had been drafted and introduced by Harris-Topping, who was allowed to introduce bills but could not vote. Stemming from the petition, the new bill had rekindled the statehood crusade. The legislation would transform the mayor into a governor and turn the City Council into a House of Delegates. The state would have an attorney general and would no longer rely on the U.S. attorney's office to prosecute crimes.

After a series of hearings conducted by Joseph Mareno, chairman of the House District of Columbia Committee, the committee voted for it. Pushed by Democrats, who saw a new state that would perpetually send Democrats to Congress, the House passed the measure. Lawson had offered the Senate version as an amendment to the District of Columbia appropriations bill. A pro-statehood vote in the Senate would mean that the District of Columbia became the state of New Columbia. No ratification by state legislatures would be needed.

Some Republicans and most Democrats in the Senate, led by Lawson, backed statehood. But opposition was strong. One unspoken realization was that D.C. statehood would enhance Lawson's presidential ambitions among black and liberal voters. Another was that the admission of New Columbia would almost inevitably mean two black Democratic senators in the nearly all-white Senate.

There were other issues. Opponents of statehood said the District did not have a large enough economic base to support itself. Much of the property in the District was federally owned and tax-exempt. About twenty percent of the District's income came from federal funds, which had been appropriated down through the years in recognition of the fact that the District provided essential services, such as fire and police, sewers and water, that were paid for by District taxpayers, since the government paid no taxes.

To handle the issue of services, the Senate bill provided for the creation of "the National Capital Area," which would be directly funded by Congress and would be as self-sufficient as possible. A map showed the proposed area as the heart of Washington—Capitol Hill, the Mall, and a wide swath of land west to the Potomac River. It would be cut off from the rest of the District much in the way the present District of Columbia had been cut off from Maryland. It looked to Fitzgerald like a new District of Columbia with a new name.

Typically, the Senate bill differed from the House version, but proponents were confident that the differences, which included the creation of the National Capital Area, would be easily worked out. Politicians of both parties conceded that the President would have to sign it, despite his known reluctance, to please Democrats in both the House and the Senate.

Opponents of statehood, led by southern Democrats, had begun a filibuster. Under Senate rules, the sustained debate could be cut off by a vote of sixty senators. This cloture vote, which would come when Lawson felt he had the votes, would be tantamount to a vote for statehood.

Reaching the end of the report, Fitzgerald nearly skipped an appendix of legislative history on the seventh page. But his eyes fell on a familiar name. The appendix listed bills by their numbers and hearings and mark-up sessions by their dates. Lawson's legislation was actually a bill that had been written several months before. The original author of the New Columbia Admission Act, Senate Bill S. 836, was Senator Charles Curtis Bristow.

17

THREE CHAIRS were lined up in front of Fitzgerald's desk. In the middle one sat Sergeant Stephen Williams, president of the Capitol Police chapter of the National Black Police Association. To his left sat another black sergeant, the secretary of the chapter; to the right was Boomer Hawkins, brought along, Fitzgerald assumed, as a rank-and-file member of the chapter. Williams was reading a statement and Fitzgerald was taking notes on a yellow legal pad.

". . . the issues involved affect directly the dignity, self-respect, and economic well-being of black Capitol Police officers. And it is for this reason we are bringing our general grievances, and this particular one, to the attention of the House District of Columbia Committee." Williams paused, put the statement in the briefcase on his lap, and said, "Well, that's it, Chief. We wanted you to hear it before I testify."

"I appreciate that, Steve," Fitzgerald said. He put on his glasses and looked down at his notes. "And I'm not going to try to talk you into changing a word. You're too tough a guy for that."

Williams smiled. He was the leader of an emergency response team, an organizer of the black police chapter, and a skilled contract negotiator. "I think I hear a 'but' coming, Chief."

Fitzgerald smiled. "You're right. Two 'buts.' First, the matter of Lieutenant Phelan. I know that you know that her case is not a very good one for you. She was first in the test by a very wide margin. I made the appointment on that basis. And—"

"And you're as bad off in the female promotion department as in the black promotion department. But—"

"Wait, Steve. Hear me out. We've got the murder of a member on our hands. She's the best investigator I've got. She'll have to deal with the FBI, Metro police, maybe the Secret Service before we're through. You know damn well she'll have more clout as a lieutenant."

"You think you have to tell *me* that?" Williams said, his voice suddenly no longer reasonable. "Or Emory here?" He gestured toward the other sergeant. "That's the whole point—respect and self-respect."

"Okay," Fitzgerald said, whipping off his glasses and leaning forward. "Okay. When I came here there weren't any real examinations for promotion. There was cronyism and nepotism all over the place. I'm fixing that. You concede that much at least, don't you?"

Williams shrugged and slightly tilted his head.

"Thanks for the silent assent. Okay. The second 'but.' This is a bad time, a very bad time, for the department to be in the spotlight on the Hill. I'm wondering if we can't settle one grievance right now in exchange—"

"Chief, right at the beginning I said we didn't come here to negotiate anything."

"Hear me out, Steve. I'm asking for *time*. Can you possibly postpone the testimony before Mareno's committee for, say, two weeks?"

"And what's the grievance you want to settle?"

"Beards."

For months Fitzgerald and Williams had been exchanging memos and holding meetings about the question of beards. Williams had produced medical evidence to show that nearly ninety percent of black men have *pseudofolliculitis barbae*, or PFB, a skin condition that can make shaving extremely painful. PFB sufferers have tightly curled facial bristles. When these are shaved, the sharp ends enter the skin, become ingrown, and cause discomfort and in many cases infections and scars.

Capitol Police regulations allowed neatly trimmed moustaches like Fitzgerald's but prohibited beards. The issue had become symbolic of misunderstandings between black officers, who made up about thirty percent of the force, and their predominantly white superiors and the all-white Police Board, headed by Mason.

"You're lifting the beard ban?" Boomer Hawkins asked, rubbing his scarred cheeks.

"I'll put out a special order at tomorrow morning's roll call," Fitzgerald said. "It will say that anyone who produces a physician's statement recommending against shaving will be allowed to grow a neatly trimmed beard."

"And Mason will back you up?" Williams asked.

"The personnel policies of the force are my responsibility, not the Police Board's."

Williams looked at his two companions, shrugged, and said, "It's a deal. I'll call Mareno's office and get the testimony postponed. Two weeks. No more."

A few minutes after the delegation left Fitzgerald's office, Phelan called to say she had set up a meeting with Tolland.

"Fine," Fitzgerald said. "And talk with Haverlin. Tell him you want to go over his statement in case he wants to amend it. That always scares 'em."

"I've got a call in to his office," she said. "But he's all tied up with the memorial service this afternoon."

"So am I. We got pretty damn short notice. We're expecting most of the Senate at the cathedral. We're talking heavy security. I want you there, too, Alix. Keep your eyes open. You know the routine."

18

ALEXANDRA PHELAN confessed to only one weakness: Gothic churches. It was not a matter of religion with her. It was the soaring towers and steeples, the graceful, vaulting lines that lifted her gaze toward the heavens. No space was left without embellishment. Outside, ugly stone gargoyles poured rainwater. Some of them were a touch obscene, but they inevitably provoked her laughter. Inside, stained glass windows captured light in a way that seemed to send them spinning in color. Statues, paintings, carved pulpits and pews, elaborate chapels and gilded columns—they took her breath away.

And none more so than the National Cathedral in Washington. Eighty-three years to the day in construction, the sixth largest cathedral in the world occupied 83,000 square feet on Mount St. Alban, with its highest point soaring almost 700 feet above sea level. Phelan knew the cathedral's statistics by heart. Several times a year on her days off she would spend hours there, photographing the hundreds of stone angels and grotesqueries, focusing binoculars on the ceilings, ribbed vaults, and stone carvings of Biblical tableaus high above the nave. Once she waited nearly two hours to catch the setting sun's rays through the spectacular west rose window. She was almost tempted now to steal a glance at the elaborate balconies and triforium arcades in the transepts. But today was all work.

The memorial service for Senator Julia Bristow was in progress, and more than two dozen of Phelan's colleagues were present to protect the ninety-two senators who had traveled by bus from Capitol Hill to the cathedral. Sergeant Fred Mathewson's CERT team was in the choir's vestment room. Other heavily armed officers huddled in granite niches throughout the cathedral.

The President, with a stronger-than-usual Secret Service detail, was in attendance, as were the governors of Louisiana, Texas, and

South Carolina, each accompanied by state troopers. Security was drum-tight. Media speculation had murkily linked Julia Bristow's murder to opposition to statehood. Racial tension had enveloped the city of Washington. There was also the possibility of an assassination or a terrorist bomb whenever so many powerful people collectively went outside the protective walls of the White House and Capitol Hill.

Phelan stood to the right of the pulpit, her eyes scanning the faces of the congregation, which must have numbered more than two thousand. She was alert for any sudden movement—a raised hand, a gesture that signaled danger. Oblivious to the sweeping sentiments expressed by the eulogists, she watched senators and congressmen fidget, whisper, look sad, adopt poses. Although she knew little about Senator Julia Bristow, the thought occurred to her that it was fortunate that the eulogies were not under oath.

The service, she knew, would last about one hour and forty-five minutes. After nearly an hour she switched places with another officer so that familiarity with the crowd would not breed carelessness. Then she returned to her original station. Finally it was over, and most of the congressional delegations started to file out of the western entrance and head toward the buses.

Most, but not all. Phelan noticed two men strolling leisurely behind the altar and down toward the Bethlehem Chapel in the crypt, where the first bishop of Washington, Henry Yeats Satterlee, was entombed. She recognized both of them. The white-haired and distinguished-looking man was James Nadeau, the governor of Louisiana. The other was Congressman Michael Royal. The two men walked solemnly and talked quietly, occasionally pausing by a stone sculpture or a painting. But Phelan's instincts told her they had more than sightseeing on their agenda at the moment.

She moved closer to the chapel. Walking on her toes while trying not to appear secretive, she could pick up only fragmented words from one of the voices. The words were indistinct, unconnected. "Christ . . . not cold . . . unseemly . . . soon . . . a week, ten days . . ."

Then the other voice, a gravelly, angry whisper. "No! Bullshit. Now . . . Lawson will move . . . People of Louisiana . . . never forgive." It was clear that one of the men was being pushed and he did not like it.

There was a break in their exchange, a sudden silence, as if the two men sensed the presence of an intruder. Phelan inhaled quickly and then walked boldly into the chapel.

"Oh, Governor Nadeau, Congressman Royal—there you are. Lieutenant Phelan, Capitol Police. I'm sorry, but the buses are getting ready to leave. And Governor, your chauffeur is waiting for you at the south entrance." She was guessing at this, but added, "But the Secret Service may have made him move because of the President's motorcade."

Both men wore the masks of tourists and feigned surprise that they had dallied so long. They assured Phelan that they would be with her momentarily.

"Are either of you going to Senator Bristow's home for the reception?" she asked.

Royal looked at Nadeau and shrugged his shoulders. "Why, I hadn't planned to, but why don't I go with you in your car, Governor? I think it would be a nice gesture."

Nadeau's expression turned to a forced smile like a grimace. "Why, yes, yes," he stammered. "That would be a nice thing for us to do."

As soon as the buses arrived back at Capitol Hill and discharged their passengers, Phelan placed a phone call to Philip Dake. She next called Tolland and made an appointment to deliver evidence to him.

Dake had been the Washington *Post*'s premier investigative reporter and, as a victim once said of him, had more scalps of prominent heads hanging from his belt than a Comanche warrior. While still on the *Post* he had written two best-sellers about Washington scandals. The previous year, without explanation, he had quit the newspaper and announced that he was going to work full-time on another blockbuster book. Phelan had heard that it was about Congress.

Periodically, Dake was sighted at a congressional hearing, surveying witnesses and their congressional tormentors. Funerals were not his known specialty, and it had struck Phelan as odd when she had spotted him sitting at the very back of the National Cathedral. He may have been using the memorial as a place to run into a potential source. Maybe he was only paying tribute to Julia

Bristow. Something told Phelan, however, that Philip Dake was not one to pay respects to dead politicians.

He accepted her invitation to meet for drinks at five at La Colline, an upscale restaurant near Capitol Hill frequented by some of the Senate lions. Phelan arrived first, and asked the maître d' to place her at a corner table in the front. From there, if she turned slightly, she could see the dome of the Capitol in the distance and keep an eye on the street traffic on North Capitol Street, as well as on the incoming clientele.

She ordered a wine spritzer and had just started to sip it when Dake sauntered in, his jacket over his shoulder. He stood for a moment waiting for his eyes to adjust to the interior light. Tall, dark-haired, about forty, he was handsome in a way that most women probably could not explain.

Phelan had helped him out once when he had been investigating the check bouncing scandal that involved some of the most powerful members of Congress. He immediately picked her out from the gathering end-of-the-day crowd. He shook hands with her, not in an austere or formal way, but as if to suggest that he considered this a business encounter. While Dake gave the impression of professional nonchalance, he was always wary and protective. He was used to asking all the questions and was not inclined to answer any. But he owed her, and he always paid his debts.

First they exchanged familiar small talk. Then Phelan got to the point: "I saw you at the National Cathedral today."

Dake's lips turned into his patented Mona Lisa smile while one eyebrow arched. *So?* he said, without uttering a word.

"I need your help. I understand you're working on a book about Congress."

Dake nodded, drinking deeply from the vodka-tonic he had ordered.

"I'm guessing you were paying more than respects today . . . I'm curious."

Again Dake remained silent, his expression disclosing nothing.

"The chief's got me working on the Julia Bristow case. But frankly, I don't know where to begin on this one. I need to know about the politics of the Senate. Who the players are. What drives them."

Dake smiled his little smile. "It's not hard to figure out. You just have to keep your eye on who has the power and who wants to get it. It used to be a club—very exclusive, very male, very self-protective, with established rules to play by. Today it's more like a rugby match."

"Rough enough to include murder?"

"Passions have run pretty high in the past. Even to duels. But no senator has ever resorted to murder." Dake's lips spread to a full smile. "Now you've got me curious. You think Bristow was murdered by one of her colleagues?"

"I don't think anything yet," she said. "There are no clues. No witnesses. Just the body. I'm just trying to run down every possible motive. You know, the classic test: motive, ability, opportunity."

"But what can I add to that?" Dake asked.

"Let's start with who gets Senator Bristow's seat."

"Whoever gets appointed will serve until the next general election," Dake replied. "My guess is that the governor will appoint Congressman Royal in the interim. Give him the advantage of incumbency."

The image of Nadeau and Royal whispering in the National Cathedral chapel was still fresh in Phelan's mind. Their words made sense now: *Christ, let the body grow cold for a week or ten days.*

"But why would he appoint Royal?" she asked. "He's pretty conservative even for Louisiana, isn't he?"

"Nice way of putting it."

"So why would the governor appoint him?"

"He really doesn't have any choice," Dake said matter-of-factly. "Look, politics is pretty byzantine in Louisiana. Eight months ago, Charles Bristow stunned the politicians down there by introducing a D.C. statehood bill. It ignited a hot campaign for an issue that has been on the back burner for a long time. Most of the locals thought Bristow brought it up because he wasn't going to run for reelection and wanted to stake out a position in the history books as a statesman. A profile in courage."

"Sounds to me like you don't buy it."

"No. There had to be something in it either for Bristow or for Louisiana. Daniel Lawson wants D.C. statehood bad. Statehood will give him two more Democrats, and that is bound to make a

Senate majority leader take notice. More important, he gets two blacks in the club—great politics for him when he launches his presidential bid."

"But what was in it for Bristow? Besides the profile in courage?" Phelan asked.

"I'm not sure. There were rumors that Bristow was having financial problems with his family business back home. But I haven't figured out any money angle on this one yet. Lawson is straighter than a redwood. He wouldn't be involved in any kind of a money payoff. But he's not above making political deals. My guess—and it's only a guess—is it was something big for Louisiana. Maybe that new super computer center the Senate just authorized. If Lawson cut a deal with Bristow and that center was to be built in Louisiana, Bristow could hold himself out not only as a statesman but as one who delivered the pork to his constituents. Thousands of jobs would be involved."

"So you think that's why the governor appointed Julia?"

"In politics, there's always more than one reason. Do you know how Charles Bristow died? He drowned on an alligator hunt in the bayous. In four feet of water. And at LSU he was the captain of the swim team."

"You mean *he* was murdered, too?" Phelan asked.

"No. I checked it out. Accidents happen. The autopsy showed that prior to drowning he had a massive heart attack."

"So what does that have to do with the governor's appointing Julia?"

"Everyone expected Royal to get the appointment. But there was an embarrassing problem. Royal was in the boat with Bristow." Dake held up his hand. "Don't jump to conclusions. Royal wasn't implicated. The media left him alone. But the governor felt that it wouldn't look good to appoint him right away. He wanted a decent interval. So he gave the seat, on a short-term basis, to Julia, as a cheap and easy sop to the women's vote for his own reelection campaign. Supposedly, he got a pledge out of her that she wasn't going to run for the seat on her own. He figured she'd be seen as a caretaker until the next election. He could tell everyone that D.C. statehood wouldn't come up for serious consideration until Royal occupied the Senate seat."

"And the governor secretly figured that Lawson would bring up the statehood bill and pass it with Julia's support."

"That was the game plan, only . . ."

"Only?" Phelan pressed.

"Only Julia decided to cross the governor. That's my guess. Two weeks ago she gave an interview to the *Times-Picayune* and said something about hoping that Lawson wouldn't press the D.C. statehood bill to a final vote. She said she was inclined to vote against cutting off the filibuster. As a result of that interview, her popularity in Louisiana went off the charts."

"Leaving the majority leader hoisted on a very sharp petard," Phelan said. She drank deeply from her wineglass and shook her head. "It doesn't make any sense to me. Why would she vote against her husband's wishes?"

"Julia and Charles kept up a good front, but some of my sources say she felt . . . how should I say it? . . . neglected. Or maybe she didn't like the deal Lawson had engineered. Maybe she planned to go back to Louisiana to live and didn't want to have any burning crosses on her lawn."

Dake said this matter-of-factly, but Phelan sensed disbelief in his voice. "You think it's something else, don't you?"

He tipped his tall glass to his lips and drained what little vodka was left. "Maybe there was no deal at all. Maybe Charles Bristow was just a statesman who was going to retire from office."

"Or maybe . . ." Phelan said, pushing Dake to complete his speculations.

"Maybe Julia Bristow was intoxicated with the smell of power. It happens all the time in this town. And if Julia was making plans to run in the next general election, an antistatehood stand would give her a simple way to crowd out any competition."

"But if that was the case," Phelan said, "I'm back to square one on motive, which is nowhere. Whoever murdered her would be a proponent of D.C. statehood."

"Not necessarily. Julia said she was *inclined* to vote against cutting off debate, not that she would. That's a politician's classic stall to keep everyone off-balance until the vote actually comes."

"Then she might secretly have been planning to vote for it?"

"Or maybe the guy who knocked her off just wanted her job."

"Royal?"

107

"Possibly. But I wouldn't start typing up an indictment just yet."

Phelan saw that Dake was gathering up his suit jacket and was about to get up from the table. "Philip, this is all terribly helpful. I'm really indebted to you. I won't discuss any of this with anyone but the chief. If I could impose a bit more . . ."

"Sure," Dake said, signaling to the waiter for the check.

"How soon will Royal be appointed?"

"Ordinarily, decency would demand a week or so. But these aren't decent times. If Governor Nadeau waits, the District will probably be a state. So, I'd say soon. Real soon."

"Could you fax me whatever you've got in those famous files of yours on Royal? Only the chief and I will see it, I promise."

"I don't fax anything that's confidential," Dake said. "Those machines have a nasty habit of treating your papers the way airlines treat your baggage. They usually end up in exotic places. I'll send it up by messenger."

He refused Phelan's offer to pick up the tab and paid in cash. The two of them then passed through the glass entranceway and onto First Street. Dake shook Phelan's hand and hailed a cab.

As he opened the door to the cab, he turned to Phelan and said, "By the way, while you're checking into Royal, the *Post* is checking into your chief."

"About what?"

"About someone he was watching over who got killed."

"You mean the FBI agent," Phelan said. "That's old news."

"But I'm told there's new news about the old news." Again the enigmatic smile.

19

FITZGERALD took off his tie and opened another shirt button, then polished off a well-loaded pizza from Armand's, across the street from his office. The air conditioning had gone on the blink for the second time in ten days. The engineers blamed the failure on the unusually warm weather, but the breakdown had been all too typical of similar recent power crashes.

He rolled up his sleeves, turned on his computer, and keyed in a listing of the most recent criminal activities on the Hill. Robberies were up dramatically, and there had been three rapes this month. One robbery on Second Street had turned into the rape of a seventy-four-year-old woman in a wheelchair. Last month, a Maryland man had managed to sneak a .44 Magnum pistol into the Dirksen Building. He had had a list of half a dozen senators he wanted to shoot because of their abortion votes. Early the previous week, some whacko from San Francisco had walked into Senator Wiley's office and started breaking up the furniture because Wiley was stealing his ideas for a book by mental telepathy. He had kept the CERT team at bay for more than three hours with a threat to blow up the office with a bomb. It turned out to be a phony. And then there had been Preacherman and his undetectable plastic gun.

As Fitzgerald watched the case files flow across the screen, he saw beyond them and became convinced that the world was in an advanced stage of moral rot. Banks and investment firms mugging the public; narcotics traffickers turning white powder into greenbacks; drive-by shootings; gang wars; teenagers being blown away for a pair of vanity sneakers or for looking the wrong way at somebody else's girlfriend; the District drowning in drugs; mental hospitals dumping patients out onto the street like so much garbage. Forty percent of the homeless were chronically ill, thirty-five percent were mentally ill, and fifteen percent were HIV positive. Now this—murder right in the U.S. Capitol . . . He punched the exit key hard, then turned off the computer.

"Hey, Chief." Phelan had knocked and was halfway through the door before Fitzgerald looked up. "All work and no—"

"No results," Fitzgerald said, not hiding his exasperation. "You know, sometimes I think my mother was right. I should have become a priest."

Phelan smiled. "Somehow I just can't see you in a stiff collar." She slipped into the chair alongside Fitzgerald's desk and told him about the scene at the memorial service and her meeting with Dake. "He'll be sending over copies of materials from his files on Royal," she concluded. "He's a piece of merchandise, that Royal.

109

He's been preaching a sophisticated form of racism that makes the Klan look old-fashioned."

"Yeah," Fitzgerald grunted. "He was a Klansman until a few years ago. And he may be the biggest bastard this side of the French Quarter. But motive is the key, remember?" It was not a question or a putdown but a reminder, to himself more than to Phelan. "Is Dake sure about Julia Bristow's crossing the governor and getting ready to run in the next election?"

"He said he was guessing," Phelan said. "But his guesses are usually worth betting the mortgage on."

"And the tip-off was her doubletalk on statehood?"

"Right. If she voted against statehood, and decided to run, there's no way Royal could beat her. Then she'd get a full six-year term, and Royal would lose all the momentum he's built up by using the statehood issue to stir up antiblack emotions. There's motive there, and—"

"What Dake gave you is a start, Alix," Fitzgerald interrupted. "But we'll need a lot more than this. And we've got to be real careful how we handle Royal. We could start a bonfire if word got out that we even consider him a suspect." He paused. "Anything else on her?"

"Not much. But I did find one odd bit. She was preparing a financial disclosure statement that had to be filed next month. It basically lists what she inherited from her husband. Apparently he left most of his estate to her and very little to his kids by his first wife."

"And?" Fitzgerald asked, a hint of impatience in his voice.

"And I decided to take a look at Charles Bristow's last financial disclosure statements. Some stock that she lists in her statement— it looks like holding company stock—he did *not* list in his statement. He was withholding information about his business dealings."

"Shady deals? On the Hill?" Fitzgerald shrugged. "Don't give that much priority. Focus on her and what she was up to just before she was killed. What have we got from the hideaway?"

"Specimens I took to Tolland." Something in her voice caught his attention.

"What specimens?" he asked.

"I'd rather not say now. It all could be nothing."

"How about telling me about it over a drink?" He looked at his watch. "I'm supposed to meet Tolland at nine. Down at the Dubliner?"

"Kind of noisy. How about the Monocle?"

"Okay," he said, smiling. "See you about ten-thirty."

As soon as Phelan left, Fitzgerald turned back to the computer. But all he could do was stare at the screen. *Time. There's never time. Solve it, Lawson said. Solve it. Chance is what solves things.* Everything seemed like pure chance in his life. Where was choice? Suppose everything was predetermined at that slap-on-the-ass moment, and all the rest—the twists, turns, and pirouettes—was not random at all?

From the beginning, it seemed, his choices had always been wrong. His father scoffed at his mother's wishes. *Priest, hell.* He should follow in his father's footsteps and be a cop. But from the moment he entered Boston College, he had set his sights on law school. He could still hear his father's voice. *A lawyer? A liar. A shyster, you mean! They don't give a damn about justice. They'll defend any scumbag as long as they get their dough up front.*

Any hopes he had for law school faded when he received his draft notice. He rushed to the Navy recruiter, figuring that his chances of surviving the Vietnam War were better at sea than in a rice paddy. But after boot camp, his competitive instincts pulled him to volunteer for Special Forces training as a Navy SEAL. During a practice drop from a CH-130 helicopter, his parachute did not fully open, and he hit the deck hard enough to break his hip and shoulder, which washed him out of the program. He finished his tour of duty as a shore patrolman—*at least I'm a Navy cop, Dad*—stationed at Subic Bay in the Philippines. Then he returned to Boston.

By then law school was no longer on his wish list, and he worked three years as a credit investigator, which included such exciting work as repossessing cars. That job in Dorchester proved more dangerous than duty in the Philippines.

The police commissioner, Sean Dugan, a former FBI agent and a friend of his father's, recruited him under a Bureau policy that allowed men without a law degree to join the FBI if they had had three years of law enforcement work and were recruited by an ex-agent in good standing.

Although Fitzgerald never took a vow of celibacy, his mother wondered whether he had signed a covenant of permanent bachelorhood. Then, in 1981, while assigned to the FBI field office in Philadelphia, he met and married Helen Whiteman, the Protestant daughter of a prominent neurosurgeon. Neither family approved of the marriage. Two years later, he was the father of a little girl they named Maureen.

Fitzgerald almost became a statistic when he and a fellow agent crossed signals during the arrest of a bank robber. He took a slug in the shoulder, and it was only Perkins's fancy work at St. Luke's Hospital that saved him from being a cripple. In an effort to redeem himself in the eyes of his superiors, he became obsessed with his work.

As he spent more and more time away from home on assignments, the weaker the ties of his marriage became. Fitzgerald's reassignment to Washington after the Alice Tyle disaster finally did it. Helen did not come with him.

Fitzgerald sighed and tried to haul himself out of memory by turning the computer on again and typing questions and answers on the screen.

Who? Someone she knew, according to film. Why? Political views? Why mutilate with knife? Black man? Unlikely. Knife used to make it look like rage? White racist against statehood? A crazy? Connection between Bristow and prostitutes? Serial killer? Copy-cat?

He knit his fingers behind his head and stared at the screen. Maybe he was giving too much time to motive and not enough to who did it. Maybe . . . His thoughts started to blur and merge together as a dull ache took form somewhere in his head.

The phone rang. He waited for Margaret to get it, then remembered that he had told her to go home. He picked up the phone and said, "Fitzgerald here."

"Good evening, Chief," a voice said. Fitzgerald immediately recognized the anchorman's delivery of James Davis. "I'm on my way over with a camera crew," he said. "I have a tape recording from Senator Bristow's killer."

Fifteen minutes later, Davis arrived, along with a camera operator, a sound man, and a producer. "Just sit right where you're sitting, Chief," the producer said. "We'll wire you up and get this over with as quickly as possible." He signaled to the sound man and the camera operator. Camera on her right shoulder, eye to the lens, she was writhing about, aiming at Fitzgerald, filing cabinets, the coffee counter.

Davis sat in a chair in front of the desk, his firm jawline softened by a dimple and a narrow moustache over thin lips. Before he could say a word, Fitzgerald said, "I understand you have a tape about the Bristow case."

20

KYLE TOLLAND was waiting for Fitzgerald at the visitors' reception lobby of the J. Edgar Hoover Building, headquarters of the FBI. Fitzgerald, although in uniform and a chief of police, had no official status there, so he had to be treated as an ordinary visitor who happened to be entering the building after regular office hours, as a maintenance man might be called upon to do.

He wanted it that way. He signed a register handed to him by a young man behind a chin-high console. Tolland apparently had already done some paperwork, for the young man handed Fitzgerald an identification tag and instructed him not to clip it on yet.

"He knows the drill, Chambers," Tolland said sternly to the young man.

He motioned Fitzgerald to turnstiles that stood beside a corridor leading to the interior of the building, slipped his laminated identification card into a slot in one of the turnstiles, and clicked through. Fitzgerald did the same. Somewhere a computer had registered Tolland as Fitzgerald's escort. If either one of them attempted to leave the building without the other, the automatic security system would lock the exit and alert an armed guard.

Fitzgerald slowed his step as they approached the elevator. He was six or seven inches taller than Tolland, who walked with a short, quick stride. He had a sharp chin and the pale skin of a man touched more by fluorescent light than by sunlight. His gray-white, unparted hair rolled in a high wave.

They got off the elevator at the main entrance to the lab, turned left, then right, then left again through a warren of corridors to Tolland's office. He suddenly stopped in the middle of the last corridor and made signs for Fitzgerald to lean down. "There's a move to leak the internal report on you and the Yosemite case," he whispered. "It's been misfiled. It will slow things but not necessarily stop them. Don't talk about this in my office."

He continued down the corridor, unlocked a door, and motioned Fitzgerald to a chrome-framed leather couch. He went to a counter, poured water from a carafe into a small yellow enamel pan, and put it on a hot plate before going to a matching leather chair that faced the couch across a low glass-topped table. "Well," he said as he sat down, "have you decided who did it?"

"What I have decided at this point, Kyle, is that this is not just a murder. You told me a long time ago that nothing ever happens in this town that isn't politics. That's all I keep thinking about: politics."

"Assassination?" Tolland shook his head. "For what? What did she have a chance to do? Who could be holding a grudge? Now, her husband, Charles Bristow—well, he was in the game long enough to make enemies. But Julia Bristow killed by an assassin? I doubt that very much."

"I don't mean assassination," Fitzgerald said, sensing the familiar pattern of a conversation with Tolland: you say something; he gives it a spin; you respond to the spin; he takes you someplace else.

"What you are trying to say, Fitz, is that this isn't just a homicide by some nut who happened to come upon a victim by chance." He stood and went to the counter. "Another one of those brainless murders that's giving murder a bad name. What you mean is"—he turned and smiled—"that this is one of those *delicious* murders that you need brains to solve."

"Yes, Kyle. I meant to say something exactly like that."

Tolland poured the hot water into a two-cup Finnish coffeemaker whose mechanism Fitzgerald had never been able to figure out. All he knew is that it made the best coffee in the world. Tolland opened a cupboard above the counter and took out a white mug bearing a decal of the FBI shield. Written under it in indelible black ink was FITZ.

It had been a ritual. Some people earned their name on one of Tolland's mugs and some people didn't. Fitzgerald had never quite known how he earned it, but he thought that it had something to do with being shot. After he had been wounded in the Philadelphia bank shoot-out, he had been temporarily assigned to headquarters under what vaguely appeared to have been a cloud. He had killed the man who had shot him; his action clearly had been in self-defense, and the slain robber had a bag of money and a criminal record. But the conventional wisdom of the FBI was that its agents did not get into shoot-outs, especially with young inner-city blacks, and even more especially when the Bureau was being criticized for its indifference to racial issues.

Fitzgerald had been assigned, with some sense of bureaucratic irony, to Weapons Identification Analysis, and that move had put him in frequent contact with Kyle Tolland. Bullets fascinated Tolland. He had been shocked to learn that Fitzgerald did not cherish —or even possess—the slug that had been extracted from him. Tolland had tracked it down and presented it to him, along with the mug he now held in his hand.

"I would have thought that you'd have thrown this away," Fitzgerald said, raising the mug.

"Yes, that is exactly what you would have thought. I never throw them away. Smash them sometimes. But I never throw them away."

Fitzgerald took the package containing the tape from his pocket, explained how Davis had said he obtained it, and asked, "What can you get out of this for me?"

"This is the original?" Tolland asked. Fitzgerald nodded. Tolland looked up at the ceiling, then at a far wall, barren like all the wall space in his office. "The usual analysis: brand name of the tape, whether it's new; if not, maybe fragments of what has been erased on it. A voice signature, in case you get something you want to compare this voice to. We'll run it through the accents and dialect library, maybe get some potential identification data on the voice. Then I'll pass it along to the Behavioral Science Unit at Quantico and ask them for a voice analysis—stress, possibility of impersonation, and a comparison with the voice signatures in their collection. Does he say anything pertinent?"

"Nothing obvious. Sounds a bit like a crazy. Or someone wanting us to think he's a crazy. You'll hear it all on Davis's eleven o'clock show."

"And now let me tell you what I have for you," Tolland said. "By the way, that's a very bright investigator, your Alix Phelan. And an interrupted autopsy. Oh yes, this is a delicious one." He picked up a file folder from the table between them. Fitzgerald recognized it as the kind used for lab reports. But the label on it was blank.

"You notice the label," Tolland said, opening the folder. "Officially, this does not exist." He squinted at Fitzgerald to make sure he was paying attention. "Now, up on the Hill, you're going to have to tell some smart people and some cretins about DNA analysis. So I pulled something out of a report that *Congress* ordered published. The Congressional Office of Technology Assistance, to be exact." He handed Fitzgerald a sheet of paper, which Fitzgerald folded twice and put in his inside jacket pocket.

"All you need to know for the exam is this: genetic evidence that is acceptable in court can be produced from the DNA in a semen stain. Remember, *the FBI lab* says that," he emphasized, giving the three words the weight of a divine pronouncement. "And when we get a semen *sample* from a vaginal smear, instead of just a scraping from a stain, well, it's like having a full portrait in living color instead of a murky little snapshot."

"Okay," Fitzgerald said, tapping his jacket pocket. "And what have I got?"

"Not so fast. This is murder. We go carefully and with stately grace." Tolland put the mug and the folder on the table and leaned back. "Perkins, who is very, very good, found no scratches, no blood or flesh under the fingernails. Not even a *broken* fingernail. So we can assume that there was no struggle. Right?"

"Possibly," Fitzgerald said. He stood, stretched, went to the counter, and picked up the coffeemaker and the yellow pan. He told Tolland about what appeared on the surveillance camera tape. "We can build a scenario that says she knew her killer, obviously didn't fear him. It would be a better scenario if she voluntarily had sexual intercourse before her death. No struggle."

"So Alix told you what we have here?" Tolland stood and darted to the counter. "Let me do that. You'll break something." He poured water into the pot and put it on the hot plate.

Fitzgerald stepped back and leaned against the counter. "No. She sounded like she wasn't sure. But I know there was hope the vaginal swab from the autopsy would show something. And you've started giving me your DNA lecture. So it figures—"

"You don't know *what* it figures yet," Tolland said. "Be patient. Alix delivered a vaginal swab from the autopsy and scrapings from a semen stain on the couch in Mrs. Bristow's hideaway. If the two semen samples came from the same man, the genetic signatures of the two samples would be the same."

"And?"

"They were. Someone, let us call him Mr. A, definitely had intercourse with Senator Bristow shortly before her death." Tolland paused. "But who is Mr. A? Well, I get that information if I get a chance to compare the semen on the swab and the semen from the couch with a sample of blood from the man on the couch."

"And a DNA comparison of semen and blood holds up?"

"Read your paper. To put it in terms even a jury would understand, DNA is extracted from the semen sample and from the blood sample." His voice took on the tone of a witness giving testimony, a familiar role. "The method for finding the DNA is the same for both. You can get the evidence from bone marrow, hair, saliva, urine, the pulp of a tooth, besides blood and semen. DNA is DNA, no matter where it comes from."

"Okay. Okay. So what's the bottom line?"

"Our conclusion," Tolland said, continuing in his testimonial voice, "is that the DNA pattern obtained from both the vaginal swab and the couch stain matched the DNA pattern obtained from the blood that was submitted to the FBI laboratory. In other words, we know, within a probability of something like one in one hundred million, who made love to Mrs. Bristow within two hours of her death."

"*What* blood? Where did you get the blood?" Fitzgerald spun toward Tolland.

"Didn't Alix tell you?" Tolland asked innocently.

"No, she did not."

"It seems that the physician's office has a House blood bank. The Secret Service started it, storing blood from members who are in the line of succession. Some others picked up on the idea— members paranoid about being shot at, I suppose, and maybe members who figure that if they ever need blood, these days the safest blood is the blood that comes out of your own veins."

He poured hot water into the coffeemaker, manipulated it, and refilled Fitzgerald's mug. He put down the coffeemaker and went back to his chair. Fitzgerald knew there was no use in asking any more questions. Tolland was in what Fitzgerald called a Nordic saga mood.

"Your ingenious Alix managed to get a blood sample from the blood bank. And she passed it on to me," he said. He paused, folded his hands, and, smiling sublimely, said, "The lover on the couch was the honorable Michael Royal, the congressman from Louisiana and the Ku Klux Klan."

21

THE MONOCLE, next door to Capitol Police headquarters, was a watering hole for lobbyists, members, and Hill staffers. Capitol Police officers, who felt more comfortable in the beery din of the Dubliner, rarely patronized it. Fitzgerald had been there only a few times, twice with Lawson, the other times with other members who chose it as a convenient place to discuss matters off the record. The Monocle was that kind of place, off the record, and perhaps that was why Fitzgerald did not feel at ease there.

He sat now at the bar, which was two steps higher than the restaurant section, finishing a vodka martini.

"Evening, Chief," a member called out as he passed by. Fitzgerald nodded, trying to remember the man's name. A New York Republican. But his name? His name? Funny being able to remember numbers better than names. A shrink could probably make something out of that.

"Another, Chief?" the barman asked. Fitzgerald nodded again.

He wished he had been able to go home, grab a quick shower, and get out of the goddamn uniform.

The barman gently lowered a glass onto the bar. Fitzgerald let it stand there, glistening, icy, for just a moment. Then he picked it up and tolled it slightly to hear the faint clink of the perfect cubes. He pulled out the blue toothpick thrust through the unfashionable olive and was slowly raising the drink to his lips when a voice at his side said, "Looks luscious. I'll have one."

He turned to see Alix Phelan slipping onto the seat next to him. She wore a sleeveless, high-necked blue dress that did not quite cover her knees and rose a few inches when she crossed her legs. He saw this, he believed, in the lower edge of his vision, for he was looking directly into her eyes. It was only an instant. He looked quickly away, toward the barman, signaling superfluously, for the barman was quick. Phelan's vodka martini, on the rocks and with an unfashionable olive, was already being created.

"You made quite an impression on Tolland," Fitzgerald said.

"I like him. He's smart, gracious, and tough, a combination you don't see much in this town."

"He wouldn't tell me how you got Royal's blood sample." He waited for a response. There was none. "Now maybe *you'll* tell me about it. I wish you had—"

"Not much to tell," Phelan said. She looked around, a quick sweep of the room, then turned her eyes on him. She had a way of pulling a person toward her, Fitzgerald thought, certainly not in a coquettish way, but through a kind of strength or energy.

"I'm sure Tolland told you it was from the infirmary blood bank. It was a hunch. And I knew that when Royal was elected to the House he was paranoid about being a 'target.' That was his word. There were death threats during his campaign. So I checked with our Threat Assessment guys and found out that he was one of their best customers. Nut letters; boxes of feces, horse and human. Nice people down there in Louisiana. Then I checked the infirmary, expecting that Royal would have signed up for the blood storage." She paused to sip her drink.

"How did you talk the medics into handing over a sample?" Fitzgerald asked.

"I told a nurse I was carrying out a very confidential request from Threat Assessment. I said Royal wanted a blood sample because he had cut his finger when he cut the string on a box of feces some constituent had mailed him, and he was afraid he might have AIDS. I said his doctor wanted to check his blood today against the blood-bank blood to show him that he was still okay. Well, the nurse was black, and she laughed and said, 'Serves the son of a bitch right. He hands out so much shit.' And she got me the sample."

Fitzgerald tried to hold back, failed, and erupted with laughter. Phelan laughed with him. It was over in a moment. Fitzgerald made his face stern. "But it's *wrong*," he said. "What you did is *wrong*. You know that. The evidence is tainted. And if we—"

"Tolland didn't think it was tainted. And he's as FBI as you are," Phelan said, her voice hardening. She took another sip. "The point is, we can get to Royal with this. The semen that we got is admissible. We can get a blood sample from him under court order by showing probable cause."

"Keep your voice down. This place is full of ears. What probable cause?"

"We can push Haverlin for a statement about Royal and Julia Bristow's being lovers and using the hideaway as a rendezvous. I can get it out of him."

"You can get it out of him? Come on, Alix. This isn't a goddamn Rayburn Building office theft. We've got to do this by the book."

"For God's sake, Chief. Forget the book for a minute. If the blood and the semen match, we can put Royal in Julia Bristow's hideaway just before her death." She dropped her voice. "And they do match, don't they?"

"Yes. They do. But I like to play it straight. Your little caper did make me laugh. But we can get in trouble, big trouble, if we botch this one."

"We won't botch it. I know I've never botched anything. And I'm sure you never have."

"That's where you're wrong, Alix. Dead wrong." He drained his glass.

Phelan switched to a neutral topic: movies. But she had seen many and he had seen few. Then she tried leisure. She talked of hiking the C&O Canal near Harper's Ferry. He had walked along the canal towpath in Georgetown but had never gone beyond.

Phelan abruptly changed the subject. "I took an immediate liking to Kyle Tolland. He called you 'Fitz.' I never heard anyone call you Fitz. It's a very Boston name."

"Well, it ought to be. I'm originally from Boston."

"I know."

The way she said it made him think that she had somehow looked him up. Maybe she had.

"And your name," he said. "It sounds . . . it sounds like there's a story in it."

"Not much of one. All too typical, I'm afraid. My father wanted a boy. They got me and named me Alexandra. My mother liked the sound of the name and my father liked it because he could make a boy's name out of it. So they called me Alix."

"Not a saint's name. Odd in a Catholic family."

"I wasn't raised a Catholic."

"But Phelan—it's an Irish name."

"I was raised a Unitarian. I still am one. But I did go to Boston College. My father, who *was* brought up Catholic, wanted me to get a Jesuit education."

"BC. That's my school, too," Fitzgerald said.

"I know," Phelan said, smiling. "I'm surprised you didn't know *I* went there."

"What do you mean you're surprised?"

"I mean, why don't you know more about me? Didn't you just go through my personnel files? I would have thought—"

"I didn't have to go into any files about you. I start with my own instincts. If I size somebody up and I don't like what I see, I drop it, and I don't have to go through all that paper. When I like what I see, then I move, and forget the paperwork."

"Well, do you like what you see?"

Fitzgerald looked back at her, perplexed. What he saw was a tall woman, not slim—lean. Black hair, straight and framing an oval face. Not beautiful, not cute. Pretty. Lovely. Green eyes, he thought, but he did not want to stare and confirm the color. It would be in the personnel jacket. "Yes," he said. "I think I have to do some reading about you."

"Okay. Just don't believe everything you read."

"I think," he said after an instant's pause, "that we should start talking about the case."

"Let's start with the camera tape," she said. "Royal would probably know about the camera angles in the corridors. He could have checked them out in advance. After being with her in the hideaway, he leaves and comes back to the subway, avoiding cameras and standing out of sight of the one in the corridor. He waits there and calls her over. He kills her in the ladies' room and then dumps the body in the subway and goes back the way he came. Or to the House parking garage. We should check his car for bloodstains."

"Not so fast, Alix. Remember, he's a member of Congress. We'll take it slow. Have a chat with Haverlin. That little snake knows a lot more than he's telling us. But let's do all we can without spooking anybody. We follow all the routines. We'll have to show we took other paths before we took the one to Royal."

"Okay. I'll do some follow-ups. Like the prostitute murders that Perkins mentioned."

"That's exactly the kind of thing I mean. Those similarities in the wounds—we've got to check that out. But don't get us mixed up with the Metro cops. Stick with Perkins."

"Why? I thought we're supposed to be entering an era of good feeling with them. I know someone in Homicide who could—"

"Forget it," Fitzgerald said with a slash of his right hand. "Asking them about those murders would get us nowhere. The murder rate in D.C. is climbing. There are two, three a day, and it's been that way for two years. Metro Homicide is one of the worst in the business. I can't remember the last time they solved a murder, a real murder."

"They used to be damn good," Phelan shot back. "The closure rate on murder cases was eighty-nine percent. Then came Mitchell. About the first thing he did when he became mayor was start ruining the police force."

"Mitchell was elected mayor ten or eleven years ago. You weren't around then."

"No. But my friend was."

"Your friend in Homicide?"

"Yes. I . . . dated when I first came to D.C. We're still friends. He's got a caseload of fifteen or twenty all the time. They've cut the homicide squad to the bone."

"So what? A good detective's a good detective."

"Come on, Fitz. You know damn well a cop's got to have backup. The guys in Homicide make arrests. But the perps walk because there's no cooperation between the Metro cop brass and the U.S. attorney, and he makes no bones about trying to nail Mitchell for corruption." She drew a breath. "Well, you know all this. But I just had to spout off."

"So it's 'Fitz,' is it?"

She smiled and said, "Sorry."

"I don't expect *sorry* is a word you say very often."

"No. It isn't. My only excuse is that I heard Tolland say 'Fitz' so much, I guess I started thinking of you that way."

"So you heard a lot of Nordic sagas from him, including some about me."

"Correct."

Fitzgerald looked at his watch, signaled for the bill, and, looking away, said, "Well, don't believe all you hear. I think we'd better get over to my office. I want to see what Davis is doing with that tape."

Phelan dug into her purse for her wallet while Fitzgerald reached into his back pocket for his. He grabbed the bill. Phelan slapped her hand on it, startling the bartender. "It's Dutch," she said.

"It's Fitz. You let me pay and I'll let you call me Fitz when . . . when we're off-duty. A deal?"

Phelan was reading the bill. She put down three fives, looked up, and said, "You owe me seven-fifty and you can leave the tip. I don't make deals. It's Fitz from now on, when I feel it's not going to turn your face red. Like it is now."

22

THROUGHOUT THE EVENING, Fitzgerald's words—"I understand you have a tape about the Bristow case"—were used as a sound bite in a promotion for "a Channel 3 exclusive: Capitol Hill killer tape!" At the top of the eleven o'clock Channel 3 news show, the largest news-watching audience in the Washington market saw Fitzgerald at his desk, with his words being played as a voice-over.

The scene shifted to Davis, who told how the tape had been delivered to him by messenger that morning. The messenger then came on screen and said that during his rounds on Capitol Hill he had been stopped on the sidewalk by a man who handed him a small package and fifty dollars and asked him to take the package to Davis at Channel 3. After a commercial break, Davis came back and finally played the words on the tape: "All women like her must die. The world belongs to men."

Fitzgerald switched off the television set in his office and turned to Phelan. "Did we get anything on the messenger?"

"He's no cherub. He's been arrested on a couple of minor drug charges. I talked to a Metro undercover man I know, who says they have suspicions about a few messengers, including this one. Delivering drugs downtown and on the Hill."

"What do you think about his story?"

"I assume he didn't know who hired him," Phelan replied. "I'll get someone to talk to him, but I don't think we'll get anywhere chasing him down. I'm more interested in the tape. You got the original?"

"Yes," Fitzgerald said. "Davis wanted to palm off a copy. I threatened to hold him here as a material witness unless he came across with the original. I had three copies made and stowed away. Tolland's got the original."

They talked awhile, mostly about the case, and Phelan left. Fitzgerald finally signed off on the computer, after copying his Bristow files onto disks and locking them in a drawer. Then he walked home, hoping that he would be able to fall asleep more quickly than usual. He had an eight o'clock meeting with Mason in the morning.

Shafts of light from the front bay window fell across the roses, casting a tangle of shadows across the walk. As he unlocked the front door, he heard Mrs. Darwin's door open.

She was standing in her doorway when he entered the hall. "I . . . want to talk to you," she said. "Something has come up."

He bolted into her room. "Someone called? Communications should have—"

"Calm down, Jeffrey. It's just something I have to tell you."

"But Mrs. Darwin, it's so late. I—"

She directed him to one of the chairs at the table near the bay window. On the table were several outsize playing cards, some face down, some face up, showing strange scenes. A man in what looked like a tomb. Flaming swords. A cavern. He did not immediately realize what he was looking at. Then it dawned on him. Tarot cards.

Still standing, he pointed to the cards. "Something to do with them?"

"Yes, in a way. Please sit down."

"Look, Mrs. Darwin, I've had a long day. I can't believe anything coming out of Tarot cards."

"Yes, I know that, . . . Jeffrey. But please sit down. This is important. I think I know something about the murder."

Fitzgerald slumped into the chair, exaggerating his fatigue. He glanced at the cards, ten of them laid out in a crude cross on a black gossamer cloth. Two were turned over. One showed a black-haired woman rising from the sea. Next to that one was a card showing a king on a throne. He looked up at Ellen Darwin. She looked as she always looked: pleasant, quick, trustworthy. He could almost see the words in his mind. *How can this nice old lady be a damn fortune-teller? Why should I give her any time?*

He shrugged, with another touch of exaggeration. "Mrs. Darwin, I am sitting here, and I am going to listen to you because I like you and want to be courteous. But I don't believe a damn thing about the occult."

"As I said, I know that." She settled in the opposite chair and looked as if she were about to pour him a cup of tea. "I sensed when you first showed up on my doorstep that something like this would happen between us. I can *feel* your cynicism, your disbelief. I ordinarily would not try to persuade an unbeliever. But there is something terrible here, Jeffrey. Terrible."

"And what is that, Mrs. Darwin?"

"Please don't patronize me. Just listen to me. The murder of Mrs. Bristow—it is part of a chain, a chain going back and a chain going forward. I can feel it. Almost see it."

"And what is it that you see?"

"I see killing, more killing, all part of a chain."

"Can you be more specific?"

125

"Yes, I think I can. I can see two women. A woman and blood on bricks. A woman and blood on marble."

"And did you happen to see the eleven o'clock news on Channel 3, Mrs. Darwin?"

"Yes. That tape. That voice. *'All women like her must die. The world belongs to men.'* Yes, Jeffrey, that is part of it. Part of what came together for me tonight."

"And don't you think that the tape is what . . . what set you off?"

" 'Set me off'? It's much, much more complicated than that."

"Mrs. Darwin. It's been a long day. I appreciate your interest in the case. But—"

"But what? You don't believe in psychic phenomena? I am not asking you to believe. I am asking you to listen."

"I'm sorry, Mrs. Darwin, but I don't see any point in listening." He stood. "Good night."

Before he could turn toward the door, she touched his right arm. "Look at this, Jeffrey." He looked down at a card that she turned over. The figure on it looked like a tall, slim image of the devil. She touched the card with the index finger of her left hand. "You aren't seeing it all. You are acting as if you don't care about the truth. You're thinking only of yourself. You're being very selfish."

Before he could speak, she raised her hand to his other arm and lightly held him. He started, then tried to look impassive.

"I can feel your muscles tighten. Please sit down. Give me just another minute."

He sat down, his eyes on her face.

"I think you need convincing, Jeffrey. I can tell you things about yourself. I can go back, into your past. If you are closed, it's hard to penetrate. But I can go back. I can see."

She let go of his arms and leaned back in her chair. "I'm not going to try to prove myself. I am just going to show you that I know some things about you."

He did not take his eyes from her.

"Your sister, Catherine—Kate—started calling you Fitz when you were about ten. You objected, and she said, 'Well, okay. I'll make it Fritz. And how would you like that?' And you said, 'No. Don't call me Fritz. I'm Irish.' And Kate laughed and said that she was going to be the only one who could call you Fitz. And you agreed. Isn't that what happened?"

Fitzgerald rubbed the back of his neck with his right hand. "It's an old story in my family," he said. "I must have told you something about it and you made up the rest. You've heard me mention Kate. You must have seen the letters I get."

"You never told me that story, Jeffrey. And you know that you didn't." She gathered up the cards on the cloth, put them in the deck, and began shuffling. He watched her, wondering what cards she would put down on the cloth. Instead, she put the deck on the table, at the edge of the cloth.

"You still resist. Very well." She seemed to be looking just past his right shoulder, into the darkness framed by the bay window.

"I see bodies on the ground," she said. "Two women. A man. One of the women and the man are in some kind of uniform. Not soldiers. I see a man coming out from behind a tree. There is a gun in his hand. He has just fired it, just killed with it. You turn toward him and you fire your weapon. Once. Twice."

Beads of sweat appeared on Fitzgerald's forehead and cheeks. She lowered her voice.

"The man falls, face up. He is a young, good-looking man. Your two shots hit him in the chest. Heart shots. You know he is dead. You walk over to him. His eyes are open. You want to say something to him, but you can't. You shoot him once more in the chest. Then you shoot him three times in the face. The first shot penetrates his right eye. The second—"

Fitzgerald was on his feet, his hands still gripping the table. "You *can't* know this," he said, his voice almost a scream. He was breathing hard. "You were told," he croaked, trying to get his voice under control. "Kyle told you. That's it. You know Kyle. The two of you sit around talking like a pair of old biddies. That's it. He told you."

"Would you like a drink, Jeffrey?"

He sank back into the chair and nodded.

Mrs. Darwin went to the kitchen and returned quickly with two glasses. "Sambuca for me," she said, smiling. "I'm an old biddy. For you, vodka on the rocks."

Fitzgerald took the glass with a shaking hand and drank nearly half. He put it on the table but still held it. "Sorry about 'old biddies,'" he said. "You gave me quite a shock."

"I meant to. I'm sorry, too. Usually that's the only way."

"What do you mean, 'only way'?"

"Jeffrey, I don't expect to convert you. I just want you to understand, in your mind and heart, that I can see and sense things."

"A psychic. You're saying you're a psychic."

"If that's what you want to call me, fine."

"I'm stunned, all-out stunned by what you told me, Mrs. Darwin. But I can't buy it. Never could."

"You must know about the use of psychics by police."

"I've heard about it, read about it. Never saw it and never believed it," he said, his voice and breathing nearly back to normal. He took a sip of vodka.

"And you do know that the FBI has used psychics on occasion, and that psychics have lectured at Quantico."

"Maybe I heard that."

"Of course you heard it. Just as you've heard of the Behavioral Science Unit and the National Center for the Analysis of Violent Crime."

"You seem to know a lot about the FBI. Kyle's a great one for sagas. Nordic sagas, I call them."

"Yes, I know. And how do you think I met Kyle? At some senior citizens' club?"

"I don't know how you met. Never gave it a thought. It's a small town that way. People meet. I don't know."

"I met him at Quantico, at a seminar on violent crime."

"You? At Quantico?" He pictured the sprawling FBI training establishment at Quantico, Virginia, and could not picture her in it anywhere.

"Try Building 428," she said. "That's where the seminar was. Kyle was in the audience, on the right side of the auditorium. About the eighth row back. He came to hear me speak."

Fitzgerald shook his head, started to say something, then sagged back in his chair.

"We moved here when I was a child, as you know," she said. "When I started living in this house, this house that had already seen so much, I began to realize that I could see things, feel things, sense things. I could be in various places. Sometimes I was on the ceiling, looking down, sometimes on the floor, looking up. I couldn't control it. I was frightened, and I told nobody about what I was feeling.

"What I felt was that I was using some kind of energy. But as I grew up, I forgot all about it. I remembered it as a kind of dream. I married young, and it was a strong, powerful love. More energy, I guess. Then, when Fred went overseas—he was in the OSS—it all started to come back. I could feel, painfully feel, the danger he was in. I could see him plunging out of the plane, his parachute opening up. The guns down below." She picked up her glass of Sambuca. "I knew he was dead before I got the telegram. I knew how he died. Saw how he died."

Between sips she told Fitzgerald about her gradual acceptance of what she called her gift, about her quiet readings for close friends, about her introduction to area police and then to the FBI. "It has all been very discreet. I am no Jeane Dixon."

"Jeane Dixon?" Fitzgerald asked.

"A Washington psychic who predicted John Kennedy's assassination."

"I sort of remember hearing something about that. But believe me—"

"Don't worry, Jeffrey, I'm not going to give you any prophecies. That's not where my gift takes me. I see the present. I see the past. I see people walking through doors to changes in their lives. But prophecies? No."

"What about those?" Fitzgerald asked, pointing to the Tarot cards.

"The cards make my reading easier. I can read people without them, but once I start working on the cards, my visualization improves, and so does my ability to tap into a person. Sometimes things just come to me, and I like it that way. But sometimes I have to work for it. These cards"—she brushed a hand across the pack—"just tell me where I am, where my mind is. As I work with someone, I get a feel for that person."

"I guess you know, Mrs. Darwin, that you're never going to work with me."

She laughed lightly, a laugh hardly more than a smile. "We'll see about that, Jeffrey. We'll see." She motioned toward his glass. He shook his head. She rose and went into the kitchen, where she poured another glass of sambuca. When she returned, she stood by the window and looked out into the night.

"Louisiana," she said, her head still turned away from Fitzgerald. "There are strange places, strange sights there." She swung around and gazed at him. "You've never been there."

"That's right. And you?"

"Not physically," she said, looking away.

"You mentioned a chain, something about a chain," Fitzgerald said. "Does that have anything to do with Louisiana?" Even as he spoke, he wondered why he was letting himself be pulled into this.

"This all goes back into the past. Senator Charles Bristow was once involved in a scandal. There was a murder." She returned to her chair. "That was the beginning of the chain. Bristow's father owned a big contracting company that did a lot of state road work. He spread money around—political contributions and outright bribes—and he got state contracts. It went on like that for years.

"Years ago, when Bristow entered the Senate after three terms in the House, his father was retiring. The new senator was taking over the business. Well, the rules said that even though you may have bribed your way to a state contract, you were expected to be honest from then on—do honest work for the state, use real concrete instead of oyster-shell tabby stuff. It seems that Senator Bristow started using two kinds of concrete, the kind that the inspectors saw on top of the highway, and some stuff that was tabby underneath.

"There was a young inspector who wasn't fooled very easily. He got a look at some of that funny concrete and he told his boss, and his boss called Bristow's father, who was old but still had all his marbles. And Daddy, well, he just raised general Hades about it."

"Excuse me, Mrs. Darwin," Fitzgerald asked. "But I have a feeling that I could look all this up. Louisiana, I'm sure, has a fine old tradition of bribing state officials. And maybe Charles Bristow wasn't the most honest politician who ever came down the pike. But I don't see the chain you mentioned. I don't see where anything you're telling me has anything to do with his widow's murder."

Mrs. Darwin continued as if there had been no interruption. "It seems that this young inspector disappeared. He left his house one day, waved goodbye to his wife, got in his car, and drove off to the highway department office where he worked. But he never got there. He simply disappeared. When he didn't come home at the end of the day, the wife called his boss, at home, and the boss asked her the same thing she was asking him. Where was Bobby? That was his name. Bobby Lee Turner."

Fitzgerald had taken his notebook out of his pocket. He wrote *Bobby Lee Turner* on a blank page. He did not quite know why he was writing this, but he vaguely thought that it would please Mrs. Darwin.

"The wife—her name was Lori—called the sheriff," Mrs. Darwin continued, "and he just sort of shrugged and said not to worry, that men had a way of going off and then coming back in a few days. But that wasn't enough for Lori. She—"

"Excuse me again, Mrs. Darwin," Fitzgerald said. "But I was wondering, how does this fit in here and now? I want all the background I can get, but this background is a bit deeper than I expected."

"I suppose you want me to speak a little faster and—what's that phrase? Cut to the chase?" Mrs. Darwin said. "All right. Let me tell you that Lori Turner is a benefactor."

She paused for Fitzgerald to say exactly what she expected him to say: "A benefactor?"

"Yes," she said. "Some psychics call them clients. I call them benefactors because 'client' sounds as if I charge them, when actually they give *me* something, a feeling of helping. Well, to continue, when Lori got nowhere with the sheriff, she called her mother, who knew about my gift. Lori's mother heard about me through the Louisiana community here in Washington. A lot of people here are from Louisiana, you know—lobbyists, journalists, former congressmen. Their sons and daughters get married and stay here. Well, that's how I came into this." She shifted her gaze to his open notebook, and he dutifully wrote *Lori. Louisiana. What's the point?*

"The point," Mrs. Darwin said, "is that the violence in Bristow's life may have had something to do with the murder of his widow."

Fitzgerald looked up, startled. From where Mrs. Darwin sat, it was impossible for her to see what he was writing. He shifted in his seat, as if to shield himself from her gaze.

"Well, Lori sent me a picture of her husband, and I had a friend get me a U.S. Coast and Geodetic map of the area."

She picked up her Sambuca, took another sip, put down the glass, and resumed speaking, a bit more slowly. "I felt that he had been killed with a knife. I got the impression that the knife had been used to skin alligators. I felt that Bobby had been stabbed in the neck and chest. I saw that, and I saw where the killer put his body, near the curve of a river. I looked at the map and figured it out, and I told them where they could find him."

Fitzgerald knew she was waiting for him to ask if they did find the body, but he knew that they did. He felt as if he had entered an unknown dimension. The room around him no longer seemed familiar.

"They found Bobby's body the next day, right where I said it would be. There were two knife wounds, one in the neck and one in the chest. Well, there was plenty of talk, of course, but no one was able to pin anything on Bristow or any of the shady men he knew. The state contract was quietly canceled, and the family contracting firm just as quietly went bankrupt. So Senator Bristow was left with his Senate salary as his only dependable income."

Fitzgerald began writing rapidly. He looked up and was about to ask a question when Mrs. Darwin said, "No. I'm not suggesting that the man who killed Bobby killed Mrs. Bristow." She hesitated and returned to her story. "I couldn't give them much of a description of Bobby's killer. I could see a tattoo of the number 13 on his upper left forearm, and I sensed what it meant. The thirteenth letter is M. I knew that he had the 13 tattooed when he was in reform school. Well, it wasn't a regular tattoo, it was punched deep into the skin with a needle dipped in regular ink. Guards thought it meant 'murder,' but it really only meant 'marijuana.' Well, that's all I saw, the 13 on his arm. And that wasn't enough, and they never found him."

She waved vaguely with her right hand. "He can't be your murderer. I am quite sure that he's dead. A motorcycle accident, I believe—drunk. No, he is not the point. The point is *violence* and *greed*. That's it, Jeffrey. Greed. Murder motivated by greed. I feel that it has happened again."

"I appreciate your help, Mrs. Darwin. But I . . . I can't see how a murder years ago down in Louisiana is going to help me with a murder here. Besides, if you do see things—"

"This is so difficult to explain. A psychic, if that is what I am, does not *solve* crimes, does not suddenly blurt out the murderer's name. Psychics feel things, see things, and then, if they are working with the police, pass these things on. I am not saying there is a direct connection between the death of Bobby Lee Turner and the death of Charles Bristow and the death of Julia Bristow. I am saying that there is the same kind of *energy*—a pattern, an aura, whatever you want to call it—around all the murders. Greed."

"If you saw this connection, or nonconnection, why didn't you tell me all this before?"

"I knew it would confuse you, send you off on the wrong track. Looking for connections." She hesitated again, and Fitzgerald felt she was going from one place in her mind to another. "There is no passion here, Jeffrey. No evil passion, no mad passion. That is why it is so difficult to see. This is not someone killing for passion. There is a terrific energy in that kind of murder. The energy here is weak, murky. Greed is like that."

She hesitated again. "And then, today, I began to see the chain, the chain to past and present and future. A chain whose links are greed. I saw a knife, a broken knife, and a woman bleeding, and another woman bleeding. Both of them bleeding. A woman bleeding on bricks. A woman bleeding on marble. And the chain suddenly went back to Bobby Lee Turner. And the chain had to do with greed and killing. Those women, bleeding—both of them bleeding."

"I thought you couldn't see into the future."

"I can't. I move from the present to the past. But I see doors open. I see tunnels into darkness."

Fitzgerald stood and walked to the door. He hesitated. *Doors* and *darkness* reverberated in his mind. He knew he would have trouble falling asleep.

Inside his apartment, he picked up a book he had started weeks ago and headed toward his bedroom. On the way, he glanced at his phone and its built-in answering machine. No blinking light. Thank God for that. And then it hit him. *The redial button.*

He pictured in his mind the phone in Senator Bristow's hideaway. It did not have a redial button like the one on his phone here. It was like the one in his office. New phones . . . to redial, you hit the number sign twice.

He reached for the phone and hit the button that rang in the operations room. The watch captain answered.

"Phil," Fitzgerald said, his voice tense and tired, "I need the key to the lock on Bristow's hideaway. Right. Get someone to deliver it to me and drop me at the Capitol. No. It's a shot in the dark. There's no need for anyone else. Just drop me off. Right. Thanks."

In a few minutes he was heading toward the Capitol. The driver left him at the deserted plaza, and Fitzgerald sent him back to headquarters. He had radioed ahead to the checkpoint. A new man let him into the entrance behind the stairs.

There was enough light for him to make his way quickly to the door directly across from the police command post that led to the hideaways nestled in the Capitol's basement. Ordinarily the post would have been a center of activity. Tonight, still boarded up from the recent electrical fire, it was as hushed as the corridor.

As he reached for a light switch near the short flight of stairs going down to the hideaways, Fitzgerald heard something, the sound of wood sliding. A desk drawer closing? But where? He paused on the stairs, holding his breath in the darkness. Then he saw it: a flash of light beneath the door to Julia Bristow's hideaway. Then darkness, then light again. Someone was in the room. But how? It was supposed to be sealed, with a new lock that replaced the temporary padlock and hasp.

Fitzgerald quietly slipped his .38-caliber pistol from its holster. While his officers were all outfitted with new .9mm sixteen-shot Smith & Wesson semiautomatic handguns, he held on to his six-shot revolver. The semiautomatics provided more firepower, but they had a tendency to jam.

Fitzgerald held his gun beside his right ear while he slowly turned the door handle and applied a slight pressure. The door was locked. He saw no more light coming from underneath. He heard nothing inside. Whoever it was knew that he was outside. He'd be a shot-through-the-door target if he stooped to use the key.

He stepped back. He knew the door was not solid. One strong kick and he could smash it open. His heart was pounding now. He inhaled and held his breath. Gently lifting his right leg, raising it almost chest high, he jammed his foot just above the doorknob with the full force of his 190 pounds behind it.

The panels splintered as the lock flew off the doorjamb. Fitzgerald hesitated momentarily, allowing the door to swing all the way to the side wall, which assured him that no one was hiding behind it. "All right, come out of there!" he shouted. No one answered. Nothing moved.

With his left hand he groped for the wall switch just inside the door, holding his gun steadily in his right hand. Moonlight filtered in through the two tall windows, casting Bristow's desk and high-backed chair into silhouette.

Just as he located the switch, Fitzgerald saw movement in the darkness. Then something hard cracked viciously across his shins, and he dropped in agony to his knees. He heard the sound of something swooshing in the air. The blow followed immediately, and pain shot through Fitzgerald's forearm, forcing him to drop his gun. "Son of a bi—" A hammerlike kick aimed at the base of his head sent him sprawling forward on his face into the thick carpet. Nausea gushed up the back of his throat as he fought not to lose consciousness.

In spite of his ringing ears, Fitzgerald heard heavy footsteps on the stairs, then the sound of someone running on the concrete floor of the basement. A big man running, the sound growing fainter.

He pulled himself to a sitting position. His brain felt as if it had exploded. Holding on to the wall for support, he managed to stand, found the switch, and flicked on the ceiling lights. He retrieved his gun. "Fuck!" he shouted. "Dumb son of a bitch." He rubbed his right forearm and checked the back of his head to see if he was bleeding. He wasn't.

He staggered up the stairs and looked to the right. He saw nothing. Not sure of what he was doing or why, he started to trot down the long corridor to the left. He listed to the side, like a bird with a broken wing. His footfalls echoed like rifle shots in the empty basement. But it was more than an echo. He heard it again, picking up speed. Someone else was running!

Then he saw him. In the dimly lit corridor, another man was running, his heavy boots clumping loudly. The pain in Fitzgerald's legs had eased. He picked up speed. Now only steps behind the heavy-shouldered man, Fitzgerald leaped, tackling him at the waist.

The man screamed as he went tumbling face down onto the cement floor, Fitzgerald riding him all the way. Moving swiftly, Fitzgerald grabbed him by his thick hair, then shoved the .38 to the base of his neck. "Don't move, you son of a bitch," Fitzgerald yelled, "or I'll spread your brains all over the walls!"

He could feel the man's body go limp, then start to tremble. He jerked his head sharply to the left so he could see his face.

"What are you doing to me, you goddamned fool!" the man shouted. "What are you doing?"

Fitzgerald felt shock spread throughout his body as if he had been hit by another blow. There on the floor, with a pistol shoved under his ear, lay James Barclay, the senior senator from Wyoming.

Nearly an hour later, after he had called the car and got Barclay to his home, after he had seen to it that the senator was not injured and at least somewhat mollified, he went back to the hideaway. He ordered a guard at the shattered door until it could be patched up and relocked in the morning. Then he went back in, stared for a moment at the phone on the desk, and, holding a handkerchief over his finger, hit the number sign twice.

"You have reached the office of Representative Michael Royal," said a mechanical voice. "The office is closed right now. The office hours are . . ."

Fitzgerald hung up the phone, just as Julia Bristow had when she made the last telephone call of her life.

Thursday, April 9

23

AT 7 A.M. Fitzgerald walked quietly down the hall, opened the front door and then the front gate as silently as possible, and turned left onto the sidewalk to avoid passing in front of the bay window. He wanted no encounter with Mrs. Darwin this morning. His head throbbed and his arm ached. He had done the best he could when he got home: a couple of vodkas, a plastic bag of ice cubes on the bump on the back of the head, liniment on the arm, cold compress on the black-and-blue shins. He would live.

He strode through the rapidly warming morning at a pace that looked more confident than he felt. His father had instilled in him the Irish Catholic inclination to be irreligious about religiously sponsored mysticism, scoffing at pious accounts of statues of the Blessed Virgin with tears running down their plaster cheeks, of polio victims throwing away their crutches at Lourdes. But his people were religious about avoiding the occult. He learned at an early age that Ouija boards and fortune-tellers and palm readers and Tarot cards were dangerously sinful, the works of Satan.

Fitzgerald was passing the court-of-Neptune fountain, which bulged from a wall on the broad sidewalk in front of the Library of Congress and which he usually passed without noticing. In the center was a giant Neptune holding court over green sea nymphs, horses, snakes, turtles, and frogs. The huge crouching turtles, shadowy green like the other figures, spouted water at Neptune, a

vibrant god with wild, flying hair. *Like something on a Tarot card,*
Fitzgerald thought.

He continued down Second Street to D Street and turned left to
headquarters. The sergeant at the door duly logged him in, and he
climbed the stairs to the top floor, where he walked past empty
chairs and silent cubicles to his outer office. The only sound came
from overhead, where the transformers of the fluorescent lights
faintly hummed. He went to his desk, for a moment savored the
stillness, then called Kyle Tolland.

"I'm calling for some personal information," he explained. "It's
about Mrs. Darwin. Ellen Darwin, my landlady."

"I know who Ellen Darwin is," Tolland said, impatience edging
his voice. He did not mind a telephone call at any hour of the day.
But he did mind people not getting to the point.

"How do you know her?"

"What do you mean?" Tolland asked irritably. "We met years
ago."

"Have you ever . . . worked with her?"

Fitzgerald heard a deep sigh, a sure sign that Tolland was decid-
ing on the exact wording of an indirect answer.

"She has done a lot of work for some interesting people," he
finally said.

"What kind of work?"

Another sigh, then, "Work that's not well known. On-the-fringe
stuff. But really reliable. Does that answer your very vague question?"

"Only vaguely," Fitzgerald replied. "I really called to see what
you turned up on the tape."

" 'Really' usually means 'not really.' But I'll let that go," Tolland said. "I've got a draft, which is the technical boys' way of
saying we may not have spelled everything right. You'll get a copy
one of these days. The gist of it is that it is a high-priced but
everyday tape. It was never used before, so there's no chance of
tracking it down. The voice is that of, and I quote, a stressed
Caucasian male of probable northeastern origins. Unquote. The
stress comes not from that cheerful little message but from at-
tempting to disguise his voice."

"If there is another one," Fitzgerald asked, hesitating between
words, "will they be able to verify the voice?"

140

"Probably. Why do you ask? Expecting another one?"

"No. Just curious."

Fitzgerald hung up and swiveled his chair around. The window framed blue sky and glistening marble and more windows. Somewhere out there was the man with the knife. Was he going to use it again?

Fitzgerald's mind summoned up a feeling he had had many times before. It was not quite an image; it was in his mind's eye—that was his mother's phrase. But it had become, like numbers, something he could put words and ideas to and almost see: a set of nesting boxes, or boxes that were supposed to nest. And the feeling was that he was trying to fit them together. The trick was to figure out how they fit, even though they did not seem to have dimension. There was one box that no other box could fit into because it contained things. And that was the hardest one to deal with, for it was the last, and unlike the others it was not empty.

Now, thinking about that box, he tried, as he had tried many times before, to look into it and see what it contained. *Politics.* Boston politics he understood: the Irish against everybody else. For anything more complicated than that he would have to depend on experts, on the practitioners—Lawson, Royal, Mareno. But talking to one of them was like talking to a doctor or a lawyer. Well, they were all lawyers, anyway. He looked into the box again. *Sex.* Julia Bristow and Royal; they got along in bed but not in politics. That happens. Still, Royal was married, had a wife and kids back in the bayous somewhere. Maybe he was trying to get out of it. That facelift Alix mentioned—Bristow could have been getting desperate, called him to the hideaway for a showdown: me or your wife.

He called Phelan's extension. "I saw your name on the roster when I came in," he said. "And I thought *I* was early." He told her about the redialed phone number and his encounter in the hideaway.

"And you're okay?" she asked. He was surprised that the concern in her voice cheered him.

"Fine. No problem. I want to get back to the hideaway, but I'm pretty well booked up to the rally. What's on your agenda?"

"Haverlin. I'm going to the hideaway, too. I thought I'd question him there."

"Okay. But have the evidence boys go over it first, on the outside chance that my visitor left prints. See you at the rally. I'll be wandering around."

When he heard Margaret enter the outer office, he called her on the intercom and asked her what he had on today besides Mason and the statehood rally.

"You'd better head over to the architect's office right now," she said. "You've got the rally at noon, the swearing-in of"—a disapproving pause—"Senator Royal at two. You said you wanted extra security in the gallery, and I assume that means you. And I've set up a meeting with the new senator at four o'clock."

"I'll want Mathewson with me for that," Fitzgerald said. "Be sure to alert him. And what else?"

"I'm putting everything else on hold."

"Thank you, Margaret. And what is on hold?" As he spoke, he stood and put on his uniform coat and hat.

"Adam Morrison, about getting his sergeants-at-arms on our police roster."

"But they're already deputized. Sworn law officers. Gun permits. The whole bit."

"It's something about pensions, Chief."

"Can you buck it to Koch? Say I want a legal opinion first?"

"I'll try. But Koch's on the calendar, too."

"What's he want?"

"Human rights. The Committee for Creative Nonviolence is complaining about our handling of Mr. Bones, and—"

"They can go to hell."

"Maybe so, Chief. But Koch says he needs to talk to you to try to stave off a suit."

"Jesus! We've already got a policy that you can't touch a homeless person unless he's up a tree or peeing—sorry, Margaret. Okay, get Koch in here sometime after the rally. Maybe I can duck in. What else?"

"Cathy Owens and Steve Williams. From the unions. An urgent request on a health matter. According to the contracts—"

"Yeah, yeah, I know. So we get the black union and the white union at the same time? How come?"

"It's about the lead in the water, Chief. You got a report the day before yesterday and—"

"And I didn't read it."

"Well, it says there are unhealthy concentrations of lead in the water, because of old lead pipes. It's like the asbestos scare in the old building, I guess."

"Well, what the hell can I do about the goddamn pipes?"

"*I* am not the one to yell at, Chief." Margaret waited for his apology, got it, and then went on. "I believe that they want bottled-water coolers installed where there are drinking fountains in headquarters and the police rooms in the House and Senate. It seems that Capitol staffers are making similar requests."

"Okay. I guess I've got to read about the water and I guess I've got to meet with them. Set something up. What else?"

Margaret's list went on. A preliminary disciplinary hearing for two officers who had staged a mock arrest to liven up a bachelor party for an assistant Senate sergeant-at-arms; one officer and the victim had been slightly injured. A need to answer a memo from Mason, who was surprised and indignant to see beards sprouting on officers.

"Okay, Margaret. I get the picture—it's going to be a long day. You make me look forward to Mason and the goddamn rally. I'm off."

He cut across the parking lot behind headquarters to the Hart Building, boarded the subway, got off at the Capitol, and walked rapidly across the polished stones of the crypt, where rows of pillars upheld massive groined arches supporting the Rotunda. An inconspicuous stairway led to the empty tomb, where George Washington was to have been enshrined. Just beyond was Mason's office.

Fitzgerald managed to slip into the room just before Mason plucked a paper from the leather folder in front of him and announced that the meeting would begin. Running a meeting was one of Mason's favorite tasks. Once a month, in this office, which he called the wardroom, he assembled around a long table the managers of the varied enterprises in his domain. The men sitting around the table supervised the construction, maintenance, and remodeling of all federal structures on Capitol Hill, including the Supreme Court and the Library of Congress; tended the acres of lawn and gardens that graced the Hill; ran the Capitol power plant, which heated and cooled all the buildings on the Hill; provided paper, pencils, computer terminals, and telephones to the 535 members and the 24,000 people who served them; operated the Senate restaurant, the House members' dining room, the House beauty shop, the House and Senate gyms, and the Capitol subway system; furnished every nook and cranny in the Capitol and its buildings; supervised the guides and pages of the Capitol; and watched over the 10,000 species of plants in the U.S. Botanic Garden, at the west end of the Capitol grounds.

To Mason's left was Adam Morrison, the Senate sergeant-at-arms; at his right was Paul Constantino, the House sergeant-at-arms. Mason usually went around the table clockwise, asking each person one or two questions. The sergeants-at-arms and the managers—nine men, two women—had little to say, but most of them handed Mason a report in a gray folder bearing the stamp of the architect of the Capitol.

Today Mason turned to Fitzgerald and said, "You have a lot on your plate already. I'm going to try to make this a fast meeting." He looked around. "Anything more than mere routine?"

Jerry Sumter, the chief engineer, a stocky, round-faced man wearing gold-rimmed glasses, raised his hand. "It's all these electrical problems, Captain. There are gremlins in the system. I try to fix one thing—the blown-out circuits into the Cannon Building, say—and the next thing I know the air conditioning is out in Russell. Even though I must say that, well, with the weather being so unusually hot and all, that—"

"Surely you can come up with something more specific than gremlins," Mason interrupted. "Antiquated equipment? Inexperienced workers?"

"There are some things, Captain Mason, that even money and hard work won't fix. And as for—"

"Well," Mason interrupted again, "if money and work won't fix our system, I wonder what will."

"As you know," the engineer went on, "we've got two coal burning boilers and a couple of oil and gas boilers for backup. We produce enough steam to take care of the heating needs of most of the buildings on the Hill, along with heating and cooling their water supplies. But we stopped generating electrical energy back in 1951. We're still buying that from Pepco. At one time we thought that maybe the answer was to go back to what we used to do."

"And what was that?" Mason asked.

"Generate our own electricity. We even looked into getting another power station hooked in, one for electricity. We talked to the electric company and—"

"Very interesting, Jerry," Mason broke in. "But perhaps it would be best to put this in a report and send it to me by e-mail."

No one else had anything to say. When all the reports had been turned in, Mason adjourned the meeting as abruptly as he had begun it and nodded for Fitzgerald to stay as the others filed out. Fitzgerald thought he knew what was coming. Preacherman . . . a senator murdered . . . and now a senator mugged.

He could not believe it, even now. Senator Barclay had been working late in his hideaway. As he was leaving, he heard someone running in the basement. It was dark and he was alone. When he heard the footsteps, he thought it might be a mugger, and as he said, "given what happened to Julia Bristow," he panicked and started running, hoping he would find a police officer on duty somewhere. He looked back once and saw a burly figure behind him. Then the man disappeared. At least Barclay thought he disappeared. Moments later he heard footsteps again, so he just kept running—until he was hit from behind by Fitzgerald and found himself flat on the concrete floor.

It had taken all of Fitzgerald's limited persuasive powers to calm him down. Fitzgerald had apologized again and again, explaining how he had mistaken Barclay for the man who had assaulted him, the one who might have murdered Julia Bristow.

Barclay had at first been infuriated. "I'll get your goddamn badge and your goddamn head for this," he had said. Within minutes, however, Fitzgerald had learned why the senator was so revered by his colleagues. Dabbing his nose, which had been bloodied when he hit the floor, Barclay even apologized to Fitzgerald, for being so rash with his initial threats.

Now, awaiting Mason's first words, Fitzgerald was furious with himself. One word from Barclay about what had happened, he told himself, and Mason would send him out of town on the first Amtrak. Once again he had acted on instinct. Maybe it was time to get into a new line of work.

Mason leaned forward and said, "Jeff, we have a problem." Then he tilted his chair back, head against leather, eyes toward the plaster carvings on the ceiling—another of his calculated pauses. The impudence of command. Fitzgerald had heard that Mason kept an admiral's uniform in the office just in case the Navy called him back and gave him stars.

Fitzgerald was about to begin his defense—*I thought he was the intruder, I had to move fast*—when Mason resumed speaking. "The problem is this. The *Post* is sniffing around. About you. About one of your undercover policemen being found in the District Building trying to buy drugs."

A wave of relief washed across Fitzgerald's mind as a new wave of anxiety loomed.

"Did you authorize the operation?" Mason asked.

"Yes. Drug sales on the Hill have been increasing. You've seen the drug arrests in my monthly reports."

"Yes, yes," Mason said impatiently. "But an attempted drug purchase in the District Building?"

"We have reason to believe that there's a protected source of drugs, coming out of the District to the Hill."

"Protected?" Mason asked. "Meaning what?"

"We believe that an official in the District Building is involved in drug trafficking."

"Someone in the *District Building?*" Mason leaned forward, then snapped back in his chair and began staring at the ceiling again.

"I am sure," Fitzgerald said, "that you are aware of the rumors about a Justice Department investigation of Mayor Mitchell's personal involvement in drugs. On the basis of that—"

"What I am aware of, Jeff, is that there's enough going on around here without straying off the Hill. I've talked to the mayor. He's holding off the *Post* as best he can. He's on our side, Jeff. Believe me." He paused. "In fact, the mayor told me something that may be related to your investigation of the Bristow murder." He paused again. "Which, I assume, is going well?"

"We're doing well in tracing Senator Bristow's last hours," Fitzgerald said cautiously. "You've seen the report I e-mailed."

Mason pointed to the computer terminal next to his desk. "Yes, I've read it. No names yet? No suspects?"

146

"Nothing firm," Fitzgerald replied. "And what does the mayor have to offer?"

"As you may have heard," Mason said, "District citizens around Thomas Circle are trying to get rid of the prostitutes in their neighborhood." Thomas Circle, about five blocks north of the White House, had for many years been a pickup point for prostitutes, who got into customers' cars and drove off, usually to seedy nearby hotels where pimps leased rooms. "It seems that these people have been taking down license plate numbers and even videotaping prospective customers to embarrass them and drive them away. And one of the citizens turned a videotape over to the mayor. It clearly shows a prostitute—a *black* prostitute, I might add —getting into a car with Louisiana license plates. And the driver of the car was Michael Royal."

"But . . . but what does Royal have to do with—"

"Come now, Jeff. No need to be discreet. You're placing him in the hideaway on the night Julia Bristow was killed."

"I didn't put a name in my report to you."

Mason waved the remark away with a flick of his wrist. "Be that as it may. The tape is being sent over by the mayor. This is extremely confidential: no connections with the mayor. Understood?"

Fitzgerald nodded.

"Fine," Mason said. "And now—"

One of the phones on his desk rang. Fitzgerald recognized it as the kind that had a built-in scrambler. Mason picked up the handset and listened without giving his name. "I'm quite aware of the problem," he said. "I am working on it. Yes. Yes. I can't speak now. I'll call you back. Where are you?" He jotted a number on a pad. "Right. I'll call you back in"—he looked at Fitzgerald—"two minutes." He hung up.

Fitzgerald stood. "There's something you could help me with," he said.

Mason, who seemed to have mutely dismissed him already, had begun reading a report on his desk. In the instant before he looked up, Fitzgerald saw the phone number on the pad. He thought he had seen it before.

"And what is that?" Mason asked sharply.

147

"That computerized model of the Capitol and its grounds—I'd like to try to trace Senator Bristow's movements on it."

Smiling at a chance to show off his proud possession, Mason said, "Certainly. Good idea." He touched a button on the console on his desk and said, "Henry, I'm sending in the chief. He wants to see the 3-D Capitol image." Mason pointed to a side office. "Just go right in. Henry will do his stuff. Every time I see it, I see something new and marvelous. I'm sure you'll recognize the image this evolved from. The modified hologram in the headquarters conference room? That was, so to speak, the grandfather of this beauty."

Henry's fingers were already fluttering over the keyboard when Fitzgerald entered the small, windowless room. The computer operator motioned for Fitzgerald to sit next to him before a large-screen monitor. A series of images flashed by so fast that Fitzgerald felt as if his eyes were seeing things but his brain was not quite registering them.

"What we've done," Henry said, turning to look at Fitzgerald, "is digitized a lot of images, including blueprints, wiring diagrams, old architectural designs, landscaping sketches, that sort of thing. In other words, we converted a lot of images to the kind of data that a computer can handle. Things will calm down in a minute or two."

Fitzgerald leaned forward. The images did seem to be slowing down.

"We grab the old images and interface them with images taken by videocameras. That gives us some motion and some up-to-date imagery. Here's what we wind up with."

Shimmering on the screen was what first appeared to be a version of the image in headquarters. But unlike that sterile, sharp-edged picture, this one pulsed with life. Quarter-inch cars moved up and down Independence and Constitution avenues. Tiny pedestrians darted across streets at crosswalks. Four people walked diagonally up the broad stairs of the Supreme Court building.

Henry touched two keys. The image on the screen grew larger, blurred, and then seemed to veer. The viewpoint now was that of a pedestrian crossing First Street Northeast near Constitution Avenue and walking rapidly toward the west front of the Capitol. The viewpoint kept changing—a look to the right toward Union Station, a look to the left toward a low stone wall and a mass of magnolia trees in bloom, a glance up to the Capitol dome.

Then, just as suddenly, the pedestrian seemed to whirl around the Capitol and come to a stop at the east front. The Capitol, with its two symmetrical white wings for House and Senate, filled the screen. It flickered, and slowly the upper portion opened like the top of a treasure chest. For a moment all was still within the unroofed building.

Then the viewpoint shifted again, moving to a point directly over the House chamber, then dropping down to the public gallery. At that moment the chamber came to life. A member left his seat and strode to the microphone before the Speaker's dais. Other representatives ambled to and from their seats. A ghostly figure wearing a high collar and a black suit glided down an aisle and began ascending the steps to the dais. "Henry Clay," Henry said. "A little joke."

Now the hovering viewpoint moved with a quickening pace through Statuary Hall, skimming past the statues of Liberty and Clio in niches above the doors, then flying across the checkered floor amid the pedestals with their marble busts and bronze figures. Next came the Rotunda and a roller-coaster swirl through its band of paintings and, high above, the dome's fresco of gods and mortals—Minerva and Benjamin Franklin, Aphrodite and Robert Fulton. The sweeping view passed over the small Senate rotunda, the Senate cloakrooms, and finally the Senate chamber, which, like the House chamber, came to life as senators rose and spoke and pages scurried down the aisles.

"That's the exciting part," Henry said dryly. "Now comes the meat and potatoes."

The image of the complete unroofed Capitol returned, and with representatives and senators still talking and moving in their chambers, the first floor of the Capitol folded back on an invisible hinge. Now the subterranean House and Senate appeared as a labyrinth of corridors, cubbyholes, vaults, arches, and columns.

"I assume this is about the murder of Senator Bristow," Henry said.

Fitzgerald nodded.

"She was in her hideaway, right? Well then, let's start there." The image of a corridor filled the screen. Fitzgerald recognized the

Capitol Police station near Senator Bristow's hideaway. The viewpoint shifted to the hallway just outside the hideaway. Henry hit a few keys and the screen divided into four sections, each containing a three-dimensional image.

"We've developed software that lets us take blueprints and photos and sketches and meld them into 3-D images," he said. "This one is the corridor outside the hideaway, not as a video image but as a holographic image. That means you can sort of spin it around and see it from various angles." Other images appeared on the screen.

"Each of the screen's viewports, or windows, as some people call them, shows a specific image from a different angle," he went on. "You can get a kind of X-ray view, looking down on it from the floor above. Or a view as if you were standing in it. Or a look at fine details, like this closeup of the nonskid material on that stair. And finally, a view as if it were suspended in space. Just touch the window and you get a bigger, more detailed look at what's there."

Fitzgerald touched the suspended-in-space window. The other windows disappeared and the corridor filled the screen. "Now," he said, "give me the view down this hallway, toward the Senate subway entrance."

The translucent outline of a corridor swung around in the fathomless black space of the screen, and a blank yellow wall appeared at the end.

"No subway at the end of this one," Henry said. "Let me open it up a bit. There. See? There's a crossway near the end. That takes you to a parallel corridor." He touched two keys. "Now, here are the two corridors, looking down on them." He touched two other keys and a rectangle appeared at one end of the left-hand corridor.

"Or she can walk down this corridor and cross over here," he said as the rectangle moved. "That takes her to the right-hand corridor leading to the subway." A closeup of the wall showed a sign: TO SUBWAY. He touched the keys again. "Or she can walk all the way down this corridor, past the Senate Recording Studio"—that sign appeared—"and cross over here to get to the subway."

"I wish I could see that again," Fitzgerald said.

"No problem. I'll save everything we've done onto the hard disk, then copy it to a floppy disk and send it over to you. There'll be a READ ME file. Bring that up, maybe print it out, and you'll get the commands for handling this. It's like a computer game, really. You just slip the disk into your computer and—"

Henry picked up the phone next to the computer on the first ring. "Schultz here. Right. You've got him." He handed the phone to Fitzgerald.

"Good tracking, Margaret," Fitzgerald said to the voice on the phone. "Okay. Okay. I'm on my way."

"End of session?" Henry asked.

"I'm afraid so. It's back to the real world, such as it is."

24

PHELAN WALKED ACROSS the plaza to a tunnel under the massive steps. An officer threw her a casual salutation that was more wave than salute and opened the same door that Fitzgerald had entered the night before. Phelan entered a low-ceilinged corridor that looked as if it had been burrowed through the Capitol's stone foundation. She turned right and walked down a second corridor, badly lit and cluttered with abandoned desks and stacks of cartons. She passed supply rooms, a janitorial office, a cubbyhole for Capitol guides, and an open door bearing a charred wooden sign saying CAPITOL POLICE. The door behind the sign was patched with a sheet of plywood, but she could see workers inside replastering a wall.

She turned left to an unmarked set of doors. As she turned the doorknob, a police officer rushed out of the patched door and shouted, "You can't go—oh, excuse me, Lieutenant." He took up his post as she opened the door and went down the six carpeted stairs to the short passageway. Along it were three plain white doors marked with numbers and a fourth door leading to a bathroom.

Haverlin was standing at a water cooler filling a paper cup. Next to the cooler was a shattered door. The crime scene team apparently had left it ajar. There were traces of fine white powder on

151

the brass knob. She had told Haverlin to meet her *at* the hideaway, and he had taken her at her word. Or maybe he just did not want to enter the room alone. She ushered him in.

"I still hardly see why we—" he began.

"We went over that on the phone, Mr. Haverlin. Let's not waste time."

Haverlin took a step toward the sofa facing the windows. But Phelan pointed to a straight-backed chair at the mahogany desk and turned it around so that its back was to the view. The window on the right framed the distant Washington Monument at the end of the Mall. Rising in the foreground and dampening the terrace were the mists of an unseen fountain. Phelan placed another straight-backed chair in front of Haverlin but just to the edge of his vision. To talk to her, he would have to turn slightly to the left and face her.

"In your statement," she began, "you say you brought correspondence over here for Senator Bristow to sign. I asked you to bring along copies of that correspondence."

Haverlin pulled from an inside pocket a single, triple-folded sheet of paper and handed it to Phelan. She unfolded it, glanced at a list of a dozen or so names, and looked across at Haverlin, who was contemplating a large, signed political cartoon on the opposite wall. It portrayed Senator Charles Bristow as a bull in Ye Olde Liberal China Shoppe. The bull was smashing pieces of crockery labeled *Quotas*, *Pro-Choice*, *Gun Control*, and *Ecology*. Under the cartoon was the caption " 'Liberal? Hell, I'm the biggest damn liberal in Louisiana.' —Senator Charles Bristow, responding to a question at Thursday's press conference."

"I asked you to bring the correspondence," Phelan said.

"I am not at liberty to disclose confidential matters between the senator and her constituents." Haverlin began the statement while looking straight ahead and ended it with his head turned slightly toward Phelan.

"Who told you not to turn over the letters?"

"Told me? No one told me. This was my decision." He turned back to look at the wall.

"You're in charge now? Is that it? After years as a cog, you're now a wheel?"

"I naturally assumed responsibility." He had a way of raising his voice at the end of a sentence, giving it the effect of a question.

"And you naturally assumed that Michael Royal will hire you on?"

Haverlin swung his head and looked toward her, but directed his gaze over her right shoulder. "I have no crystal ball, Lieutenant. It may happen. It may not." He again looked away. "And I fail to see what this has to do with the investigation into the senator's death."

"It wasn't just a death, Mr. Haverlin. It was a murder, an assassination perhaps."

He spun around and leaned toward her, his well-manicured hands grasping his knees. "Assassination? She was murdered, like all the other folks who get murdered in this city. Sounds to me like you're wasting your time looking for a Lee Harvey Oswald when you should be rounding up all the Willie Hortons and asking them where they were when she was killed."

"So then, Mr. Haverlin, your theory is that Senator Bristow, after her tête-à-tête with you, went—"

"Tête-à-tête?" He started to rise, then sat down. "What are you trying to imply?"

"I'm not trying to imply anything. But as a matter of fact, I would like to know a few more details about your last meeting with the senator."

"What details? What are you trying to get at?"

"Well, one detail is this: did either you or Senator Bristow consume any liquids? Coffee, perhaps?"

He reached up a hand and swept it through the air. "Look for yourself. There's no fridge, no bar, like in some of these hideaways. No sink. I did not have any so-called liquid and neither did Senator Bristow. I told you, we talked. I sat on this chair—on this very chair—and she sat in that little easy chair there." He pointed to a chair covered in the yellow floral fabric that also covered the sofa. "We talked just a bit. I handed her the sheaf of correspondence." He moved his hand in pantomime. "And she signed the letters and talked, small talk mostly, as she signed them. And then she sat back for a few minutes and she talked a little about whether she was going to run on her own or not. Sort of musing to herself. I offered to wait for her and walk her to her car, but she said she was going to stay here a while—those were her actual words, I believe, 'stay a while.' And I got up and I left."

"You have no idea, then, how a stain got on that . . . love seat?" Phelan pointed to the sofa.

"I believe that you are referring to the sofa, or maybe you call it a couch?"

"Call it what you will, Mr. Haverlin." Phelan rose, walked over to the sofa, picked up the middle cushion, and turned it over. "This side was up when our evidence technicians examined the room the morning Senator Bristow's body was found," she said. She carried the cushion over to Haverlin and pointed to where a piece of silver gaffer's tape covered a hole about one inch square. "We removed the stain for analysis by the FBI laboratory. Our preliminary belief was that it was a bodily secretion, possibly semen. Senator Bristow wasn't just talking, was she?"

Haverlin jumped up, almost knocking over the chair. "You goddamn dirty-mouthed bitch. I never . . . never!"

"Sit down, Mr. Haverlin." Phelan carefully replaced the cushion. "As I am sure you know, there is another explanation: you were not the last person to see Senator Bristow in this room."

Haverlin sat down sideways, putting his left elbow on the desk and heavily leaning his head on his hand, riffling his blond hair.

"Did Senator Bristow act as if she was expecting someone after you left?"

"No. But, well, now that you mention it, she was fussing with her hat. She had it off when I came in, I think. And when she handed me back the letters, she picked it up and was holding it. And I expected her to put it on. She nearly always wore a hat, you know. But I think that when I said goodbye and left, well, she didn't have it on."

"So you're saying that if she was about to leave, she would have put on the hat?"

He nodded. Phelan stood and looked out the window. Three women and a man, all wearing identical red peaked hats, walked along the portico, oblivious to the curtained windows of the hideaway. "Hats," Phelan said, half to herself. Her back was to Haverlin.

"What kind of jewelry do I have on, Mr. Haverlin?"

"Nothing around the neck. No gold chain or anything. A little pin, gold, diamond-shaped, on your left lapel. I think it has your initial in it. *A*. Right?"

"Right." She turned and smiled. "So you do notice little things, don't you?"

"Well, I guess I do. At least on ladies." He sat back and smiled up at her.

"Mr. Haverlin," she said, taking her notebook and pen from her pocket, "I want to believe you." She flipped the notebook open. "Who told you to stop the autopsy and destroy any evidence of Senator Bristow's sexual activity on the night of her murder? Who told you to call Gardiner and get that court order?"

"You've got that wrong, Lieutenant. It was my . . . I was carrying out the wishes of the family."

"So stopping the autopsy was your idea?"

"Yes."

"Mr. Haverlin, I find that highly unlikely. It was not your idea. It was somebody else's. That person may have gotten you into a great deal more trouble than you can imagine." She snapped the notebook shut. "For starters, we'll want a blood sample from you. And hair, both head hair and pubic hair. I will make the necessary arrangements with the infirmary. You'll—"

"Now just hold on there, Lieutenant. That's self-incriminating, and—"

"We've got the courts on our side on that one. Look it up when you get back to the office. Or call Gardiner, if you like." She walked to the door. "I think that's all for now."

Haverlin stood and looked out the window. "Beautiful day on the Mall," he said. He looked at Phelan, who was standing by the door. "It was Congressman Royal. Congressman Michael Royal. I was just doing what he told me to do." He looked at her, a pleading look twisting his face. "Do you still need the samples?"

"Appointment postponed, Mr. Haverlin."

25

MARGARET'S CALL to Fitzgerald was an order for him to start for the statehood rally. He left the architect's office and headed out of the circle at the base of the Rotunda, then abruptly turned down a low-ceilinged corridor and rapidly walked the short distance to the charred sign saying CAPITOL POLICE. Battered old desks had been moved in, and behind one sat an officer who looked up, started to salute, then gestured toward the stubble on his chin and smiled. "Morning, Chief," he said.

Fitzgerald nodded and pointed to the phone. The officer stood and walked away. Fitzgerald sat, pressed the numbers of Barclay's office, and identified himself to a secretary. "He's right here," she said. "I'll put him on."

A new pain shot through the back of Fitzgerald's head as Barclay boomed, "Well now, Chief, and how are you feeling this bright spring day?"

"Not so good, Senator. And you?"

"A little stiff, but nothing shows. To tell you the truth, it takes me back to my younger days. Started out in this game as a sheriff, you know."

"No, I didn't know that, Senator," Fitzgerald said. He realized he was speaking slowly, as if to pace the words to the throbs in his head. "Senator, I called to make an appointment so I could apologize in person for what happened."

"No need to do that, Chief. It's between me and you, and it's over. Give it no more thought. And good hunting."

Fitzgerald hung up and returned to the corridor, his headache gone. He suddenly remembered reading that the same thing, an instantly cured headache, had happened to U. S. Grant when he got the surrender note from Lee.

At the door leading to the hideaways was the officer who had been at the desk. Fitzgerald opened the door and, stabbing his finger toward the hideaway below, said, "That is where you're supposed to be." He would have said more, but he was in a hurry. The officer stepped aside, then followed him down the stairs.

He stepped into the hideaway and checked the broken door. The hasp and lock were still intact on one of the door's shattered panels. It had been locked from the outside. The only other way into the room was through one of the two windows that looked out on the stone-railed terrace. He scanned the room. There was no sign of a ransacking. The books in the case along the wall looked undisturbed.

He walked to the windows, which were about waist-high, with broad interior sills. Three tourists stood on the terrace looking out toward the Mall and the Washington Monument. The woman and one of the two men turned and leaned against the rail; the other man stepped back and aimed a videocamera at them. He was so close to the window that if it had been open, Fitzgerald could have touched the blue letters, BALLSTON SPA CHAMBER OF COMMERCE, on his orange T-shirt. The broad back nearly blocked the lower half of the window.

Fitzgerald leaned closer to the window. Layers of cream-colored paint covered the closed latch and the seams between the window sashes and their frames. Decades of painting had effectively sealed the window shut. He went to the other one. Along the bottom and sides of the lower sash, the paint had been carefully sliced away by a razor. No, Fitzgerald suddenly thought, it was too tough a job for a razor. A knife, a sharp, thin-bladed knife. Paint had also been peeled away from the latch, and it was open.

He waited for the Ballston Spa visitors to move on. Then, wrapping his handkerchief around his right hand, he braced the heel of his hand against the upper frame of the lower sash and pressed. The sash smoothly slid upward.

Fitzgerald stuck his head out of the window and, still clutching the handkerchief, reached up to pull down the upper sash. It too slid smoothly. He swung a leg across the sill, ducked, grabbed the outer stone edging for leverage, and pulled himself out of the hideaway to the terrace. It was empty in both directions. He slid the lower sash closed, and by tugging on the vertical frame inched it open enough to get his handkerchief-covered fingers under it so he could slide it back up. He did this three times, opened the

157

window, crawled back in, went to the phone on the desk, stared at it for a moment, then sprinted to the stairs and back to the corridor.

He asked for the radio of the officer in the hall and called communications. "This is the chief. Patch me through to Lieutenant Phelan." She answered on the first ring.

"I'm at the hideaway," he said. "Get out the evidence photos and see if you can tell from any of them whether either of the windows in here was unlocked at that time. Get enlargements made if you need them. And get Stan to make a careful fingerprint check on the inside and outside of the unlocked window. I doubt if he'll find anything, but it's worth a try."

"What do you think the guy you ran into was doing in the hideaway?" Phelan asked.

"I don't know. My hunch is that our lover boy got in and out that way." He looked at his watch. "I'll be here for a little while. See you at the rally."

Back in the hideaway, his back to the windows, Fitzgerald swept his eyes slowly across the room. He walked to the sofa and knelt in front of it. The right front leg was still centered in the dent it had made in the carpet.

Suddenly two sharp buzzes sounded from the clock above the sofa. He instinctively looked up. Throughout the Senate wing were clocks like this, clocks that both told time and told senators the status of events on the Senate floor. Irish had explained them to Fitzgerald. Halfway between the numerals 2 and 3 was a red light that glowed when the Senate was in session. Between the numerals 9 and 2 were six yellow lights. One light signaled that a vote was in progress; two, a quorum call on the floor; three, a demand for a live quorum, which called for the presence of all available senators; four signaled adjournment or recess; five, that a vote was half over; and six, that morning business was finished.

The buzzer transmitted the same signal: a long buzz for a vote; two buzzes for a quorum call; three for a live quorum. The lights stayed on after the buzzer gave the signals.

Fitzgerald looked at the clock again. Only one of the red lights was lit, but he had heard two buzzes. He climbed up on the sofa, put on his glasses, and looked carefully at the face of the clock.

The second yellow bulb, which should have been glowing like the one near the 9, looked slightly different from the others.

Fitzgerald jumped down from the sofa, went back outside and up the stairs to the officer, and again took his radio. "This is the chief," he said. "Get me somebody in ECS." The Electronic Countermeasures Section had been set up by Fitzgerald to investigate suspected electronic monitoring of members, congressional offices, and hearing rooms, along with taps on telephones and computers. The team regularly swept rooms at the request of members, sergeants-at-arms, or the architect.

"This is Chief Fitzgerald. Who is this?" Fitzgerald asked when a new voice came on the phone.

"Brooks, Chief."

"Brooks, I want you to come over to Senator Bristow's hideaway. You know where it is?"

"Sure. We've got them all mapped."

"Okay. Bring equipment for a sweep."

Fitzgerald handed the radio back to the officer. "What do you know about access to the terrace out there?" he asked, pointing in the direction of the hideaway.

"Access?"

"Yes, access," Fitzgerald said. "Getting to the terrace."

"Oh, the terrace," the officer said. He took off his cap, wiped his bald head with a handkerchief, and put the cap back on. "Well, the only way a tourist could get there that I know of is to go up the east front stairs on the House or Senate side and walk around to the west. That's if you're a tourist. Now, if I wanted to get out there, or if you did, or anyone, well, we would get out through the doors in offices that open onto the north, south, and west sides of the terrace. Now, if you want, I can go get you a map and—"

"Never mind the map," Fitzgerald said. "The point is that even when the offices fronting on the terrace are closed—at night, or on weekends, say—somebody could get there just by walking up the east front stairs and walking around to the terrace."

"Well, they'd have to get past us, past the guards."

Fitzgerald was going to make a comment but changed his mind. "And typically how many guards would there be on the terrace, say, early in the evening or late at night?"

"There's a shift that ends at six, usually, when the House or

Senate is in regular session. The officers on that shift, there would usually be two outside, and one of them would walk the perimeter, including the terrace, about every hour or so."

"No standing post? No call-in station?"

"No. It's a roving foot patrol."

Fitzgerald thanked him and returned to the hideaway. The lowest possible priority for these guards, he knew, was what was called roving foot patrol. Inside the Capitol buildings they had regular posts and orders to check in at stations so that patrols could be monitored and logged. Outside, unless security had been raised above normal, the watch was irregular. So just by staying in the shadows and watching for a few minutes, anyone could easily wait for the unguarded moment to go up the stairs, onto the terrace, and through the window.

Brooks arrived a few minutes later. He was in plain clothes, carrying a lawyer's attaché case. He easily blended in with the three-piece-suit brigades of the Hill.

"Give this place a sweep," Fitzgerald ordered. Brooks put his case in the middle of the room, opened it, and turned two dials on a built-in amplifier, then took a wandlike object out and attached it to a thin cable. Beginning at the wall containing the windows, he held the wand a few inches from the surface and began moving it up and down in the motion of a painter.

After hearing a faint buzz from the case, he approached the sofa, raised the wand, and moved it through the air. The volume of the buzz increased as the wand neared the clock. "Bingo!" he said. He climbed up on the sofa and looked carefully at the lights. "Beautiful," he said. "Absolutely beautiful. Shall I remove it?"

"Not yet," Fitzgerald replied. "It's potential evidence. So is that phone." He told Brooks about the number-sign redial system and asked whether he could establish what number was on the redial mechanism.

"Sure," Brooks said. "What else?"

"Get Lieutenant Phelan over here with a photographer and an evidence technician. I want her to see exactly where the device is, whatever it is, so she can testify about it if necessary. Tell her I want it shot *in situ* and checked for prints. Then you remove the clock and the phone and take them back to your shop. Take out the device, and take all the usual chain-of-evidence precautions.

When you're through, give the device and the clock to Lieutenant Phelan to log in to the evidence vault. I want a briefing on this before the end of play today."

He looked up at the clock. "I've got to go."

26

FITZGERALD CURSED under his breath. Tension. Heat. People yelling. People with murder in their eyes. But no matter how much he wanted to be away from Capitol Hill at that very moment, no amount of cursing was going to help.

It was only April, and the heat was almost as malevolent as in July. The thick soup enveloping the city tried to masquerade as early morning fog, but it was nearly noon. Besides, fog wasn't yellow. The macadam had turned in places into black putty. The soles of his feet felt blistered. He knew it was only his imagination. His feet weren't on fire. It was his mind that was burning up.

The demonstration taking place at the east front of the Capitol should have been canceled, or at least postponed. The west front was closed to the public because of repairs. It had been a long-standing policy not to allow more than thirty people to congregate as a group to protest or demonstrate on the east side of the grounds. Politicians liked to say they wanted to remain close to the people, but for Fitzgerald, proximity to the masses—especially those who hadn't been searched or passed through a metal detector—only ratcheted up the danger. *Like the goddamn heat*, he thought.

But Lawson had said danger be damned. And Fitzgerald had to listen to the Senate majority leader. Sure, as long as security wasn't Lawson's responsibility. And Lawson wouldn't care that he had violated an agreement among the law enforcement authorities limiting these mass demonstrations to weekends.

The march from the White House up Pennsylvania Avenue, then onto Constitution, had been planned for weeks. The proper petition had been filed and approved. The route had been carefully blocked off from vehicular traffic. But, Fitzgerald had argued, it had been arranged before Julia Bristow was killed, before statehood got entwined with murder. Lawson's sonorous words still echoed in his ears: "The murder of one senator, horrible as it is, does not pose enough of a safety threat to cancel the demonstration."

As Fitzgerald surveyed the crowd of more than ten thousand, he was still not sure that the Capitol Police could keep things under control. Many of the demonstrators were carrying canvas bags or wearing knapsacks containing food or diapers—or guns or bombs.

He had increased security to one notch below maximum. The Capitol was closed to the public. Not even congressional staff members' cars could be parked anywhere in the plaza. No commercial deliveries, ranging from food and bottled drinking water to toilet paper, could be made without being checked out like a Thanksgiving turkey at one of the off-site security stations. Sergeant Fred Mathewson had his three CERT teams on high alert. They were in civilian clothes, scattered through the crowd but in touch with each other. The National Park Service police had loaned a dozen steel-helmeted men on horseback. The elevation gave the riders a strategic advantage. Besides, powerful horses had a nice way of keeping crowds in check.

Fitzgerald looked out into the sea of mostly black faces. There was a smattering of whites. Liberals, no doubt, outraged by the injustice of being taxed but denied representation because of their Zip Code. At any other time, in any other place, Fitzgerald would have been sympathetic. He had seen racism up close—in college, in the Navy, in the FBI, in this city—and it sickened him. He was not a man given to philosophy or introspection. He devoted his life to separating out the good from the bad. Holding back the jungle. Doing justice. But right now his only concern was whether he and his force were going to be able to contain this mass of humanity in the sweltering heat.

His eyes settled on the center of the plaza, where a speaker's platform had been erected and an elaborate public address system had been installed. A large, stately black woman was speaking. Her short hair was cut so that from a distance it looked like a dark helmet. Her voice was deep, resonant, lyrical, almost British in accent. It seemed to vibrate with pure power.

> If I were an old man dying now,
> I would tell of . . . time sucking life
> from old men and breathing despair
> into infants . . .

"Gordon Parks," another voice said behind Fitzgerald, startling him. It was Phelan.

"She's Gordon who?" Fitzgerald said sarcastically, trying to mask his embarrassment at not having seen Phelan approaching him.

She poked him gently in the ribs. "No, that's Gwenda Harris-Topping, our delegate to Congress. She's reading Gordon Parks, poet, playwright, photographer, musician, Mr. Everything."

> And I would speak of summers lived
> through the lash and sickened mobs and . . .
> where I prayed beneath broken flesh
> swinging black from a south tree branch . . .

There was a stir in the audience. Men and women were shouting. "Yeah. Yeah. Sing it, sister." People started to sway to the cadence of the words.

The speaker stopped cold. She would brook no intrusions. She wanted them to listen, not to turn the rally into a revival meeting. The crowd fell silent.

> If I were an old man dying now,
> I would tell of black jungles
> where on asphalt meadows
> stood my prison home, crumbling
> in mortal chaos around me.

The words were enunciated with a razored clarity. They were clipped, powerful, full, not of hate but of rage.

163

Then climbed to fatherless rooms
My hopes compressed between mean streets
and rooftops where the death peddler waited.

Fitzgerald was astonished at the hushed silence, which he thought was impossible in a crowd of this size. He finally started to enjoy the moment, with Phelan standing next to him. His eyes drifted up to the top of the dome of the Capitol glistening in the sun. There stood a nineteen-and-a-half-foot, cast-iron statue of Freedom. Another woman, in another era, who stirred controversy. Fitzgerald had read that the sculptor, Thomas Crawford, originally had the statue crowned with a Phrygian cap like those worn by freed slaves in ancient Rome. But the Secretary of War at that time, Jefferson Davis, who was in charge of the Army Corps of Engineers constructing the Capitol, protested that the symbolism would inflame the debate over slavery. The sculptor yielded, giving Freedom a helmet that carried an eagle's head and feathers surrounded with stars. From a distance, most viewers thought the headdress was that of a Sioux warrior.

Something caused Fitzgerald involuntarily to look at the crowd —a slight movement off to the left. "Here comes trouble," he said.

Phelan followed his gaze. Moving slowly, surrounded by several beefy aides, was Congressman Michael Royal. A few feet behind him, inconspicuous but looking as alert as a panther, was Mathewson.

"Jesus!" Fitzgerald exclaimed. "If Royal says or tries to do anything in this crowd, we're going to have a goddamn riot on our hands!"

Phelan reached out and gently touched his arm. "Take it easy, Fitz. He'd like nothing better than to have all those TV cameras showing him under attack by a black mob. But it won't happen." She spoke with surprising conviction.

"What makes you so sure?" Fitzgerald asked, not taking his eyes off Royal.

"Royal can't be sure that he'd survive—not that he doesn't have total confidence in your force," Phelan said, smiling. "And everyone in this crowd knows what's at stake. If they let Royal bait them, they can kiss statehood goodbye."

Royal, only hours from becoming a senator, stayed on the fringes of the crowd, but close enough to be caught in the telephoto lenses of the network television cameras. He then moved off. He would have his ten seconds of exposure on the evening news. At no cost. And no harm. Phelan had it figured perfectly.

From the speaker's platform, Gwenda Harris-Topping continued her recitation:

> Knife and bullet formed my law
> and plunged me into darker darkness . . .

27

THE ORNATE CLOCK above the dais showed precisely two o'clock. To Fitzgerald's surprise, the Senate's galleries were barely filled. About a dozen members of the press looked down like carrion birds from their perch high over the dais. Only a handful of senators were in the chamber as the president pro tempore, after the chaplain's prayer, banged his gavel hard to establish order. Fitzgerald wished the gavel would bring some cool air, too. Heat enveloped the gallery. The air conditioning was down again.

On more than one occasion, Fitzgerald, while dressed in civilian clothes, had slipped into one of the Senate galleries to watch the people he was charged to protect grinding away at the legislative process. In college he had studied giants—Clay, Webster, Calhoun, La Follette, Taft. But he didn't see men of that stature in the chamber or walking the corridors of power today. Maybe, he thought, history just exaggerated the talents and accomplishments of those Olympians. Or maybe the people just expected more of their leaders then and saw less of them. Maybe television had reduced would-be myths to ordinary men. And women, he had to add, thinking of Julia Bristow.

To be sure, there were some talented people down there. Daniel Lawson, for one—butter-smooth, sharp as hell. And the minority leader, another of those men who could stride through the glass-paneled doors of the Senate with the self-assurance and the unstated assumption of superiority. Maybe a dozen others of varying degrees of competence. But more and more blow-dried mannequins were filling the chairs now, preening for the remote-control television cameras, reading speeches drafted by zealous college grads who didn't have a dime's worth of experience of how the world really worked. Maybe that's why the whole process of government seemed to be breaking down. There were no more giants, just a lot of pygmies tying up the country with trivial pursuits. But what did Fitzgerald know about it? They were down there and he was in the gallery.

He watched Congressman Michael Royal, accompanied by Governor James Nadeau and the senior senator from Louisiana, Carl Ropers, advance to the desk of the Vice President. The president pro tempore administered the oath of office, and Royal wrote his signature in the official oath book. The senators witnessing the ceremony broke out in polite applause. Then Senator Lawson, slipping a small microphone onto the breast pocket of his suit, asked to speak.

Standing behind the majority leader's desk in the front row, just to the left of the center aisle, Lawson was an imposing figure, even from a distance. Gripping the podium with both hands, he began to speak. "Mr. President, the Senate has suffered two great losses in less than a year. Tragically, we have lost both members of a wonderful family, our beloved Charles Bristow to a bizarre accident and now his lovely wife, Julia, murdered by some savage beast . . ." Lawson paused, clearing the catch in his voice.

"Each of us knows we stand on the edge of crumbling time, that no day is promised to any one of us. But we also know that the great blessing of democracy is that it is ever-replenishing. And so today, even as we continue to mourn the loss of Charles Bristow and Julia Bristow, we are fortunate to have been given Senator Michael Royal by the people of Louisiana."

The words kept coming. They were all there, Fitzgerald thought, but Lawson's voice was flat, mechanical, without even a hint of joy. Lawson welcomed Royal as his colleague with about as much enthusiasm as he would welcome a deadly disease. Royal meant not only the end of D.C. statehood; his brand of politics was going to speed up the Senate's decline. And it was clear that Lawson was deeply offended by the rapidity of Royal's appointment. It was an act of indecency—one directed not only at the Senate as an institution, but at him personally. He had no intention of moving forward with the statehood vote before Julia Bristow's successor was appointed. But it was clear that Governor Nadeau did not trust him to wait.

Fitzgerald glanced over at the gallery reserved for family members of senators or their special guests. In the first row he saw nine young men with short haircuts and dressed in dark blue suits. Probably members of Royal's staff. They could barely contain their sense of pride and a now invigorated mission. They reminded him of Nazi thugs all scrubbed up in their Sunday best.

He fought to push these thoughts out of his mind. They were poisoning his judgment, his investigation. It wasn't necessary for him to be here. He had seen enough of the Senate's ponderous formalities, the insincere flatteries that could spread like an Alaska oil spill. But he wanted to find out as much as he could about Michael Royal. He had studied Royal's face throughout the ceremony, listened to his voice as he repeated the oath of office, and watched his body language, looking for anything that might tell him something about the man.

Royal certainly had had a motive to kill Julia Bristow. Maybe others had, too. Or maybe there was no motive. Maybe it was just one of those goddamn wackos who wander all over the Hill—Mr. Bones, Crazy Eddie, Preacherman. But would Julia Bristow walk toward one of them, as she did on that surveillance-camera tape?

Several other senators welcomed their new colleague with brief remarks, then Royal made a short speech thanking them and promising to follow the distinguished service and standard of excellence set by Charles and Julia Bristow. Another polite smattering of applause came at the conclusion of his remarks. Then the president pro tempore once again banged his gavel, restoring order just before declaring that the Senate would stand in recess until three o'clock.

The ceremony was over. There were backslaps, handshakes, and good wishes. Michael Royal left the chamber and headed toward his new suite of offices. Fitzgerald looked at his watch and wondered how many times he had done that today. He had time to talk to Phelan, put together a carefully worded report for Mason, scratch off some of the items on Margaret's long list of appointments, put his uniform back on, and still make his date with Royal.

28

THE STATE MOTTO, "Union, Justice, & Confidence," unfurled across the state seal of Louisiana. Taped beneath it was a rectangle of white cardboard with SEN. MICHAEL ROYAL lettered on it in black Magic Marker. Under the cardboard, Fitzgerald knew, was the still shining name of Julia Bristow. Sergeant Mathewson opened the glass door to the reception room and stepped back to let Fitzgerald precede him. Fitzgerald wondered if Royal would recognize the man who had been guarding him at the rally. Maybe, he decided. Whether Mathewson was in his uniform, as he was now, or in civilian clothes made no difference. He was one of those cops, Fitzgerald thought, who looks like a cop no matter what he wears.

A young woman with extraordinarily long blond hair knelt at a large cardboard box. She looked up, flustered, and said, "How may I help you, sir . . . I mean, Officer?"

When Fitzgerald gave his name and told of his appointment, she sprang up and went to the cluttered desk in the center of the room. She searched around for a moment among the stacks of papers, looked up helplessly, and said, "You know, Chief Fitzgerald, what I am going to do is just simply send you right in there to the congressm— I mean, the senator." She pointed toward the inner office, silver bracelets gently tinkling as she moved her arm.

Fitzgerald told Mathewson to stand by and walked through the hustle of moving day toward the inner office. He passed through the outer office suite, which teemed with activity. Boxes stacked on dollies were moving in and out of the double glass doors with the speed and precision of a military operation. The queen was dead. Long live the king.

Two young men cautiously navigated a huge framed photograph

of their hero through a knot of staffers. It showed Royal standing on a platform, grinning broadly, his right fist raised in some kind of victory gesture. The photograph itself was benign enough, not very different from those that adorned hundreds of other congressional offices. But Fitzgerald imagined it to be far more sinister. A salute to Royal's past—or to the Grand Wizard, or maybe to the Führer. Or maybe a rallying call to the future.

His thoughts were interrupted by a tall, lithe blonde poured into a navy blue skirt whose hemline reached just above her knees. Her expensive silk blouse was thin enough to reveal a touch of lace beneath. Royal's staff members and supporters were said to be evangelicals, but this lady could stir lust in the coldest Christian's heart. "Come right this way," she said lyrically, ushering him around modular partitions being erected along a narrow path to the rear of the suite.

One of the eight-foot-high mahogany doors was open, allowing Fitzgerald to make eye contact with Michael Royal, who was leaning back in a large leather chair, talking on the telephone. He beckoned Fitzgerald in, rapidly concluded his phone conversation, and rose in greeting, leaving his suit jacket draped over the chair; he seemed to relish projecting an image of casual, down-home informality. The monogram MR on the breast pocket of his tailored dress shirt struck Fitzgerald as a little more upscale than Basin Street.

"Welcome, Chief," Royal said, smiling broadly as he extended his hand. "I hope you'll forgive the mess out there. There's going to be a few days of pure hell before we get settled in. And then, I'm told, they'll move me right out again." He chuckled with professed amusement at the injustice of it all.

After a few more acts from the good-ol'-boy routine, he turned serious. "Now, how can I help you?"

Fitzgerald began tentatively. "I understand you were quite close to Senator Bristow."

Royal smiled again, his gray eyes suddenly alive with the desire to challenge the innuendo in Fitzgerald's words. "Why, Chief, you're right. The senator and I were real good friends. We used to confer quite a bit. After her husband died, she sought some counsel and some comfort, and I hope I was able to provide both. Anything wrong in helping a widow, Chief?"

It was Fitzgerald's move. If he even hinted that Royal was a suspect, he would have to give him a *Miranda* warning. *Bring a lawyer in now*, he thought, *and I can kiss this investigation goodbye.*

"Nothing wrong at all, Senator," he replied, forcing hostility out of his voice. "I was hoping that you might be able to establish a motive. Any enemies she may have had? Threats, that sort of thing?"

"Chief, there wasn't a soul who didn't love Senator Bristow. She was a grand lady. A true southerner. Woman of great character and principle . . ." Royal was off on a preaching routine, the honeyed words of praise so effortless they seemed prerecorded. "Now, we all get threats from time to time. Had more than a few myself. There are lots of fruitcakes out there, you know. She never spoke of any, but . . ."

"But what?"

"But there are a lot of folks who want to see this District of Murder become a state."

"You're right, Senator," Fitzgerald said. "As a matter of fact, we think it would be wise to set up some special protection for you. I would like to have officers from our Threat Assessment Section sit down with your staff and work out arrangements. I've brought along one of our protection specialists, Sergeant Fred Mathewson, who is out in your reception room. I'd like—"

Royal waved a dismissive hand. "Thanks, but no thanks. You have enough on your hands without babysitting U.S. senators." He pointed through the door to a man Fitzgerald recognized as the bodyguard who had been puffing behind him on his morning run. "We do our own protection around here. Good boys, well trained, well aware of who I *really* have to worry about. And I'll tell you this, Chief: if that creature who killed Julia tries it on me, Bobby there, or one of the other boys, will take care of him, and you won't have to worry about getting evidence and having a trial."

As Fitzgerald turned to go, Royal said, "Hold on, please." He walked to the door, closed it, and stood with his back against it. "I know your people have been talking to Craig Haverlin. I intend to hire him as my administrative assistant. I made a pledge to keep on all the people on Julia's staff."

"I was the first to talk to Haverlin," Fitzgerald said. "We have a statement from him. He appeared to be the last one to see Julia

170

Bristow alive. We will keep talking to him and to anyone else who can help us solve this crime, Senator."

"Just make sure you do, Chief."

"And what do you mean by that, Senator?"

"What I mean is that I hope this is an equal opportunity crime and you talk to black boys as well as to white ones." Royal laughed and clapped Fitzgerald on the shoulder. "That's all I mean, Chief."

29

WHEN THE DAY was finally over, Fitzgerald made himself a pot of coffee, sat down at the computer, and brought up on the monitor several reports on the Bristow case. One of these was his own running commentary; to it he added Tolland's findings about the tape. Then he reread Phelan's summary on Royal. He unlocked the lower left drawer of his desk and took out Dake's memo and package of photocopied newspaper clippings on Royal, which he went through again, then replaced in the drawer.

From the same drawer he took out a three-and-a-half-inch microdisk, which he put in a slot in the computer. After calling the READ ME file up to the screen, he read the list of commands, saved the file, and called up one called XRAY. He tapped a few commands, and the spectral outline of the Capitol and its grounds appeared on the monitor. Using the arrow keys on the keyboard, he manipulated the model, peeling and twisting it until he had on screen the corridors leading from the Bristow hideaway to the Senate subway.

He retraced Senator Bristow's probable routes several times, satisfying himself that there were only two. Then he stood and from a bookshelf took down the *Congressional Directory*. He looked up Royal's House office and returned to the computer, where he moved the image around until he found a subterranean route from the Cannon House Office Building to the House side of the Capitol. Evading the surveillance cameras shown on the image, he continued following the route, which twisted under the House chamber, under Statuary Hall, under the Rotunda, under Senate conference rooms, into a corridor leading to the hideaway area, and finally to the Senate subway platform.

He replaced the disk in the drawer and locked it. Then he went back to reading the piles of printouts strewn across his desk. The phone rang.

"Go home, Margaret. That's an order," he said when he picked it up. She agreed, after announcing that Sergeant Brooks and Lieutenant Phelan wanted to see him. He told her to send them in, "and then, for God's sake, go home."

Brooks handed Fitzgerald a plastic bag containing a black metal box about the size of a cigarette package. "It was a bug," Brooks said. "First-rate. A commercial product that's been modified by a real pro."

"Traceable?" Fitzgerald asked, knowing the answer before he heard it.

"These things never are," Brooks said. "Usually they're the work of guys who go straight for a while, learn the trade in the nice world, and then drift over to free-lancing. They know how to buy without a trace, how to make safe contacts with a client, how to customize. This was a beaut. Whoever put it in that clock is a pro."

"But if he is a pro, would he break in like that, rough up the chief?" Phelan asked. "I mean, it's one thing to be an expert on bugs and another to be an expert on breaking and entering."

"Comes with the territory," Brooks said. "At least breaking and entering does. Rough stuff? Kind of unusual. I think what happened was the client had it put in, maybe on a long-range basis, a kind of eavesdropping stakeout. Then came the murder, and someone, maybe the panicky client himself, tried to get it out before it was found. And you"—he pointed at Fitzgerald—"caught him before he got to it."

"So," Fitzgerald said, "maybe the client is the murderer, and maybe not. But he certainly isn't a good citizen who wants to come forth to help us." He turned to Brooks. "I suppose we're not so lucky that it was a tape recorder."

"No such luck," Brooks said. "It's a low-power transmitter, voice-activated and able to run for maybe two or three hundred hours on a tiny battery. It broadcasts a signal with a radius of about three to five hundred feet."

"Then somewhere within that radius there's a receiver and a tape recorder," Fitzgerald said.

"Not anymore. I tracked for pickup signals. But it was a lost cause. Whoever wanted to get that out of the clock would have removed the pickup receiver first, and probably at low risk. The way this works, the receiver is usually in a much safer place than the bug."

"Okay, Brooks. No report on this. I may get back to you later to arrange an FBI lab checkout of the bug, just in case similar ones have shown up somewhere else."

When Brooks closed the door behind him, Fitzgerald told Phelan about his meeting with Mason and the videotape from the mayor.

"Does it really exist?" Phelan asked.

"Yes. I've seen it. It's in the evidence vault. No copies. It's just what Mitchell said it was."

"It's definitely Royal on the tape?" she asked.

"Definitely. The car has a Louisiana plate—'Sportsman's Paradise' it says on it—and is registered to his bodyguard goon."

"I'm willing to bet," Phelan said, "that Mitchell knows about the possible tie-in between the prostitute murders and the murder of Bristow."

"And maybe he even knows we're taking a hard look at Royal," Fitzgerald said. "So he digs into his blackmail trunk and gets out the videotape. God knows how many other tapes he has."

"Lot of high-tech stuff going on," Phelan said, her voice trailing off. "Bugs. Security cameras. Videotapes." She stood and walked to the counter to fill a coffee mug. Fitzgerald followed her with his eyes. He was still staring at her when she turned and asked him if he wanted some. He shook his head and looked away, feeling like a schoolboy.

She smiled and returned to her chair. "I've been thinking about the bug in the hideaway," she said. "Something bothers me."

"What's that?"

"Let's suppose that the killer planted the bug and decided to come back to retrieve it by entering through the window. And by the way, we don't get any prints but yours on the window."

173

"I tried to be careful."

"That's what all the men say," she said, laughing. "Okay. The killer comes back, at great risk, to retrieve the bug. *Why?* Why take the chance when there was nothing that bug could give us? It doesn't make any sense to me."

"I had one answer," Fitzgerald said. "I thought he might have had the same idea I had about redialing. But obviously that wasn't it. If it were, he would have snatched the phone or dialed some meaningless number. No. He was there for the bug."

"But why?"

"Get me the answer to that and a few other questions, and we'll have it all figured out," Fitzgerald said.

She looked around the office. "End of the day for you?"

"Not quite. Got some writing to do. I want to keep Lawson and Mason informed. But not too much."

"I'll be at home. If anything—"

"Don't worry," Fitzgerald said. "I'll call."

He was digging into his second carton from the Chinese takeout place when the phone rang. It was Lawson. Fitzgerald felt his stomach tighten. "What do you have?" Lawson asked.

"We're building a case," Fitzgerald said. "Making definite progress."

"Don't give me cop-talk bullshit," Lawson said. "I'm getting calls from the *Post* I'm not returning. The President has called in the House and Senate leadership for a showdown on Monday. The word is we've got to let the FBI in. What can I stop him with?"

"Let me call you back later on," Fitzgerald said. "I might have something." His mind was racing ahead with a decision to placate Lawson by giving him everything that implicated Royal.

"Call me by eleven-thirty," Lawson said. He hung up without saying goodbye.

Less than half an hour later the phone rang again. Fitzgerald looked at the clock on his desk: 9:24.

"Doyle here, Chief. A woman's body has been found on the grounds. It looks like murder. There's a car waiting for you."

The grounds. He thought of the rolling lawns of the Hill. And he thought of what Mrs. Darwin had said: "A woman and blood on bricks." *Well, at least that's wrong.*

174

Rather than wait for the elevator, he took the stairs, then ran through the lobby and out to the curb, jumped in next to the driver, picked up the microphone, and flipped a switch. "Communications. Chief Fitzgerald. Get me the watch commander. Doyle, stand pat. I'm covering the scene. Contact Lieutenant Phelan and tell her to round up a crime scene team and get there. Also tell her to get Perkins, the medical examiner. Field any media queries to me at the scene."

30

THE CAR SPED down D Street, screeched left at First and then at Constitution Avenue, on the Senate side of the dark Capitol Hill. About halfway down the block, near the bottom of the hill, Fitzgerald could see the flashing red, white, and blue roof lights of a patrol car pulled up diagonally athwart the sidewalk. A civilian car, its driver's door open, was parked at the curb, facing the wrong way.

Fitzgerald's car parked behind the patrol car. Fitzgerald jumped out, vaulted the low stone wall, and ran toward the beam of a flashlight. A thin mist rose from low sprinklers scattered about in the grass like brass mushrooms. The mist glazed Fitzgerald's shoes and cuffs as he cut across the rolling lawn. He could see the outline of a small, vine-covered brick pavilion. The flashing lights of the two police cars sent shadows shimmering across one of the arches of the pavilion. Silhouetted there at the edge of darkness, like figures at the entrance to an ancient grotto, were three men. As Fitzgerald approached, he saw that two of them were Capitol Police officers, Sergeant Fred Mathewson in civilian clothes and an officer he did not immediately recognize. The third man was Senator Michael Royal.

Behind them, a wrought iron gate gaped. A damp gravel path led from the sidewalk to the pavilion, a vague shape in the darkness. Mathewson stepped forward, nodded to the chief, and swept his flashlight beam along the path and into the darkness beyond the gate. The path ended at a circular brick floor that surrounded a semicircular wall with two water fountains. The light moved down the wall to what looked like a shadow. When the light moved again, Fitzgerald saw a face, eyes open, mouth wide. The light wavered for an instant and Fitzgerald saw flesh, coffee-colored flesh, and blood. *Blood on bricks. My God. Blood on bricks.*

Mathewson flicked off the light. "I'd finished my shift, changed clothes, and was driving home," he said. "I had my window open, and I heard a scream when I was coming up Constitution, so I jumped out of my car and ran here. When I flashed my light inside, I could see a body, inside the . . . the little brick building."

"The pavilion," Fitzgerald said. "They call it the pavilion." While Mathewson spoke, the other officer began stringing the CRIME SCENE DO NOT CROSS tape from tree to tree.

"Right, the pavilion," Mathewson said. "The lock on the gate was hanging there, broken I guess, and I went inside and I could see that the woman was dead. So I stepped out of the pavilion and left it the way it was. I saw Senator Royal standing here, so I asked him to stay where he was. I ran back to the car, called in a ten-six for backup on my CB, and requested an ambulance."

A gray Honda and a Capitol Police car screeched to the curb. The siren of a D.C. ambulance wailed in the distance. Fitzgerald could see Phelan running across the lawn from her car, and the two men of the crime scene team, carrying aluminum cases, emerged from the police car and walked up the sidewalk.

After nodding to Fitzgerald and Mathewson, Phelan stopped at the entrance to the pavilion, played a small flashlight over the body, turned to the officer stringing the tape, and said, "Get the on-duty CERT team on the radio and tell them to get a van here with lights and a generator." The officer dropped a tangle of tape and trotted back to his car.

"Let's just stand by until we get some lights up here, Stan," she said to one of the technicians.

Fitzgerald gave Phelan a brief review of Mathewson's report. She aimed her flashlight's beam at the body again. "My God!" she said. "That's Gwenda Harris-Topping, the delegate. The bastard propped her up, just like Julia Bristow."

Phelan turned to Royal and took out a notebook and pen. Fitzgerald shifted around so that his back was to the body and Royal faced it.

"Now, Senator, I'd like to ask a few questions," Fitzgerald said. "Lieutenant Phelan here will be writing down your answers and they will be incorporated in a formal statement we will be asking you to make later. Understood?"

"Understood," Royal said, his voice low, his eyes turned away from the body and toward the deep darkness of the trees beyond the pavilion. His lightweight tan suit was showing the wrinkles of a long day. Thin stripes of sweat showed through his white shirt, and his bright yellow tie was speckled with black dots. He reached into a back pocket of his trousers, took out a damp handkerchief, and wiped his brow.

"Sergeant Mathewson says he found you standing here when he discovered the body," Fitzgerald said. "Would you mind telling me why you were here?"

Royal carefully folded the handkerchief and put it back into his pocket. "About five this afternoon," he said, "I was on the floor of the Senate when a page brought me a note saying that I had an urgent call. I went to the private lobby and called my office. My secretary said she had received a call from someone who insisted that he had to speak to me, that it was extremely urgent. I get a lot of calls like that, and I usually take them. She put him through, and when he started talking it sounded just like that voice on the tape that the TV station got after Mrs. Bristow's murder. He said—"

"Just a minute, Senator," Fitzgerald interrupted. "You immediately had that thought, that the voice sounded like the voice on the tape?"

"Yes. Yes, I did."

"And what did the man want?"

"He didn't want anything. He said he had important information for me."

"What kind of information?" Fitzgerald asked.

"That . . . is not pertinent, Fitzgerald," Royal replied.

"Not pertinent, Senator?"

"That's right, not pertinent."

"All right. Please go on."

"The man said he would call me with further instructions on

how to meet him. At about six o'clock the Senate adjourned. I went to my office to pick up some paperwork and lock up. I left, switching on my answering machine the way I usually do. At about eight o'clock I got a phone call at my home. It was the same voice. He told me to go back to my office and listen to my answering machine, then he hung up. I called my machine at the office and heard his voice again, this time telling me to be here—at the pavilion here—at eight forty-five."

"Was there anyone else in your home?"

"To verify my story? No. I was alone. I was told to come alone."

"Senator, exactly what did the man say? How did he describe the place to meet him?"

"He said there was this brick structure on the Senate side of the Hill, near the bottom of the hill. I vaguely remembered seeing it, and I more or less knew where it was."

"And so you arrived here? Around eight forty-five? Without your friend Bobby, who carries that small Gatling gun?" Fitzgerald asked. He could see the ambulance pulling up to the curb, followed by what looked like a van from one of the television stations.

"I told you, I was told to come here alone. I got here maybe five minutes early. I left my home just before eight thirty."

"And your home is where?"

"It's on East Capitol Street, between Third and Fourth."

"You walked?"

"Yes. I enjoy walking."

"So you came here and stood just about where you are standing now?"

"Yes. I paced up and down. But I was always just about here, in front of the pavilion."

"And what did you do when you heard the scream from inside the pavilion?"

"I didn't hear any scream."

Phelan looked up from her notebook. "Would you mind repeating that, Senator?"

"I said that I did not hear a scream."

The ambulance attendants were approaching, rolling a gurney across the lawn. Behind them were three people from the television truck. Fitzgerald recognized James Davis, the Channel 3 anchorman.

Suddenly cupping his right hand under Royal's right elbow, Fitzgerald propelled him diagonally away from the pavilion. "Hold the fort, Lieutenant," he said. "Nobody talks to Davis except me. Nobody. I'm getting the senator out of here."

He hurried Royal along the edge of a line of high shrubbery and onto a sidewalk that led to Constitution Avenue. The officer who had been sent to call for lights was getting out of his car. "Hold it for a minute, Hessman," Fitzgerald ordered. "I want you to take Senator Royal here home."

To his left Fitzgerald could see two figures crashing through the shrubbery, one holding a television camera, the other a microphone boom. He pushed Royal into the car next to the driver and said, "Get the hell out of here." The car sped off. At the same time, two television vans arrived, closely followed by three civilian cars with press signs on their visors.

As Fitzgerald turned back toward the pavilion, out of the shrubbery stepped the camera operator and sound man who had been in his office. Behind them, zigzagging through the sprinkler mist, trying to keep his feet from being sprayed, was Davis.

"Did you get it?" Davis called to the camerawoman.

"Yeah. Sound, too, right, Jack?" He raised his microphone boom like a lance and smiled.

Davis stepped in front of Fitzgerald, and the other two adroitly took up their familiar positions to record the standard shot: James Davis confronting authority.

"Who was that man you just bundled into a police car, Chief Fitzgerald?" Davis asked in a booming voice that seemed to resonate with outraged virtue.

"A person aiding police with their inquiries," Fitzgerald said dryly. He had often playfully used this British detective-story line with his FBI colleagues.

"A person who was at the scene of this crime?"

"I am not going to discuss this matter further at this time, Mr. Davis."

Davis swung away from Fitzgerald, who jogged back to the pavilion. He ducked under the tape and turned. Looking full into the camera, Davis was saying, "And so, for the time being, the

179

mystery man at another Capitol Hill murder remains unidentified by police."

Davis and his crew trailed Fitzgerald back to the pavilion. When they approached, bathed in camera lights, Fitzgerald motioned for them to stop at the tape. Davis pivoted to face the camera and began to speak again. "We are at another crime scene"—the camera zoomed in on the tape—"on Capitol Hill, waiting to find out who the victim is." He began ad-libbing a brief recollection of Julia Bristow's murder.

As two CERT men arrived to set up a generator and lights, Fitzgerald took Mathewson aside. Phelan, holding a flashlight, was on her knees inside the pavilion, looking at but not touching Harris-Toppings's body.

"Let's go over this again, Fred," Fitzgerald said. "You rushed up here after hearing a scream?"

"Right, Chief."

"And you're sure that the scream came from there?" He pointed to the pavilion.

"Yes, very sure. It was a scream with a sort of gurgle. An awful scream. Like it was full of blood."

"Okay. I just wanted to be sure, because your report apparently is not going to jibe, at least on that account, with Senator Royal's."

Mathewson nodded rapidly, then said, "There's something else, Chief. I saw it, but I didn't want to touch it." As he spoke, he began moving toward the pavilion. Fitzgerald followed him to a stretch of drenched lawn on the side of the pavilion nearest Constitution Avenue.

Mathewson pointed his flashlight at an object on the ground. Fitzgerald's shoes sank into the soft, wet grass as he hunkered down and put on his glasses. The object was a special Capitol Police badge, a commemorative issued for the most recent presidential Inaugural.

"Stay here," he ordered. He trotted back to Phelan, who, intent on looking at the body, was oblivious to him. When he tapped her on the shoulder, she turned, startled.

"What's up?" she asked.

"Mathewson spotted something. We'll need a technician over there to photograph it."

"Right," she said, standing and brushing off the knees of her jeans. "Stan's done about as much as he can until Perkins has come and gone. What's the something?"

"An Inaugural badge."

"What the hell does that mean?" she asked.

"I don't know yet. Tell Stan to photograph it and then carefully remove it and photograph the ground underneath it. And find out when those sprinklers went on. I assume they're turned on and off automatically and there'll be some kind of record."

"Right," she said as Fitzgerald walked toward Constitution Avenue, where Perkins was emerging from his car. Behind it two more mobile television units were arriving.

Fitzgerald shook hands with Perkins and told him about the discovery of the body.

"You're sure it's Gwenda Harris-Topping?" Perkins asked, with a rare look of shock.

"Not sure enough to announce the identification. Alix—Lieutenant Phelan—recognized her first. When she did, so did I. She spoke at the rally."

"Yes, I know," Perkins said, still looking shocked. "I . . . I knew her—not well, but I knew her. A fine woman, really fine." He squared his shoulders, as if that gesture would change him back to the imperturbable medical examiner. "Okay. Let's take a look."

The generator was chugging, and two lights rigged in nearby trees shone down on the pavilion. One of the technicians was photographing the lock on the wrought iron gate. He stepped back when Perkins approached.

Perkins, his shadow long in the harsh light, walked through the open gate and stood for a moment, head bowed. Then, crouching, he spread a handkerchief on the bricks and shifted around so that he did not block the light. He pulled on translucent yellow gloves and gently touched the body of Gwenda Harris-Topping. The bodice of her dark blue silk dress was slashed and stained with dried blood.

"Lieutenant," Perkins said, turning to Phelan, "will you please shine a flashlight here?"

Phelan crouched next to him and shone the light where his sheathed finger was pointing. The light revealed a dark slit that ran along the arc of the left breast. A segment of the coffee-colored flesh hung open, exposing a dark weave of muscle. "Breast partially severed," Perkins said to the tape recorder in his left hand. He moved his finger, and Phelan moved the circle of light to a gaping wound at the throat. "The fatal wound appears to be a throat wound. This appears to have been caused by a deep knife thrust. There seems to be a hilt bruise at the point of entry."

Perkins looked over the body for a few minutes, then stood. "I'll need to move the body to complete this preliminary examination," he told Phelan, "so tell your photography boys to finish up their shots. And I think you have something here to establish identification." He moved his finger again, and the circle of light moved to something pinned onto a shred of the dress. It was a rectangular white card in a plastic holder. Two dark streaks ran diagonally across the plastic. The white card said, in printed words, SOCIETY OF AFRICAN-AMERICAN LEADERS. Written below, in a clear, neat hand, was GWENDA HARRIS-TOPPING.

Phelan stared at the card for a moment, then switched off the flashlight, stood, and headed for the technicians. Perkins stepped outside the gate and took deep breaths of the cool evening air. Fitzgerald walked over. "How similar?" he asked.

"Very," Perkins said, staring away. "You know, I gave up smoking three years ago, and this is the first time I can remember wanting, really wanting, a cigarette." He turned to Fitzgerald. "Major throat wound, same as Bristow. Breast mutilation, same as Bristow. Killed somewhere else, same as Bristow."

"Killed somewhere else. That's what it looked like to me, too," Fitzgerald said. "But the officer who found her said he heard a scream from here."

"No way. My God, her vocal chords were severed. She may have screamed when she was killed, but that wasn't here. For one thing, just like Bristow, there's not enough blood here. The body was placed here."

Perkins told Fitzgerald about the name on the card. "It looks like she may have been at some kind of meeting," he added. "You can probably easily track down her whereabouts."

"What else do you think you can give me on this?"

"Not much," Perkins said, shrugging and shaking his head. "The only thing—well, I can't promise. There's a hilt mark. I might be able to prove that the same knife was used for both murders. I can't make that promise until the autopsy." He turned to Phelan, who had just approached. "You'll be at this one, too? Let's say nine o'clock tomorrow morning."

Phelan looked quickly at Fitzgerald, who said, "Okay. Then report directly to me. I'll be in my office. Now I think I'd better talk to the media ghouls."

He took two steps toward the crime scene tape. The camera lights flared on, and microphones and tape recorders were thrust into his face. *A feeding frenzy*, he thought. He held up his hands against the torrent of questions and briefly described the finding of the body, without naming Mathewson or Royal. He said that Perkins was completing his preliminary examination. As he spoke, the ambulance attendants brought up the gurney, and the cameras switched from Fitzgerald to them.

"The victim was a woman," Fitzgerald continued. "We have a tentative identification."

The cameras swung back to him, and the murmur stopped as he paused.

"From identification found on the body, we believe the victim is Gwenda Harris-Topping."

"The D.C. delegate?" Davis said. "But I saw her alive just hours ago." Unadorned by stagecraft, his voice sounded small.

"Where? What time?" Fitzgerald asked.

"There was a reception for black leaders in . . ." Davis pulled a piece of paper from the inner pocket of his blue blazer. "In room EF100 in the Capitol." As he spoke, he began recovering his professional voice.

"I'll want to talk with you off-camera," Fitzgerald said. He turned away from Davis and back to the other reporters. For fifteen minutes he answered or ducked questions, then he declared the session over. Taking Davis aside, he told him to pass his information on Harris-Topping to Phelan. The print and television herd moved toward the sidewalk and their vehicles, preparing to ambush him whenever he headed for a car.

Fitzgerald walked back to the pavilion, where Phelan said, "I had a quick talk with Perkins before he took off. He's beginning to think serial murder."

"Or maybe copy-cat," Fitzgerald said. "Look, I want to bounce something off you. When you wind up here, can you drop by my place?"

"Sure. I'll be there," Phelan said.

Fitzgerald headed toward the sidewalk. He thought of walking home, but when he saw the reporters lined up, he signaled for an officer to precede him to a car. As he was about to get in, Davis burst from the pack and confronted him. Speaking both to his microphone and to Fitzgerald, the anchorman said, "The man, the man who was spirited away in the Capitol Police car. Who was that man, Chief?"

"I have already said that I cannot discuss that matter, Mr. Davis."

"The African-American community and the District of Columbia's statehood forces have lost their most distinguished voice," Davis said. "A black leader has been struck down by a man with a knife. I ask again, Chief Fitzgerald, who was that man who was spirited away—who was that *white* man?"

Without answering, Fitzgerald got into the car and sped away.

31

MRS. DARWIN was standing at her half-open door when Fitzgerald entered the hallway. "Would you care to stop for a drink, Jeffrey?"

"No thanks, Mrs. Darwin. I'm still on duty. I'm going to be meeting with Lieutenant Phelan for a while. There has been another murder."

Mrs. Darwin grimaced. "I understand. There was a bulletin on the news. I didn't know the victim or follow her career, but . . ." Her voice began to trail off. Then, sharply, she added, "If you want help—"

"I'm sorry, Mrs. Darwin, but I have to get going," Fitzgerald said, and continued down the hall to his apartment.

Phelan pressed the doorbell that rang in his apartment about half an hour later. By then Mrs. Darwin had climbed the stairs to her bedroom on the second floor. She had an inner spiral staircase. The hallway stairs led to a hallway of locked doors, one of which was the door to a room Fitzgerald was allowed to use for storage. The other apartments could have been rented out, but Mrs. Darwin had told him that she wanted only one tenant, and he was, she said, the perfect sort.

He had showered and changed to jeans, moccasins, and a short-sleeved yellow shirt. He let Phelan in, led her down the hall to his open door, and pointed to an overstuffed chair he had moved next to his rolltop desk at the far end of the long living room. She sat and looked around the apartment. "This is exquisite, Fitz," she said. "What a nice snug place."

He stood beside her, leaning a hand on the edge of the desk, which gaped to reveal piles of papers and the kind of old-fashioned calculator that had a crank on the side.

"I suppose you were expecting a Sears sleeper sofa and bullfight posters on the wall," Fitzgerald said, his hands sweeping to encompass the room. "Well, the desk's mine. It belonged to my mother's father. The rest I can thank Mrs. Darwin for. She advertised the place as unfurnished, but when she found out that all I had was the desk and a portable TV, she decided to trust me with some of the pieces she had stashed away. Can I get you something?"

"How about some coffee? And would you have the makings of a sandwich? I never had a chance to eat."

"Coffee it is. Cheese okay? I think that's all I've got. Mustard?" She smiled and nodded.

He returned from the kitchenette carrying two thick sandwiches and a ceramic bowl full of pretzels. From a slot on the left side of the desk he slid out a writing board. After putting the bowl on it, he sat on a wickerback oak swivel chair in front of the desk and spun toward Phelan.

"Interesting bowl," she said. The bowl was thick-walled and squat. The surface was a medley of browns swirling around pockmarks in some kind of a design.

"My daughter made it in her pottery class," Fitzgerald said proudly.

185

Phelan tried not to look surprised. She knew that he was divorced but not that he had a child. "I didn't know—"

"Well, yes. Maureen. Almost ten. But there's work to be done." He picked up a yellow legal pad, took his half-lens glasses from his pocket, and scanned the page he had been writing on before she arrived. "What I did," he said, looking up, "was start on two lists: similarities between the two murders and what we have to do about the second murder." He told her about the similarities that Perkins had seen and added, "Do we have a serial killer on our hands?"

"I've been thinking about that, too," Phelan said. "Our two murders and the murders of the prostitutes."

Fitzgerald tossed the pad onto the desk. "What have you got on them?"

"All three women were black. The cases were shelved as low-priority murders, which means sometimes there's not even a follow-up to the original crime scene investigation."

"What about copy-cat crime?" Fitzgerald asked.

"Doesn't seem likely. A copy-cat needs something to copy. He reacts to publicized crimes. There was nothing on the prostitutes except the usual two-paragraph story on an inside metro page. And from what Perkins—"

The phone rang, and Fitzgerald's pager, lying on the desk, began to beep. He walked across the room to the phone. "Yes. Just back from there." He looked toward Phelan and mouthed a name: *Mason.* "Yes. Terrible. Yes. Yes." He nodded his head vigorously. "No, I'm not planning a press conference. Yes. Well, I would rather not speak about that on the phone. Yes. There will be an autopsy at nine o'clock tomorrow. There was a witness at the scene whom I must interview again. Give me tomorrow morning to work on this. How about one o'clock in your office? Fine. Yes. Thanks."

He hung up. "Mason seems about ready to call in the Marines. Or at least the FBI. He wants a one-on-one talk, as he puts it, on the investigation." He went back to his chair. "Now where the hell were we?"

"I was saying that Perkins seems to have seen the same kind of wounds he saw on Julia Bristow. That would mean the same hand, not a copy-cat."

"Right," Fitzgerald replied vaguely, his thoughts drifting back to the sight of Julia Bristow's body lying sprawled in the subway car. His next few words struck Phelan as being oddly disconnected and out of focus. Fitzgerald seemed to be clinging to the wreckage of the Bristow murder to avoid having to confront tonight's new horror.

"We're avoiding murder number two," Phelan called out to his back as he got up and left the room.

"I know," he answered from the kitchenette.

He returned with two cups of coffee, then handed one to her and raised his own. "Thanks for being here. One murder, I thought I could handle. Two, and maybe more to come—well, I don't know."

"You're imagining somebody running around out there killing women on the Hill for months," she said. "And then one day a cop just happens to knock on a door to tell somebody that the lights are on in the car in front of the house, and standing there is some loony with the knife in his hand and pictures of his victims on his living room wall. A case broken by a fluke. That's what you're seeing?"

"Yes. You hit it exactly. I'm not just worried that the bastard will kill more people. I'm worried that I won't be the guy who grabs him."

"What about Royal? What do you think?"

"Sure. A damn good possibility. Especially with that video hanging around his neck."

"Well, what about Royal? Let's start with him at the scene."

"I treated him like a member," Fitzgerald said. "Maybe he was in danger. I got him out of there to get him away from Davis. Now I wonder about my judgment. Christ! What if Royal did it?"

"Get on him first thing tomorrow. Check him out right away. That business about not hearing the scream—"

"Neither one of them could have heard it," Fitzgerald said. "She was dead when the killer put her body there. And somehow he got in and out through the locked gate. How the hell did he do that?"

"I took a good look at the lock. It didn't look like it was broken. It looked like it was just hanging open," Phelan said. "Anybody with a paper clip could open it. And the screams? There are enough screams in this town for Mathewson to have heard somebody else's. He might have heard some scream and then be drawn to that body by . . . by instinct."

"But he described the scream so vividly. 'Like it was full of blood,' he said."

"Things like that happen," Phelan said. She stood and went to a window framed by light green drapes. She pulled one aside and stared out, her face dimly silhouetted against the glow of a street-light.

"Meaning what?"

"What I mean," Phelan said, turning to look at him, "is that some people manage to touch things, see things, hear things that other people don't notice." She stepped toward him.

He looked up at her, startled, and at that moment decided to tell her about Mrs. Darwin. "She rattled me, really rattled me, when she told me about something only I knew." He waited for a moment, but Phelan did not ask what Mrs. Darwin had revealed. "And then there was the thing connected directly with this murder. She said there would be two more women, 'a woman and blood on bricks' and 'a woman and blood on marble.' Tonight—well, you saw it. Blood on bricks."

Phelan returned to her chair and picked up her coffee cup. She held it in her left hand, tapping its rim lightly with her right. "You wouldn't be the first cop to use a psychic."

"I know that. But I never believed any of that stuff. Now I wonder a little. Just a little. But I can't afford to be caught using a goddamn fortune-teller. The media—Davis—would have me for breakfast. I can't tell anybody."

"But you're telling me."

"You're not just anybody. I . . . I trust you."

"Thank you, Fitz." She finished her coffee and stood to carry it to the kitchenette.

Fitzgerald rose from his chair and laid his hand on her left shoulder. "I'll get that later," he said.

She reached up and touched his hand. "No. I want another cup of coffee anyway." She turned her head to look at him, pulled his hand from her shoulder, and gave it a squeeze. She was in the kitchenette before he could move.

"Get one for me, too," he called to her.

They settled opposite each other, each holding a cup, each, for a moment, surprised to be looking at the other.

"I may not be the best one to ask about psychics," she said. She hesitated, apparently sifting through thoughts.

"Tell me about it," he said. He sounded interested but dubious.

"You may not want to hear it. You want less doubt. I may be giving you more. Besides, you need to concentrate on the murders, not on this side issue."

"You're a practical-sounding, practical-acting person, Alix. That's why I like you as an investigator. And I consider you a friend, outside of who we are professionally. So . . ."

"Okay, Fitz. It happened when I was looking for my birth parents." He looked puzzled. Drawing a breath, she rapidly continued. "I was adopted. I had fine adoptive parents and all that, but when my father died, I decided to search for my . . . for the woman I was born to. I found a little information, but here I was, a trained investigator, and I couldn't get the name I needed. If I could get the name on my birth certificate—the original name, before the Phelans adopted me—then I could track down my other mother." She raised the cup to her lips, inviting a question if Fitzgerald had one. He did not speak.

"I joined a group of adoptees who were searching. One of them told me she had finally broken through with the help of a psychic. I was skeptical, but I was getting desperate. So I called her and told her I would like to see her. Her name was Sarah. She's dead now. The *Post* wrote a feature on her when she died, about how she worked with area police on missing-person cases, how people came to her to get personal information. She lived near Antietam—the Civil War battlefield, up near Harpers Ferry?"

"I've been there," Fitzgerald said.

"Well, that's where Sarah lived, on land where the battle was fought, near one of the cemeteries. I told her what I wanted. She looked at me for a long time. She was a small woman with big dark eyes. Something seemed to be tugging at my mind. I know that's not a very scientific description, but that's what I felt. Something rummaging through my mind.

"We met three times. The third time was along a sunken road that was part of the battlefield. It was called Bloody Lane. We sat on a couple of rocks, and she began telling me about the battle, as

189

if her eyes could see it. And in between, as if she were weaving two sets of memory, she said she was seeing my mother and finding out about her.

" 'I can see her here, Alix,' she said, 'because she is of the earth now, like the men who fell here.' When she said that, I began to cry, and she put her arm around my shoulder and said, 'She died three years ago, in New Britain, Connecticut, and she knew about you. She went to Hartford once in a while to see you, at the park near your house, at high school. And once, in your freshman year at Boston College, she followed you down Commonwealth Avenue when you and a friend went to get a pizza.' She told me details like that casually, almost as if it were something we had always known together. Sometimes the details broke my heart. She was telling me there were times I could have turned around and seen my mother or taken a step and touched her. She gave me my mother's name, the name of her boyfriend. When I checked it all out, it was all true."

"What about your mother seeing you, following you?" Fitzgerald asked. "Could you establish that?"

"Not factually. I got the factual information, following up on the bits she gave me. I got my birth certificate, and the death certificates of my mother and the man I assume was my father. But the stories about my mother seeing me, those I couldn't prove. I knew, though, emotionally knew, that they were true. I just knew it. Couldn't prove it, but knew it." She cupped her hands around Fitzgerald's right hand. "I haven't helped you, have I?" she asked.

"You said you might not be the one to ask," he replied. "But I think you were exactly the one to ask. Will you go with me when I talk to Mrs. Darwin?"

"Yes. But don't forget, she might not tell you anything new. Looking back at what Sarah told me, I wondered if somehow I knew what she was telling me but had missed the cues. I wondered if I had known that some strange woman kept appearing near me and I had decided not to notice her. I mean, was Sarah telling me something I already subconsciously knew? That's the way it can be, you know."

They continued to talk for a few more minutes, never straying far from the second murder. Finally, the contemplation of a 9 A.M. autopsy, along with a need for sleep, dragged Phelan from the chair. Fitzgerald walked her to her car. He was reluctant to let her go. When she got behind the wheel, she rolled down the window. Fitzgerald reached in, held her face in his hands, and softly kissed her.

He stood at the curb for five minutes after she was gone.

Friday, April 10

32

FITZGERALD was behind his desk at 7:15. He turned on the computer and wrote a one-page report on the murder of Gwenda Harris-Topping. He printed it out, made a few corrections in pencil, transferred them to the computer file, and printed out a new page. Mason liked pieces of paper, and this might save Fitzgerald a verbal debate. *There's not much on this sheet,* he thought. *I've got to get more, got to end this.*

At 7:45 he consulted his directory of members' private phone numbers, called Royal at his home, and agreed to meet him at his office at noon.

Phelan appeared shortly after ten and gave him a briefing on the autopsy. He took notes on the computer as she spoke. "Similar wounds, possibly the same knife," he repeated as he typed. "How does he come up with the same knife? I thought the tip was broken off. And any more mention of the prostitute murders?"

"Two questions, two answers. First, he thinks the killer resharpened the knife used on Julia Bristow, getting a new tip on it; he probably did that rather than use a new knife because he's particularly attached to it. Second question: I told Perkins I wondered how the same killer could shift from prostitutes to a U.S. senator and a congressional delegate."

"What did he say to that?" Fitzgerald asked.

"He said it bothered him, too. But he had a hunch. The three

195

prostitutes and Gwenda Harris-Topping were all black. She wasn't as much of an exception as Julia Bristow was."

Fitzgerald raised his fingers above the keyboard, pivoted to his desk, and leaned his head on his hands. "I can't get into that," he said, explaining that he was trying to write a report for Mason and simultaneously do some thinking. "Tell me about the similarity of the wounds."

"Perkins had assumed that there would be little in the files about the prostitutes. But he ran into some luck. His assistant, a very sharp doctor named Douglas, did the autopsy on one of them. She got curious—not from a crime angle but for a paper on knife wounds for the *Journal of Forensic Pathology*. She became a walking encyclopedia on knife wounds and has been gathering information from all over the country. When Perkins said he wondered about the similarities of the wounds, it turned out that Douglas was way ahead of him but hadn't mentioned it. She's a very scientific type, and didn't want to say anything until she had enough data. Perkins says that at least one of the wounds on each of the prostitutes bore a peculiar bruise. Douglas says the bruise is what she calls a hilt mark—an abrasion caused by the hilt of the knife scraping the skin as it is completely inserted."

"Right to the hilt," Fitzgerald said softly. He typed a few more words into the computer.

Phelan looked down at her notes. "The photographs of the hilt marks indicate that the same hilt, and therefore the same knife, was used in all three prostitute murders. And when Perkins and Douglas compared those marks to the hilt marks on Julia Bristow and Gwenda Harris-Topping—bingo!"

"Terrific," Fitzgerald said, pounding away at the keyboard. "All five, same knife." He stopped suddenly. "Why am I happy, for God's sake? We've got a guy who killed five people and who's probably planning some more."

Phelan ignored Fitzgerald's remarks and kept reading from her notes. "Also, the MO is the same in all five cases. Strangulation, apparently manual. Then, when the victim is dead or dying, a savage knife attack. And then he takes the body and puts it somewhere."

"Anything else?" Fitzgerald asked.

"Well, he's smart, killing in one place, moving the body to another. And there are no broken fingernails, no flesh under the nails, no indication that the victims struggled. Even a big, strong woman like Harris-Topping."

Fitzgerald pivoted back to the desk. "Meaning?" he asked.

"It probably means that somehow they did not initially fear this guy."

"I have trouble with that, Alix. It's one thing for a guy to pick up a whore on a street corner, take her in his car someplace, and tell her . . . well, you know, to get undressed, and then wham! he strangles her. That's one thing. But Julia Bristow walking in a Senate building? And Harris-Topping? Where was she grabbed, do you think?"

"I'm working on a minute-to-minute of that reception she was at just before her death. I assume you didn't see what James Davis put on Channel 3 last night. Ted Ringle taped it and left it for me. I went to the autopsy straight from home. I found the tape on my desk when I stopped by before coming here, so I brought it along. Want to see it?"

"Sure. Mason mentioned seeing something on Channel 3. Is this it?"

"I think it was broadcast as one of his specials, after the regular local news."

She reached into her large brown leather handbag and handed Fitzgerald a videotape. He opened a cabinet opposite his desk that contained a television set and a VCR, inserted the tape, and took the remote control back to his desk. Phelan turned her chair around and slipped on a pair of glasses "Movie glasses," she said.

The tape opened with a short teaser that showed Gwenda Harris-Topping in a dark blue dress, smiling her wide, honest smile. People with wineglasses in their hands were walking up to her and speaking. The movements were in slow motion, and the distinctive voice of James Davis was intoning: "Heroine of the civil rights movement. Godmother of D.C. statehood. Murder victim." His voice quickened. "Stay tuned. After the local news, a news special: Murder Encore on the Hill."

"Encore!" Fitzgerald exclaimed. "All of that guy's taste is in his mouth."

The tape sped ahead to the beginning of the special, a logo next

197

to the words *Murder Encore on the Hill* and a white silhouette of the Capitol with blood running down the dome.

"It looks like that goddamn paint commercial," Fitzgerald muttered.

The scene of the reception returned. The focus shifted from Harris-Topping to other faces, smiling, talking, clustering around her as if to gain strength from the energy of their champion. The murmur of voices and the faint clinking of glasses faded away and the voice of Davis returned to tell his audience that he had been at the reception. Then he was on-screen, speaking to Harris-Topping as a young woman in a bright red cocktail dress walked into camera range on the right side of the screen. The young woman whispered something to the delegate, who excused herself, announcing that she had to take a phone call.

The rest of the telecast consisted of Davis reviewing the two murders. He ended with the image of Fitzgerald shoving a man into a Capitol Police car. "Who is this man?" Davis asked. "Why was he spirited away from the scene of the crime?"

Fitzgerald clicked off the VCR. "Get an ID on that young woman in the red dress and find out about that phone call," he said. "And run a copy of the tape past somebody in the Threat Assessment Section to see if there are any familiar nuts in the crowd."

He turned back to his desk and placed his hands flatly on top, pushing against them as he spoke. "Getting back to your theory about the victims not fearing the killer, or apparently the approach of the killer: we know a little more now. Assuming that the phone call lured her somewhere, Harris-Topping may have gone off to meet the killer. See if anyone overheard anything."

"Right," Phelan said. She hesitated, then said, "Lured . . . That tape of Senator Bristow turning her head, walking toward her killer—the same thing seems to have happened to Gwenda Harris-Topping. She went off to meet her killer. There are no indications of a struggle. Initially at least, neither one of them had anything to fear."

"I can't see it, understand it," Fitzgerald said.

"Then maybe we should go talk to Mrs. Darwin," Phelan said.

Fitzgerald, smiling, put a finger to his lips. He unlocked his drawer, took out a transparent plastic bag containing the badge found at the crime scene, and said, "Okay. Let's go."

33

MRS. DARWIN opened the door at Fitzgerald's first knock. He had the impression that she had been there waiting for him. As he ushered Phelan through the door, he said, "Mrs. Darwin, this is—"

"Lieutenant Alexandra Phelan," Mrs. Darwin concluded with a warm smile. "I feel I know you already. Please come in." She gestured toward the table and chairs at the bay window. "Now you both sit there while I put on tea." She disappeared into the kitchen, leaving Phelan to admire the room and Fitzgerald to pace.

When Mrs. Darwin returned, she opened the drapes and sat forward on her chair, framed in the radiance of the morning light.

"Mrs. Darwin," Fitzgerald began, "we need—*I* need—your help."

She smoothed her gray skirt and waited for him to continue.

"We have reason to believe," he said in his best policeman's voice, "that the person who killed Julia Bristow and Gwenda Harris-Topping also killed three prostitutes in the District in recent months."

Mrs. Darwin opened a drawer in the table and removed a deck of cards wrapped in a gossamer black cloth. Her studied movements unreasonably irritated Fitzgerald, who tried not to show it.

"Now don't let these cards bother you, Jeffrey," she said. "I told you I don't need them. I just feel more comfortable with them." She started slowly shuffling them.

"I think, Mrs. Darwin," Phelan hesitatingly began, "that Chief Fitzgerald can't quite put what he wants into questions."

"I understand, dear," Mrs. Darwin said. She was putting nine cards face down in an arc along the edge of the table. She turned over the card in the center of the arc. It showed a beautiful black-haired woman rising from the sea; in her hands was a golden cup.

199

Mrs. Darwin turned over a card at one end of the arc. This one showed a regal figure wearing a golden crown and sitting on a golden throne; an eagle perched on his shoulder.

"There is a great deal of falsity here," Mrs. Darwin said, a sharpness to her voice. "And danger. Danger to you both. You both must be on your guard." She turned toward Fitzgerald and held out her right hand. "You have something to show me."

Fitzgerald took the bag containing the badge from his pocket. "Do you want me to take it out?" he asked.

"That won't be necessary," she said. She closed her long fingers around the bag and held it for nearly a minute.

"More falsity," she said, handing the badge back to Fitzgerald. "Nothing is as it seems."

"Well, Mrs. Darwin," Fitzgerald said, recovering his skepticism, "that's often true in murder cases."

"I realize that," she replied, embarrassing him with her smile. "But I am trying to tell you that there is something more to the pattern here, something fraudulent, something underhanded."

"The badge is a fake?" he asked, putting the bag back into his pocket.

"The badge is real, as a badge. But I see a hand going into a drawer and taking it. It is attached to something black. The black . . . the black holder is ripped. The hand takes it and closes the drawer. The desk is in a room with many photographs on one wall."

She paused and leaned back. Now the light, which had made an aura of her white hair, fell across her face and grazed the gold frames of her glasses. She seemed to be looking over Fitzgerald's head. Then suddenly she looked directly at him. "You are there, standing there, by the bricks. A man is standing next to you. He is speaking. He is connected to the badge, but you do not talk to him about it. You will talk to him about it today."

"That man," Fitzgerald said. "That man by the pavilion. Is he the killer?"

Mrs. Darwin gathered up the cards, wrapped them in the sheer black cloth, replaced them in the drawer, and spoke, her head down, her eyes focused on the marble tabletop. "I . . . I do not like this man. He is part of the falsity, part of the lies, telling lies, an object of lies. He—"

Fitzgerald lunged forward, a desperate look on his face. "Can you tell me who the killer is?"

Mrs. Darwin, startled, pulled back. "I tell you what I see," she said. "That is all I can do. I see a man walking, a man talking, a man with a knife. That is the man. But he is hidden by another. You must look underground. The answer is underground. Underground." She sounded tired.

Phelan reached over and touched her clasped hands. "Thank you, Mrs. Darwin," she said. "Thank you very much." She adroitly shifted the conversation to the decor of the room and the paintings on the wall. She and Mrs. Darwin chatted for a few minutes while Fitzgerald sat staring out the window.

Finally he rose. "I have to go, Mrs. Darwin," he said. "Thank you." Phelan stood and they made their goodbyes.

As soon as they reached the sidewalk, Fitzgerald said, "Well, I guess I blew that."

"No," Phelan said. "You got information. You got confirmation of what you must be suspecting. You know there's something fishy about the badge."

They began walking toward First Street. "What's on the agenda?" she asked.

"For me, Royal and Mason. For you, to pin down the whereabouts of Harris-Topping and find out whatever else you can get about her. And another thing—get the dates of the prostitution murders from Perkins. I want to ask Royal where he was on those nights."

At First Street, they turned toward Constitution. "Okay. I'm heading off to see Irish," Phelan said. "He was involved in setting up security for the reception." She waved vaguely and ran diagonally across the street toward the Capitol.

Irish. Fitzgerald realized he had not had a chat with Irish Lunigan since Preacherman was killed. Fitzgerald and Lunigan had known each other since the first hour of Fitzgerald's first day on the job, when Irish had welcomed him with a natural, deeply ingrained cordiality. To that had been added genuine friendship and respect. Fitzgerald made a mental note to give him a call and continued walking along Constitution.

At the Supreme Court, men and women, some with signs on sticks, some with signs hung on their bodies, swarmed on the wide marble steps and spilled across the sidewalk. A Capitol Police officer spotted Fitzgerald and rushed over to clear a path through the crowd.

"What's the beef today, Morse?" Fitzgerald asked.

"From what I can gather, Chief, it's a combo today; the anti-abortion crowd and the pro–capital punishment folks both got permits. We thought they might get to arguing about who should be here, but they seem to get along fine. There's nothing going on inside, so we figure, why not let them have their fun?"

Fitzgerald picked up his step. He wanted to finish the report to Mason before going to Royal's office. And he had a phone call to make.

Back in his office, he called Kyle Tolland, who answered on the first ring, as usual. "The minute I picked up the *Post* this morning, I knew what you'd be thinking, Fitz," he said. "Let me say first of all, no matter what the media may be trying to sell, this doesn't sound like you're on the ground floor of a murder series. For one thing, it's happening too quickly. For another, there's a drastic change in venue and type of victim: from red-light district to Capitol Hill, from anonymous whores to famous women. There's something else going on."

"Like what?"

"I don't know. I attended a meeting with our Behavioral Science Unit a while back. They were looking at *false* serial murders. It seems that sometimes—"

"Wait a minute," Fitzgerald interrupted. "Why did you suddenly say *false?*"

"Because, Fitz, *false* was the word I wanted to use. I'm trying to tell you that even just sitting here, without knowing more than what I read, I feel something odd is going on."

"That's just what . . . just what I've been thinking," Fitzgerald said. "Something false. Any suggestions?"

After a moment, Tolland said, "Treat them as separate murders. Not as a murder series."

Fitzgerald told him about the hilt marks and the badge, information not released to the media. He thought about mentioning Royal's presence at the scene, but decided against it.

"Interesting," Tolland said. "But I still have a feeling this isn't serial."

"I've got to get more than feelings and intuition," Fitzgerald said, his voice rising.

"Well," Tolland said, "If I'm not giving you what you need, old pal . . ."

"Sorry, Kyle."

"I bet you've had a session with Ellen. I can see why you're worked up. She gives you a peek but never a perp. That's what a guy here once said about her. But he also said that she helped him a lot, Fitz. Helped him to open up. Think about that. Open up. At this point, that's about all I can offer."

34

ROYAL'S BACK was turned when Fitzgerald was ushered into his office. He was standing on a chair taking photographs off the wall, which was checkered by the faint outlines of vanished moments in the lives of the two Senator Bristows. *A room,* Fitzgerald thought, *with many photographs on one wall.*

Royal turned at the sound of Fitzgerald's entrance, jumped down from the chair, walked around his desk, and extended his hand. "Glad to see you, Chief. I want to thank you for getting me out of there last night."

Fitzgerald shook hands and said, "I got you out of there, Senator, because I was not sure what was going to happen next. When in doubt, get a member away from a scene of violence."

"And from that big black man with the microphone," Royal said, smiling. *He looks like a man who practices smiles in front of the mirror,* Fitzgerald thought.

Even after he left the FBI, Fitzgerald continued to study the psychological profiles of some of the most notorious killers in American history. Mass killers tended to live in the South or in California. They usually had some military background or some familiarity with weapons. The typical mass killer was a white male, single or divorced, a loner who was socially maladjusted but did not appear to be demented. Ordinarily, some personal crisis would trigger a passionate outburst that in turn triggered a murderous rampage, within a matter of minutes or hours.

Serial killers were different. It was not anger or the need for revenge that set them off. They killed for pleasure, coldly, methodically, taking great care to plan the almost ceremonial execution of their victims. And while a serial killer might select victims at random, he wanted the act of murder to be intimate. Jeffrey Dahmer carried that sense of intimacy to nightmarish extremes by eating part of a victim or by having sex with one after killing him, so that he might relive the experience of knowing him. But it was not Dahmer that Fitzgerald had in mind at this moment. It was Ted Bundy.

Dark, as handsome as a model, and celebrated by the Jaycees as one of that organization's outstanding young men, Bundy could pass as a junior executive in a major corporation—or as a politician destined for stardom. In fact, he had once been the state of Washington's Young Republican of the Year, and when he was caught, he was toying with the idea of running for office. Bundy seemed genuine but was absolutely amoral, able to lie without detection, guilt, or remorse.

Royal sat on the big leather chair behind his desk, leaned back, put up his feet, and motioned Fitzgerald to a chair in front of the desk.

"Senator, there are two things I have to check out about last night," Fitzgerald said, sitting on the edge of the chair and bracing his hands against Royal's desk. "First, we will need the tape from your answering machine for a voice comparison test with the tape that was given to Channel 3. I know you're aware of that tape."

"You're damn right I'm aware of that tape. And it got me to thinking about whether there is a black vendetta against Louisiana's congressional delegation. Or maybe against southern members of Congress. The voice on that tape on TV, well, it sounded like a *colored* voice to me."

"We have had the voice analyzed by the FBI lab, Senator. The lab says Caucasian."

Royal waved his hand in front of his face as if he were brushing away flies. "Some linguistic experts in white coats? *I* know a colored voice when I hear it."

"Even without the voice analysis, we decided the killer is more likely white than black," Fitzgerald said.

"What makes you jump to that conclusion?" Royal asked.

"It's not a jump, Senator. We have evidence that the person who killed Senator Bristow was very familiar with the Capitol."

"Lot of blacks fit that bill."

"More whites fit it."

"Well, the proof will be in the pudding, Chief. Whoever it is, I sure hope you get him." He paused. "What else can I do for you?"

"Senator, I am going to ask you some questions whose answers may be of a self-incriminating nature. You may want to defer answering them until you have an attorney present."

"Well now, Chief. It looks like this is going to be what I suppose is an *interrogation*. Okay. Fire away! I've got nothing to hide." A pause. "I don't believe you'll mind if I record this, will you?"

"No objection at all, Senator."

Royal reached into his top drawer, took out a small tape recorder, and inserted a microcassette. "Okay, Chief. We're on the record."

"Let's start with last night. You said the first call came about five o'clock."

"Right."

"Then, about eight o'clock you got that angry call at home because the man failed to find you in your office." Royal nodded and Fitzgerald continued. "So you called your office answering machine and got the message that he left." Royal nodded again. "Senator, tell me exactly how you did that."

"I call my office and when the answering machine responds, I dial—well, you know, hit three numbers, my identifying numbers, and the unit rewinds its tape and plays back the message. Simple as that."

"And you got the message about meeting at the pavilion?"

"Yes. Look, Chief, we went over all this last night."

Fitzgerald, glad to see some nervous response, looked up from his notebook and said, "Sorry, Senator. I'm trying to get this absolutely clear so there will be no misunderstandings. After all, you were at the scene of a murder and you and the victim did have serious differences about D.C. statehood."

Royal suddenly stood, started to say something, took a breath, and sat down. "There was nothing personal about those differences. She knew what I felt about statehood, and I knew what she felt."

"I am just pointing out, Senator, the circumstances that exist. That's why I want to get this tape matter absolutely clear. It's a key piece of evidence."

"Okay, Chief. I see your point. Maybe what we should do now is listen to the tape. I haven't touched it or the machine, by the way." He pointed to a beige tape machine on a small table next to the console phone on his desk. Every member had more than one phone. One was hooked into the House or Senate phone system and the other was a private phone connected directly to the C&P Telephone Company, which served the Washington area. Some members, particularly those on committees dealing with defense or intelligence matters, had still another phone, especially secured against tapping.

Royal's two phones were connected to the answering machine. He picked up one of the receivers, hit a button, and said, "Hold up all calls, Julie." Then he pointed to a rectangular button marked *playback*. He looked at Fitzgerald, who nodded. Royal hit the button. A beep came from the machine, then the sound of a spinning tape. Then silence and two more beeps. Royal punched *rewind*, waited for a beep, then hit *playback* again. A beep, silence. Then two beeps and silence.

"There's . . . there's no message," he said. "There's nothing." His face was as frozen as a mask.

"You are absolutely sure that this is the tape that was in the machine last night?"

Royal slouched back in his chair, his eyes on the answering machine. "I'm as sure of that as I am of anything else. I locked my door when I left last night"—he pointed to the thick wooden door to his private office—"and I unlocked it when I came in around eight o'clock this morning."

"Does anyone else have a key?"

"Craig has one. And I have this one." From a trousers pocket Royal fished out a key ring on a gold chain. "I told him that I always locked and unlocked the door to my private office at the House and I wanted to continue that here."

"Is he here?"

"I assume so."

"Call him in."

Royal picked up a phone, hit a button, and said, "Craig, please."

An instant later the door opened and Haverlin came in. He gave Fitzgerald an almost imperceptible nod and walked to the desk, facing Royal.

"One question, Haverlin," Fitzgerald said, "and then you can go about your business outside."

The aide looked questioningly at Royal, who pointed a silver letter opener toward Fitzgerald. Haverlin half-turned and said to Fitzgerald, "And what would that question be?"

"The tape in the senator's answering machine," Fitzgerald said. "Did you or anyone else change it since, say, three o'clock yesterday afternoon?"

Haverlin quickly looked back at Royal, who was studiously examining the letter opener, and then turned fully toward Fitzgerald. "No. I didn't change the tape. I don't do housekeeping chores like that, anyhow."

"Well, would whoever does do the chores around here have changed it?"

"I have given everyone, and I mean *everyone*, specific orders that no one sets foot in this office unless either the senator or I ask them in," Haverlin said, his voice strengthening. "As a matter of fact, I do believe that the senator himself handles most things that have to do with . . . with the immediate proximity of his desk."

"Thanks, Haverlin," Fitzgerald said. "You may go now."

Without turning to get Royal's approval of the order, Haverlin walked out of the office and closed the door behind him.

Royal dropped the letter opener onto the green blotter. The sun streaming through the window caught it for a moment, and a patch of reflected light played across his chin. "Well, Chief, it looks like my AA has tossed the mystery right back to me." He shrugged his shoulders and smiled. He seemed outwardly calm, and Fitzgerald wondered just how deep the composure went.

"As I am sure you can see, Senator, there are three possibilities," Fitzgerald said. "One, you were lying about the tape. Two, someone switched the tape. And three, it was erased, either by you, accidentally or on purpose, or by someone else."

"I'm not lying," Royal said in a low, calm voice.

207

"All right. So let's count on three being what happened. May I use your phone?"

Royal nodded. Fitzgerald hit Tolland's number, got the usual response, and said, "I have a tape here, from an answering machine. There may have been an erasure. Can the lab bring it up?" Fitzgerald twisted his head to read the make of the answering machine. "Panasonic, KX-F155. Yeah. One of those small ones. Microcassette? Right." As Fitzgerald spoke and then listened to Tolland's responses, he watched Royal's face. There was no change of expression. "Okay. I'll have an officer get it to you right away." He hung up, dialed another number, and ordered a patrol-car delivery of the tape to Tolland at FBI headquarters. When Royal heard "FBI," his expression did change: his eyebrows briefly lifted.

Fitzgerald returned to the chair in front of the desk and sat down. "Let's assume for the moment that the lab finds the erased message," he said. "And let's put aside for the moment how, if there was an erasure, it could have happened. That could mean that the murderer was luring you to the scene, that it was part of a frame." He paused, waiting for relief to play across Royal's face. It was still a mask. "But, Senator, we have several other matters to go over." He took his notebook from his pocket and flipped back three pages. "You say you did not hear a scream. Correct?"

"Correct. I heard nothing except, well, traffic noises, that sort of thing, until I saw that officer—Matthews?—come running up to the pavilion."

"Mathewson. Sergeant Mathewson. What exactly happened at that moment? What did Sergeant Mathewson say?"

"He said something like, 'A scream. Who's screaming?' Before I could answer, he flashed his light into the pavilion and—well, it was funny, but just in that quick flash you could see it was a body. He turned his light onto my face and said something like, 'Please stay here, Senator,' and he hightailed it to his car and ran right back. And we both just stood there until the other police, and then you, got there."

Fitzgerald continued writing for a moment after Royal stopped speaking. Then, with great deliberation, he put the notebook on the edge of the desk and reached into his uniform coat pocket. He took out the transparent plastic bag containing the Capitol Police badge. Royal looked at it curiously.

"This is a badge issued as a commemorative for the presidential inauguration," Fitzgerald said. "Recognize it?"

"Well, I know what those badges look like. Sure. Lots of members have them. One of your cop— one of your officers got one for me as a souvenir."

"Would you mind showing it to me, Senator?"

"Sure. I kept it right in my top drawer in my other office." He slid open the top desk drawer. "I think I just tossed it in there the day I got it, and like a lot of other stuff I accumulate, it just . . . I just never figured"—he slid the drawer out farther—"Well, I thought that I moved everything in that desk to this desk." He began rummaging through the items in the drawer and took out a small black leather case. "Damn. The goddamn badge, it was in this thing. Look." He tossed the case onto the top of the desk. "See the little holes? See where it was ripped? Goddamn. Now you're going to tell me . . ."

"Tell you what, Senator?"

"Tell me that goddamn badge there has something to do with . . . with what happened last night."

"This badge, Senator, was found at the scene by Sergeant Mathewson. There is a number on the back, and I am sure that this will enable us to trace it to the person it belonged to."

"Oh, I'm sure of that, Fitzgerald," Royal said. He stood, went to the window, and turned his back. Fitzgerald could see a faint reflection of his face. He was clenching his teeth, squinting. Then he spun around. "Christ! They're framing me. Can't you see that those fuckers are framing me?" A spray of spittle glistened in the shaft of sunlight streaming across the desk.

"And who would 'they' be, Senator?"

"You know fucking damn well who 'they' are. The liberals of Chocolate Town, my goddamn so-called new colleagues who don't want me in their club—that's who 'they' are."

Fitzgerald looked down at his notebook, then looked up, eyes locked on Royal's face. "Senator," he said quietly, "in your statement at the scene, you said that the voice on the phone had information that was not pertinent. I believe that it may well be pertinent."

209

"Well, we have a disagreement, then."

"Isn't it true that the man on the phone mentioned information regarding Julia Bristow?" Before Royal could answer, Fitzgerald lunged forward to ask, "And isn't it true that the man on the phone said he knew you were with Julia Bristow in her hideaway on the night she was murdered?"

"The phones! The goddamn phones are tapped!" Royal exclaimed, pounding his fist down on the desk. In an instant he realized what he had said, and his face paled. He fell back against the puffy black expanse of his high-backed chair.

"This is not from a phone tap, Senator," Fitzgerald said. "I was only assuming that the man on the phone knew something about you that we have recently learned. You were with Julia Bristow on the night of her murder. You had sexual intercourse with her on the couch in her hideaway, and you entered and left by the window, as you frequently did in the past."

Royal did not respond. He sat still, as if he were strapped into the chair.

"Senator," Fitzgerald began in his gentlest voice, "we can place you in that room on the night of April 6. We can show that you attempted to obstruct justice under the guise of stopping the Bristow autopsy. We can—"

Royal shot forward, stretched across the desk, grabbed a fistful of Fitzgerald's tie and shirt, and shouted, "Goddamn you! Goddamn you self-righteous son of a bitch!" He let go and slumped into the chair. "You don't understand. Where I come from, you don't let a black doctor touch a white woman, dead *or* alive."

"And where I come from, innocent people don't try to destroy evidence."

Royal ran a hand through his hair. He was regaining his cool demeanor. "And what evidence would that be, Fitzgerald?"

"Your sperm, Senator. Which you had reason to believe would be found in a vaginal smear during the autopsy."

"Jesus Christ!" Royal's right arm shot out and swept to the floor a marble slab adorned by a golden pelican, a clock, and a pen-and-pencil set with a golden plaque that said *Sportsman of the Year*. He did not seem to notice. "Jesus Christ!" he repeated. "You dirty-mouthed son of a bitch."

Fitzgerald stood. "You are out of control," he said, "and I will

210

not take advantage of your state. This conversation is over. I advise you to contact your lawyer and prepare a statement regarding your whereabouts on the evening of April 6 and *exactly* what happened last night."

He walked to the door, opened it, closed it quietly behind him, and walked through the outer office past the stares of staff members looking at him from their cubicles. *They'd better start updating their résumés,* he thought.

35

FITZGERALD consumed a sandwich, a candy bar, and two cups of coffee at his desk while he updated his computer file with a digest of the Royal interview. He was nearly finished when the phone rang.

Uncharacteristically, Lawson did not start with a friendly remark or a bit of small talk. "I thought you were going to call me," he began. "Well? I'm waiting."

"I need a few more minutes."

"I don't have a few minutes. Get over to my office as fast as you can." He seemed to hear himself for the first time. His voice slowed down. "Jeff, something has come up. It's *extremely* urgent."

"I'll be there in five minutes," Fitzgerald said.

A few minutes later an aide ushered Fitzgerald into the inner office of the majority leader's suite and then returned with a tray, which he placed on a small round table next to the chair Fitzgerald was sitting in. He poured Fitzgerald a cup of coffee, handed it to him, then fixed a coffee with cream for Lawson, who remained behind the desk.

Lawson waited for the aide to leave the room and close the door before saying, "I got some information a few minutes ago, Jeff. I called you right away. I wish I had gotten this from you."

"And what's the information, Senator?" Fitzgerald knew that it would be about Royal.

"That our new senator, Michael Royal, was at the scene of the murder last night. That you bundled him out of there. And that the media is poking around and trying to get this out." Lawson took a sip of coffee. "Well?"

There were times when Fitzgerald felt that he was an interchangeable part in the machinery of the Hill. *"Well?"* made him just another of the 20,000 people who made their living by bowing and scraping and answering to their 535 congressional masters. He had not yet drunk any of his coffee, and he decided, as an irrational gesture of protest, not to touch it.

"Yes, Senator Royal *was* found standing by the pavilion last night," he began, speaking slowly. "Yes, I did get him away from there, to protect him from whatever danger might still be present and from the media. And if the media are poking around"—he cherished his correct *are* to Lawson's *is*—"it's because somebody leaked this, just as somebody apparently leaked it to you. May I ask who told you?"

"You may ask, but I'm not going to tell you. The fact of the matter is that there's a firestorm building about a possible cover-up of the murders and their possible ties to statehood. That's what I'm looking at."

"Senator Royal is not a suspect," Fitzgerald hedged, then added unconvincingly, "not at this point." *I wonder if he knows about the badge.*

"I understand a badge was found. And what about that? It belonged to him."

"You're ahead of me on that one, Senator. I have not yet established positive identification on the badge."

"Well, I have. We're going to have to go public on this, Jeff. As I understand it, Royal's story doesn't hold up very well. And then there's the matter of that videotape."

"So somebody leaked that, too. As for Senator Royal's presence at the— just a minute, Senator. I just thought of something. May I use your phone?"

Fitzgerald stood, reached across a surprised Lawson, and hit five buttons to reach his communications center. "This is the chief. Get me Senator Royal on his private line." Lawson stood and began making gestures of protest. "Senator. This is Fitzgerald. Let me talk, please. You said a Senate page handed you a note saying that you had an urgent phone call. Yes. What did you do with that note? Yes. Yes. Thank you."

"What the hell was that all about?" Lawson asked.

Fitzgerald rapidly told Lawson what Royal had said about the phone call in the private lobby. He did not tell him about Royal's presence in Julia Bristow's hideaway. "I want to check Royal's desk," Fitzgerald said. "He said he thinks he tossed the note in there, or in the wastepaper basket under the desk."

"Jesus, Jeff!" Lawson said, his voice quivering with exasperation. "You've got two murders on your hands and you want to poke through garbage." He stood, walked to a window, and stretched out his hands, as if to embrace not only his suite of power but also the Senate and his ambitions beyond.

"I'm sorry," he said, sounding as if he meant it. "All this is weighing heavy today. I know that sounds pretentious as hell. But I mean real weight, something I can feel pushing me around, cuffing me. It's not power that we get here, Jeff. What we get is freight —all the burdens and blame that nobody else wants to wrestle with."

Fitzgerald waited a moment before he spoke. "I didn't tell you about Royal because I don't tell you or any other member about ongoing investigations. Michael Royal was at a murder scene, and that automatically makes him a target of the murder investigation. At this stage I can say, confidentially, that a pretty good case can be built against him. But I'm looking over the horizon, so to speak. I'm trying to make sure that an arrest will hold up and lead to a conviction."

Lawson looked at Fitzgerald as if he expected more words. When none came, he said, "Okay. I should have learned a long time ago to let the professionals handle this. I should have let the FBI in from the beginning." He walked back to the desk.

"How much time have I got before the FBI comes in?"

"I'd count on Monday, after the leadership meeting with the President."

"Well then, Senator, I'd better get to work."

Before Lawson could speak, Fitzgerald slipped out the door, his face flushed with anger. He had no doubt that Lawson's source was Mason. He could imagine Mason privately interviewing Mathewson, getting the information about Royal and the badge. Mason

213

had done it before, stepping in to show his power. Most of the time Fitzgerald had not cared. But now he wanted to be in charge, to show he could run a murder case, to show them all.

He glanced at his watch. He just had time to get back to the office and pick up the report he wanted to give Mason.

When he got there, he hurried past Margaret, telling her to get Phelan on the phone. He touched up his report, printed it out, and was putting it into one of his gray folders when his phone rang.

"Alix," he said. "Things are moving about the guy at the pavilion. Do you have those dates I asked you to get?"

"Yes, I have them," she said.

"Hold them tight. Don't talk to anyone about this. Got it?"

"Got it. When can I see you?"

"Let's say here in my office at five. But check with Margaret first. I've got to run." He hung up and headed out the door.

36

FITZGERALD recognized the signs of Mason's displeasure. The architect raised his left hand silently and pointed to the inquisitorial chair that had been placed in front of his desk. He kept his head down and did not speak. He looked up once, as if to speak, then looked down again, indicating that what lay before him on the desk was of far greater importance than the person who sat in the chair. Then, when he felt that he had inflicted enough discomfort, he looked up, placed his pen in the holder, and reached for the gray folder.

The report described the murder scene, including Royal's presence, but did not mention the badge, Fitzgerald's interview with Royal, or the evidence that put Royal in Julia Bristow's hideaway on the night of her murder.

Mason's eyes swept over the two single-spaced pages. "Thin, Fitzgerald. Very thin," he said, placing the report in the top drawer of his desk. "And deceptive." He let the word sink in, waiting for

Fitzgerald to say something, but Fitzgerald remained silent. "The badge, Royal's presence in Julia Bristow's hideaway, the semen identification—why are you holding all that back from me? I want an answer."

"I am not holding anything back. This is a report on an ongoing case. The information you mention—information that you got from someone other than me—is raw. I don't put raw data in a report like this. The badge, for example: I haven't identified its owner yet."

"Well, *I* have. It was quite simple." Mason reached into a side drawer of his desk and took out a piece of green-and-white computer printout and handed it to Fitzgerald. "I kept very complete records of those commemorative badges. As you recall, Inaugural officials gave a badge to each Capitol Police officer to wear during the ceremonies. There was a great demand for them, and another 457 were made. Most of them went to dignitaries and to members of Congress who requested them. The requests were channeled through my office. Each badge had a number. Look on that page and you will see that number 447 was issued to Representative Michael Royal."

Fitzgerald stared at the page, then handed it back to Mason. "You're one step behind the investigative process," he said. "That badge may have belonged to Royal, but when I talked to him a little while ago, he told me that it had been stolen. The leather case he kept it in was in his desk. The badge had been torn from it."

"And you believe that?"

"It isn't a matter of belief. It's a matter of building a case. An investigation is not based on belief. It's based on evidence, statements—incriminating information that can lead to a conviction. I'm not doing a character analysis of Royal, or of anybody else. I'm trying to solve two murders."

"Exactly!" Mason said harshly. Then, catching himself, he continued. "Look, Fitzgerald, you didn't ask for this. Your people are not up to this sort of thing. It was unfair to ask you to—"

"It's time to put cards on the table," Fitzgerald interrupted. "You're moving in on me. You've been talking to Mathewson and others. You've lost confidence in me, and the FBI's in the wings. So why the hell don't you just say so?"

215

Mason's expression feigned hurt, but he did not sound hurt when he spoke. "All right. The situation comes down to this: the only way to keep the White House from sending in the FBI is for you to arrest Royal right now—today. And if you want cards on the table, all right. What about your evidence that puts Royal in the hideaway? What about the FBI lab tests of Royal's semen?"

"Royal was having an affair with Julia Bristow," Fitzgerald answered. "But I don't see what it has to do with the murder. I have asked him to make a statement. I had intended to use the statement as leverage to get more information about what went on that night."

"Chief," Mason said with a smile, "it's time to do what you have to do. Royal must be arrested. There's a firestorm building."

Fitzgerald was not surprised to hear *firestorm* again. Obviously, Mason and Lawson were having back-alley talks. "There will be a worse firestorm if I arrest Royal and we can't make a case. I have a feeling, a gut feeling, that he's being set up. Give me until Tuesday. If I'm satisfied that Royal's our man, I'll arrest him by then. If I'm not, I'll hand the case over to the FBI and they can do what they want from then on." Fitzgerald stood. "Now I'd like to get back to work."

Mason put down his head and made a waving motion. Fitzgerald walked out.

37

AT FOUR O'CLOCK, Channel 3 began running promos for James Davis's regular Friday night show, "Washington Insider." Against a film clip showing Fitzgerald pushing someone into a police car, the promos asked a question—"Who is this mystery man?"—and answered it: "Get the name tonight on 'Washington Insider.'" The screen then showed the now familiar logo with blood dripping down the Capitol dome, and on the screen came the words "Murder on the Hill: New Revelations."

Shortly before five, Mason called Fitzgerald, told him about Davis's promise to reveal Royal's name, and again demanded that he arrest Royal. After a similar call from Lawson, Fitzgerald charged out of his office, telling Margaret over his shoulder, "When Lieutenant Phelan comes in, tell her to meet me at the pavilion." He had to get out in the air, away from the phones, away from the people who always knew what to do. He walked in lengthening strides to the pavilion. He had been there only a few minutes when Phelan's unmarked police car pulled up at the curb on Constitution Avenue. As she cut across the grass toward him, he remembered another bit of information he wanted.

"Have you heard about the Davis show?" she asked as soon as she reached him.

"Yes, goddamn it," he said. "Why am I the only person in Washington who didn't know about that show?"

"I guess you don't watch enough television," she said. "I found out about it from Davis. I was getting a statement from him about his talk with Gwenda Harris-Topping at the black leaders' reception. All of a sudden his camera crew popped in and filmed me with him. Then he started asking me about Royal, about the badge. I said I would not talk about an ongoing investigation. How did he—" Suddenly, as if she had just noticed the pavilion, she pointed to it and asked, "Why are we here? Is there something new here?"

They both ducked under the yellow crime scene tape woven through the trees. Fitzgerald stood facing the gate, which still hung ajar. Something in his expression drew Phelan's eyes to the gate.

"I came here to get away from the phone calls," he explained, turning his head slightly to look at her. "Everybody's on my a— my back. I don't trust the goddamn phones any more than Royal does." He took a step toward the gate. "It's like some kind of puzzle that someone designed for me to solve, but solve wrong."

He pushed the gate wider and went inside. In daylight the pavilion had the beauty of a grotto. The gravel path led to a brick archway framing a four-foot-high circular brick structure about six feet in diameter and topped by a deeply greened bronze plaque decorated with entwined vines and flowers. Around the wall were two drinking fountains and benches made of bricks. Beyond the circular structure was what had once been another entrance to the pavilion; it was now sealed by gleaming black iron grillwork. Over-hanging the outer wall was a tile roof, and deep in its shadows were other brick seats.

Phelan walked into the shadows. "Such a beautiful little gift of Olmsted's," she said. "The Hill was like a big backyard gone to seed until he came here. He designed this grotto—that's what he's supposed to have called it—as a retreat from the care of govern-ment. And now this." Her voice sounded sad, strained. She emerged from the shadows and sat next to Fitzgerald on one of the seats along the inner wall. He told her about the meetings with Mason and Lawson.

"I see two possibilities at this point," he concluded. "Either Royal is being set up, or he's made it *look* like he's been set up. So we're caught either way. We don't move on him because we think he's been set up. Or we do move on him, and in court his lawyers use a frame-up defense."

"You do think it's a setup, don't you?" Phelan asked.

Fitzgerald got up and walked over to the gate. "When you looked at the lock, you said something like 'Anybody with a paper clip could open it.' Had it been picked?"

"I'll have to double-check. It's in the evidence vault. But just looking at it hanging there, I thought it was an old lock that would be easy to open."

"Suppose it *was* open," Fitzgerald said. "Suppose someone for-got to lock the pavilion, or whoever killed her had a key."

"But Mathewson said it was broken," Phelan said.

"He may have made the same assumption you made. It was open, so it was broken."

Fitzgerald returned, sat down, and said, "Let's see the dates on the prostitutes." Phelan flipped through her notebook, found the page she wanted, and handed him the open book. He glanced at the page and said, "Two found on Sunday, killed on Saturday. One found on Monday, killed on Sunday. Weekend pattern. What else have you got?"

"Davis gave me a copy of the videotape in which he interviews Harris-Topping. I'm passing it along to Threat Assessment so they can look over the crowd for any known bad characters. Irish helped me track down the young woman who called Harris-Topping to the phone at the reception. She said it was a male voice. She's coming in later today to listen to the tape that Davis got after the first murder and compare the voices. She worked for Harris-Topping and worshipped her, so she's pretty broken up."

"What did Davis tell you about the show tonight?"

"Nothing much. I think he'll identify Royal. And from what I overheard of a producer's phone call, our esteemed mayor will also be on."

"For what?"

"Exposure, I suppose. Davis is a popular anchor in this town."

"Any idea of how he got the information?"

"No," Phelan replied. "He's fairly tight with the mayor, but I don't think he has any big contacts on the Hill."

Fitzgerald stood and stretched his arms. "He's got someone very much inside the case. But who? Mathewson and a couple of other officers at the scene knew Royal. Any of them could have leaked, though I don't know why." He took a step toward the gate. Phelan followed him. "But I told no one about the badge. Mason had to have learned that from Mathewson. So Mason probably somehow got the information to Davis to put more pressure on me to arrest Royal."

He looked up the Hill. The Capitol loomed through the trees. "Some town we have here, Alix. Everybody's either on a string or pulling one."

"Maybe," Phelan said, determined not to surrender to what she could see was Fitzgerald's darkening mood. "But there's still time for us to cut a few of them."

38

THE SHOW OPENED with the blood-on-the-Capitol logo fading into the film clip showing Fitzgerald pushing someone into a police car. Then the film was frozen, and superimposed on it was a C-Span clip of Michael Royal being sworn in as a United States senator. After he said, "I, Michael Thomas Royal," his voice faded away and the voice of James Davis came up: "Yes, Michael Thomas Royal, the new senator from Louisiana, the former Ku Klux Klansman, was the man who was found standing by the bleeding body of the godmother of D.C. statehood, Gwenda Harris-Topping." The image changed again, first to the resplendent delegate at the reception, then to the pavilion and the dark form lying within it.

Davis appeared in closeup, seated at his anchorman's desk. Mayor Lydell Mitchell was seated at his right. "We are here tonight," Davis said, "to try to find out why Senator Michael Royal was spirited away from the murder scene, why he was there in the first place, and why he was the last person known to see this woman—alive."

It was all so predictable, Fitzgerald thought. He sat before the TV set in his office, watching the show with Phelan. Davis asked the mayor what would have happened if a black man had been found standing near the body of a white woman. "Well, Jim," Mitchell answered, "he certainly wouldn't be shielded from the media. He'd be taken off to jail."

Once again Davis ran the film showing Fitzgerald pushing a man into a police car. The scene remained frozen behind Davis and Mitchell as they continued speaking.

Fitzgerald glanced away from the screen, then looked back intently and pointed to the freeze-frame. "Alix—that night. Running across the lawn, you got your feet wet, right?"

"Yes. The sprinklers were—"

"But look," Fitzgerald said. "Look at Royal's cuffs. And mine."

As the freeze-frame disappeared, she got an instant's look at the cuffs of Royal's tan suit. "They're dry. Yours are wet."

On-screen, Davis was back. "Yes," he said, "that is Chief Fitzgerald *personally* pushing Royal into the car. And when I asked the chief about that man—"

Fitzgerald was getting up to switch off the set when a huge image of an Inaugural badge filled the screen.

"The badge," he said, pointing at the image, "was in the wet grass. Royal couldn't have gone into that grass."

"He could have killed her somewhere else, put her there, changed his clothes, and come back," Phelan said.

As the show continued, Davis pointed to a window of Senator

Bristow's hideaway and told his audience that she and Royal had spent "her last night on earth together, first as lovers, and then? . . . Michael Royal is the last person known to have seen Julia Bristow alive. Now stand by for more about Senator Royal, and the murders of three District women."

As Davis faded from the screen, a shadowy videotape came on. In a series of jerky frames it showed a woman wearing a loosely tied red halter and a silvery microskirt approaching a car.

The show broke for a commercial, and in Fitzgerald's office the phone rang. It was Lawson.

"Jeff, I'm sure you've been watching Davis," he said. His voice sounded tightly controlled. "We've got to move. We've got to do something before this city explodes."

"Do what, Senator?" Fitzgerald asked. "What I'd like to do is haul that son of a bitch Davis in here and find out how he learned so much about an ongoing investigation."

"Forget Davis. You've got to arrest Royal. You have Sergeant Mathewson's report. You have that badge. You have motive. Royal is a *killer*, a man killing with immunity."

Lawson waited for a response. There was none.

"You can close this case," he continued. "You can give what you have to the U.S. attorney, and he can bring it before the grand jury. And we'll be done with this."

"I just don't like the feel of this, Senator. I—"

"I want him arrested *now*," Lawson cut in. "I want you to do it."

"I'm sorry, Senator. I don't have enough evidence to arrest him."

"Very well, Jeff. You force me to take other steps." He hung up.

The Davis show resumed with the flickering videotape. As the woman in the microskirt walked toward the car in extreme slow motion, Mayor Mitchell's voice provided the commentary, explaining how "a citizen" made the tape and "provided it to your District government. I have shared it with Jim Davis because it shows, better than any words I could speak, the contempt that our masters show for their plantation on the Potomac."

The camera veered to the car's Louisiana license plate. Then it rose to the open window on the driver's side. The smiling face of Michael Royal appeared. His lips moved and he leaned to open the passenger door. The screen filled with an enlargement of the time-and-date stamp on the lower right of the tape. *10:49 02/08.* "On this date," the mayor continued, "a young woman got into a car at Thomas Circle. She was found dead the next day. She had been strangled, stabbed, and mutilated, just like—"

"That's one of the dates, isn't it?" Fitzgerald said, turning to Phelan.

Without taking her eyes from the screen, she nodded. "The second one. Killed that night."

While the videotape ran again at normal speed, Davis read Metropolitan Police reports on the murders of the three prostitutes.

"They're tightening the noose, Fitz," Phelan said. "Before this show is over, they'll have you *and* Royal tried and convicted."

"And maybe they'll be right," Fitzgerald said.

Saturday, April 11

39

FITZGERALD ARRIVED at the majority leader's office suite at 8 A.M. He vaguely recognized the young, harried staff member who greeted him and took him to an anteroom outside Lawson's private office. "I'm Louise Duncan," she said. "The senator is in conference. He asked me to brief you on—"

"Spare me," Fitzgerald interrupted. He sat down in a gold-and-white-striped wing chair by a marble fireplace and picked up a copy of the *Congressional Record*. "What he actually told you," he said, "was to snatch me up and bring me here in case Jim Davis or some other media type crashed into the outer office and found me sitting there."

Louise Duncan did not indicate that she had heard. "The senator," she repeated, "asked me to brief you on legal questions regarding the arrest of a member of Congress." She took a sheet of paper from a file folder she carried and, glancing down, said, "As you know, a member has constitutional immunity from arrest while Congress is in session 'and in going to and returning from the same.' But an arrest of a member can be made—"

"Just a minute, Miss Duncan," Fitzgerald said. "Who says there's going to *be* an arrest? As far as I know—"

The door to the private office opened and Lawson emerged with the minority leader, two other senators, and two staff people. They all wore the standard uniform of Washington officials called in to duty on a Saturday: crisp chinos and well-pressed sports shirts. The uniform supposedly signaled to TV-viewing constituents that some weekend recreational activity had been interrupted by the call to service. The Saturday toilers walked past Fitzgerald and Duncan as if no one were in the room.

Lawson stopped at the outer door, said his goodbyes, closed the door, and turned to Fitzgerald and Duncan. "Okay," he said, "let's go in." He briskly led them into his office and pointed to chairs in front of his desk. Standing behind his desk and leaning on his chair, he said, "Louise here will be handling the press on this, Jeff, so I decided to have her sit in on some of it. Any problem?"

"The only problem I have, Senator, is with the presumption, which you raised in a phone call last night, that I am going to arrest Senator Royal and charge him with murder. I told you then and I tell you now that I can't do that on the evidence I have."

"The Davis show last night speeded up the timetable. Once he put out the name and the business about the badge and that video-tape, we had no choice but to move on Royal. This town can go up in flames. Congress giving sanctuary to a murderous Klansman? I've been on the phone with the leaders of the Black Congressional Caucus, and they're holding it together for as long as they can. They talked to Mayor Mitchell, and he talked to me. I told him an arrest was imminent."

Fitzgerald looked up, stunned. "Imminent?"

"Well, tomorrow. But I didn't tell him that. We need a buildup. I contacted Bill Mason late last night and through him got a Capitol Police surveillance unit watching Royal's house. They're camped out there with the media right now. Royal's in his house. I'm going on 'Face the Nation' tomorrow morning and will go public with a hint of an arrest. That will build the pressure on Royal. We'll—"

"Wait a goddamn minute. The surveillance unit was put on without checking with me?" Fitzgerald asked. "What the hell is going on?"

"Things are moving quickly, Jeff. Mason called the watch commander and got the surveillance people there." He was speaking rapidly, and Fitzgerald felt like a bound-and-gagged body thrown into a deluge of words and deals.

"Mason also tells me that your Threat Assessment people have traced some vicious pieces of mail Julia Bristow's office got just before her murder. The mail threatened a lynching—well, a 'media lynching,' but still a lynching. It came from some outfit set up by one of Royal's leading supporters. So let's get that into your statement at the press conference."

He paused for an instant and looked at Duncan. "Okay, Louise. Start taking notes for the background we'll need at the press conference." Then he turned to Fitzgerald and began speaking rapidly again. "I've talked to Roy Koch and got a legal opinion: the Capitol Police, as a creature of Congress, cannot empower one of its officers to arrest a member of Congress. So that will be your out."

"What do you mean, my out?"

"Simple, Jeff. We'll follow Koch's suggested procedure. I call in the Senate sergeant-at-arms and he takes Royal and delivers him to FBI agents waiting outside the chamber. All you have to do at the press conference is say you turned the evidence on Royal over to the FBI—notice you say 'evidence' and not 'case'—and on the advice of your police counsel you've had the arrest made by the Senate sergeant-at-arms."

"Pretty simple," Fitzgerald said.

Lawson nodded.

"But," Fitzgerald added, "I'm not going to be speaking at any press conference."

He unpinned his badge from his uniform coat and put it on Lawson's desk. Then he stood, reached under his coat, and unholstered his .38. After deftly removing the bullets, he placed them and the gun next to the badge. "Call an officer and have him take custody of the gun and rounds," Fitzgerald said. "It's against the law to have an unauthorized gun in the Capitol." He took a step toward the door. "I'll get a formal letter to you before the end of the day."

"What should I say in the release?" Duncan, unperturbed, asked him.

"Just keep it simple," Fitzgerald replied. "Say I resigned because I had stomach problems. I wanted to throw up."

He walked out the door, leaving it open, and headed down a hallway leading to an exit from the Senate wing. He stopped suddenly at the entrance to the Senate reception room, just outside

the chamber, where senators often rendezvoused with constituents. There, amid the splendor of Brumidi frescoes, gilded walls,
and glittering chandeliers, was Irish Lunigan. Arms outstretched,
white mane bobbing, he was showing four well-dressed tourists
around the room. "At our feet are nineteenth-century Minton tiles,
whose intricate patterns in blue, red, and cream—"

"Irish!" Fitzgerald called into the room. Irish, a rare look of
irritation on his ruddy face, turned, saw who had called, and, turning back to his visitors, said gravely, "Excuse me, ladies and gentlemen. Senate business."

He hurried to the open doorway and grasped Fitzgerald's forearm while shaking his hand. The onlookers got the impression that
he was meeting someone he had not seen for a long time. "Jeff!"
he boomed. "You look like you need help. What can I do?"

"Irish, I've got to go into the chamber."

"No problem." He strode back to the other end of the room,
apologized to the visitors, went to a highly polished mahogany
desk that stood beneath a gilt-framed portrait of Senator Robert A.
Taft, and phoned for an assistant to take over. Then he returned to
Fitzgerald and pointed to the place where the badge had been on
Fitzgerald's uniform coat. "So it's another badge lost?"

"That's right, Irish. You'll find out all about it at Lawson's next
press conference."

"When they get the Senate SAA to collar Senator Royal?"

"News travels fast around here."

"Just a guess, Jeff. Just a guess. Now, what can I do for you?"

They walked out of the reception area and into the corridor. To
their right were the double doors leading to the Senate chamber.
Irish opened one of these and motioned Fitzgerald in.

"I want to see Senator Royal's desk, Irish."

The chamber was empty. Above, clusters of tourists filed in and
out of the galleries, passing through wooden double doors flanked
by niches containing marble busts of early Vice Presidents. Irish,
an authority on Senate lore and history, pointed up and said,
"They come and they go—the tourists and the Veeps."

He led Fitzgerald to a desk in the third row to the right of the
rostrum. Like all of the other desks, it was equipped with an inkwell, a pen holder, and a crystal shaker for dispensing blotting
sand. "One Bristow, another Bristow, now Royal. This is going to

get to be a very historic desk," he said. "It's one of the originals, you know, bought for thirty-four bucks apiece when they renovated the chamber after the British burned the Capitol in 1814." He swung open the hinged top, exposing a drawerlike box. "They added these writing boxes in the 1830s." He stepped back and Fitzgerald looked inside.

"What are these, Irish?" Fitzgerald asked, pointing to names written or carved on the bottom of the drawer: *John W. Bricker, Karl E. Mundt, Marlow W. Cook, Charles C. Bristow.*

"Previous occupants," Irish said. "It's a tradition that goes back to early in this century, maybe before." He hesitated for a moment, then took a ballpoint pen and printed *Julia Bristow.* "I guess she kept postponing doing it." He turned to Fitzgerald. "Looking for anything special?"

"Just a piece of paper," Fitzgerald replied. The desk contained a book on Senate rules, two yellow pads, two ballpoint pens, an open package of Wrigley's chewing gum, a crumpled Milky Way wrapper, a week-old copy of the *Times-Picayune* sports section. But no note from a Senate page.

Angry and frustrated, Fitzgerald turned away, bumping Irish, who was about to hand him a pamphlet on the history of Senate desks. The pamphlet dropped, and Fitzgerald, embarrassed, stooped to pick it up. As he reached for it, he felt a draft coming from a grille set in one of the risers that form the broad levels of the well of the Senate. He looked up, and before he could ask about the draft, Irish said, "That's part of the chamber's original air-conditioning system. There's a tunnel that runs under the grounds, and—"

Under the grounds, Fitzgerald thought. *Underground.* "Take me to it," he said.

"What?"

"Take me to it, to the tunnel. I've got to see it."

Irish looked at the glint in his eye and said, "It's Saturday. I'll have to track down Jerry Sumter."

"Thanks," Fitzgerald said. "But don't use any Capitol phones. Possible?"

"More than possible. I'll just go over to my house and phone his house. If he's not home, believe me, then he's here, and I'll track him down discreetly. Where will you be?"

"I've got to go back to my office and start packing. Then I'll be heading home. Stop off there and leave a message with Mrs. Darwin about Sumter. Tell him not to mention this to anybody. Think he'll go along?"

"Have no fear. I'll let him think it's a hush-hush security matter."

"Well, Irish, it is."

40

FITZGERALD did not want to make phone calls from any Capitol building, so he walked to the Monocle and found a pay phone. He called Phelan at home and told her where he was. Standing just inside the Monocle's door, he watched the street, waiting for her to drive past. The Capitol Police headquarters and its parking lot were next door.

She saw his furtive wave from the corner of her eye, did not acknowledge it, drove into the lot, and parked her car. Fitzgerald could see her enter the glass entrance door, drop off the keys, and check in with the officer on duty. Then she cut across the lot to the Monocle. Fitzgerald stepped into the vacant bar, where a waiter who had arrived at work early looked at him in surprise.

Phelan slipped onto a stool next to him and said, "What's going on?" Then her eyes fell upon the empty spot on Fitzgerald's jacket.

"You're looking at an ex-chief of Capitol Police," he said. He told her what had happened in Lawson's office. "But I think I'm on to something, and I've got to keep going."

"What can I do?"

"Well, to keep your job, report to Mason. Do what he tells you to do. I assume he'll just want you to get everything ready to turn over to the FBI. As I said, they're planning to arrest Royal, probably tomorrow. Lawson will have to line up senators to support him, and that means a lot of phone calls and meetings."

"I figure that one thing you want is Mathewson's personnel file," she said. "I've already checked the roll call. He's off-duty today and tomorrow."

"You're ahead of me on that. Finding that badge, hearing that scream: I've got to find out about him, talk to him, even if I don't work next door anymore. And another thing. When you talk to Mason, tell him you consider that videotape of Royal and the prostitute important evidence. Better still, see if you can get Roy Koch to subpoena the original from Davis or Mayor Mitchell. I'm sure now that what we've got in the evidence vault is a copy."

"With a patched-on date?"

"Right. I assume that the FBI lab can prove the date's a phony add-on."

The waiter drifted in and went behind the bar. "We're closed, you know," he said. "But look, if it's a quick eye-opener you want—"

Fitzgerald laughed his first laugh of the day. "No thanks, friend. One of us is on duty."

"We've got to figure a way to keep in touch," Phelan said when the waiter left. "No phones, even pay phones."

He told her about Irish and the tunnel. "I have no idea what I'm going to find," he said. "But I'm going there."

"After the tunnel, back to the house?"

"I don't think so. There's a chance somebody will be watching it. Irish has a tiny office just behind the Senate reception room. I'll wait for you there, and we'll figure out what to do next."

Fifteen minutes after Phelan left the Monocle, Fitzgerald walked into the main entrance of headquarters. The murder of Gwenda Harris-Topping served to throw gasoline on the city's burning emotions over the statehood filibuster. Fitzgerald had ordered his force to remain at full staffing levels over the weekend. He started to sign the visitors' register, but the embarrassed duty officer, who had obviously heard the news, pulled it away from him and gruffly said, "You're the *chief* until somebody tells me otherwise."

By the time he got off the elevator on the top floor, word had passed through the building. About a dozen officers and civilians were standing at the door when he opened it. They all began talking at once, lamenting, complaining, swearing. He walked through them, shaking hands with the men, getting kissed by the women, and all he could say, over and over again, was "Thanks, thanks, thanks."

He hesitated as he approached Margaret's desk. She had been crying, and now, looking up at him, she burst into tears again. She came from behind her desk, threw her arms around his neck, and kissed him square on the lips.

"What will your husband say, Margaret?" Fitzgerald asked when she let him go.

"Mr. Retired Fireman, the TV fan?" she said with a jut of her chin. "I don't give a damn what he'll say. This is a rotten day, Chief. I've already put in my papers. I know I'll never work for a finer man, so I'm taking the pension."

"That's damn rash. I don't know what to say."

"You've said enough with the look on your face, Chief." She glanced over her shoulder, then, lowering her voice, said, "Irish stopped by a minute ago. He said to tell you 'two o'clock in front of Taft.' That's all he'd say."

"Thanks, Margaret. Now I've got to write Mason a letter, with copies to the SAAs and Lawson. Any word from him?"

"Not a word. Ted Ringle was the first to hear, I guess. He called to say that the local AP wire had a story that was speculating on your . . . your—"

"Getting canned."

"—on your forced resignation. Then a couple of minutes ago he called to say there was an advisory on the AP Hill wire saying that Lawson would be making an important announcement tomorrow when he's on 'Face the Nation.' Ted wants you to call him right away. He said the queries are building up."

"I'll bet they are. I've got nothing to do but clean out a desk and write a letter. Tell him he can drop by anytime."

Ringle wheeled in a few minutes later. They prepared a press release that simply said that Fitzgerald had resigned.

"You're getting a raw deal on this, Chief," Ringle said as they shook hands at the door.

"Well, all it is, Ted, is that I lost my job. It's not the first time."

41

BETWEEN taking phone calls and visits from well-wishers, Fitzgerald worked at his computer, transferring all the murder files
from the hard disk to floppy disks, which he put into his briefcase,
along with the Dake file from the locked drawer. Then he erased
and reformatted his hard disk, obliterating all information that had
been on it. He put his uniform cap in his private drawer and
scooped his few personal possessions into the briefcase.

He said his final goodbye to Margaret and, slipping into the
stairwell, managed to leave headquarters with a minimum of handshakes and hugs. Carrying his uniform coat over his shoulder, he
walked home. He had expected to feel regret or anger as he
trudged this familiar route, but he walked confidently, head up,
strides long, surprised at his exhilaration. At the mythological fountain outside the Library of Congress, he stopped and enjoyed the
cool mist hovering in the air. He smiled at a tonsured, brown-robed
young man passing out leaflets about redemption through medita-
tion. "Bless you, sir," the young man said, and Fitzgerald replied,
"And bless you, too."

Mrs. Darwin was standing in the hallway when he entered the
house. Somehow she had heard what had happened.

"You fought the good fight," she said.

"I'm still fighting it," he said, following her when she beckoned
him into her apartment. She had laid two places for lunch. In the
center of the table was a bottle of wine and a bowl of one of her
specialties, Peking chicken salad. He started to ask her how she
had known he would be coming home at lunchtime, smiled to
himself, and decided not to ask.

"A very genial gentleman named Irish stopped by," she said
when they sat down. "He said to tell you—I hope I've got this
right—that Mason has fired Koch for saying that an arrest of Royal
will not hold up in court. I asked him to write it down, but he said,
'No paper, no phones' or something like that. Mysterious doings."

"Maybe dangerous ones, too," Fitzgerald said. "Don't let any-one into the house, no matter what their story, except Irish and Alix. Don't say anything about the murders on the phone. But it will be over soon. I think things are coming to a head."

"So do I, Jeffrey," she said, laying her hand on his. "There *is* danger, deadly danger."

"Maybe, Mrs. Darwin," he replied with a smile, "it would be better to talk about what kind of season you think the Orioles will have."

Shortly before two, Fitzgerald, in jeans and a plaid sports shirt, walked into the Senate reception room. He was still carrying his briefcase. Irish and a young woman were seated at the desk under the portrait of Senator Taft. Standing off to the side, admiring the gilded frescoes, was the chief engineer, Jerry Sumter, who turned his head when Fitzgerald entered. Sunlight streaming through a north window reflected off his gold-rimmed glasses, momentarily glazing his stare.

Irish whispered something to his assistant, stood, and with a nod of his head led Fitzgerald out of the room and toward a cross-corridor that led past the old Senate chamber and the Rotunda. Walking behind them at a discreet distance was Sumter. They descended a staircase to the crypt beneath the Rotunda and went past the massive columns thrusting from the black stone floor, past the iron gates before the tomb intended for George Washington. Irish, ever the historian and guide, pointed to the darkness beyond the gates. "Inside there," he said, "is the catafalque that held Lincoln's coffin. And Jack Kennedy's."

Down a side corridor, he opened an unmarked door at the head of a stone stairway. A few steps down, they waited for Sumter. "I've told Jerry this is off the record," Irish whispered. "He's all engineer, you know. No nonsense."

The door opened and Sumter appeared. He closed the door behind him and walked down to the step above them. "Irish tells me you're interested in our underground," he said, shaking hands with Fitzgerald.

"That's right, Jerry. I'd like the fifty-dollar tour."

They filed down the stairs to a low-ceilinged passageway lined with unmarked doors. "Supply rooms, mostly, along here," Sumter said. He stopped at one of the doors, snapped a key ring from several dangling from his belt, unlocked the door, and switched on a light.

The room was small and longer than it was wide. Along one of the walls was a wooden bench. Over it were several metal cabinets, out of which ran silvery, wrist-thick conduits. "This is one of my outposts," Sumter explained. He swung an arm toward the cabinets. "I share it with some of the power hodgepodge down here." A government-issue metal chair with worn green armrests stood in front of an old, scarred wooden desk, on the top of which rested a computer, a telephone console, and a wooden tray full of papers.

"Where *are* we?" Fitzgerald asked.

"It's easier to show you than tell you," Sumter said. He flicked on the computer and, after touching a few keys, brought up a menu. Looking over his shoulder, Fitzgerald saw a file named XRAY. "Mason's Capitol cutaway show," he said, surprised.

"Right," Sumter said. "Use it all the time. Here it comes." His fingers flitted over the keyboard, and the Capitol image began gyrating. Sumter stripped back the roof and the first floor and brought up a schematic, three-dimensional view of the Senate underground. He touched two keys to create a yellow, translucent rectangle.

"We're here," he said, "and the tunnel is here." A labyrinth of corridors peeled away. "We'll be entering from a door along here." The corridors returned. He turned to look at Fitzgerald, who seemed to be absorbed in what he saw—on the screen or somewhere. "What's up?" Sumter asked softly.

Without moving or changing his expression, Fitzgerald said, "Can you find me Room EF100 in the Capitol?"

"Sure," Sumter said. Irish, who had plumped down on the wooden bench, looked up sharply, walked over to the desk, and leaned over his shoulder.

The images reeled around again, and a long, richly decorated Senate corridor appeared. "Here's Room EF100," Sumter said, moving the yellow rectangle to a doorway. "Where now?"

"Take that yellow tag to the tunnel." The rectangle moved swiftly along the route the three men had taken. "Stop!" Fitzgerald said. "Stop at the crypt." He stared at the screen and seemed to be speaking to it. "She gets a phone call—a call so urgent that

235

she's pulled from the reception. What did he say? What would lure her? 'I've got something that will guarantee statehood.' A document, maybe a videotape. Maybe a threat: 'I'll kill X or Y or Z if you don't come.' He says something that convinces her. Maybe identifies himself. He tells her to meet him—or maybe someone who will lead her to him—at the crypt. She goes there and meets someone she recognizes or trusts. He explains that he cannot disclose the information in the open. So he takes her . . ."

Sumter, caught up in Fitzgerald's narrative, moved the rectangle to the door leading to the stone stairway. "Even if she's suspicious, she still follows," Fitzgerald continued. "Even if her trust is waning, she still goes. She gets to this corridor." The rectangle moved to the door of the room they were in. "He leads her to the entrance to the tunnel." The rectangle stirred. Fitzgerald's left hand came down hard on Sumter's right shoulder. "Damn! Where does that tunnel lead?"

"Lead?" Sumter asked. "Well, it goes out under the grounds, under the west, well, the northwest side. And then it just stops. I think we'd better look at it."

He shut down the computer, picked up the phone, and punched a number that Fitzgerald recognized: the Capitol Police communications center. "Sumter here," he said. "Request a turn-off of detector 14W." He waited a moment, then said, "Thanks."

"What was that about?" Fitzgerald asked.

"There's an intruder-presence alarm down there. If it's not turned off and you go down there, the comm center responds awfully fast, with a CERT team, the whole works. But I guess you know that. We've got intruder-presence alarms in the unpatrolled tunnels, like the one we're going to. Stirred-up dust will set them off. Gas, chemicals. Anything that could be introduced into the tunnels and enter the House or Senate chambers through the old air-conditioning system."

"You can't just turn off the alarm from here, right?"

"Right. It's tied to the comm center. You just request a turn-off of a detector and they do it from there." He took a flashlight out of the desk and turned toward the door. "Let's go."

Fitzgerald left his briefcase with Irish and followed Sumter. They hurried down the passageway to a locked door, which Sumter unlocked using one of his key rings. The door opened into darkness. Chill, moist air swept past them. Sumter switched on the light, which feebly lit a metal platform connected to the top of a spiral staircase. As he started toward the staircase, Fitzgerald touched his arm.

"Hold it just a minute, Jerry. Can I borrow the light?"

He shone the light along the door jamb. There was no sign of forced entry. "Who has keys to this door?" he asked.

"Truth?" Sumter asked. "I have no idea how many. For starters, there's a set of keys for all the corridor doors in that police cubby-hole down near the architect's office. The one that had the fire? And officers on regular patrol usually have sets. I used a specific key for this door, but the truth is, these doors are so old that most of them will open with the same basic key."

Fitzgerald got down on his knees and methodically examined the platform. He ran the beam of light along the railing that extended from the door to the staircase.

"Looking for anything in particular?" Sumter asked.

"I'm not sure what I'm looking for. Wait." He pointed the beam toward a stretch of railing clear of dust. "How often does anyone come in here?"

"Depends. I don't get here that much. Until recently, I hadn't been in this tunnel for . . . what? three, four months. I've sent electricians around lately to work on the gremlins that have been making my life a living hell. I'm usually in here Saturdays now, and lots of times on Sundays."

Fitzgerald crawled along the platform to the staircase, scrutinizing every inch under the flashlight's beam. On the top step he found what he was looking for. "Watch where you step, Jerry," he said softly. He stood and aimed the beam at what looked at first like a streak of rust. But the brownish stain gleamed dimly in the light. "We'll need to scrape that and send it to the lab. But I'm sure I know what it is." He looked over the rail to the brick floor of the tunnel, about twenty-five feet below. "It started here and ended there."

Fitzgerald handed the flashlight to Sumter and followed him down the winding stair, their footsteps clanging and setting off a faint echo below. They stepped into a blackness that seemed to engulf them. Sumter shone the light down the tunnel. The beam cut into the blackness and stopped as if it had struck a solid block of dark.

Sumter took a step toward a light switch. "Don't move," Fitzgerald said. "I don't want anything disturbed."

Sumter handed him back the flashlight without a word, and Fitzgerald crouched near the bottom stair, training the beam over the brick floor. He inhaled sharply in a kind of gasp that jolted Sumter. "She landed here," Fitzgerald said, half to himself. "There was brick dust on her dress, but the assumption was that it came from the pavilion."

At Fitzgerald's request, Sumter stepped around the blood-stained bricks and went to the light switch. The darkness turned to a dusky gloom as a string of dim lights clicked on. Each dangled from a cable that ran the length of the brick-lined tunnel, which looked to be about one hundred yards long. Sumter pointed to a spindly-legged tripod holding a short tube aimed down the tunnel. Wires ran from the tube down one leg of the tripod, along the floor to the wall, and into a cable. "That's one of the intruder-presence detectors," he said. "You'll see a couple more between here and the end of the tunnel."

"I don't see how this worked as an air-conditioning system," Fitzgerald said. He was sweeping the flashlight beam along the walls and the floor, which inclined slightly downward.

"Way back, before the Civil War, horse-drawn wagons hauled big chunks of ice in summer to a shaft at the end of the tunnel," Sumter said. "Slaves hauled the ice deeper into the tunnel and worked big canvas fans that sent cool air up the tunnel and into the Senate chamber. Later on, up until about 1912, there was a steam-driven, paddlewheel-style fan near the shaft to push the cool air rising from the ice." He pointed to a perpendicular shaft almost directly over their heads. They could see a dot of light at the top of the shaft. "That's light from the chamber, coming through the grillwork in the steps. That's where you felt the draft of cool air."

"Who knows about this?" Fitzgerald asked.

"Well, I guess just about all of us in engineering and mainte-nance. But even the few people who know about these tunnels avoid them. They say a couple of slaves died down here, and there's talk of ghosts. I didn't pay much attention to that, or to the history. To me, this is just another source of headaches."

"Why?"

They had gone about halfway along the tunnel, Fitzgerald judged. Sumter nodded toward clusters of big silvery pipes that seemed to burst through the wall. "Some of the electrical power from the outside world—we get Pepco power, just like everybody else—comes in through those conduits. Lately they've been the source of a lot of our troubles. That's why I've been recommending that we do a major overhaul."

He went up to one of the conduits, which ran along the wall about four feet up from the floor. "See those patches?" He pointed to lengths of cable that looped between holes in the conduits. "We had to run new wiring around stretches of old wiring that went bad. And that made the wiring even more vulnerable. Some of the cables hanging out like that have been cut and then rewired so carefully that the cuts are hard to find. That's been the source of a lot of the electrical problems."

"Deliberately cut? Sabotage?" Fitzgerald asked. "Why haven't you—"

"Why haven't I done anything about it?" Sumter said. "Well, I hate to bring up an embarrassing matter, Jeff. But the fact is, I *have* reported it. Nothing's been done about it. Except, of course, for the investigation that Sergeant Mathewson's been making." They resumed walking.

"Mathewson? He's in CERT. And I've never heard of any sabotage investigation. Who did you report this to?"

"Well, to my boss, Captain Mason. And I just assumed—"

"Goddamn it, Jerry, I never . . . What's that?" The last ceiling light dimly illuminated a brick wall directly in front of them.

"End of the line," Sumter said. "That's the shaft that was used for dumping the ice down and bringing the slaves in and out. It's been closed up since before my time." In the middle of the brick shaft was a wooden door. On the door frame hung a broken padlock.

"Jesus!" Fitzgerald exclaimed. "Another tunnel. Where does this one come out on the surface?" His heart was racing, for he felt he knew the answer.

"At a little pavilion on the grounds—you know, where Gwenda Harris-Topping was found."

"None of your men ever go into that shaft?"

"When we come down here—and we usually don't come down here much—we just check up to that point back there where the Pepco conduits come in. We have no need to go any farther."

"Can you get back without the flashlight?" Fitzgerald asked.

"Sure. Why?"

"I'm going out this way," Fitzgerald said, touching the door.

Sumter hesitated for a moment. "Well, all right," he said. "In case you can't get out that way, I'll leave the hall door unlocked." He turned and began walking rapidly down the tunnel.

Fitzgerald wrapped his handkerchief around his hand, pulled open the thick wooden door, and shone the light around. The shaft was shaped like a silo, with a squared-off section to accommodate the door. Piercing the darkness, Fitzgerald saw a steep, narrow stone staircase, the slaves' passageway. Each movement of the flashlight revealed another blot of blood on a stair.

He entered and slowly ascended, his mind's eye seeing Harris-Topping's body being dragged up the stairs that had been used by so many of her people. The shaft was about twelve feet in diameter and twenty-five feet high. Something metallic grazed his head at the top. He ducked and saw what he assumed to be the circular bronze plaque that capped the brick structure in the center of the pavilion. Olmsted must have made the old brick shaft the core of the pavilion, then sealed it with the decorated bronze plaque.

A broken lock lay on the second step from the top. Shining the light around the edge of the plaque, he saw a hasp that had been crudely welded onto it. The loop of the hasp curved out from an iron plate set into the brick. He imagined the killer putting the body on a stair, breaking the lock, and then pushing the plaque away.

With his handkerchief draped over his hands, Fitzgerald pushed upward. The plaque gave way easily. Carefully getting a grip with one shrouded hand, he slid it sideways, raised his head, and breathed in the warm spring air. A startled mockingbird flew out of a drinking fountain. Fitzgerald slipped out of the shaft, replaced the plaque, and trotted up a path to the Capitol.

He entered the Senate side at the tourist entrance. The two officers on duty looked at him curiously as he put the flashlight on the conveyor belt of the X-ray machine and walked through the

240

metal detector. When he picked up the flashlight and hurried off to the Senate reception room, he heard one of the officers say to the other, "Wasn't that the chief?"

42

IRISH TOOK Fitzgerald to his cubbyhole off the reception room. "All you need is here, Jeff: telephone, TV, refreshments." He pointed to a small refrigerator and a shelf with a coffeemaker and cups. "If you want me, I'm right outside the door."

"Thanks, Irish. I think I'll make some coffee. And I need some more help. Can you bring someone here for me?"

"Sure. I'll get someone to take over for me in a jiffy. And then would you want me to track down Lieutenant Phelan for you?"

Fitzgerald grinned. "You're always one step ahead, Irish. Yes. Go to Margaret—"

"A fine woman. And you want me to ask her to direct me to Lieutenant Phelan, without using a phone, and get her over here? Is that it?"

"That's it," Fitzgerald said, and Irish slipped out of the door, closing it noiselessly.

Twenty minutes later he opened the door, silently ushered Phelan into the cubbyhole, and closed the door behind her.

Fitzgerald recounted what he had found in the tunnel, then asked, "Anything come in from Tolland?"

"A messenger delivered it to me a couple of hours ago."

"Great. I needed it yesterday," Fitzgerald said.

"Well, it's a preliminary report, Tolland said. The lab technicians lifted ghosts of words from Royal's tape and amplified them. I took notes from the report and then put it in another case's files in the evidence room." She flipped through her notebook. "There were three messages on the tape. One said, 'Michael. Julia. Call me, you bad boy.' The second was 'Senator, Craig. It's the Baton Rouge people. Senate dining room at 1 P.M.' We'll be able to pinpoint those messages to specific times. They also found the come-

241

to-the-pavilion message—same thing, by lifting ghost words. They found an electronic pulse that shows that the messages were erased not by pressing the button on the answering machine itself but by sending a signal over the phone line."

"So it could have been erased by Royal or by someone else."

"Right. Provided someone else knew the phone's remote-control code. And there's more. The speaker on the phone did not use the word *pavilion*. He hesitated and said, 'The little brick place, you know, near Constitution Avenue.' Sound familiar?"

Fitzgerald looked puzzled.

"Mathewson," Phelan said. "At the scene. He didn't say *pavilion* until you did, unconsciously prompting him."

"Jesus! So Mathewson is the voice on the tape?"

"Could be. It would be easy to get a snippet of comm center tape with his voice on it and get the FBI lab to see if it matches the voice on the answering machine tape—and on that tape that Davis got."

"Did you get Mathewson's personnel file?"

"No. It's been cleaned out."

"What happened to it?"

"It's obviously been pulled. I tried the computer. Same thing. He's been wiped out of the computer, too."

"He must be planning to bolt. Do we know his address?"

"There's a duty roster in the CERT ready room with phone numbers. I put his through the D.C. crisscross directory and got the address. Eleventh Street, just off East Capitol."

"I've got to see him, question him," Fitzgerald said.

"How will you handle it?" Phelan asked. "You're just a concerned citizen now, you know."

"I'm the citizen, you're the cop. We talk to him, and when he's finished talking, you arrest him. Let's go."

"Wait a minute. Arrest him for what? What have you got on him?"

Fitzgerald thought for a moment. "You have a friend in the comm center. See if they keep a record of who asks to have that detector system in the tunnel turned off. It's called 14W."

"I'm off. Are you staying holed up here?"

"Yes. Goddamn it, I wish we could use phones."

Phelan returned about half an hour later, breathless and clutching a computer printout.

"Luckily, Cathy was on duty. That made it simple. I told her what I wanted without telling her what I wanted it for. It turns out there was a log for turning off good old 14W. When someone asks for the turn-off to go into the tunnel, the comm center puts the requester's name and the time in the log. And in the past five months, the name found on the list most frequently is . . ." She dramatically flipped the computer printout, which unfolded like an accordion. "Sergeant Fred Mathewson."

43

ON THE WAY to Mathewson's in Phelan's car, they went over the case. "We've got evidence that at least implicates Mathewson," Fitzgerald said. "The motion detector log shows that his last request for an alarm turn-off was just after the phone call to Room EF100. We've got that and the tapes. Voice tapes hold up well in court, and you've got that woman who answered the phone call to Harris-Topping. She'll give a positive voice ID, I'm sure."

"But," Phelan said. "There's a big *but* behind every word you're saying. But no motive, right?"

"Right."

"Sometimes there isn't any. Sometimes it's just crazy."

"Not this one," Fitzgerald said, shaking his head. "This is not a guy who killed just to get his kicks. Something more is involved. My guess is that someone hired him."

"Rent-a-killer-cop?"

"It happens," Fitzgerald said.

Phelan had been reading the numbers on the houses as they drove down Eleventh Street. When she saw Mathewson's building, she pulled over, parking alongside a fire hydrant. Fitzgerald instinctively reached for a holster that was not there. "You armed? I'm not."

Phelan nodded, patting her left shoulder.

243

"Okay. When we knock on his door, you have that gun out. It's a Glock, right? And take that goddamn fuzzy safety off. Stand back from the door in case he fires through it, and—"

"Fitz, please. This is no time for police academy." She touched his hand. "I can take care of myself. *You* watch out, Mr. Citizen."

Mathewson's three-story apartment house was several blocks east of the Capitol, where the neighborhood quickly changed from yuppie and gentrified to shabby and dangerous. Two blocks away, only three nights before, a car had slowly cruised down a street and the driver had casually leaned out the window and sprayed two teenage boys with an Uzi. The dead young men had made some business error in their short careers as drug dealers. Their killer, like nearly every other killer in Washington, had not been caught.

Phelan found Mathewson's name on a mailbox in the hall. Ignoring the black button over the name, she tried the hall door. Its lock had been broken long before. They walked up to the second-floor landing and found his door, battered and peeling like the others. She pushed the door button, heard the buzz inside, and stepped to the side, her gun raised. Fitzgerald flattened against the wall on the other side. They waited for a full minute.

"Not a sound inside," she whispered.

"Lean on it," Fitzgerald said.

Phelan pressed the button and shouted, "Mathewson! It's me, Lieutenant Phelan. Answer the door." Then they both took up their positions.

The next door down the hall cracked open and an unseen woman said in a sleepy voice, "He ain't been up all day. But he's in there. I know that."

"How?" Fitzgerald asked.

"The messenger boy. He rang and he got let in. One of them dudes in those shiny, tight-ass clothes. Big black boy."

"When was this?"

"This mornin'. Early this mornin'. Woke me up, him poundin' on the door."

"And Mathewson opened it?"

"It wasn't anybody else."

Fitzgerald raised his right foot high and kicked at Mathewson's door. It flew open on the second kick, and both Fitzgerald and Phelan pressed themselves against the wall. Phelan dropped to one knee and for an instant leaned forward, gun aimed at the point beyond the door where someone's chest would be. Fitzgerald, crouching and ready to spring, looked in as soon as she withdrew her head. Hunched over, she dashed in and ducked behind an armchair. "Mathewson!" she called.

Fitzgerald leaped in and with a single rolling movement got to the wall next to a doorway on the other side of the room. He and Phelan waited a full minute before they stood and advanced slowly into a small hallway, which led to a kitchen and bathroom on one side, a bedroom on the other. The bedroom door was open. Lying naked on the rumpled bed, arms outflung, eyes staring at the ceiling, was Mathewson.

Except for the unmade bed, the room was extraordinarily neat. On one wall were three masks that looked as if they had come from an Asian country, maybe Bali or Thailand. On the opposite wall was a copy of the stark hologram rendering of the Capitol that hung in the conference room at headquarters. An exercise bicycle stood in front of a cabinet holding a television set, VCR, and tapes. In a corner was a rowing machine and a racked set of barbells. On a small table alongside the bed was a brass lamp with a prim white shade and a stack of magazines, fanned slightly so that the titles of two could be seen: one on body-building, the other an obscure pornographic publication. Next to the magazines, lying on a blue plastic saucer, was a syringe. It was empty.

Fitzgerald bent close to Mathewson's left arm. "Pretty fresh blood around the needle hole," he said. "Looks like an overdose. Any experience with drug deaths?"

Without touching the syringe, Phelan sniffed it, bending to examine it closely. "Not much," she said. "But I agree. I'd say OD. No marks on the body. Whatever killed him came from the inside." She looked around the room. "I'd better call Perkins."

She found a pair of transparent plastic gloves in her pocket, put them on, and went to the phone in the living room. Fitzgerald wrapped his hand in his tattered and grimy handkerchief and examined the objects on Mathewson's bureau: a gold ring with a sapphire stone flanked by small diamonds, keys and coins in a small wooden dish, a Swiss Army knife, a black leather wallet. In the wallet he found Mathewson's driver's license, several credit cards, eight twenty-dollar bills, three ten-dollar bills, two fives, and six ones.

"Well, it sure as hell wasn't a robbery," he called to the other room. An uncashed check for $3,500 was folded in half amid the currency. On an invoice attached to the check was the printed notice *The Attached Check Is in Settlement of Items Listed Below.* Typed below that was *April Advance Payment for Security Consulting.* Across the top of the invoice was the name of the firm, Monument Associates, with a Trenton, New Jersey, post office box as an address.

Phelan returned to the bedroom and looked over Fitzgerald's shoulder. "Monument," she said. "Sounds familiar . . . Wait a minute. That's the name of the company on Julia Bristow's financial disclosure statement. Remember? I told you that she listed a company on her financial disclosure form that Charles Bristow had not put on his."

"Why in hell would Mathewson be drawing down heavy money —that's about forty thousand a year, right?—for a company the Bristows had an interest in?"

"Whatever the reason," Phelan said, "it's a connection."

"That's what the messenger was," Fitzgerald said. "Mathewson's drug connection. Like dialing up a pizza, I guess."

"There's a number written on a pad near the phone," Phelan said. "Want to try it?"

"Yeah, let's try it," Fitzgerald said. He went to the living room and dialed it.

"Urban Redevelopment." The voice was male.

"What?" Fitzgerald asked.

The voice repeated the words, and Fitzgerald gave the number he had just dialed.

"That's this number, mister. If you don't know what you're doing, maybe you shouldn't call it anymore."

Fitzgerald hung up and said, "That's the name of the office!"

"What office?"

"The Office of the Assistant to the Mayor for Urban Redevelopment—the place where our undercover cop got scammed when he tried a buy-and-bust in the District Building. And that number . . . that number. I've seen it before. Mason jotted it down when I was in his office. He was talking to somebody and was so guarded about it that I wondered. It's the number."

"Mason a druggie?" Phelan said. "Come on!"

"Not a druggie, maybe, but someone in a tight little game with Mitchell. But why does he have this number?"

"There could be some answers here," Phelan said. "I'd like to look around. I told Perkins that I found a body, that the victim was connected with a Capitol Police Department case, and that he could decide when he got here whether to call in the D.C. cops."

"So you, as investigating officer, have a right to do some looking around?"

"Right. Come on, Fitz, let's lift this place."

Fitzgerald took the bedroom, Phelan the kitchen. She had been there only a few minutes when she called him.

She found the knife wrapped in a blue-and-white dishtowel and stuffed into an empty Cheerios box on a shelf in a kitchen cabinet. It was a hunting knife with a bone handle, a broad hilt, and a six-inch blade. "Check the tip," she said, holding the knife, still in the towel, under the kitchen counter's flickering fluorescent light. The blade's graceful symmetry ended in an awkward tip formed by uneven angles.

Fitzgerald shuffled through the tools and scraps of wire and bits of metal jumbled in a wooden box under the sink. He found a quarter-inch electric drill and a slightly worn grinding-wheel attachment. "Carborundum, I think," he said. "The lab shouldn't have too much trouble proving that this is what put the new tip on the knife. And there's the hilt mark, too. I guess we've got him."

"How about a little enthusiasm?" Phelan said.

"Let's assume that Mathewson killed the prostitutes. Assume he was a sicko, hated prostitutes. But Senator Bristow? Delegate Harris-Topping?"

"Why not just leave it that he killed women?" Phelan asked. "He felt the law coming and he killed himself by overdose."

"Overdose is for amateurs. Let me show you something." He went into the bedroom and returned with an expensive black leather attaché case, which he carried open. "Found it in the closet," he said. "His stash."

The case had a combination lock under the handle. "He left it unlocked?"

"Most people use their birthdays for the numbers," he said. "I got it from his driver's license."

247

Fitzgerald set the case on the kitchen table. It looked empty. He reached in and pressed a catch hidden under the gray fabric, then pulled the back of the case forward. Neatly arranged in the hidden compartment were eight small transparent plastic bags full of white powder, a small plastic bottle containing capsules, and a leather case. Fitzgerald snapped open the case. In it were three syringes and a plastic box that contained extra needles.

"A guy this organized, a guy who's savvy enough to evade our drug testing, a guy with what looks like a steady source of extra money—a guy like that is no chump overdoser."

"Then how did he die?"

"Let's wait and see what Perkins says."

Fitzgerald returned to the bedroom and continued his methodical rummaging through Mathewson's bureau. In the bottom drawer was a metal chest with a small brass lock. He selected a key from the cluster on top of the bureau and opened it. As he began riffling through the papers inside, a buzzer sounded. He stuffed a packet of papers into his pocket and ran into the living room.

Phelan was already there, behind a chair, gun leveled at the door. "Who's there?" she shouted.

"Perkins, Alix."

She eased the door open on its chain, saw the medical examiner, and unchained the door. He walked in, followed by two attendants with a gurney. After listening to Phelan's account of finding Mathewson's body and the knife, he went into the bedroom and briefly examined the body, concentrating on the eyes and the left arm. "You two are messing up a crime scene," he said, looking around the room.

"You're saying crime, not accidental OD or suicide?" Phelan asked. She stood by the door, her eyes moving from the body on the bed to Perkins.

"Toxic heroin," he said. He pulled a sheet over the body, slipped off his plastic gloves, and tossed them on the bed. "I've seen six, maybe seven people killed by it." He pointed to the syringe. "Methyl fentanyl, a tranquilizer used mostly in surgery cases, blended with pure heroin. It makes a hit that's about thirty times more potent than heroin. Knocks out all the opiate receptors in the brain, and that causes breathing to stop."

248

"But it looks like Mathewson was streetwise. He'd never take that stuff," Fitzgerald said.

"He didn't know what it was," Perkins said. "Nobody sells this on the street. It's a lethal poison. You get some guy to mix it up for you and you slip it to the dude you want to kill. It's a murder weapon to use on addicts."

"Somebody wanted to shut him up," Phelan said.

"That's my guess," Perkins said. "Any candidates?"

"Yeah," Fitzgerald said. "The guy who hired him."

Phelan told Perkins about the phone number.

"You mean you think Mitchell set this up? Could be," Perkins said. "The word on the street is that His Honor has some pretty good drug connections." He looked at the bed. "We've got to keep the D.C. cops out of this."

"Can you do it?" Fitzgerald asked.

"Sure. I just have the body delivered to a pal at Georgetown and tell him to keep his students away from it. No problem."

"Okay," Fitzgerald said. "We can get the FBI to claim it later." He turned to Alix. "Hold the fort. If D.C. cops show up, just tell them Perkins took the body."

"You sound like you won't be here," Phelan said.

"I won't," Fitzgerald said.

As he turned to go, Phelan noticed the packet sticking out of a back pocket of his jeans. All she could read on it was *U.S. Navy*.

44

FITZGERALD walked rapidly down Eleventh Street to Pennsylvania Avenue, where he found a pharmacy with a phone booth. After calling information for the number of a Thomas R. Sanders in the District, he dialed, praying that Sanders would be home.

"Tom, Jeff Fitzgerald. Yeah, long time. Listen, I need help—fast. Can you meet me right away? It's a big one." A pause. "Well, this has got to be better than washing your windows. Right. Hawk and Dove? Thanks and more thanks."

Lieutenant Commander Tom Sanders was an up-from-the-ranks officer in the Naval Investigative Service. They had known each other during Fitzgerald's brief career as a SEAL, and when he arrived in Washington, they had renewed their friendship and had occasionally been able to help each other.

Fitzgerald walked down Pennsylvania Avenue to the Hawk and Dove, where he waited for Sanders in a cool, dusky booth and ordered a draft beer and a hamburger. He was halfway through both when Sanders came in. A broad-shouldered man with graying black hair and a neatly trimmed moustache that was grayer than his hair, he wore the standard chinos and sports shirt.

After ordering two more beers, Fitzgerald took the packet from his pocket and spread its contents on the table between them. "I'll tell you more about this later. Right now I want to know what you make of this guy."

Sanders put on a pair of black-rimmed glasses and scanned the papers. "Convenience-of-government discharge," he said, putting one paper aside. "Means this guy Mathewson was a bad guy but the Navy had nothing it could arrest him for."

He picked up Mathewson's personnel record, several papers stapled together and folded. He unfolded them and quickly flipped through them. He looked at the last page and exclaimed, "*Puget Sound*! Yeah. A bad guy. The Ship of Ghouls."

"What?" Fitzgerald asked.

"That's the name some of us in the NIS gave her," Sanders said. "She's cleaned up now, but she was notorious. A guided-missile test ship. Because she wasn't a combat ship, there were a lot of women aboard—lesbians, straights, a mixed bag. She was one of those ships where things suddenly get out of control. Drug-dealing, rapes—homosexual and boy-girl—and two deaths. Murders, we thought."

"What kind of murders?"

"No one will ever know," Sanders answered. "Two women missing at sea. I wasn't directly involved in the investigation, but I remember it pretty well. It was the talk of the Navy at the time." He paused. "You think this guy Mathewson was involved? If you've got anything, we'd love to take a crack at it. No statute of limitations on murder, you know."

"Mathewson's dead," Fitzgerald said, and quickly told Sanders about finding the body and the personnel file. "This is the one I'm interested in." He pointed to the name of Mathewson's commanding officer on the *Puget Sound*: Commander William P. Mason.

"Oh, yes, the distinguished architect of the Capitol," Sanders said. He took a sip of beer. "Didn't you know about his checkered career in the Navy?"

"All I know is that he retired from the Navy as a captain and then went to some defense agency—"

"DARPA," Sanders said. "The Defense Advanced Research Projects Agency. Right. As I remember, he was posted there while he was still in the Navy. The gossip was that the Navy offered him to the electronic spooks at the National Security Agency, but they looked into his *Puget Sound* background and turned him down. He was supposed to be brilliant, absolutely brilliant, about computers, electronics. That's why he was CO of the *Puget Sound*. She's full of electronics."

"Tell me about the murders."

"You'll want copies of the investigation files. But right now you just want recollections, right?" He tapped his forehead.

"Right."

"A buddy of mine was in charge of the investigation. It was quite a few years ago. It started when a Wave in Norfolk was stabbed—"

"Stabbed? Killed?"

"No. Badly stabbed, but she survived. She said she was sure she had been stabbed by a crewman of her ship, the *Puget Sound*. She said she had been planning to come to us, the NIS, and tell us about what was going on aboard the ship."

"Did they find out who stabbed her?"

"Not as I recall. But her story stood up. There was a drug gang aboard. She said that the other crew members called them the Dirty Dozen. At sea they roughed up both men and women, raped Waves, blackmailed gays—that's still a sure ticket out of the Navy, you know. And she said that one woman was killed and her body thrown overboard. There *was* a Wave who turned up missing. The shipboard report said she had been swept over the side in a storm. Our informant said there was blood all over one compartment on the night she disappeared."

251

"You said there were two murders."

"The ship was scheduled to be deployed to missile tests off Florida, I think. We had to postpone the investigation. But we got an undercover Wave aboard before she sailed. That woman was lost at sea, too." He looked at the papers lying on the table. "Goddamn it! Goddamn it!" he said softly.

"What's wrong?"

"Mary Ann Choates. I helped train her. A kid from Spokane, from a Navy family. After it was all over, I called up the reports. I wasn't on the case, I just wanted to know what happened to Mary Ann. There was a suicide note, typed and unsigned, that said she was despondent, or some bullshit. I never believed it. But there was an accompanying statement from the commanding officer. He knew that she was NIS undercover. Telling the captain is standard policy. He said that she had come to him and had said she was under a terrible strain. He confirmed her despondency and ratified the suicide verdict. Well, that satisfied the Navy brass. No mess. Except for one thing."

He drained his beer and thumped down the mug. "There's a procedure for keeping clandestine notes during a mission like that. You keep a diary, but part of the diary is written in a book code. You know, with references to pages and lines in some ordinary book that both you and your control have. You sprinkle numbers, like dates or the number of dolphins seen or whatever, through the diary, and those dates are in book code. Well, the diary disappeared along with Mary Ann."

"What about the investigation? Didn't Mason get grilled about this?"

Sanders looked grim. "In the Navy, Jeff, you don't grill commanding officers. And when an investigation gets too messy or too complicated, our masters want it wrapped up fast and neat. Look at what happened to the investigation of the *Iowa* gun explosion. So that's what NIS did."

"So Mason commands the Ship of Ghouls and that's that?"

"Not quite. He was taken off the ship. Not relieved of command, but taken off and given a shore job, something in the Pentagon that had to do with electronics. He got his four stripes as captain on time, and it looked like the Ship of Ghouls was being forgotten. He was in line for rear admiral. Even bought the uniform, I've heard. But there was no way he could get flag rank."

"Because of the *Puget Sound*?"

"That and, I suspect, other things. He wasn't very social. He was NROTC from MIT, not Annapolis. He never married. And admirals need to have wives. The Navy discreetly got rid of him, tried to palm him off on NSA, and finally got him into DARPA."

"But why didn't Congress know all this?"

"Oh, it's like firing a guy and then giving him a recommendation for his next job. You send along a warm note and give a lot of commendations so that you don't look bad for having hired the guy in the first place." He paused. "Another round?"

"I'll take a raincheck, Tom. I've got to move on this fast."

"Too bad. I was going to ask you for a recommendation. I'll be retiring in a couple of months. I've had enough of it."

Fitzgerald called for the check and laughed. "So have I," he said. "I was forced out today. A recommendation from me will do you about as much good as one from the Three Stooges."

45

FITZGERALD hitched a ride in Sanders's car to Lawson's townhouse in the most fashionable neighborhood on Capitol Hill. The Lawson maid answered the door. Recognizing Fitzgerald, she told him that the Senator had left earlier without saying where he was going, but she thought he might be at his office as Mrs. Lawson was away for the weekend. "Any message?"

"Tell him *I* called in the FBI. And if he wants to talk to me, not to use the phone. Got it?"

"Sure. It makes about as much sense as a lot of other messages I've given him," she said, smiling. She shut the door, and Fitzgerald trotted out to First Street and down the hill to Union Station, where he found a taxi. He gave an address on upper Connecticut Avenue.

A few minutes later he was telling a woman behind a counter in

Kyle Tolland's apartment house that he wanted to see him. She did not like the looks of his jeans and sweaty shirt. On an intercom she told Tolland that there was someone in the lobby to see him. "He says," she reported in a disbelieving voice, "that his name is Fitzgerald."

Fitzgerald was standing close enough to the intercom to hear Tolland's reply: "I think, Miss Thompson, that I had better not invite him up. I will be right down."

The elevator door opened and Tolland appeared in flannel slacks and a tweed jacket, with a paisley foulard tucked into his gleaming white shirt. "I'll handle him, Miss Thompson," he said in a stage whisper as he walked past her and pointed Fitzgerald at two lobby chairs. Before Fitzgerald could ask any questions, Tolland insisted that he tell him about the circumstances of his resignation.

"All right, now I understand your somewhat dubious status. And just what is it you want now?"

Fitzgerald plunged into a report on what he and Phelan had found at Mathewson's apartment and what he had learned from Sanders. "I need to get all I can on Monument Associates. It's connected to the murders. I'm sure of it."

Tolland looked at him blankly for a moment. "You want me to run Monument Associates through the Racketeering Section. It has a database on all registered U.S. corporations, and lately it's been used as much as the fingerprint files. All right, I'll take care of it. But I can't get anything done until Monday. The white-collar computer crime boys don't work on weekends. Anything else?" He looked at his watch. "I'm due for tea with the vicar of the National Cathedral."

"Just call me a cab."

He took the cab to the street behind his home, walked through an alley, climbed over Mrs. Darwin's stockade fence, and knocked at the back door. Mrs. Darwin, evincing little astonishment, took him into her living room, where Phelan was waiting. They brought each other up to date while Mrs. Darwin was in the kitchen brewing coffee.

"What's next?" Phelan asked.

"We wait. I need to find the undercover cop who was scammed

by Mitchell's guys—Charles March, in the Intelligence Section. He'll remember the dial-for-drugs number that went right into the District Building. I'm sure that it's the same as the one we found in Mathewson's apartment. Can you try to find him?"

"Sure. Are you going to hole up here?"

"No. I want to talk to Royal."

"Why?"

"I think I can clear up some things."

Phelan left before Mrs. Darwin returned with the coffee. Fitzgerald politely accepted a cup, though his mind was racing ahead to what he had to do. He told her about his resignation, but he held back on his trip into the tunnel until she asked, "And underground? You discovered truth there?"

"Yes, Mrs. Darwin. I found truth. Some questions, some answers. And truth."

"Good. Now, no more need to be polite. I can feel you moving out there." She looked toward the window, already beginning to dim in the late afternoon sun.

He showered and changed into a gray suit, white shirt, and blue-and-red tie, put on sunglasses, and hoped that he could get to Irish without being recognized.

When Irish saw him entering the Senate reception room, he stood and went to his cubbyhole, gesturing for Fitzgerald to follow. "Rumors are flying," he whispered, closing the door behind them. When he handed Fitzgerald his briefcase, his suit coat flared open, and Fitzgerald saw the holstered Smith & Wesson. All qualified assistant SAAs had recently been armed, but Fitzgerald was still not used to it.

Irish began speaking rapidly in his normal voice. "Everybody's expecting a break in the case. There are lots of comings and goings in the majority leader's office—White House types, the FBI's congressional liaison man. What's up?"

"I can't tell you anything now, Irish. Any word on Royal?"

"He walked in bold as brass, with a gaggle of tourists from New Orleans. All full of 'Good morning, Irish,' like he's been here for years. Apparently, he's entertaining some of the hometown folks over the weekend. Like they say, the devil never takes a holiday."

"Think he's in his office?"

"I can check easily enough," Irish said, reaching for the phone.

255

He had memorized every senator's office number. "Now would this be Senator Royal's secretary? Well, yes, hello, Julie. This is Irish Lunigan. From the Senate reception room? I just want to know whether the senator is still in. I saw some lovely New Orleans people wandering the halls, and I'd like to give them a few of those free maps of Washington. In the senator's name, of course." A pause. "Yes, thank you. Thank you."

Irish hung up and turned to Fitzgerald. "The son of a bitch is in his office," he said.

46

ROYAL'S RECEPTIONIST was startled to see Fitzgerald, as was Haverlin, whom she sent for when Fitzgerald asked to see the senator.

"Are you here to arrest the senator?" Haverlin asked.

"Haven't you heard, Haverlin?" Fitzgerald asked. "I'm no longer chief."

"Then why are you—"

"I'll tell that to the senator," Fitzgerald said, pushing past him and striding down the cluttered aisle to the door to Royal's private office. Haverlin followed. Fitzgerald opened the door, and the two men stepped into the office almost simultaneously.

Royal looked up from his phone. The receptionist had given him a warning. He hung up, pointed to the briefcase, and asked, "You got another videotape in there?"

"I had nothing to do with that, Senator, and I think you know that. I'm no longer a police officer, but I came here to ask you some questions."

"And why are you doing that, Fitzgerald? Who sent you?"

"No one sent me," Fitzgerald said, opening his briefcase and taking out a sheet of paper. "I have three dates I want to ask you about."

"Sit down. You, too, Craig. Now, let's say that I do answer your goddamn questions. What are you going to do with the information?"

"If the answers are what I think they are going to be, I will give them to the FBI, which is about to take over the Bristow and Harris-Topping investigations."

"The FBI!" Haverlin exclaimed. "What in the hell are—"

"Shut up, Craig," Royal said. "Let me get this straight. You expect me to give you some information so that the Federal Bureau of Investigation can have even more on me than it has now?"

"Senator, I think that someone is trying to frame you. If I'm right, there'll be no FBI investigation of you."

Royal rubbed his chin and picked up the silver letter opener. "And suppose you're wrong?"

"Well, then, Senator, you are in a lot of trouble."

"Senator, I think—" Haverlin began.

Royal ignored him. "I'll give you a date, Fitzgerald. I'll give you February eighth, the date on that goddamn videotape."

Fitzgerald looked down at the paper he held, looked up, and nodded.

"February eighth was one of the days of Mardi Gras," Royal said. "I figure that about two hundred and fifty thousand people saw me in New Orleans that day."

"I thought that the date on that tape was faked, Senator. I'm sure if the FBI lab checks the original, they'll find that the date was dubbed in. Mardi Gras clinches it."

"What are the other dates?"

"Saturday, January eleventh, and Sunday, February 2."

"Fitzgerald, I got to tell you, I sure don't like to spend many weekends in this city," Royal said, his voice swiftly changing from rage to relief. "Craig, go out to Julie and ask her to get out my House schedule and phone logs for those days. Fast."

When Haverlin left, Royal leaned back in his chair, put his feet on the desk, and said, "Now, what else?"

"The night of Julia Bristow's murder, Senator. I realize that this is a very private matter. It may well be that it will never become public."

"Don't give me any bullshit. That goddamn video, it became pretty damn public."

"That video may give you a lot of trouble with your supporters,

Senator, and most assuredly with your wife. But I want to ask you about Julia Bristow."

Royal looked out the window at the Capitol, the dome gleaming with startling purity against a sky of perfect blue. He leaned forward, touched a button on the phone, and said, "Tell Craig to stay outside until I call him." He motioned Fitzgerald to a chair directly in front of his desk.

"I tell you, Fitzgerald, it was that window, I guess, that started me out. I mean, in and out of a window like a goddamn Romeo." His waxy face burst into a grin that seemed boyish and genuine. "And, well, she was a damn . . . *active* woman, if you know what I mean."

"How long had it been going on?" Fitzgerald asked.

"It went back a ways. She and Charlie, well, they stopped sleeping together when she found out what *he* was up to. And then she got sort of interested in me, and I can't say I discouraged her. Fact is, I didn't think much of Charlie, either."

Fitzgerald had taken out his notebook but had not written anything down. "Senator," he said quietly, "I want to know about the last night, about what you said and what she said. I have a very good reason for this, believe me."

"It was all over. It was fun while it lasted and all that, but I knew that she was about to take me on politically, and I knew that we couldn't keep up the other business."

"So you saw her on the night she was killed, and you told her then that it was over."

"Yes. You see, I just can't sleep with somebody who double-crosses me. It's not in my nature."

"How was she double-crossing you?"

"She told me that she had decided to run for the Senate on her own. She wasn't going to step down, like she promised the governor—and promised me, in private, in bed."

"Wouldn't her change of mind have gotten her in trouble with the party?" Fitzgerald asked.

"The party leaders would have been pissed off at first, and then they would have come around. Hell, that's what they did with me when they stopped worrying about the black vote. Politicians come around to winners. And I gotta tell you, she was beginning to look like a winner."

"Meaning that you couldn't have beaten her?"

"I can't really say that I could. Julia would have given me a fight, a real fight. She was getting heard and she was getting respect, on women's issues and all that. And she was looking like she was going to do a turnaround on her husband's stupid goddamn stand for D.C. statehood."

"And that would take the statehood issue away from you if you ran against her in the primary."

"Right."

"Did she tell you that night that she had changed her mind about running—and about statehood?"

"Yes. But I knew she was holding off, dangling Lawson about her vote on ending the filibuster, playing games with the media back home. She was good at playing games."

"But what reason did she give for going back on her husband's stand on statehood? Wouldn't it sound to her constituents like she was going against her husband's memory? Wouldn't that hurt her?"

"That's exactly what I said." Royal looked toward the ceiling. "And then she told me that she had a bombshell. A real bombshell."

"And what was that, Senator?" Fitzgerald asked. He edged forward on his chair, a move that drew Royal closer. He leaned across his desk.

"She said that she had found out something that would show why Charlie had supported statehood. She said she had evidence of corruption. Those were her words, as I remember them, 'evidence of corruption.' "

"Did she tell you anything more than that?"

"Well, let me tell you. When she said 'evidence of corruption,' I just laughed. I mean, corruption, an issue? In Louisiana? And that got her mad, and she said, 'This is no piddling stuff, Mike. This is big. Like the S and L's.' And then she gave me a hint. She said that statehood was just a cover for a deal that involved billions."

"And that was it? That's all she said?"

"Pretty much. But she did say that she was going to make her revelations—that's what she called them, revelations—the next day."

"Did she show you a copy of her speech?"

259

"Didn't have one. She said she was going to give it extemporaneously—right from the heart, she said."

"Did you ask Haverlin about this conversation?"

"Yeah, I did. Next morning. In fact, I was on the line talking to him when he got the call about her being dead."

"Did he know anything?"

"Not a damn thing. And I had to believe him. If he had anything to tell me, well, he would tell me."

"No mention of a company called Monument Associates?"

"Never heard of it."

Fitzgerald looked down in his notebook for a moment, then looked up and asked, "Senator, when you left the hideaway that night, did you leave by the window?"

"Sure. She insisted on it, and like I said, I got a kick out of it, too."

"That's about it, Senator. Now, how about those dates?"

Royal called Haverlin. He came in carrying printouts of Royal's appointment calendar and phone log. Fitzgerald glanced through the pages. They showed that Royal had not been in the District on any of the three dates.

Fitzgerald left the Hart Building by the visitors' entrance and walked down C Street to a block given over to grass, shrubbery, and small gardens. At the end of the block he turned toward Union Station, then skirted around a semicircle of briskly flapping state flags and darted through traffic to the North Capitol Street entrance of the Dubliner.

He found a pay phone, called Lawson's Senate office, and instead of a secretary, got a recording. "This is Saturday, and the office is closed," a young woman's voice said. He next called the majority leader's office and got a similar message from a similar voice. He ordered a beer, drank half of it, and went to the pay phone again. He called Lawson's townhouse. "This is the gentleman who rang the bell," he told the maid, who answered. "Please don't use my name on the phone. Just tell the senator that I can prove he has the wrong man. He knows how to reach me. And he needs to reach me."

Reach me, he thought as he picked up his beer. A worrisome thought. If Lawson's phone was tapped or Royal's office was

260

bugged . . . He hurried out and walked rapidly home. He saw no signs of surveillance as he looked down the block, but he decided not to take any chances. He again used the alley and climbed the fence. When Mrs. Darwin opened the back door, he told her, "I want you to leave the house, just for tonight, Mrs. Darwin."

She looked him directly in the eyes for a moment and nodded. "There is danger," she said. She quickly agreed to spend the night with her niece in Virginia and not to phone her in advance. Fitzgerald called for a cab, telling the dispatcher he wished to be taken to National Airport. Mrs. Darwin looked curiously at him, then smiled.

When the cab arrived, they both got in, each carrying a small bag and Fitzgerald still clutching his briefcase. The driver's route sheet would show that he dropped them off in front of the American Airlines entrance at National Airport. From there Mrs. Darwin called her niece and said she would be seeing her in a few minutes. "It's nothing to be alarmed about, Elizabeth," she said. "Just some police business."

Fitzgerald helped her into a cab and went to a battery of phones in the main terminal, where he made a reservation at the Americana, a nearby motel in Crystal City. Then he dialed his answering machine. No call from Lawson. *He's ducking me.* Fitzgerald hailed a Red Top cab outside the terminal. Five minutes later he checked into the Americana and called room service. He needed more than a drink right now, but the drink would have to do.

47

AT TEN O'CLOCK, Fitzgerald was slumped in front of the television set at the motel, just beginning to do battle with his third vodka. He fingered the remote control, idly searching for something other than the Clint Eastwood reruns the networks and cable companies sent out to what they assumed would be mostly empty households. The best that HBO had to offer was *Rocky V*—or was it *VI*?

He felt light-headed, but despite the alcohol, tension remained tightly wrapped around his back and neck muscles. He got up from his chair, paced the room, sat down again. Maybe he had it all wrong. Maybe he was chasing red herrings while the big fish was being hauled in by Lawson. But Mathewson had to be the killer, not Royal.

Mathewson had had no discernible motive to murder Bristow and Harris-Topping. He had been street smart, but not smart enough to have masterminded those murders. Someone must have paid him. Someone far cleverer. Mayor Mitchell was the best bet. But why? Would he kill for statehood? No, it had to be more. Michael Royal in the Senate did not give Mitchell statehood. A dead nonvoting delegate did not give Mitchell statehood. There was something else. But what?

"Damn," Fitzgerald cursed audibly, as if his anger could force the answer to the surface. He drank deeply from his glass. What a joke. He was out of a job again, out on a limb, for what? To do justice? To protect a certifiable Klansman who was caught on video without his robe, picking up a black prostitute? *Hypocritical bastard! Hope his Nazi skinhead friends are having some chest pains about their hero . . .*

Fitzgerald hesitated, then picked up the receiver of the telephone and punched a ten-digit number. After three rings, a voice answered in a slightly bewildered tone.

"Hello, Alix. Sorry to call so late. Listen, how about meeting me at the Monocle for a drink?"

"Anything else on Mathewson?"

"No. Just . . ." Fitzgerald could feel a sudden touch of remorse creeping into his brain. "Actually . . . no, it's probably too crowded there tonight."

"Fitz . . . Look, I'm just about to step into the shower. Why don't you come to my place? I mix a vodka martini that will make you plead for mercy." Her voice took on a sudden musicality, a light playfulness that was just short of laughter.

Fitzgerald had never been to her apartment. As chief of the Capitol Police, he had always made sure to keep a professional distance between himself and his subordinates. Especially female subordinates. But he was no longer Alix's boss, he quickly reminded himself. After a momentary hesitation, he agreed and jotted down the directions to her place.

She lived in one of four apartments in a big old townhouse on Belmont Avenue in Adams-Morgan, a neighborhood known for its ethnic mix and fine restaurants. She buzzed him through the lobby door and he walked up one flight to a door that opened as he neared it.

She was wearing a white terrycloth robe that, in the dimly lit foyer, dramatically set off her olive skin. Her dark hair, still wet from the shower, was slicked straight back from her forehead, accentuating high cheekbones and widely spaced eyes. Green eyes, Fitzgerald thought, shining like precious gems.

He was slightly unsteady as he walked to the living room and looked around for a place to sit. The sofa and the two armchairs looked as if they had come from a solid, comfortable living room in a big old Connecticut farmhouse. A basket of white and yellow daffodils graced a low table in front of the sofa. There was a piano in the corner of the room, with a dozen small, silver-framed photographs on it. On one off-white wall was a starkly geometric ceramic hanging that conveyed a sense of landscape. On another wall was a painting full of color and shapes that made its kitchen table look mysterious and somehow alluring.

Alix was standing close to Fitzgerald now, so close he could smell the fragrance of her wet hair. Roses. Crushed roses, he thought. He could feel a familiar tingling start to surge throughout his body, a feeling that had been missing for nearly a year now, suppressed by—what? Guilt, anger, remorse, work? He wasn't sure. He knew only that it felt like a flame spreading through his entire being, threatening to set him on fire.

Alix stepped quickly away and moved to the kitchen, directing Fitzgerald to make himself comfortable on the couch. The sound of an electric harp floated softly from a large oak armoire in the corner. The melody was haunting.

"Who's playing?" he asked.

Alix, returning from the kitchen, carried two glasses that had been chilled in the freezer. "That's *Caverna Magica*, my favorite album. It's by Andreas Wollenweider. Has an ethereal quality, doesn't it? Sometimes I close my eyes and I can see flowers dancing to the strings."

Fitzgerald stood up as she handed him his drink. They clinked glasses in a silent toast and drank deeply. "Whew," he gasped, fighting back a cough. "That's deadly!"

"I warned you. Ten parts vodka, just a whisper of vermouth," Alix said, smiling broadly.

"Mercy. I surrender." Fitzgerald laughed.

He stared into her eyes, emerald eyes that drew him deeper into their light. He tried to look away, but his eyes came back to hers as if pulled by a magnet. His head was swimming now, intoxicated by the alcohol, the music, her fragrance. Everything was spinning. He reached out and cupped the back of her head, the wetness of her hair deliciously cool. He felt himself start to harden, and when he began to pull away, Alix slipped her arm behind his waist and drew him tight against her, pressing her pelvis against him.

Fitzgerald kissed her, gently at first, then more forcefully, his tongue probing, fencing with hers, sliding along the front of her teeth. He could feel her begin to tremble with excitement.

Setting his drink down on the coffee table, he slipped his hand inside her robe and massaged her breasts until the nipples turned hard. She moaned softly as he began to kiss them. Her robe fell open as he lowered himself to run his tongue along her quivering stomach. He ran his hand along the back of her legs, drawing his fingers lightly across her skin, and then sank them into her. He felt her go wet with desire, and sounds started to bubble up from her throat.

She pulled him up, tearing at his shirt, his belt. His clothes seemed to fly away. Then he drew her to the floor and entered her, gently at first, then with a force that was pure lust and fury, altering rhythms, moving deeper, slower, longer, then deeper again. Their bodies glistening, they pounded against each other.

When it was over, Fitzgerald started to talk, but Alix put her fingers to his lips. "No," she whispered. "No words. Just stay with me in the magic cavern."

He fell back into her arms and lay with her for a long time, letting the music take him to a place of warmth and absolute serenity. Later they moved into the bedroom and made love again, this time more slowly and lovingly, until they fell asleep, exhausted.

Fitzgerald dreamed that night. He heard a cry, a gull's song, the bird's wings white against a liquid blue sky. Then riderless horses, wet with lather, raced along a beach, whirling, pirouetting with enormous grace, yet leaving no tracks along the sea-washed shore. A woman's voice called. Flowers . . .

Sunday, April 12

48

THE SMELL of fresh-brewed coffee caused Fitzgerald to stir. He opened one eye slowly and saw Alix hovering over him, a breakfast tray in her hands, a white gardenia in her hair. "Looks like you missed your morning run, Chief," she said as she handed him the Sunday *Post* and set the tray on his lap. Then she reached over and snapped on the bedroom television set. "You're just in time for 'Face the Nation.'"

Fitzgerald winced, not quite believing that it was almost eleven-thirty. Alix sat next to him on the bed and they glanced through the *Post* together. Mathewson's death was reported briefly on an inside page of the metro section. "The cause of death," the story said, "is being investigated." Nearby was a three-paragraph story on Fitzgerald's resignation "for personal reasons." The story mentioned that he had been leading "the preliminary investigation" of the two Capitol Hill murders and that there was "speculation that the FBI will take over the investigation."

"Lots of investigations going on," Alix said. Fitzgerald picked up the sports section to check on the Orioles. Then, sipping coffee and munching toast, along with hundreds of thousands of other Washingtonians, they began watching Majority Leader Daniel Lawson on "Face the Nation."

Like all skilled politicians, Lawson was an alchemist with reporters' questions, transforming them into rhetorical stepping-stones for the path he wished to take. To each of the first two questions—Is Royal a suspect? Are the murders linked to the statehood filibuster?—he gave not answers but statements. From them he reconstructed the facts of the two murders, vaguely mentioning the FBI lab in such a way that it appeared the FBI was already conducting the investigation. He also built up an aura of suspense as the first commercial break neared. That was one reason he was among the guests adored by the producer. The guests who returned again and again knew that you didn't give it all away in the first twelve minutes.

"Do you think he'll announce Royal's arrest?" Alix asked during the commercials.

"Maybe," Fitzgerald answered. "I'm sure he knows I've been trying to reach him. He must know that I've got something. If I had gone to the studio, he'd probably still have managed to duck me. I know him. When he sets a course, he doesn't change. He's out to get Royal, no matter what."

Lawson returned to another round of questions, which he assembled into a narrative about the progress of the filibuster on statehood. "Julia Bristow would have been the key vote for closing debate," he said, ending his narrative. "And as you all know, Gwenda Harris-Topping, the great champion of statehood, introduced the House bill. Their murders made them both martyrs for statehood."

He paused just long enough for a question: "If I might shift the questioning, Senator, there is a growing belief that you will be a candidate for Presi—"

"Before I answer that question, Jack, I'd like to take a moment to get back to my Senate concerns. As you know, during the filibuster the Senate has stood in recess on weekends until the call of the chair. That call, scheduled for Monday, was changed after I consulted this morning with the minority leader. The Senate will be called into an extraordinary Sunday session at two o'clock this afternoon."

Lawson's failure to answer the question was forgotten in the uproar of new questions about the significance of a Sunday session. From the hubbub emerged one question that he chose to answer: "Why the Sunday session, Senator?"

"To consider," he said, "a new and grave matter concerning the murders of Julia Bristow and Gwenda Harris-Topping."

The producer also liked guests who used the show as a place that made news.

Shortly before two o'clock, an ex-senator, hastily called in by C-Span as an expert on Senate protocol, set up the proceedings for the audience, one of the largest ever to watch a Senate session. He spoke in a studio, an image of the Senate chamber behind him. "Twenty minutes ago," he said, "Senator Lawson made a brief appearance on the floor. He said he had a matter of greatest urgency to discuss with his colleagues and suggested that every senator come to the floor immediately. He then asked the clerk of the Senate to order a live quorum, meaning that each member will have to record his presence or be counted as absent. I'm told that only two senators are missing, as Lawson is about to begin his presentation."

The commentator disappeared from the screen, and live coverage of the session began. A loud murmur filled the chamber, as if the members of a small community sensed that a storm was approaching but were unsure of the direction from which it was coming or how much force its winds would carry.

The presiding officer banged his gavel down harshly three, four times. "The Senate is not in order!" he proclaimed. "The majority leader has an important statement to make. But he will not proceed until there is order!" Again, down came the gavel in successive whacks.

Finally there was silence. "Mr. President," Lawson began solemnly, "for far too long violence has stalked the streets of this great city. Senseless violence has been driven by poverty, drugs, guns, by the virtual breakdown of the family and of law and order, by reasons too manifold to reiterate here today."

He paused and surveyed his colleagues. Gone was the amiable chatter and good-natured joking that normally gripped this group of lawmakers. He saw only stern, unsmiling faces.

"Many of us have remained indifferent to the violence, to the heartbreak, to the victims," he continued. "After all, this is not really *our* city. Those who live here are not really *our* constituents. And after all, they could stop it if they had the will to do so . . ."

271

Lawson's voice trailed off, as if he knew that he was in danger of politicizing his remarks, of chastening his brethren for benign neglect. He had not summoned them here to preach to them.

"Until the seventh of April, each of us remained isolated from, insulated against, this rising floodtide of violence. But a madman is loose now in this city on the Hill. He has murdered two distinguished women with an unspeakable savagery. A United States senator and Washington's distinguished delegate . . ."

His voice cracked with emotion. He paused, sipped from the glass of water on his desk, then gripped the podium. On it rested a single sheet of yellow paper bearing several handwritten notes.

"For the past twenty-six days, the Senate has been engaged in a great, historic debate on whether to enfranchise the people of the District of Columbia by granting it statehood. That debate has been carried on in the finest traditions of the Senate. There are legitimate arguments that can be made, and have been made, by members on both sides of the aisle, by liberals and conservatives alike. And I want to commend my colleagues for adhering to the Senate's highest standards."

This was one of those false flatteries that Senate leaders so often find it obligatory to loft. In fact, the rhetoric had been florid, heated, nasty, and at times vicious. There had been speeches of scholarship and quiet reason, but the debate had not set many high marks for excellence.

Stanley Ichord, an Arizonan whose face looked like a mudslide in motion, all lumps and wrinkles sagging at once toward a narrow, weak chin, coughed volubly, a signal for Lawson to cut short the rhetorical foreplay and get on with the business that the Senate was called to discuss on this Sunday afternoon.

Lawson turned toward the rostrum, looked up at the senator seated there, and continued, paraphrasing Justice Louis Brandeis. "Mr. President, we who hold public office are the keepers of the flame. If we break the law, we breed only contempt for the law. The privilege of our office does not place us above the law. Indeed, our so-called immunity under Article I, Section 6, Clause 1 of the Constitution is greatly exaggerated and misunderstood. Even the importance of legislation pending before the Senate would not insulate a member from arrest for speeding, for that is a breach of the peace that is not protected. But treasonous or felonious conduct, of course, is so reprehensible that no one could conceivably raise doubts about legal accountability."

Lawson could hear soft muttering spreading in the chamber. He saw several members shift in their chairs, trying to suppress their growing agitation at the glacial pace—and perplexing pertinence—of his comments. He wet his lips before proceeding. "Every person under the law is presumed innocent of a charge, however high his position, however heinous the alleged crime. And we must bear this in mind throughout what undoubtedly will be a long ordeal." Satisfied that he had laid out in sufficient detail all the precautionary warnings, he spoke more rapidly. "It is with great personal regret that I must announce that there now exists sufficient evidence to charge one of our distinguished colleagues for the murder of Julia Bristow."

Now it became clear to everyone why Lawson had been so cautious, so solicitous, so fulsome in exculpating his colleagues from base motivations: he did not want any of them to question his own. The quiet muttering suddenly erupted into a raucous babble, prompting the presiding officer once again to gavel the Senate to silence. Minutes passed before order was restored.

"Accordingly," Lawson said with the finality of a judge pronouncing a death sentence, "when the Senate goes into recess, I will ask that member to proceed voluntarily to the U.S. attorney's office for the District of Columbia. In the event he fails to do so, I have instructed the sergeant-at-arms to forthwith deliver that member into the custody of the United States attorney."

All eyes turned immediately toward Michael Royal, searching his face for—what? An admission of guilt? A protestation of innocence? A display of outrage?

Although Royal's face was fully flushed, he remained remarkably calm. Rising from his chair, he asked, "Would the majority leader yield to me?"

"I would yield for a question."

"Mr. President, this is hardly the place for me to defend my innocence or honor. But let me say that I do indeed have a question." His calm erupted into red-faced, searing anger. "I question the majority leader's motives," he began. "I question why he would be so driven by his desire for D.C. statehood that he would be a party to this conspiracy to indict me, not for the murder of

273

Julia Bristow, which is just a charade to take me off the Senate floor and deprive my constituency of a strong voice on this issue, but for defending the honor of my convictions!

"Mr. President!" he exclaimed, turning not to the rostrum but first to the visitors' galleries, then to the packed press gallery. "The people of this nation want no part of racial quotas or racial politics. They want equal opportunity for all, based on merit, competence, skill—the values that have made this country strong—not on skin-toned, preferential policies. What profit will there be to our party to pick up two Senate seats if we lose our soul in the process? The soul of our party consists of working men and women, middle-class, church-going, God-fearing men and women of all colors. And I find it strange indeed that the majority leader, who could not shut off the right of the people to have statehood debated fully by hook, has decided to do so by crook. Yes, I have a question, Mr. President," he thundered. "How could the majority leader stoop so low?"

Ken Sewall jumped up and shouted, "Mr. President, the senator from Louisiana is out of order!"

"The senator from Iowa is correct," the presiding officer shouted above the din. He banged the gavel hard, threatening to breach Senate custom by publicly naming those senators who refused to remain silent.

"Mr. President," Lawson responded, not looking at Royal. "The junior senator from Louisiana is understandably angry. As I tried to say at the outset, each of us must be presumed innocent, just as each of us must be held accountable for our actions. The charges against Senator Royal are truly extraordinary, indeed, unprecedented. But justice must be permitted to take its course. I must also add that justice has been delayed too long for the people who reside in the District of Columbia. The cloture vote on the issue of statehood has been set to occur tomorrow at eight P.M. I intend to have the Senate proceed with that vote as previously ordered. In addition, I intend to request the Ethics Committee to meet in executive session to determine whether the junior senator from Louisiana should be deprived of any of his senatorial privileges pending a resolution of the charges against him. I now ask that the Senate stand in recess until eight P.M. tomorrow."

With the smack of the presiding officer's gavel, the press gallery erupted, as each reporter raced to a computer terminal to file the congressional story of the decade.

Angrily shouting words that no one listened to, Michael Royal refused to move from his seat when the Senate sergeant-at-arms, Adam Morrison, his face contorted by loathing, touched him on the shoulder and asked him to leave. Morrison signaled to his assistants in the chamber, and three of them, led by Irish Lunigan, swarmed around Royal, pulled him from his seat, and half carried him out. They propelled him through a gauntlet of Capitol Police officers into the Senate reception room, where a white male FBI agent read him his rights while a black female agent pulled his hands behind his back and handcuffed him.

Fitzgerald turned to Alix, whose eyes had not left the screen. "Suppose I'm wrong?" he said. "Suppose Royal made it look like he was framed?"

Monday, April 13

49

AT 9:30 A.M. Fitzgerald checked the answering machine at his flat. He recognized the voice of Kyle Tolland, who had not left his name or number. Fitzgerald went to a pay phone at a gas station a few blocks from Phelan's apartment. "Are you sure your phone's safe?" he asked when Tolland answered.

"Well, I do have a certain feeling of security in this place," Tolland said. "Let's dispense with paranoia and get on to business. I had one of my workaholic friends in the Racketeering Section run a check through the database on all registered U.S. corporations. Even crooks have to have corporations, you know. He started at seven o'clock. Took him two hours before he turned up Monument Associates, a New Jersey corporation that is an off-spring of something called an anstalt."

"No connection with Royal?" Fitzgerald asked.

"No connection with anybody, Jeff," Tolland said. "The racketeering boys tell me an anstalt is a legal gimmick invented by Liechtenstein to shield identities. Like in Switzerland, but more so. All that shows up in the U.S. is a limited partnership in New Jersey. And under Jersey law, only the name of the general partner must be disclosed. The Jersey partnership is called River Associates, and the papers on file in Trenton show that its general partner is Monument Associates—of Liechtenstein."

"And that's all?"

279

"That's all. Unless you tell me more, I can't get you more."

"Thanks, Kyle. I'll dig for more."

When Fitzgerald returned to the apartment, Phelan was standing in the kitchen, gulping down a cup of coffee and obviously ready to leave. He told her what Tolland had found. "What this means to me," he said, "is that somebody went to a hell of a lot of trouble to keep something secret."

"But who?" Phelan asked.

"We'll find him," Fitzgerald said. "What are you supposed to be doing this morning?"

"Officially? Talking to Internal Affairs about finding Mathewson's body. I'll have to do some fancy stepping there. And wrapping up a brief for the FBI to hand over the cases. I'm supposed to be liaison."

"So you're officially off the murders?"

"Not exactly," Phelan said. "If you mean will I be able to track down Officer Charles March, ex–bicycle messenger, and ask him something, the answer is, just ask." She put down the cup and slipped on the jacket of her uniform. "Can I give you a lift?"

"Well . . . look, I had no intention of spending another night here. I just—"

She kissed him on the cheek, pulled back, and said, "It's business time, Fitz. You want me to find March and see if he'll confirm the phone number of the District Building drug drop, right? See if it's the same one as the number in Mathewson's apartment?" He nodded. "Okay. Will you be home?"

"No. I'm still checked in at the motel," he said. "But right now I need a lift to the District Building."

Byron Brown, Mayor Mitchell's security chief, was sitting in Mitchell's outer office when Fitzgerald arrived. Brown was a very large man, officially a plainclothes Metropolitan Police officer but much better known as a retired Redskins linebacker. He moved quickly, putting his considerable bulk between Fitzgerald and the door to Mitchell's office.

"I've come to see the mayor," Fitzgerald said.

"You don't have an appointment, Fitzgerald. You don't even have a job."

"Well, maybe I'm looking for one, Byron."

Brown laughed a laugh that sounded more like a cough. "Look, man. It's simple. No appointment, no getting in."

Two women looked up from their desks. They did not often hear Brown speak to anyone a second time.

"I'm going to reach into my coat pocket, Byron," Fitzgerald said slowly, "and I'm going to take out an envelope. There's something inside the mayor will certainly want to see. All I want you to do is give it to one of the young women here and ask her to take it in to the mayor. If he does not immediately let me into his office, you can personally throw me down that beautiful staircase outside."

Brown contemplated Fitzgerald's deliberate movements, accepted the envelope, looked at it, then looked at Fitzgerald. He tapped the envelope against his hand for a moment, then, without taking his eyes from Fitzgerald, said, "Alice, take this in to the mayor."

Alice emerged twenty seconds later and said, "The mayor says send him in."

Mitchell was standing behind his desk, holding the envelope in one hand, a sheet of paper in the other. On the paper was written the phone number Fitzgerald had dialed at Mathewson's apartment.

"What the hell is this about, Fitzgerald? Some kind of threat? You're in no position to—"

"It's no threat, mayor. It's a chance for you to stay out of jail for murder."

Mitchell moved slightly, his right index finger searching for a button under his desktop. The door flew open, and before Fitzgerald could react, Brown grabbed him from behind, threw him to the floor, dug a knee into his back, grabbed him under the chin, and jerked his head upward.

"Easy, Byron," Mitchell said. "I just want to see if the Feds wired him."

Brown shifted slightly and, still holding Fitzgerald's neck in one hand, lifted up his jacket and pulled out his shirttail. He ran his hand up Fitzgerald's bare back and across his chest. "Stand," he ordered.

"If I can," Fitzgerald said, slowly getting to his feet. He swiveled his head left, then right.

"Spread your legs," Brown said, running his hands up the inside

281

of Fitzgerald's legs, then heavily patting his buttocks and the outside of his legs. "He's clean," he said, looking down at Mitchell. He turned and left the room.

"Take a chair, Fitzgerald," Mitchell said. "I can give you a minute."

Fitzgerald painfully lowered himself into a chair to the right of the mayor's massive desk. "That number," he said, "was found in the apartment of a Capitol Police sergeant named Fred Mathewson. Name familiar?"

"I hear lots of names, meet lots of people."

"Well, you might remember Mathewson because you are an accessory to his murder."

Mitchell's expression did not change.

"You got a call from a friend—let's call him Mr. M," Fitzgerald began, speaking rapidly. "He told you that Mathewson was panicking and was about to talk. Mr. M said that Mathewson needed to be kept quiet, permanently. And you said you'd help out. You had as much at stake as Mr. M. Then you—"

"Look, Fitzgerald, you want me to call Byron in and have him give you a real workout?"

"Then you got your connection to fix up something special for Mathewson, and you got one of the connection's bike messengers to deliver it."

Mitchell sat down. "You can't prove any of that shit."

"I don't have to, Mr. Mayor. The FBI will be doing the proving. They've got that number on a pad in Mathewson's apartment. They've got Mathewson's knife, the one that killed Bristow and Harris-Topping. And probably those three D.C. prostitutes you talked about on Davis's show. The FBI's got the cases now, including the murder of Mathewson. Everything's been handed over to the anticorruption task force that's been on your ass all these months."

One of the phones on Mitchell's desk buzzed. He picked up the receiver and shouted, "No calls! I'm in conference!" He slammed it down and looked back at Fitzgerald. "I thought that Royal . . . I mean, they *arrested* the son of a bitch." He gazed down at his hands, splayed on the mirrorlike surface of the desk. Then he looked up again and said, "What the fuck *do* you want, Fitzgerald?"

282

"What I want is to solve these murders. And if you help me, you probably won't go to jail. Now that sounds pretty good to me."

"I think I'd better call my lawyer and get him over here," Mitchell said, reaching for the phone.

"Hold on," Fitzgerald said, placing his hand on the phone. "Let's just do this man-to-man and see about lawyers and U.S. attorneys later. Okay?"

Mitchell thought for a moment. Much of his political success had been based on his skill at thinking on his feet, on making momentous decisions based on little more than his own instincts. "Okay," he said, leaning back and looking both wary and relieved.

"There was something else in Mathewson's apartment," Fitzgerald said. "A check from a company called Monument Associates. Recognize the name?"

"Mason said it was foolproof," Mitchell said.

"And a bonanza, right? Mason told you statehood for the District was going to be a bonanza," Fitzgerald said. "I see you've got one of his holograms of the Capitol." He gestured toward the wall between two windows looking out on Pennsylvania Avenue. Framed there, over a print of L'Enfant's original plan for the District of Columbia, was a copy of Mason's hologram-based rendering of Capitol Hill.

"Yeah," Mitchell said, turning to stare at it. "Have you seen Mason's computer show?" Fitzgerald nodded. "Well, you remember seeing the part where the Capitol and the grounds sort of fly up into the sky?" Fitzgerald nodded again. "Well, that was the basis of the idea. The National Capital Area, he called it."

"Sure, I remember that image, that flying Capitol," Fitzgerald said. "It looked as if it had been ripped out of the District. The National Capital Area—that's mentioned in the statehood bill. But it takes in a lot more than Capitol Hill."

"You're goddamn right," Mitchell said. "The idea was that when the District became a state, the heart of the District—Capitol Hill, the Mall, and most of the land west to the Potomac— would become the National Capital Area. Mason's idea was to make what he called a federal city. He said it would be like an island. That's what he called it, the Island, like a name. It would be completely independent from the rest of the District, with its own utilities, its own transportation, its own little hospital and school.

"At first when he told me about it, it was like a big dream, a big computer dream. He was like a salesman making a pitch. I'd seen hundreds of guys like that. Blue smoke, mirrors—bullshit. But Mason, he was different. He told me there was a statehood bill in the works, that he and some senator named Bristow had put it together. He told me about the National Capital Area idea, the Island. And he said it was the key to getting statehood. Now don't forget, I've been campaigning for years for statehood. I *want* statehood. And anything that would make that impossible thing happen . . . well, I had to listen.

"He said that the *reality* of the Island, yeah, the *reality* of the Island, had to be a secret that only he, me, and this Bristow knew. He said that the Island was a treasure island—he laughed at that. Yeah, every once in a while, in the middle of saying something, he would laugh." Mitchell paused, suddenly realizing that he was letting the story pour out.

Fitzgerald felt the tension, sensed the crucial psychological pivot as Mitchell changed from a man telling a political tale to a criminal launching a confession. He knew that an interruption now could seal Mitchell's lips. His mind swarming with dozens of questions, he remained silent, waiting for the mayor to begin his confession.

"The second time we met," Mitchell continued, "Mason said he'd like to show me something on a computer. He sent it over just before the meeting. That's the first time I met Mathewson. I didn't know he was one of your cops. He was in civilian clothes. He introduced himself as an assistant to Mason, and he wheeled in this big computer on a dolly. Mathewson was a real piece of work. Big, quiet, with a funny way of looking at people.

"Anyway, Mathewson leaves and Mason shows up and he starts playing that computer like it was a synthesizer. The old Capitol spinning around and all—well, you've seen it. And then all of a sudden the Capitol and a lot of land around it lifts up, and attached to this big hunk of land are a lot of pipes and cables and tunnels: the Island. It was like a castle with a moat around it. Mason knew he could get those scared white folks on the Hill to buy that. And then, while that picture is frozen on his big screen, he tells me that he figures the Island, with its own independent electric power, its own subway tied to the D.C. Metro, that it's all going to cost, well, something like five *billion* dollars.

"He lets that sink in, and when I say where's that kind of money going to come from, he says that it's easier to get Congress interested in billions than millions. He said no one had ever made D.C. statehood look attractive before. He said he had enough clout to talk turkey with important congressmen, and he could sell them on giving statehood to the District while making *their* turf, the Island, safe and absolutely independent of D.C. Well, I wondered what was in it for me—and for him and his pal Bristow."

Mitchell paused, and this time Fitzgerald reacted with a question in the form of a statement: "Monument Associates."

"Right. He said it was legitimate. He showed me a statement he had dredged up from some database. It was some case in Atlanta or somewhere. A U.S. attorney issued a statement saying that there was no federal, state, or local law that keeps public officials from conducting a business. Mason told me that Monument Associates was a secret corporation—an anstalt, he called it."

Fitzgerald sketched what Tolland had told him about the anstalt. "So," he concluded, "nobody's name would ever appear on any U.S. piece of paper."

"Right. Absolute secrecy. Even the Feds haven't been able to crack an anstalt."

"Did you ever think this could be a scam?" Fitzgerald asked.

"You bet your ass I did. I knew the U.S. attorney and a whole damn bunch of FBIs was sniffing after me. But Mason, he was so smart, so full of *information*, that I figured he couldn't be FBI. And I knew he wasn't wired. Not in my house. And he told me things I just had to believe."

"What kind of things?"

"He said he had been in charge of putting computers and phones into Congress. He was supposed to be modernizing the place. But he said, with that laugh of his, that he wasn't just bringing Congress up to date, he was sitting like a spider in the middle of everything that went on. He played me tapes of phone calls—some pretty wild stuff—and he showed me stuff he lifted off computers."

"Like what?"

"Like the draft of Mareno's budget plan for D.C. It came off his computer, with 'Chairman of the District of Columbia Committee, U.S. House of Representatives' right across the top. I mean, that was real nice to have before Mareno started his hearings last year."

"What else?"

"I think I better get my lawyer over here," Mitchell said. But he did not reach for the phone.

"Look, Mr. Mayor," Fitzgerald said. "You're going to have to go over all this again. You know that. And when you do, that's when you need a lawyer." Having remained impassive through Mitchell's explanation, he now allowed a friendly smile to cross his face. "What you're doing now is rehearsing, getting your story lined up. That's what you're doing. You're a smart guy. You know that."

Mitchell smiled back, and Fitzgerald knew he had him. "Well, let me tell you, Fitzgerald, that man Mason, he was talking about a *lot* of money, and I mean a *lot*. He had it all worked out in a big master plan, he called it. The master plan was like a secret addition to Bristow's bill. The bill said that the mayor at the time of statehood would become governor until the next election. There's a clause in that bill that says the governor would be one member of a three-member transition commission to work out how the state would be separated from the National Capital Area."

"And one of the other members of the commission would be the architect of the Capitol," Fitzgerald interrupted.

"Yeah. It's right in the bill. The other one would be a member of Congress picked by the other two commission members. That would be Charles Bristow. And there's a clause that says the commission can award contracts for whatever help is needed."

"Wasn't Lawson or any other senator in on this?"

"Lawson's a Boy Scout. He and the senators he worked with all listened to Mason and got help from his computer boys. They didn't know what they were looking at when they saw Mason's tricky stuff. It whizzed right past them, like that floating Capitol of his."

"Where did Monument Associates fit in?"

"It had nothing to do with the statehood bill that Lawson's honchoing. In the contract Mason was going to bring before the commission, Monument Associates would be the consulting contractor for all subcontractors. And Monument would get two percent of those subcontracts. You got to realize," Mitchell continued, "that the statehood bill is one thing and Mason's master plan is another. In phase one of the master plan, Bristow's statehood bill gets passed. Bristow, being a southerner, was a pivotal vote. The Democrats get two pretty much permanent black senators, the liberals get a lot of points. And a lot of senators who aren't so liberal, they see that the National Capital Area means setting up the biggest public works project in the country. I mean, breaking the District into two parts would be the biggest political pork barrel since the Panama Canal.

"So statehood passes and that's phase one. Phase two comes when the National Capital Area starts getting set up. That's where the commission and Monument Associates step in. Monument would handle the deal at two percent of the contracts it awarded. Two percent of five billion dollars—you know how much that is?"

Fitzgerald shook his head.

"It's a hundred *million* dollars. We'd split a hundred *million* dollars."

"How the hell could Mason get away with that?" Fitzgerald asked, stunned by the audacity as much as by the figure.

"He had it all figured out. He said that at the right moment he'd call in Mareno and Lawson and other big shots in Congress and tell them that for the best of all concerned, he'd be stepping down as architect to take over the job of creating the National Capital Area. He was going to *tell* them about Monument. He called it a preemptive strike. And he knew that they knew there was no other man for the job."

"And what about you and Bristow?"

"We'd each have to work out our own deals. Bristow had no big problem. He knew he couldn't get reelected. The statehood bill would put him in the history books but kill him for the voters. Me? Well, hell, I'd be *governor* of New Columbia, and I guess what I'd do is put my stock in a blind trust or something. Get a good lawyer and, like Bristow used to say, let the good times roll."

"So all was going pretty well for you three. And then Bristow died."

"Yeah. That screwed things up. Mason was like a madman about Bristow drowning like that. 'That goddamn drunk had to fall out of a goddamn boat,' he said. I remember that because Mason never swore. But then he calmed down and began speeding up the plan."

"What do you mean, speeding up?"

"He said there's stuff up there on the Hill so old it needs to be replaced. Air conditioning. Power systems. And with one of those laughs of his, he said he was speeding things up a little, making people *want* to spend a lot of money."

"Well," Fitzgerald said, "that explains why so many things are breaking down up there." He paused and made himself look as if he were relaxing. "So far, Mr. Mayor, we're looking at a conspiracy to commit tax fraud. Nothing that a little plea bargaining won't fix." He paused again. "Now tell me about Julia Bristow's murder."

"There's nothing to talk about."

"Maybe I can talk about it," Fitzgerald said. "Julia Bristow gets appointed to her husband's seat, and it looks like nothing has really changed. But for the first time in her life she's on her own and loving it. She finds out about Monument—"

"How'd she do that?" Mitchell asked, looking genuinely surprised.

"What happened, I think, is that when they were settling Charles Bristow's estate, her lawyer tried to track down Monument Associates and ran into that brick wall over in Liechtenstein. My guess is that he knew anstalts were being used by people in tax-fraud schemes. Julia probably didn't know all the details but figured that it had something to do with Bristow's sudden sponsorship of statehood. She may have had enough to ask the Justice Department to investigate. And she planned to expose the financial deal over statehood and get elected."

With a disgusted expression, Mitchell said, "Yeah. I told Mason she could screw us up. I told him he should talk to her, get her into the deal. But—"

"But he didn't want to do that," Fitzgerald interrupted. "He didn't want to take a chance that he would confide in her and she'd turn around and blow the whistle on him. She was a loose cannon. Mason knew about her affair with Royal, and—"

"You mean Royal was banging her?" Mitchell broke in. "I'll be damned."

"Mason had Mathewson bug her hideaway. One night Royal

comes in and they talk and she tells him that she's going to run on her own and that what she'll run on is a bombshell that she has found, a scandal with a tie to statehood. Mason knew that statehood was doomed if she told what she knew. So . . ."

"So," Mitchell finished, "he tells Mathewson to knock her off."

"Did you suspect that?" Fitzgerald asked sharply.

"No. Honest to God, no. I thought some nut killed her. You know, like Huey Long. I mean, it's Louisiana, man."

To keep Mitchell under control, Fitzgerald would have pretended to accept every word, whether he believed him or not. But he did believe him. The next step would not be as hard as he had expected.

"Mayor Mitchell," he said. "If there's going to be statehood, you're going to have to tell all this to the U.S. attorney. Today, before tonight's session."

"Hold on, Fitzgerald. I've got a lot of talking to do with my lawyers. And as long as just you and me know this, well, Lawson's got the votes, hasn't he?"

"I don't know about that. But I do know that if you don't do exactly what I tell you, I will go to Lawson immediately and tell him everything you've told me. And that will kill statehood for a long, long time."

Mitchell sat perfectly still while Fitzgerald picked up the phone and said, "Get the U.S. attorney on the phone and tell him Mayor Mitchell's office is calling."

He listened for an instant and handed the phone to Mitchell.

"You heard him," Mitchell said. "Do what he said."

50

FITZGERALD AND MITCHELL left the District Building by a back entrance, where a U.S. marshal hustled them into a van for a drive up Pennsylvania Avenue to the underground garage of the U.S. District Court building. They were whisked by private elevator to the office of the U.S. attorney, Harold Douglass Pearson, who stood in front of his desk, flanked by two assistant U.S. attorneys. Pearson was as tall as the mayor, whom he had known since they were classmates and teammates in the District's McKinley High School. There had been talk, when he had been appointed a year before, that a black U.S. attorney would not go after a black mayor. But the talk had stopped when Pearson had empaneled a special grand jury to investigate corruption in the District Building.

Fitzgerald was politely escorted out of the office by an assistant U.S. attorney, who took him into her office and interviewed him, with few pleasantries or preliminaries, about Mitchell's story. Next came two FBI agents, one of whom he vaguely recognized. They began with what he knew about Mathewson and then worked backward through what he knew about Gwenda Harris-Topping and Julia Bristow. Fitzgerald knew the working-back process; for some reason it was called walking the cat.

Questioning continued for the rest of the morning, Mitchell in one room, Fitzgerald in another. Coffee and sandwiches arrived around 1 P.M., and more coffee in the long hours that followed. Shortly after seven o'clock Fitzgerald was brought into Pearson's office. Mitchell was seated at a table in a corner of the long, wood-paneled room, with his attorney on one side and an assistant U.S. attorney on the other. Pearson was standing in front of his desk again, looking as if he had not moved an inch since Fitzgerald had stepped off the elevator that morning.

"All right, Fitzgerald, listen up," Pearson said in the booming voice that terrified defense attorneys. "What we have here is a mayor who is going to resign. He's gone over transcripts of what you said he said, and he has made a statement that essentially coincides with what he told you and what you told my assistant. What you did was risky, Fitzgerald, and went far beyond what I would expect a former sworn lawman to do. *I'm* the federal law in this town. If you had screwed up in your little talk with this man" —he jerked a thumb toward Mitchell—"you would have done irreparable harm to the work of a grand jury that has been investigating the Mitchell administration for months."

Pearson looked at his watch. "As far as I'm concerned," he continued, "you and Mitchell are free to go. We'll expect full cooperation from now on." He walked around his desk, sat down, picked up some papers from his in box, and began reading them.

Mitchell waited until they were standing on the sidewalk before he spoke. "Tough guy, Harold. Same as back at McKinley. He'd as soon bang a guy into the ground in scrimmage as in a real game. But he's a Washington boy, and he knows there's someplace I've got to be tonight."

Mitchell's official car, a black Chrysler, slid up to the curb, and Byron Brown stepped out before it stopped.

"It's okay, Byron," Mitchell said. "We're goin' to walk." He and Fitzgerald turned toward the Capitol, joining the small groups of people who were heading in the same direction. The necklace of lights around the base of the Capitol dome pierced the evening. Although Mitchell blended into the crowd, many walkers recognized him and assumed Fitzgerald to be a security man.

"What did Pearson say about Mason?" Fitzgerald asked.

"Well, he told me not to discuss anything with anybody but my lawyer," Mitchell said, then added with a laugh, "but I think I'll make an exception. All he said was that he'll be presenting me to the grand jury tomorrow. He acted like nothing was a surprise. He was probably faking. Anyway, he never said anything when I told him about Mason or some of the other names that came up when I talked to him."

"Other names?"

"Yeah. People I know things about. Developers, people in the District Building, drug guys. They want me to sing for my supper. My lawyer says they'll keep me guessing, but he bets I get a free ride out of town in exchange for my resignation and cooperation."

"Goddamn!" Fitzgerald muttered. "Why didn't Pearson go after Mason? The son of a bitch will be in Brazil before anybody makes a move."

"I doubt it," Mitchell said. "What's he got to run away from? What kind of a murder case can the FBI make on him?"

"Well, goddamn it, they can get him before that grand jury."

"Yeah, and get another resignation. Give up, Fitzgerald. All you got is a theory."

"Was there any mention of Mathewson?"

"Naw. That's small stuff to Pearson. Just another local murder, right?" Mitchell said. "Hi, sweetie!" he called as they passed an elderly woman selling bunches of daisies. He gave her a ten-dollar bill, took two bunches, and handed one to Fitzgerald.

A few steps farther, he presented his bouquet to a giggling girl in a parochial school uniform. "Heading for the big vote, honey?" he asked. She nodded and walked on. Fitzgerald, catching Mitchell's mood, presented his daisies to a startled police officer who simultaneously accepted the flowers and saluted the mayor.

When they reached the grounds at the bottom of the Hill, a Capitol Police officer spotted Fitzgerald and insisted on piling him and the mayor into a patrol car, which took them to the plaza. Mitchell's car was stopped at the checkpoint.

Irish was the next to recognize Fitzgerald. He took the two men to the family gallery, where they could look down at the senators beginning to assemble. Above the rostrum the clock's hands showed fifteen minutes to eight.

At one minute to eight, the Vice President took his place as presiding officer, signaling a historic occasion. Lawson stood and began speaking slowly, solemnly. No one looking at him would realize that he had spent the last thirteen hours on a whirlwind circuit of Senate offices, cajoling, pleading, and subtly threatening. He needed sixty votes to close off debate, and that vote would be tantamount to a vote for statehood. His schedule called for a vote on cloture just as soon as he finished his remarks. If cloture was invoked, then another thirty hours of debate would follow, before the final roll-call vote on the bill to create New Columbia.

Lawson had been speaking only five minutes when a movement in the far gallery caught Fitzgerald's eye. A door between the row of niches opened and Mason appeared. He took a seat in the rear row. A moment later another door opened, to the right of Mason, and Phelan stepped into the gallery. She stood next to the door, her eyes on Mason. *At least she's not letting the son of a bitch out of her sight.*

Seized by a maelstrom of emotions—anger, fear, dread—Fitzgerald began scrambling past Mitchell to get to a door and to Phelan. Across the way, Mason noticed the motion. He saw Mitchell and Fitzgerald together, and at once knew what that meant. He stood and took a palm-size phone from his coat pocket. An instant later, Phelan turned toward the door directly behind her. Mason barked into the phone, "Electric fire! Shut down!" Deep in the

Capitol, a duty electrician followed a well-rehearsed drill and pulled a huge knife switch, and the Senate chamber vanished into darkness.

Fitzgerald stumbled blindly up the steep gallery stairs, bursting through the panicked crush of people at the door. He reached the hallway and hurled himself toward the west grand staircase, running toward the beam of a flashlight and tripping once over someone who had fallen in the rush. People were shouting. Over the shouts came a strong voice. It seemed to come from the flashlight, and it was repeating, "Don't panic! Stay still!"

"Maldonado!" Fitzgerald shouted. "It's Fitzgerald!"

The flashlight beam swung around and stopped full on Fitzgerald's face. He followed it back, pushing through several people with the same idea. At the inner edge of the crowd surrounding Maldonado, Fitzgerald shouted again: "Give me the light and get to a phone! We need a CERT team to the Rotunda, and order the Big Seal." The light wavered, and Maldonado elbowed his way to Fitzgerald. As he gave him the light, a hand materialized and grabbed for it. Fitzgerald swung his left hand, connected with flesh, and grabbed the light with his right hand.

Soon he reached the top of the west grand staircase, the curving marble smooth to his touch. The gallery where Mason had sat was connected to the east grand staircase. There was no other way down for either of them but their respective staircases, which led to the central corridor into the Rotunda.

Fitzgerald fell down the last four steps, smashing his left shoulder and losing the flashlight. As he crawled to the beam slicing across the marble-floored darkness, feeble emergency lighting came on at several places. He could dimly see the corridor and the Rotunda beyond. He also heard rapidly moving footsteps—two sets, he hoped—echoing on the marble down the corridor. Then he heard Phelan's voice shouting, "Stop—police!" The sound of footsteps ceased, and he heard scuffling. Then two shots in rapid succession resounded off the marble walls and floor in the great circular hall.

Fitzgerald plunged into the Rotunda. The emergency lights faintly outlined the towering walls. A beam of moonlight streamed down from the circle of windows in the dome. Within the pale light lay Alexandra Phelan, her blood dark against the stone. One hand was under her body. Her other hand reached out, her fingers bloody from the struggle for the gun, which had been torn from her grasp.

Fitzgerald heard footsteps running in from every direction. The full lights came on as Irish, panting, appeared from a side corridor. "Get a medic," Fitzgerald shouted, "and give me your gun." Running to Phelan, Irish unholstered his gun and tossed it toward Fitzgerald, who snatched it up as he ran through the shadows to a stairway leading down to the crypt. *A woman and blood on marble.*

He could hear Mason's footsteps against the stones, then a door being slammed. In seconds Fitzgerald was at the office of the architect, pulling frantically at the big wooden door. He stepped back, shot out the lock, kicked open the door, hurled himself into the darkened outer office, and crouched behind a desk. When he felt the draft of a silently opening door to his left, he spun and fired blindly. He no longer knew or cared what his body was doing. He ran mechanically toward the spot where he sensed the opening door was. He found it, pushed it open, switched on the light, and, standing fully exposed, leveled his gun at whoever was in front of him. He was in Mason's inner office. It was empty.

Fitzgerald cursed himself; Mason had slipped out of his office through the outer door as Fitzgerald had run toward the inner one. He looked around wildly. The long cabinet doors behind Mason's desk were open, and one was swinging slightly. A wooden hanger lay on the carpeted floor in front of the cabinet.

Fitzgerald ran to the outer door and then down a corridor to the door leading to the tunnel. When he eased the door open, he could hear footsteps clanging on the spiral iron staircase. He dashed to a door that opened onto the west front of the Capitol and tried to open it, but it was locked and would not give. He smashed out the glass in the upper half with the butt of the gun and leaped through, tearing cloth and flesh and landing on the cement walk at the edge of the darkness of the west front steps.

Fitzgerald ran diagonally across the northwest grounds, crashing through shrubbery, stumbling over a sprinkler head. Somewhere behind him he could hear someone shouting at him to stop. Thoughts raced through his mind: *The Big Seal. A man with a gun will be shot down. Mason is safe underground. Not me.* He dived headlong into the lawn a split second before two loud booms from a nine-millimeter handgun sounded behind him. The slugs shredded the leaves that hung over his head. Crouching behind a tree, he saw, straight ahead, the moonlit silhouette of the pavilion.

When he heard a clanging sound and thought he saw a shadow emerge from a deeper shadow, he ran toward it, approaching the pavilion from the side. Pressed against the brick outer wall, he made his way around to the iron gate. It hung open. He took a step toward the circular structure in the center. The bronze plaque lay on the brick floor.

He ran across the grass and vaulted the low stone wall on Constitution Avenue. A block away he saw someone flagging a taxi. Gathering speed, he plunged down the hill. The man was under a streetlight. The cab stopped. The man wore a uniform. Gold stripes gleamed on his sleeve. But he was bareheaded.

Fitzgerald, his pace faltering, saw a white-topped Navy officer's cap lying on the sidewalk, its black brim encrusted with gold. At the same instant he saw the man at the curb turn and make a movement with his right hand.

Fitzgerald stopped, grasped his gun in both hands, took a deep breath, and fired four shots. The gun in the man's hand fired once as he crumpled. The cab sped away. The man fell across the gutter, his head on the sidewalk, his eyes staring up at the streetlight.

Fitzgerald staggered up, the gun dangling from his hand. It was Mason, thank God, and he was dead.

Tuesday, April 14

51

"NOW YOU KNOW what Mo Udall meant when he said he understood the difference between a cactus and a caucus," Lawson said with a bemused smile that confused Fitzgerald. The two men were sitting in the majority leader's private office. "With a cactus, the pricks are all on the outside," Lawson said, breaking into a sardonic laugh. It was his way of explaining how he had fallen six votes short on the cloture motion, a significant and uncharacteristic defeat for him.

Fitzgerald liked Lawson, even admired him. But he had never understood politicians and wasn't sure he wanted to. They were a lot like lawyers, he thought. They could shout, pound a podium, invoke the Lord's name in arguing their cause, and then, after losing either in court or on a vote in the Senate, shake hands and go out and have a drink with the guy who just beat their pants off. Rock with success; roll with adversity. A few friends, but no permanent enemies. And yet, Fitzgerald knew, that was the way it had to be.

"I don't understand why you didn't put the vote off last night," he said.

"It was a judgment call, Jeff. The city was on the verge of exploding after that Davis show. Calling in the FBI and taking your badge wouldn't hold the pressure off very long. I mean, the evidence, even if circumstantial, pointed directly at Royal. If I had delayed the vote for any length of time, the city might have gone up in flames."

Lawson opened an ornately carved wooden box on his desk, the only object on its large polished surface. He plucked out what Fitzgerald surmised was probably a Cuban cigar and offered it to Fitzgerald, who declined.

"I knew it was a gamble." He paused to clip the end of the cigar, then rolled it between his lips before striking a wooden match to light it. He drew deeply, then exhaled a thin cloud of smoke.

Fitzgerald kept watching Lawson's face, looking for some detectable sign of sorrow or disappointment. He found none. But he did not buy Lawson's reason for rushing the vote.

"You must have known that a lot of fence-sitters would see that the evidence against Royal was pretty thin," Fitzgerald said. "They'd think you were just taking advantage of his arrest to shut off debate. You didn't get to be majority leader by not being able to count votes."

"You heard what I said about the cactus," Lawson said, smiling once again.

Fitzgerald was not sure why Lawson had invited him to his office, and he did not much feel like staying. He decided he had little to lose by pressing Lawson. "If you'll pardon me for saying so, Senator," he said, "I think you decided you could still win by losing."

"Oh? And to what end?" Lawson said this in a tight, controlled tone of voice, but he displayed no change in expression.

"I don't know much about politics, but I'll bet that by making the effort, you pick up all of the minorities and liberals when you run for President. And by losing, you still get a chance to split the vote of people in the middle, some of whom don't give a damn about D.C. statehood but like your other positions. The death penalty for drug pushers. Tax cuts for the middle class. Big tax increases for fat cats. Punishing the polluters."

Lawson never flinched, but flashed a broad smile that looked more like a grimace. "Hey, that's pretty cynical, even for you, Jeff. That's the kind of stuff the *Post* prints." He paused. "But in this business you learn not to take cynics too seriously. As Lincoln said, I could swear on a Bible in front of twelve angels and it wouldn't make any difference. Either you let it slide off or you get out. And as—"

A loud ring of the telephone startled him. "Damn phones," he cursed, stabbing at a lever that muted the harsh bell. "I don't know why we ever allowed these new phones into the Senate. Sometimes they sound like a three-alarm fire. Another one of Mason's brilliant ideas." He dragged slightly on his cigar, then exhaled before picking up the receiver. "Yes, Ingrid . . . I'll be in the press gallery in about five minutes. Tell Bruce he can hand out my statement any time now. Right."

He hung up the phone and knocked off the long ash that had gathered on his cigar. "Want to join me in the gallery? I'm sure the jackals up there have a lot of questions about last night."

"No thanks, Senator. No more press conferences for me." Fitzgerald held up both hands, palms facing Lawson, who looked him over carefully, as if gauging a man he did not know.

"How did you know, Jeff?" he asked.

"Know what?" Fitzgerald said.

"Know that it was Mason. I mean, how the hell did you figure he was behind it all and not Royal?"

Fitzgerald stared at Lawson. "Actually," he began, choosing his words carefully so as not to reveal how much of it had been luck, "I can't add much to the story in today's *Post*. It kept coming back to motive. Lab tests ruled out a rape-murder but did put Royal in the hideaway on the night Senator Bristow was killed. I assumed she was killed because of her politics. She was, of course, but not in the way I first thought. Then, when we found the bugging device in her hideaway, I knew that—"

"I don't understand what you mean about her politics," Lawson broke in.

"When she was appointed to the Senate, most people assumed she would follow in her husband's footsteps and support statehood," Fitzgerald said, making no attempt to soften the edge on the words *most people*, which included Lawson. "But once Royal discovered that she wasn't going to vote to shut off the filibuster and was going to run for election, he had no motive to kill her, except pure ambition for her office. He's a bastard, but I just didn't think he'd run that kind of risk."

"But tell me about Mason," Lawson said. "Why did he want her dead?"

"A hundred million dollars is a lot of motive. She had discovered that her husband was involved in some kind of corrupt scheme. My guess is that it all began to unravel when lawyers started settling Charles Bristow's estate and she had to file her own financial disclosure form. During pillow talk, she told Royal that she had an explosive story to tell. Mason had it all on his little tape machine, and he assumed she was going to expose enough about the deal to bring it down.

"My first suspicion of Mason came when I found out that the guy who jumped me in the hideaway—it was Mathewson, who knew about the unlocked window—was trying to get the bug hidden in the clock. Why? The bug just transmitted. Why not just leave it there? Then the electronics boys told me that it could only transmit for three to five hundred feet. *That's* why the intruder was trying to recover it."

"I still don't get it," Lawson said.

"If Mathewson left the bug there, we'd presumably find it, and find out its specs. Draw a circle of three to five hundred feet and it takes in the office of the architect. The receiver could be there or at the police outpost near the hideaway—the more likely site, I thought. But Mason had ordered Mathewson to set a fire there so that no cops would be around when he stalked Senator Bristow. Incidentally, I'm sure that if the FBI searches hard enough among Mason's electronics, they'll find the clock tapes. And probably a lot more. And—"

"*I'm* sure, Jeff, that a search like that isn't going to do anyone any good."

"I see your point, Senator."

Adroitly changing the subject, Lawson shook his head in disbelief and said, "Julia Bristow must have hated Charles to want to destroy his reputation." He let out a long sigh. "You make her out to be a tough little lady, Jeff. But . . ."

"Mason thought that he still might rescue the vote and his now bigger share of the millions by framing Royal," Fitzgerald said. "He figured that some southern conservatives might be so repelled by the murder that they'd support you on the vote. I assumed he had Mathewson kill Gwenda Harris-Topping—another martyr for statehood, as you yourself said, another chance to get outraged conservatives on the side of statehood. He had Mathewson set up Royal at the murder site by planting his Inaugural badge there. Mason installed the phone-answering system, so it was easy for him to erase the message on Royal's answering machine. But the badge and the message—I just couldn't buy it."

"You said you assumed. Does that mean you're not sure Mathewson killed both women?" Lawson asked, sounding suddenly worried.

"I'm sure he killed them. He was a killer at heart. He certainly killed not just Bristow and Harris-Topping but those prostitutes. And God only knows how many more. What I meant is, I'm not sure whether Mason aimed Mathewson toward Gwenda Harris-Topping or whether Mathewson thought it up on his own as a service for Mason. They had a master-slave relationship. There were two serial killers who operated like that in California when I worked out there. You remember them. The Hillside Strangler turned out to be two killers.

"Mason and Mathewson found each other in the Navy, when Mason was the captain of a ship so full of bad characters it was known as the Ship of Ghouls. One of the electronics technicians aboard was Mathewson, who became very helpful to Mason. Mason saw that he could play master to a very dangerous slave. When he became architect, Mathewson showed up and Mason got him on the force, even made him a sergeant. I'm sure that if anybody ever looks at Mathewson's personnel file, it'll be full of fixes from Mason.

"What happened, I think, is a replay of the Ship of Ghouls. Mathewson gets out of control—the last time Waves, this time D.C. prostitutes—and when Mathewson goes psycho, his master covers for him."

Lawson's face flashed in anger. "The Navy is going to have to give me a lot of answers about how they palmed Mason off on DARPA—and then on us."

"The Navy also got rid of Mathewson without giving a particular damn about what he might do," Fitzgerald said. "The way I figure it, Mason covered up for Mathewson on the ship, maybe with a little blackmail thrown in. Whatever the arrangement, they discovered something about each other and teamed up. With

Mathewson on the force, Mason figured he could keep him on a leash and use him." Fitzgerald looked hard at Lawson and added, "Mason was good at using people."

"Well," Lawson said, inhaling deeply, regaining his sense of authority as he rose from his chair, "you did a hell of a job, Jeff. I spoke with both Constantino and Morrison this morning. Your resignation has been rejected. You're back in charge of the force."

"Thanks, Senator," Fitzgerald said, suppressing a desire to ask how Lawson could have changed his mind so drastically. "But I'm going to pass on that. Something you said a few minutes ago: that you let it slide off or you get out. It doesn't slide off me anymore."

Lawson forced a smile and grabbed Fitzgerald's shoulder with one hand while pumping a handshake with the other. "Well, you let me know if you change your mind. Take a few weeks off. Think about it. We need you here." Then, almost as an afterthought, he asked, "And the woman? The officer who was shot?"

"Lieutenant Phelan. She's going to have a rough week or two, but the doctors at Georgetown say she should recover fully."

Fitzgerald had torn himself away from the questioners who had surrounded him the night before. He had found out where she had been taken, and he had spent the night at the hospital, sick with fear that he was going to lose another one of his officers to a gun. The thought had brought him to the edge of despair. He had fought against it, trying unsuccessfully to build a wall between his emotions and Alix. But he knew he was in love with her.

52

AS THE TWO MEN entered the corridor just outside the conference room, they were engulfed by a sea of tourists. Some held the hands of children who were too tired or too bewildered to understand why it was supposed to be so important for them to walk these hallowed halls. Most people recognized the majority leader immediately, pointing and whispering to each other. Lawson flashed them an acknowledging smile, then bid Fitzgerald good-bye and strode up the marble east wing staircase to the waiting cameras and microphones of the Capitol Hill press corps.

Fitzgerald walked down the corridor, turned left, and started down the west wing staircase. He paused momentarily and looked up at the eight-foot statue of Benjamin Franklin. Franklin was rubbing his chin between his forefinger and thumb, a faint, whimsical smile on his lips, as if he found the very stuff of politics—its ideals, dreams, ambitions, and achievements—a touch amusing. Fitzgerald turned, quickly descended the stairs, and exited through the west door of the Senate.

He passed under the stone archway toward the Capitol plaza, then spun around, walked around the Senate wing, and stepped out onto the balcony that provided an unobstructed view of the long Mall and the Reflecting Pool, straight as a plumb line to the Washington Monument. He half expected to see, in protest against the previous night's vote, a massive demonstration gathered along that historic stretch of green, which had once accommodated Martin Luther King, Jr., and his dream for America. Perhaps, Fitzgerald thought, the people of the District were too stunned by the lopsided margin against statehood. Or maybe they were simply shocked by the revelations about their mayor and his forced resignation. Who could say?

Sometimes in recent nights Fitzgerald had stared at the Washington Monument and thought that it resembled a hooded Klansman, its blinking red lights like fiery eyes of hatred. But now, in the bright sunlight, the monument stood as straight and tall as truth itself, lifting his spirits as a symbol of ennobling virtue. "Seek the truth," it seemed to say, "and it will set you free." Fitzgerald was at last coming to terms with the truth. He was free now, but to do what? Go where?

Earlier that morning, after coming home from the hospital and packing for a trip to San Francisco to see his daughter, he had stopped to visit with Mrs. Darwin. He found her in the kitchen, playing with her Tarot cards. She had invited him to join her for coffee. Eager to acknowledge his gratitude for her help, he had accepted. She proceeded to explain the significance of each card.

"Now, you must understand that the cards do not predict the

305

future; they simply reflect our present conflicts, needs, and hopes."

Fitzgerald had nodded, not sure what to believe.

"There are seventy-eight cards," she continued. "But ten are usually sufficient to reflect where you are today. Think of a question, Jeffrey. But don't tell me what it is." She shuffled the cards thoroughly, then spread them out in a fan shape, face down on the table. "Now pick ten, and place them in this fashion," she said, showing him the design of the Celtic cross.

"This," she said, "is the Covering Card, the one we call the Significator. This is the Crossing Card . . ." She continued, telling him the meaning of the Crowning Card, Base of the Matter, Past and Forthcoming Influences, until she came to the card she called the Final Outcome. It showed a young man dressed in animal skins of different colors. He had vine leaves in his dark hair and sprouted small horns. The card was labeled *The Fool*.

Fitzgerald had laughed. "You're making me a believer. A fool. A joke. Seems right."

"No," Mrs. Darwin had cautioned him. "You don't understand. You see, the Fool doesn't mean that you are foolish, only that you are standing at the beginning of a new journey. The boy is stepping out from the cave of his past into the unknown. He may fall to a destructive end, but it's equally possible that he will start a new and creative career. Impulsiveness is a part of creativity. He may never arrive anywhere, but it's also possible that he will complete a safe and satisfying journey. It signifies, Jeffrey, a new chapter, but not the ending."

Maybe, he thought to himself now, as he inhaled the bright spring beauty of the nation's capital. *Maybe*. The Fool, stepping off into the unknown. He had forgotten to ask Mrs. Darwin a question: *Will Alix come with me?*

306

ABOUT THE AUTHORS

WILLIAM S. COHEN, first elected to Congress in 1972, has been a U.S. senator since 1979. He served as vice chairman of the Intelligence Committee from 1987 to 1990 and is a member of the Armed Services and Governmental Affairs committees. He is also one of the Senate's most literate members, the author of seven previous books: two novels (*The Double Man*, with former senator Gary Hart, and *One-Eyed Kings*), three works of nonfiction (*Men of Zeal: A Candid Story of the Iran-Contra Hearings*, with fellow Maine senator George Mitchell; *Roll Call*, a journal of his first year in the Senate; and *Getting the Most Out of Washington*), and two volumes of poetry. Senator Cohen lives in Washington, D.C., and Bangor, Maine.

THOMAS B. ALLEN, a former senior book editor for the National Geographic Society, is the author of *War Games*, an exploration of how U.S. policy makers and military strategists plan and play World War III. He has co-authored with Norman Polmar several books, including *Rickover: Controversy and Genius*, *Merchants of Treason*, and *Ship of Gold*, a military spy thriller. He lives in Bethesda, Maryland.